PRAISE FOR
ULTIMATE JUSTICE

"This taut, complex, and engrossing book is one of the most clever whodunits in recent years."

—*St. Petersburg Times* (FL)

"If you're craving a compelling legal yarn and a sexy love story, you'll find your fix with *ULTIMATE JUSTICE*."

—Gayle Lynds, author of *Mosaic*

"All the ingredients for a suspenseful page-turner. An attractive, bright, ambitious heroine, complicated family ties, romantic involvements, a murder cover-up, political intrigue, and danger. Filled with surprising twists and turns, the book is skillfully written and, if you are into legal innuendoes, one you will especially enjoy."

—*Sunday Oklahoman*

"The best mystery of the summer."

—Digby Diehl, KLTA-TV Channel 5 News, Los Angeles

"An engrossing tale . . . Keep[s] the pages turning."

—*The Advocate* (Baton Rouge, LA)

"In *ULTIMATE JUSTICE* Mimi Latt proves that she knows as much about the dark secrets between fathers and daughters as she does about the dark side of the law."

—Stephen White

"A taut and highly intriguing thriller that focuses on the sometimes tough issues of loyalty and morality."

—*Romantic Times*

A SELECTION OF THE LITERARY GUILD, MYSTERY GUILD, AND DOUBLEDAY BOOK CLUBS

PURSUIT OF JUSTICE

"Entertaining . . . A terrific sensual romp that should make some members of Los Angeles' legal community a little nervous."

—*Los Angeles Times*

"Riveting . . . Latt's heroine is fabulous—and so is this page-turner."

—*Woman's Own*

"Very forceful and believable . . . Although there is a lot of action and compelling subplots, the heart of this mesmerizing tale lies in the character of Rebecca . . . Latt shows that she is a real force in the legal thriller subgenre."

—*The Midwest Book Review*

"Latt gives her readers plenty of suspense, an attractive heroine, and a conspiracy plot that could have been concocted by John Grisham."

—*Booklist*

"Captures the glamour, power struggles, and sordidness of the political, legal, and law enforcement arenas."

—Nancy Taylor Rosenberg

POWERS OF ATTORNEY

"First-time novelist Mimi Latt delivers a terrific thriller ripe with romance, intrigue, and legal convolutions."

—*Publishers Weekly* (starred review)

"A perfect novel if you like steamy, romantic stories."

—*The Washington Times*

"Greed and lust among the rich and famous . . . combine Danielle Steel and John Grisham and you've got *Powers of Attorney*."

—Jonathan Kellerman

"Fascinating . . . Latt shows a natural flair for drama."

—*Chicago Tribune*

"A steamy tale."

—*Houston Post*

"There are enough machinations here to satisfy the most avid thriller fan . . . the unexpected ending will please."

—*United Methodist Reporter*

Also by Mimi Latt

Pursuit of Justice
Powers of Attorney

MIMI LATT

ULTIMATE JUSTICE

POCKET STAR BOOKS

New York   London   Toronto   Sydney   Singapore

This book is a work of fiction. Names, characters, places and incidents are products of the author's imagination or are used fictitiously. Any resemblance to actual events or locales or persons, living or dead, is entirely coincidental.

 A Pocket Star Book published by
POCKET BOOKS, a division of Simon & Schuster, Inc.
1230 Avenue of the Americas, New York, NY 10020

Copyright © 2000 by Miriam Lavenda Latt

Originally published in hardcover in 1999 by Simon & Schuster, Inc.

ISBN: 0-671-01461-7

First Pocket Books printing December 2000

10 9 8 7 6 5 4 3 2 1

POCKET STAR BOOKS and colophon are registered trademarks of Simon & Schuster, Inc.

Cover design and illustration by Carlos Beltran

Printed in the U.S.A.

QB / ✻

*To my aunt, Ruth Shapiro,
an incredible woman whose optimism
is a daily inspiration*

— ∾ —

*In loving memory of
my mother, Sylvia Lavenda,
and so many
of my dear friends
for their courageous battles
against cancer*

Acknowledgments

THIS THIRD BOOK would not have been possible without the help of these special people: Anne Sibbald, my literary agent—what a pleasure it is to hear your cheerful voice on the phone! A heartfelt thanks for your enthusiastic guidance, loving support, and constant belief in me. You never fail to put the often complicated (not to mention meshuga) world of publishing in perspective. I'm fortunate to have you in my court as both an agent and a friend. A big thanks also to Dorothy Vincent, my foreign rights agent; Tina Bennett, my audio rights agent; and the other marvelous people at Janklow & Nesbit Associates who work so hard on my behalf. Profound gratitude also to Laurie Horowitz, my dramatic rights agent at Creative Artists Agency, for the much needed education in *Selling to Hollywood 101:* Is *this* book high concept enough? Seriously, thanks for everything.

Michael Korda and Chuck Adams, editors extraordinaire at Simon & Schuster, I'm forever indebted to you both for your creative insights, continual encouragement, and warm friendship. Your incisive comments never fail to help me make my work the best it can be—despite the fact that my first drafts give us all hives. Thanks also to Cheryl Weinstein, for her valuable editorial input; Michael Accordino for the fabulous jacket; Ted Landry, astute copy supervisor; Marie Florio, for her avid pursuit of the book clubs; and all the other wonderful people at Simon & Schuster who helped in the creation of this book.

Also, a big thank you to the people at Pocket Books: Judith Curr, Publisher, and Kara Welsh, Associate Publisher, for all their support; Editor Amanda Ayers for her understanding and patience; Paolo Pepe, Art Director, for the beautiful cover; Penelope Haynes, Managing Editor, for her hard work; and all the other wonderful people within the Simon & Schuster Group who share their expertise to make my books the best they can be.

The Honorable Loretta Murphy Begen, Superior Court Judge and dear friend. I could not have written this book without your generous help and the benefit of your knowledge. I am truly grateful. Hugs and kisses also to Jerry, Sean, and Michael for their unfailing patience in light of my frequent calls. "Mom, it's that crazy writer friend of yours again." All kidding aside, I know that every minute spent on the telephone with me was a precious minute lost to your family.

Lisa Rojany, writer, editor, and good friend, I owe

you a thousand thanks for all those late nights and last-minute saves from the murky depths of the special hell known as writer's despair. Your uncanny ability to help me find the heart of my characters, stick to my story line, punch up my writing, and make me laugh at myself along the way keeps me sane. I especially like those funny little pictures you draw in the margins—I'm officially cured of flashing eyeballs, okay? Okay. What would I do without you?

Enid Zaslow, Ph.D., your psychological expertise enables me to portray my characters realistically on the page. As my best friend you also have the unique ability to keep me from sticking a fork into the surge protector and blowing up my computer when the going gets rough. Thank you, thank you, thank you.

The other experts in their field: Sandi Gibbons and Jim Jacobs, at the Los Angeles District Attorney's Office; members of the Los Angeles Police Department, the Los Angeles Sheriff's Department, and the California Department of Justice, Attorney General's Office; Juan José Garcia at *La Opinion*, and good friend Sheldon Bern, CPA—I appreciate the professional knowledge you all shared with me about details great and small. Any mistakes in the book are my sole responsibility and I promise to feel guilty forever.

My writer friends: Lisa Siegel, Ellen Jones, and Mary Firmin, our writers group was a source of constant inspiration. Your insights into my story always kept me on my toes. I also miss the weekly dishing that had absolutely nothing to do with our work—it sure was fun. You guys are the best.

All my regular friends and family: YOU know who you are, and the fact that you're still in my life and reading this is a testament to your devotion. Although I'm usually too busy to breathe, I've been organized enough (thank you, law school) to keep a list of all I owe, including: twelve dinners, twenty-four phone calls, sixty-five gifts, and assistance at three postponed nervous breakdowns. Call anytime to collect. Sorry in advance if you get my machine. Also, to Grace and Larry Latt, thanks for taking on every single holiday for our families for the last decade (or more). It allowed me the time to pursue my writing—even though I probably did us all a favor anyway, since Grace's cooking far surpasses mine any day! And thanks to Ron and Marci Bloom, and Helene and Alan Moskowitz for your special help. Kudos to all of you for hanging in there with me.

My beloved daughters, son-in-law, and grandson: Carrie Latt Wiatt, Andi, Stuart, and Spencer Price. The closeness we share and our laughter and tears are what life is all about. Remember that little saying I'm always haranguing you about—living long enough for your children to blah-blah-blah? I only mean it half the time. Thanks for always rooting for me. I love you with all my heart.

Arron Latt, my husband and best friend in the whole world, you have done more to make our lives fulfilling than anyone has a right to expect or even to ask for. Your love, support, and infinite patience sustain me. Simply said, I wake up every day and thank God for you. When I'm long gone, I'm sure you'll say the same about me. Right?

ULTIMATE JUSTICE

1

ALEXANDRA LOCKE rushed down the gray-carpeted corridor of the City of Hope Medical Center. It had already been a long day, and her body was weary with exhaustion. As a Los Angeles deputy district attorney, she'd spent most of the afternoon in court, questioning experts in an attempted murder case she was prosecuting. She'd then had to prepare a nervous witness for his next day's testimony. And once that was out of the way, she had to finish drafting a motion for another case that had to be filed the following morning. Everything was late.

Upset about her delayed arrival at the hospital and anxious to see her mother, Alexandra was startled when a heavyset nurse stopped her in the hallway. "I'm glad I caught you before you went in to visit your mother," the woman said.

"What is it? Has something happened?" Alexandra asked, suddenly alarmed that her mother, who was undergoing chemotherapy for ovarian cancer, had taken a turn for the worse.

"No. No. She's the same." The nurse, whose badge identified her as B. Stevens, R.N., gave Alexandra a reassuring smile. "In fact, she fell asleep a little while ago."

Alexandra took a deep breath and then impatiently waited for the nurse to explain why she'd stopped her.

Ms. Stevens leaned forward, her voice dropping to a conspiratorial whisper. "I was kind of hoping you'd do me a small favor."

"What kind of favor?"

"There's a patient by the name of Erica Collins and . . . well . . . she keeps insisting that she must speak to you," Ms. Stevens replied. "Could you spare a few minutes?"

"Me? Why?"

"She didn't say, just that it was important."

Looking at her watch, Alexandra hesitated. As it was, she had too little time to spend with her mother. But seeing the expectant look on the nurse's round face, and aware that Ms. Stevens had been really kind to her mother, Alexandra couldn't refuse. With a tired sigh, she gave in. "What room is this Erica Collins in?"

Ms. Stevens pointed toward a room halfway down the hall.

Noticing a sign on the door restricting the patient's visitors, Alexandra knocked softly before pushing it open.

It was dark inside, the only bit of light coming

from behind the partially closed door to the bathroom. The air in the room seemed stale and smelled heavily of antiseptic. Alexandra glanced over at the narrow hospital bed and saw a woman who appeared to be in her late sixties. It was hard to tell, though, because she had no hair and her body was hooked up to various tubes and bags.

Clearing her throat, Alexandra said, "Excuse me, I'm Alexandra Locke. Ms. Stevens said you wanted to see me?"

The woman's eyes flickered open, and with an apparent effort, she turned her pale face toward Alexandra. A slight smile touched her lips. "So you're Alexandra." She motioned for her to come closer.

When Erica spoke again, her voice was so faint that Alexandra had to bend down to hear it. "I feel I already know you from the things your mother has said."

That explained how this woman had come to ask for her, Alexandra thought. Although she didn't remember her mother ever mentioning an Erica Collins to her.

"You're very pretty," Erica muttered in the same faint voice. "Except for the color of your hair, you look just like her."

Alexandra absently pushed her dark blond hair away from her eyes. "Thank you. How do you know my mother?"

"We met here at the hospital. We both have the same kind of cancer." Erica's words were uttered slowly, as if speaking was burdensome for her.

"I've been doing my homework on you." She pointed to the metal cabinet next to her bed. "Take out the envelope in the top drawer and you'll see what I mean."

Intrigued, Alexandra pulled out a bulky manila envelope stuffed with papers, including numerous newspaper clippings.

"Go ahead and look," Erica urged.

Gazing at the first of them, Alexandra was surprised to find that the article was about her and the last case she'd handled as an assistant district attorney in New York. It had been written after her successful prosecution of a dirty cop.

Her brow furrowed, she glanced up at Erica. "I'm afraid I don't understand. Where did you get this and why have you been reading up on my New York career?"

Erica's eyes narrowed slightly. "Your mother mentioned she'd saved all of the stories on the cases you'd handled, so I asked to see them. I had to make sure you were the right one."

" 'The right one' for what?" Alexandra asked.

"To tell my story to," replied Erica. "You see, there's something I have to tell, something that's been weighing on my mind for a very long time."

Alexandra tensed; this conversation was going in a direction that made her uncomfortable. "Why don't I get the chaplain?"

"This is not about religion; it's about the law—it's you I must talk to," the woman insisted. She struggled to sit up. "You see," Erica said with difficulty, "twenty years ago my husband, my ex-husband, George Collins, killed his best friend, Jeffrey McGrath. And I . . . I helped him get away with it."

Startled by the nature of Erica Collins's admission, Alexandra stood silently for a moment considering her response. People sometimes confessed to crimes that they didn't commit, usually because they craved attention. That could be the case here. On the other hand, by admitting that she'd helped someone get away with murder, Erica Collins had opened herself up to a possible prison sentence. As a result, this type of declaration was given a certain amount of legal weight.

To make a judgment call either way, Alexandra would need more facts. "How did the two of you avoid prosecution?"

Erica licked her cracked lips, her gaze fixed on Alexandra. "We gave a young deputy D.A. a lot of money—one hundred thousand dollars in cash—so George wouldn't go to prison."

The thought of a district attorney taking a bribe sent a shudder through Alexandra.

"I think you might be interested in the rest of what I have to say," Erica said, her voice still soft but suddenly sturdier, less halting. "The deputy D.A. in charge of the case was Thomas Kendell."

Alexandra's head snapped back at the mention of her father's name. He'd been the District Attorney for Los Angeles County for twelve years. His record was spotless. Yet this woman was accusing her father of participating in a cover-up—a charge that if proven would certainly end his career. Was there even the slightest possibility that she was speaking the truth?

Alexandra tried to clear her head; she had to think over this accusation in a rational manner. "Why are you telling me instead of going directly to the police?" she asked, fixing her gaze on the woman.

"I wanted to tell someone I could trust. I want my ex-husband to spend the rest of his life in prison." She regarded Alexandra. "Your mother said you'd prosecute *anyone* if you felt that person had violated the law." Erica pointed to one of the clippings. "You're quoted here as saying *'no one'* is above the law. Is that true?" Her voice had become hoarse and noticeably weaker.

"Yes, but . . ."

"So then I've chosen wisely."

Alexandra studied the woman for a moment. "You didn't tell the authorities about this twenty years ago. Why now?"

A slight flush appeared on Erica's otherwise waxen face. "I should have done it then, but . . ." her voice faltered, "I was afraid." She exhaled loudly. "Now that I'm dying, it's different." She lay her head back against the pillows as if suddenly exhausted. "George murdered a man in cold blood. I don't want to die with that crime on my conscience."

Still dubious about the veracity of this woman's confession, and confused as to what she should do next, Alexandra frowned.

Sensing Alexandra's hesitancy, Erica's tone became more urgent. "I didn't understand then what I was getting into, and I didn't want to go to prison. But I'm dying now. I've got no reason to lie." She stopped to catch her breath before going on. "Maybe you don't care that twenty years ago my ex-husband got away with murder, or that your father accepted a bribe, but I'll bet—" Erica suddenly started coughing.

"Should I get the nurse?" Alexandra offered.

The other woman shook her head as she strained to control her coughing. "Don't bother," she finally managed to say, "there's nothing they can do."

Despite her misgivings, Alexandra opened her purse and scribbled some notes in the small notebook she usually carried.

When Erica's coughing stopped, Alexandra asked, "What evidence do you have that your ex-husband committed this murder?"

"It's your job to find evidence," Erica responded, giving Alexandra a brief, piercing glance. "But if you don't intend to do something about this, I'll go to the papers with my story. I bet Frank Sanchez would like to know about the cover-up."

Alexandra stared at the woman. Frank Sanchez was her father's opponent in his upcoming race for reelection. Suddenly Erica's confession was becoming more ominous. Still, she had doubts as to the truth of the woman's story. It was possible that she wanted revenge against her ex-husband. Or it could be that the drugs she was taking were making her delusional. There was also the chance that she could have an old score to settle with Alexandra's father.

Erica Collins had begun to cough violently again, and it took a few minutes before the seizure subsided. Fully aware that even an unsubstantiated rumor spread by a crazy woman could be harmful to her father's candidacy for reelection, Alexandra leaned forward. "If I promise to look into the matter, can we keep this between us for now?"

Fingering the thin blanket, Erica appeared pensive. Finally, she spoke. "I don't have long. I'll give you seventy-two hours to let me know exactly how you plan to proceed."

"Impossible," Alexandra replied, taken aback by the woman's ultimatum. "It will take at least a week to check out your charges."

The door opened and a nurse entered. "Time for your medication, Mrs. Collins." She flashed Alexandra a quick smile. "Could you excuse us for a little while?" she asked.

"Of course." She looked at Erica, whose gaze hardened.

"Seven days, Ms. Locke, no longer."

A short time later, Alexandra stood by her mother's bedside, waiting for her to open her eyes. Roberta Kendell's hospital room was filled with the heady fragrance of roses and other fresh flowers that stood in vases and baskets, a startling contrast to the cheerless room where Erica Collins lay dying.

Peering outside into the night, Alexandra considered her bizarre encounter with Erica Collins.

Deeply immersed in her own thoughts, she jumped at the feel of her mother's warm hand touching her own.

"Hi," Roberta said softly to her daughter. "Have you been here long?"

"No," Alexandra replied, smiling lovingly at her mother. Without the silver turban she usually wore to hide what chemo had done to her once-luxurious brown hair, Roberta looked older than her fifty-three years. She was also painfully thin—another upsetting reminder of her serious condition.

Alexandra helped her mother sit up, then fluffed the pillows behind her back and smoothed out the tangled sheets. She did her best to put a hopeful expression on her face before speaking. "Tell me what the doctor said today."

Roberta explained the details of her latest chemotherapy results. It was all very technical, but Alexandra had become as well-versed as her mother in the terminology and vicissitudes of this particular cancer and its treatment. For the umpteenth time, Alexandra tried not to ponder the injustice of why this disease had attacked her mother.

Ms. Stevens came in to check Roberta's condition. When she was through, she smiled at Alexandra. "Thanks for taking the time to see Mrs. Collins."

"No problem," Alexandra said.

As soon as the nurse was gone, Roberta gazed at Alexandra, a questioning look in her large hazel eyes. "So . . . you met Erica?"

"Yes," Alexandra nodded. "What in the world did you tell her about me?"

"Just how you left your job in New York City, where you were a star prosecutor in the political corruption unit, to come home because I was sick." Roberta's shoulders lifted with pride. "Erica was surprised that a child could be so unselfish."

"I'm hardly a child, Mother. I'm thirty-two years old."

"You'll always be my baby," Roberta countered. "Anyway, I guess I was bragging to her," she admitted with a grin. "But then, I'm very proud of you."

Her words filled Alexandra with a sudden warmth. The one constant in her life had been her mother's unconditional love, and the threat of losing that now brought tears to her eyes. Turning away so her mother wouldn't see how upset she was, Alexandra masked her fears by posing another question. "Does Erica have any family?"

"She's divorced and has no children." Roberta's voice echoed with pity. "I don't think anyone comes to visit her."

"Sad . . ." Alexandra murmured. Her mother's reply reinforced her sense that Erica could be starved for human contact. That would explain why she might fabricate a story, just to garner some attention.

"Poor Erica," Roberta continued. "She apparently slaved for years to put her ex-husband through medical school, only to have him dump her once he was established."

"He's a doctor?"

"Yes," Roberta said. "An orthopedic surgeon.

According to Erica, he's also a real louse." She lowered her voice. "Not long after he finally opened his own practice, the good doctor asked for a divorce so he could marry another woman."

This bit of information bolstered Alexandra's impression that Erica Collins might be seeking revenge. Hell hath no fury, and all that. Wondering to what extent Erica had confided in Roberta, she asked, "Did Erica ever mention why she was interested in talking to me?"

"She said that her husband murdered a man but was never prosecuted."

Alexandra's eyebrows shot up. Was it possible that her mother knew the whole story, including the part her father might have played? No, she decided. Roberta would have mentioned it at the first opportunity. Still, Alexandra needed to make sure. "Why didn't Erica speak to Dad about this? If anyone has the power to reopen an old case, it's him—not me."

Roberta's eyes focused on her daughter. "I suggested that to her, but Erica made me promise not to discuss it with him. That's when she started asking me questions about you."

Alexandra was silent for a moment. "Did Erica say anything about her having played any part in the crime?"

"Not exactly," Roberta responded. "But I could tell that she felt guilty about something and wanted to make amends."

Offering her mother a glass of water, Alexandra watched as she drank it greedily. "Mom, did Erica ever explain how her ex-husband escaped prosecution?"

"No," Roberta replied, shaking her head. "She never said a word about that to me. Why?"

"Oh, no reason," Alexandra muttered, shrugging her shoulders. Going over to the window, she gazed again into the dark night as she tried to sort out her thoughts. There was no way she could tell her mother about the accusations Erica had leveled against her father. Not when Roberta was so sick.

"Alexandra?"

She turned around to see an anxious expression on her mother's face. "Did Erica say something that upset you?"

"No, Mom." Alexandra forced herself to smile. "I'm fine. Really."

"You look tired, darling," Roberta said. "It's after nine. Get a cup of coffee before you start the drive home. And don't bother to come tomorrow. I know how busy you are."

"It's no bother, Mother. I like to come," Alexandra insisted. "And I can't believe you're worrying about me."

Roberta smiled. "Once a mother, always a mother, no matter what. Besides," she said, lifting her chin, "I'm going to beat this thing, you know."

"I believe you," said Alexandra, praying that her mother was right. She glanced at her watch. "Is Dad coming?"

"I don't know."

"Was he here last night after I left?"

"No," Roberta said, rubbing the sheet between

her fingers. "He got tied up at a speaking engagement. Winning this fourth term as District Attorney is very important to your father. By the time he finished with his speech and the dinner, it was just too late. It's at least an hour's drive from where the event was held."

Alexandra felt some of her old resentments against her father resurface. Now that her mother was so ill, she wished he could curtail his campaigning and spend a little more time at the hospital. And she wished her mother would stop making excuses for him.

When Roberta became sleepy, Alexandra gave her mother a kiss and hugged her gently so as not to dislodge her IV, then headed out into the hallway.

Passing Erica Collins's room, she hesitated. If Erica had been speaking the truth, her confession—if made public—would have powerful repercussions. There were more questions Alexandra wanted to ask the woman, but a DO NOT DISTURB sign now hung on the door. She decided it might be wiser to first do some sleuthing on her own.

As Alexandra walked to her car, she thought about her charismatic father. Although she loved Thomas Kendell, she'd never felt as close to him as she would have liked. As far back as Alexandra could remember, her father had always been busy, too preoccupied and too driven to succeed to have much time for her. But while her father certainly had his flaws, could he ever have done anything as heinous as taking a bribe to cover up a murder?

2

As SOON AS the judge adjourned court for the noon recess in the trial she was prosecuting, Alexandra grabbed her briefcase and rushed out of the courtroom. The corridor was crowded with the usual assortment of defendants, witnesses and attorneys, all waiting out the sluggish grind of justice.

Jostling her way through the throng, she eyed the large number of people standing at the elevators and felt a shot of impatience. It could easily take ten minutes to get upstairs to the Los Angeles County District Attorney's offices that occupied the seventeenth and eighteenth floors of the Criminal Courts Building in downtown L.A., time Alexandra didn't have to waste.

When Alexandra finally exited the elevator on the seventeenth floor, she noticed a cluster of deputy D.A.s standing together, talking and joking. As soon as they saw her coming, the hallway suddenly became eerily quiet.

The silence only added to Alexandra's feelings of alienation. In New York, where she'd spent the previous eight years as a prosecutor, she'd been one of the office's biggest and most popular rising stars. But here in L.A. her working environment was less than welcoming. Since she'd arrived six months earlier, the other prosecutors had been polite, but none had been really friendly. She assumed it was because her father happened to be their boss. Still, she wasn't sorry for making the move to L.A., knowing how important it was to be nearby while her mother was so ill.

Reaching her small office, Alexandra was relieved to see that her appointment hadn't arrived yet. Pushing aside some of the papers on her cluttered desk, she made room for her briefcase.

"Here are your messages," said Geena, her secretary, coming into Alexandra's office with a stack of telephone slips.

Alexandra sighed. "There's not enough time in a week to return all those calls, let alone an hour."

"Yeah, I know." Geena smiled sympathetically. "But the good news is that the witness you were supposed to see during your lunch hour had to cancel."

"Hallelujah!" Alexandra said, grinning at the gray-haired, dark-skinned woman. She was grateful to Geena not only for her competence, but for treating her just like any other prosecutor in the office, and not like the boss's daughter.

After Geena left the room, Alexandra leaned back in her rickety chair and rubbed her sore neck,

the souvenir of an old taxi accident in New York.
Her pain seemed to get worse when she was tense,
and she'd been up all night, unable to get Erica
Collins's story out of her mind.

Since her lunch hour was now free, she debated
whether there was enough time to go to the downtown library and still get back before court recon-
vened. She opened her purse and reviewed the
notes she'd made in Erica's room. She'd better start
now. With the clock running on the deadline Erica
had given her, Alexandra had to find some answers—and quickly.

On the eighteenth floor, directly above Alexandra, Los Angeles County District Attorney Thomas
Kendell was staring at the newspaper. A tall,
rugged-looking man of fifty-seven, he sported a
tanned complexion and a ready smile that he didn't
hesitate to use when setting out to charm voters.

He glanced up when his campaign manager,
Dale Jensen, came into his office. Pointing to a
headline, Thomas said, "I'm tired of reading about
our courtroom losses. Why don't they write about
our ninety percent conviction rate, or that crime in
the county has dropped significantly?"

Jensen, short and stocky and with an astute
mind that Thomas had come to rely on, squinted at
Thomas. "Because negative news sells more newspapers."

"I've done a great job, I shouldn't have to put up
with this," Thomas insisted. He thought about the
four challengers he was facing in the June primary,

now less than six weeks away. One of them, Frank Sanchez, was a deputy D.A. from his own office. Thomas's dark, bushy eyebrows drew together in an angry frown as he pushed the paper across the desk toward Dale. "Did you read the quote from Sanchez?"

"Yeah. He's coming down hard on you for accepting large contributions from powerful people," Dale agreed, shaking his head. "It's clever on his part. Since he can't attract the big givers like you can, he plays holier-than-thou by putting a five-thousand-dollar cap on donations to his campaign."

"And he's trying to make it look like the well-to-do can buy themselves access to the D.A." Thomas stood, drawing himself up to his full height of six feet two inches. "Sometimes I wonder why I need this. Plenty of law firms in the city would be more than happy to take me as a partner. I'd earn a million dollars a year instead of the lousy hundred twenty-seven thousand I make here."

"True." Dale nodded. "But my guess is you like it here too much to leave voluntarily."

Thomas knew that Dale was right. He'd been the D.A. for Los Angeles County for the last twelve years. He was proud of his record, but he wasn't done yet—there was a lot more he wanted to accomplish. With over a thousand prosecutors, his was the largest local prosecutorial agency in the world. He'd be damned if he was going to let someone else take his place and reap the benefit of his years of hard work.

"Should I order your car?" asked Dale, breaking into Thomas's reverie.

The D.A. glanced at his watch. He had another luncheon speaking engagement today. "Fine." He nodded.

A few minutes later, the two men rode down to the basement of the building while Dale outlined Thomas's itinerary for the rest of the day.

"You haven't left me a moment to breathe," muttered Thomas.

"We can't slack off," Dale said. "We've got to garner enough votes in the primary so you're not forced into a runoff in the general election."

The mere thought of a runoff filled Thomas with resolve. He couldn't let it happen. It would be too demoralizing.

Dale regarded him. "Course, chances are nobody would have had a shot at beating you if you hadn't allowed your daughter to be hired."

Thomas squared his shoulders. He didn't like being reminded that hiring Alexandra had hurt him politically. He'd known it might cause trouble with some voters, but Roberta had asked him to do it. How could he refuse his wife anything when she was so ill? Unfortunately, he'd been fighting very public charges of nepotism ever since. "It was a committee, not me, who interviewed the applicants and made the choice. Alexandra had outstanding qualifications. Why can't you get *that* message out?"

"We'll go over strategy again this Sunday," Dale promised, opening the door to a large, dark sedan.

"I'm sure we'll be fine. The nepotism issue will stay quiet as long as Alexandra does a good job and doesn't cause any kind of controversy . . ." Dale gave Thomas a meaningful look as his voice trailed off.

Rubbing his eyes, Thomas chose not to respond. He trusted his daughter completely. She would never do anything to bring the media down on her, and consequently, down on him.

Los Angeles deputy D.A. Frank Sanchez was standing amid a group of colleagues discussing the upcoming primary when he saw Alexandra Locke hurry by. Since arriving here in L.A., Alexandra had earned a reputation for being willing to tackle cases other prosecutors felt were too complex to win. Nevertheless, she was the D.A.'s daughter and Frank hadn't quite figured out yet if she was friend or foe.

"The D.A. says large campaign donations don't pose a conflict of interest, but he's full of you-know-what," Frank said, clearly aware that he had the moral support of many of the deputies in the office on this particular issue.

"Watch what you say," one of the other prosecutors warned as he nodded toward Alexandra. "She might be reporting back to her old man."

After Alexandra was gone, deputy D.A. Elizabeth Nathan smoothed down the skirt of her red suit and ventured her opinion. "You should be grateful to Alexandra, Frank. If not for her, you wouldn't have *any* chance against Thomas Kendell."

Frank scowled at the diminutive woman with the sharp tongue. He cut Elizabeth some slack because she'd had a tough time. First her husband had left her for a girl barely out of her teens and then a drunk driver had killed her only child.

"Thomas was wrong," Frank countered. "Favoritism is a bad thing. It only fuels the public's growing distrust of our justice system."

Soon, the group around him disbanded, leaving only Elizabeth. Her dark eyes appraised him. "With the exploding Latino population here in L.A., the time is ripe for a Latino D.A."

"I'd like to think that's a plus on *top* of my other qualifications," Frank stated. As one of ten children born to migrant farmworker parents, he'd been the first in his family to graduate from both high school and college. While he was proud of his heritage and was actively courting the Latino community, he felt strongly that it wasn't all he had going for him.

"So . . . with these *other* qualifications, how come you've never been offered a top post in Thomas's administration?" she said.

He gave her a wary glance. "What's your point?"

"Just that criticizing our boss is not the path to power."

"True, but I call it like I see it," he said, adjusting his tie and pulling at his collar, which seemed to be getting tighter around his throat. His wife Bianca's cooking was steadily putting the pounds on him. "And I have to use all the ammo I've got in this race, Elizabeth. You know that."

"I hope you realize that if you lose against Thomas, he'll probably demote you to issuing criminal complaints in the Antelope Valley."

He knew she was referring to a branch office in the farthest reaches of L.A. County, about thirty miles east of downtown L.A. "Is that what happened to you?"

"For one lousy year," she said. "I was just having too many courtroom victories and Thomas Kendell doesn't like to share the spotlight. On my last big case, while I worked my ass off in the courtroom, Thomas went in front of the news cameras every night, hogging all the credit. I haven't seen a good case since."

Frank wasn't sure how much of her story was valid. He'd heard that she'd had an affair with a defense lawyer and that was why she'd been demoted. But who really knew the truth? The D.A.'s office was always awash with rumors and gossip.

"How are you doing in the polls?" she asked.

"Coming up, but I still don't have enough name recognition or money," Frank admitted. "Thomas has been wooing voters for years. I need to get on television where more voters can see and hear me."

She flashed him a rare smile. "I have some ideas. Why don't we get together after work one night? We can have a drink and I'll give you the benefit of my wisdom."

"Sure. I'll check my calendar and call you."

"Do that," she said.

*   *   *

When Elizabeth got back to her own office, the morning newspaper was still lying open on her desk. It worried her that the mayors of several cities in Los Angeles County had already endorsed Thomas for D.A. If L.A.'s popular mayor were to also endorse him, it was doubtful that anyone could beat him.

In her opinion, Frank Sanchez was the only one of the four challengers with a chance to force Thomas into a runoff. The Latino vote in L.A. County was definitely an untapped resource, but she wasn't sure if Frank was clever enough to mobilize it.

Elizabeth pictured Frank with his short black hair, expressive brown eyes and mellow smile. She admired him. He'd come from the barrio and had worked his way up. She too had come from a poor family and knew what an accomplishment it was to succeed against such odds.

By comparison, Thomas Kendell's father had been a successful architect. That meant his son had had both the time and the funds to participate in all the extracurricular activities offered in college and then law school, activities she and Frank had had to forgo.

Thomas's daughter, Alexandra, had also had it too easy. While there were those who claimed Alexandra's qualifications were outstanding and that's why she'd been hired, Elizabeth didn't agree. She herself was as bright, if not brighter, than Alexandra, and it had taken her several years to become a deputy D.A. In the meantime, she'd worked as a lawyer in the private sector for a large personal injury firm, hating every minute of it.

It angered Elizabeth to see someone like Thomas use his office as a stepping stone to further his own ambitions, especially after he'd treated her so shabbily. If only she could think of some way to help Frank get elected, her future at this office would be assured.

Sitting in front of a computer screen at the downtown public library, Alexandra discovered that Erica's story was indeed based upon fact. Quickly, she scanned the twenty-year-old article she'd just found.

> Today authorities indicated they were closing their investigation into the death of Jeffrey McGrath, a successful local businessman who died last January. McGrath apparently shot himself while hunting in the Santa Monica mountains with his friend, physician George Collins. While unnamed sources have hinted that there were unexplained circumstances surrounding the shooting, the District Attorney's office has issued a statement advising that there is no evidence to suggest that this tragedy was anything other than an unfortunate accident.

Alexandra leaned back, picturing Erica in her hospital room, her face waxen as she'd said, "My ex-husband killed his best friend and I helped him get away with it." A shooting death that involved two people meant there was only one witness left to tell the authorities what had happened. That by itself, however, didn't mean there had been a murder and a cover-up.

Next Alexandra searched for and found the obituary for Jeffrey McGrath. He'd been only thirty-six years old when he died. His parents, a wife and two young children—a girl of nine and a boy of fifteen—were listed as his survivors.

She examined the vital statistic records following McGrath's death until she located the dissolution of George and Erica's marriage. The reason given was irreconcilable differences—typical legal-speak for a garden variety, no-fault California divorce.

Roberta had remarked that Erica's ex-husband had remarried. Curious, Alexandra checked until she located another entry. As the name of George Collins's second wife appeared on her screen, Alexandra sat up straighter in her chair. He'd married *Lorna McGrath?*

Why hadn't Erica mentioned the marriage between her ex-husband and Jeffrey McGrath's widow? Surely she must have realized that Alexandra would eventually discover the truth. Perhaps Erica had been afraid that Alexandra would then dismiss her accusations as being motivated solely by revenge. It was a possibility that Alexandra had already considered. But it didn't necessarily mean Erica's story was untrue.

Hurrying back to the Criminal Courts Building so as not to be late for her afternoon court session, Alexandra shook her head in dismay. She'd been hoping her brief research would provide some facts that would conclusively disprove Erica's accusations. Instead, it had only deepened the mystery, and her ethical quandary, too.

3

——— ❧ ———

FLIPPING THROUGH her mail, Alexandra started up the stairs to her small apartment, located over her landlord's garage. *Mostly junk mail and bills,* she thought, opening the door, until she spotted Kyle's handwriting and the New York return address. Kyle hadn't returned her last two calls, and as Alexandra ripped open the envelope she felt uneasy. Then, as she quickly scanned the letter, her heart sank.

Dear Alexandra,
   I guess this is a lousy way to end a relationship, but we both know things weren't going that well before you left. And six months apart is tough. I didn't intend to meet someone else—things just happened. I know your mom is sick and this is a bad time for you, but I've got to get on with my life. Marsha has a really nice place in Greenwich Vil-

lage, so I won't be needing your co-op any-more. I'll be moving out in a week and will forward the keys. Hope we can remain friends.

Kyle

Tears sprang to her eyes as she slowly let his letter drop onto a table. How could he do this to her, and in such a hurtful way? She'd been so lonely lately that she'd been contemplating flying back to New York just for a weekend visit with him.

Yanking the phone out of the charger, she punched in the number for her New York apartment. When the answering machine switched on, she waited for the beep. "I know you're avoiding me, Kyle, but I've got your letter now so you can pick up."

After what seemed like an endless few seconds, she heard a click. "Hi," Kyle said.

"Hi yourself," she replied glumly. "You know, a 'Dear John' letter is not a very sensitive or caring way to end a relationship. Why didn't you at least call?"

"I know I should have," he replied. "I'm sorry."

There was an awkward silence. She pushed away her personal feelings and forced herself to discuss the other problem. "You can't just leave me with the co-op. We had a deal."

"Hey, you're the lawyer. And besides, we never had any kind of signed agreement."

"I didn't think we had to *formalize* our understanding," she protested. "You knew I'd have to

rent another place here in L.A. You're the one who
wanted to stay in the co-op. You agreed to make
half of the monthly payments on it as well as on the
furniture we bought together." Her voice rose. "If
not, I would have sublet the place before I left."

"Yeah . . . well sometimes things change."

His attitude was exasperating. "It's only fair
that you continue sharing the payments while I try
to arrange for a sublease. It isn't going to be easy to
do from here."

"Hey, I know. And while I sympathize, I can't."

Alexandra hadn't expected him to be so totally
unreasonable or so cold. "Why not?"

"Because I've already promised to share ex-
penses with Marsha."

She was incredulous. "Can't your little friend
wait a month or two?" she asked, not bothering to
hide her increasing annoyance. At the moment she
didn't know whether to cry or start screaming at
him.

"Sorry. Listen, the doorbell's ringing. I've got to
go."

Before Alexandra could protest, he had hung up.
She swallowed her pride and pressed redial. This
time she got a busy signal. He'd obviously taken
the phone off the hook.

"Jesus! What a day!" She took the open bottle
of chardonnay from the refrigerator and poured
herself a large glass. Then she kicked off her black
high-heeled pumps and headed for the bedroom.

Gazing at her image in the mirror, she did a
frank appraisal of herself. At five feet seven and

one hundred twenty-five pounds, her figure was good. Her blond hair was thick and fell smoothly against her high cheekbones, and her large hazel eyes were arresting. While she might not be classically beautiful, she certainly was pretty. Intelligent, too. So why had Kyle chosen to leave her for another woman?

She acknowledged that maybe certain aspects of their relationship hadn't been that good before she left. And maybe she'd never been madly in love with Kyle. But he had seemed like a nice guy with some admirable qualities, and she'd been hopeful they could work through their problems. It gave her an empty feeling to know there was no chance of that happening now.

Stripping off her clothes, she drank the wine in several large gulps, then shrugged into some sweats that were lying on the unmade bed. With her failed marriage and her other short-lived relationships, Alexandra didn't exactly have a great track record in the romance department. But she had always tried to keep up her hopes that something might work out.

A surge of loneliness washed over her again. Where were all the decent men, the kind a woman could trust to be there during both the good times and the bad?

The next afternoon, when court recessed early, Alexandra went to the Hall of Records. If a file still existed dealing with Jeffrey McGrath's death, she had determined it would be in the archives.

After convincing the Supervisor of Criminal Records that she wanted to look for the file herself, she was led into a large room lined with row upon endless row of floor-to-ceiling shelves, each one filled with boxes.

When Alexandra next glanced at her watch, she realized that two hours had passed, during which time she'd been searching through torn and tattered boxes full of dusty manila folders. These old felony files were supposed to be in some kind of order, but in reality the records were a disorganized mess.

Every now and then a young woman clerk came by as if to check on her. "Find what you need yet?" the woman asked.

Alexandra shook her head. There wasn't any air-conditioning in the place and she was perspiring. The dust from the files felt like it had caked everywhere—in her hair, in her teeth, in her clothes. She couldn't wait to get home and wash it all off.

"Just remember, we close at five," the clerk said. "You gotta be signed out of here before that. I have a bus to catch."

Realizing she had less than forty-five minutes left, Alexandra grew anxious. "I understand," she muttered. So far the afternoon had been a total waste. If a file on Jeffrey McGrath's death still existed, she had not been able to find it.

At ten minutes before five Alexandra was at the end of the bottom row, sifting through a box of cases that had been filed over twenty years ago, when a name caught her eye. *Collins*.

Her pulse racing, she grabbed the manila folder with both hands and tugged, trying to pry it loose from the other files wedged tightly around it. By now her hands and fingers were covered with tiny paper cuts. A few sharp tugs past a protruding metal fastener and she had the file loose.

She hurried over to the table in the corner. Heart pounding, she skimmed the sheriff's report and noted that the first deputy on the scene had taken a witness statement from George Collins. George said his friend had been running after an animal when he tripped and fell, and his gun went off. As she read on about the shotgun she did a double take. Thinking she must have misunderstood, Alexandra forced herself to slow down and reread that section of the report.

According to the sheriff's deputy, George Collins hadn't admitted that the shot which had killed Jeffrey McGrath had come from *his* gun—not Jeffrey's—until *after* the deputy had asked him whose initials were on the second gun found at the scene.

Alexandra sat back. It was one thing when a person was killed by his or her own gun. But someone else's gun could be another story entirely—especially when George had been less than forthright about which gun was his. In her mind, these facts alone sounded suspicious enough to have warranted a further investigation into Jeffrey McGrath's death.

She searched the files for other police reports, but came up empty. Why hadn't the deputy called for detectives to come out? Where were the accounts of tests done to the weapon? And where were the autopsy findings? It was difficult to imagine the cops bringing a case to the D.A.'s office without more evidence. Something here wasn't right.

She shuffled through the papers in the thin file one more time, looking to see if there was a D.A.'s letter rejecting the case for prosecution. When she found it, she shivered involuntarily as she read her father's signature at the bottom of the page. Thomas Kendell had been the deputy D.A. who made the decision not to prosecute George Collins.

Had his decision been based on lack of sufficient evidence? Or had the evidence been presented and subsequently suppressed or destroyed? Hoping that there were perfectly reasonable answers to her questions, she decided it was time for her to talk to her father about the role he'd played in this long-forgotten case.

The armed guard sitting outside Thomas Kendell's office was a grim reminder that the District Attorney of L.A. County was a possible target for disgruntled citizens. Alexandra was just debating whether or not to ask the guard to announce her when Carol Eberhardt, Thomas's longtime executive assistant, came out of her father's office.

A tall woman with a prominent jaw and straight hair cut in a short, geometrically precise bob, Carol was adept at shielding her boss from any unpleasantness. "He's on the phone," she told Alexandra.

"I really need to see him. Could you ask if he can spare five minutes?" Alexandra pleaded.

"Let me find out if he's finished with his phone call." Carol disappeared. A few seconds later, she was back. "You can go in."

Alexandra found Thomas sitting at his desk studying some papers in front of him. She cleared her throat. "Hello, Dad."

He glanced up, a worried look on his face. "Has something happened with your mother?"

"No. She's the same. But that's not why I'm here."

"So what is this about?" There was an air of expectancy in his tone.

She sat down across from him. Then, starting with her arrival at the hospital the previous night, Alexandra proceeded to tell him about her encounter with Erica Collins. While she spoke, Thomas kept rearranging the objects on his desk, the muscles in his jaw tensing. But he made no eye contact of any kind with her.

When she was through, he remained quiet for a moment as if thinking. "You didn't mention any of this to your mother, did you?" he finally said.

"Mom had talked to Erica earlier," she explained, "but she has no idea that Erica accused you of being involved in a cover-up."

"That's good," he said, nodding. Gazing at his daughter, Thomas smiled. "I can certainly understand why this woman's accusations upset you." His voice was smooth and reassuring. "But I'm sure you realize this Erica is bitter because she's dying. I'd say she's just trying to get back at her ex-husband for leaving her."

"I thought of that too," Alexandra admitted. "But why didn't she just accuse her ex-husband? Why did she also implicate you?"

Thomas shrugged his broad shoulders. "Who knows? Maybe she's jealous because she sees that Roberta has a loving husband by her side during her illness, while she's all alone." The skin at the corners of his eyes crinkled as he smiled again.

Alexandra considered his response. He could be right. But she had a gut feeling that there was more to it. She leaned forward. "I went to the library to look up the case. And then I searched the archives for the old case file."

Thomas stood up. The smile had vanished from his face. "Why did you do that?"

"I didn't want to bother you about this unless there was a kernel of truth to Erica's story. It appears that George Collins may have had a motive for murder. Less than a year after Jeffrey McGrath's death, George divorced Erica and married Jeffrey's widow. Did you know about their relationship?"

"I don't remember."

"I'd like to hear what it is you do remember about the case, Dad," she said as nicely as possible.

Thomas stiffened. "Why?"

She didn't understand why he was putting her on the defensive. "There were many aspects surrounding Jeffrey McGrath's death that were definitely suspicious. It appeared from the file that a full investigation was never undertaken, and the rejection letter was signed by you. I'd just like to know why you decided not to proceed against George Collins and—"

"Alexandra," he said, waving his hand to interrupt her, "don't you realize that the last thing I need before the primary is for an old case to be reopened and scrutinized?"

"Of course I understand that."

"Good." He held up his palms. "Just forget about this woman and her story now, okay?"

"But Erica threatened to go to Frank Sanchez if I didn't look into the matter," she pointed out.

Thomas walked over to the window and gazed outside. Several tense seconds passed before he turned to face her. "All of this is nothing more than an idle threat from a bitter, dying woman," he said in a perfectly reasonable voice.

"Then you're saying there's absolutely no truth to any of her statements?"

He straightened his shoulders as if unsettled by her question. "Right," he replied, looking her directly in the eye.

"Then give me some facts I can take back to Erica."

"Alexandra," he said again, allowing his annoyance to show, "I've tried to reason with you, but you're not listening. I want you to forget you ever heard about a Collins or McGrath case." He paused before adding, "Am I making myself clear?"

She couldn't understand his attitude. If he had

nothing to hide, why was he behaving like someone who was guilty? Without thinking, she raised her head in defiance. "And if I don't?"

"You may find yourself without a job," he countered angrily. "Now, if you'll excuse me, I need to get back to work." He walked over to his desk and continued rearranging the papers that were already stacked in neat little piles.

His dismissal made her feel like a child again, facing a distant father who was too preoccupied with business to deal with her personal problems. But here at the D.A.'s office she had at least expected to be treated like a colleague.

As if realizing that she wasn't preparing to leave, Thomas glanced up. "Alexandra, please. I'm very busy. I've got a packed agenda today." His tone was once more conciliatory.

It was obvious that he expected her to walk away without any kind of an explanation. Under the circumstances she had little choice. She couldn't force him to tell her about the case or to reveal what he remembered. "And just what am I supposed to tell Erica?"

Thomas squared his jaw and his voice turned chilly. "Nothing. That's what you tell that woman. Nothing."

A few minutes earlier, Elizabeth Nathan had arrived at Carol Eberhardt's desk with a big red tin filled with cookies, only to find that Carol wasn't there. She heard loud voices coming from the D.A.'s office. Noticing that the door wasn't fully closed, Elizabeth glanced around quickly. After making sure that no one was nearby, she tiptoed closer.

The male voice was clearly Thomas's. As for the female voice—she wasn't sure. Then she heard Thomas say the name Alexandra, and she realized it had to be his daughter. Thomas was ordering Alexandra to stop investigating what sounded like two cases.

"Elizabeth?"

She whirled around. Carol was standing there eyeing her suspiciously.

"What are you doing?" asked Carol.

"Looking for you," Elizabeth promptly responded.

"In the D.A.'s office?"

"I heard voices," Elizabeth explained with a smile. "I thought you were in there." She held out her colorful tin. "I made you some of my chocolate chip cookies."

The suspicious expression on Carol's face slowly faded, although she didn't look totally convinced. "Come away from the door," she ordered brusquely. "I don't want the D.A. thinking you were eavesdropping."

"Oh no, of course not," Elizabeth said, shaking her head, her eyes wide and serious.

While Carol opened the tin and removed a cookie, Elizabeth's mind was whirling. Could anything she'd just heard between Thomas and his daughter be used to help Frank win the primary?

* * *

Worried by what his daughter had told him, Thomas picked up the phone to call his campaign manager on his private line.

Dale answered on the second ring. "Yes?"

"Something has come up," Thomas explained. "And I don't want to discuss it on the phone. We need to meet. *Now.*"

"No problem. I'm on my way to the Regal Biltmore downtown," Dale advised him. "We can talk there before my meeting begins."

"Fine," Thomas replied. "I'll see you in the hotel lobby in twenty minutes."

As Thomas hung up, he felt some of his tension recede. Thank goodness he could count on Dale. Without too many questions asked or answered, the man would do whatever it took to make sure that nothing interfered with Thomas's reelection campaign.

4

ALEXANDRA WAS UPSET over her meeting with her father. Why hadn't Thomas denied Erica's allegations outright and backed it up with an explanation, instead of only attacking the woman's motivations? Or why hadn't Thomas offered to check matters out in the event he'd overlooked some detail, instead of just saying it was a bad time to bring up an old case? His responses made it look like he had something to hide.

Not until Alexandra placed the question directly to him had Thomas looked his daughter squarely in the eye and said Erica's statements were not true. But even then he wouldn't give her one reason for rejecting the case. Alexandra wanted to believe him, but she couldn't ignore her nagging doubts. Would her father blatantly lie to her like that?

She thought back to another time, years ago, when Thomas had lied to her. That spring had been one of the happiest times in her young life. She'd been in her first year of college and deeply in love. Alexandra and her boyfriend, Patrick Ross, had been talking about getting married after they finished college and law school. They had been dating for about six months, but hadn't yet been intimate, waiting until it could be special.

She remembered the quaint bed-and-breakfast they had picked for spending the weekend together. It was a small place—six hours north from Los Angeles on the California coast—with only three rooms. The two of them had spent a heavenly night together, and the next morning had gone down to breakfast in the small dining room. Alexandra winced with pain at the memory. There, holding hands and sitting at a table in the corner were her father and . . . another woman. Alexandra had been shocked. She had thought her parents had the perfect marriage.

As bad as she felt about her father's actions, she'd been more upset by his words, as he looked her squarely in the eye and explained that he and the woman were merely having a business meeting—an obvious lie.

Alexandra had not told her mother because she didn't want to hurt her, but then the other woman, worried that her relationship with Thomas was over, called and begged Roberta to give him a divorce. Thomas finally admitted that he'd been involved with this other woman for over five years, and though Alexandra's mother had been devastated and her parents had separated, they had reconciled after a short time.

Deciding that she didn't want to start her career in the shadow of her father, Alexandra had transferred to an East Coast college. From there she went on to law school on the East Coast as well. Except for short visits home, she'd made a life for herself in New York.

The hardest part for Alexandra had been the end of her relationship with Patrick. He'd been the love of her life, although she hadn't realized it for many years. When they broke up, she'd been young and impetuous, wanting to escape everything associated with her bad memories.

Recalling the past, Alexandra felt an overwhelming sadness. Her father had lied to her then—what made her think he wasn't lying to her now? Yet it wasn't entirely fair to compare the two events. One had been a strictly personal matter while the situation with Erica Collins involved possible criminal acts. She wondered what had made her associate the two events in her mind. In thinking about it, she realized it was the bold way Thomas had looked at her on both occasions, as if he was daring her to prove he was lying.

The fact that her father had actually ordered her to forget about the case put her in a bind. She had no official authority to continue investigating the matter.

On the other hand, if Thomas Kendell had taken a bribe over twenty years ago to cover up a murder, shouldn't he have to answer for it? Justice wasn't an abstract idea to Alexandra. She believed in the system. A corrupt law enforcement individual to her was as bad as a murderer; she'd built her career on that belief.

Alexandra wished there was someone with whom she could discuss this problem. She considered speaking to one of the other top deputies at the D.A.'s office, but with the primary such a short time away, she wasn't sure whom she could trust to be discreet. Her other choice was to go to the Attorney General of California. Whenever the D.A.'s office had a conflict situation, the Attorney General's office could step in. But she didn't want to do anything that could harm her father unless she was absolutely sure he'd been involved in a cover-up. It seemed her only recourse was to try and find out the truth herself.

Leaving downtown Los Angeles, Alexandra drove north on the Hollywood Freeway toward the San Fernando Valley. It was one of those rare, beautiful days when the dry Santa Ana winds cleared the L.A. basin of its usual blanket of smog. Because it had been an unusually rainy year, the surrounding Hollywood Hills bordering both sides of the freeway looked magnificent in their lush greenery.

Exiting the freeway at Barham Boulevard, Alexandra drove toward Burbank and Warner Bros. Studios. She'd found out that Jeffrey McGrath's son was a director, and that he was working on a film at Warner Bros. Although the man had been reluctant to see her, she'd finally prevailed. At the gate, a guard found her name on a list and pointed out where she should park.

"Mr. McGrath is still shooting," a young male assistant informed her when she arrived at his office. "If you'll have a seat, I'll let him know you're here."

Twenty minutes later, Alexandra was led into Michael McGrath's office. The room was done in grays and blacks—muted and sophisticated—with modern paintings in somber, dark tones.

"May I see some identification, please?" he asked, his voice cool and detached.

In her experience, few people realized that deputy district attorneys, as members of law enforcement, carried a badge. Reaching into her purse, she pulled out her shield and flashed it open in his direction.

As he came toward her to scrutinize the badge, she saw that he was tall and fine-boned, with dark hair and unusual but arresting green eyes. His chin was chiseled and shadowed with stubble. A handsome man in a brooding sort of way, she thought.

After looking at the identification, he regarded her. "I thought the D.A.'s office had ex-cops to do their investigating."

"We do." She smiled. "But the investigators in our bureau often get overloaded, so sometimes we end up doing our own sleuthing."

"I see." He motioned for her to sit in one of the nearby chairs. Standing in front of his desk, he leaned back against it with his arms folded across his chest. Behind the casual pose she could see that he was tense.

Close up, his gaze was so direct that it made her

uneasy, as if he could read her thoughts. She took a deep breath and forced herself to concentrate. "Thank you for seeing me."

He nodded. "What exactly is this about?"

She found his abruptness unsettling. For some reason, her visit was making him nervous. "As I mentioned on the phone," she said, "I'd like to know a few things about the death of your father."

"I'm not sure what I can tell you. I was only fifteen at the time."

"I understand you may not remember much, but I still have some questions."

"Look, my father accidentally shot himself while hunting." A brief look of pain flashed across his face. "Why is the D.A.'s office interested in his death after all these years?"

"I'm checking out a tip we received."

"What kind of a tip?" he asked, frowning.

"Someone is claiming that your father's death wasn't really an accident—but murder."

There was a momentary flicker of surprise in his eyes before he gazed downward. "My stepfather, George Collins, was with my father that day. They were best friends." The muscles in McGrath's jaw tightened and he seemed to be carefully weighing his words. "George said it was an accident. I believed him then. And I still do."

Why was he so defensive? she wondered. She tried to put herself in his place. His father's death had to have been a traumatic experience, and George Collins might have become like a second father to him. "I can understand why you believed Mr. Collins," she said sympathetically. She paused before adding, "I'm sorry my visit is upsetting you. Please bear with me for just a few more minutes?"

He nodded grimly for her to proceed.

"You say that Mr. Collins and your father were close friends?"

"Yes. They were together a lot."

Alexandra crossed her legs and immediately sensed him watching her. "What about as a foursome? Did your parents spend a lot of time with Mr. Collins and his first wife?"

"I'm not sure."

Careful to keep her tone nonjudgmental, she went on. "I understand your mother married George Collins less than a year after your father's death. Is that true?"

"Yes." He eyed her carefully. "She was lonely and George spent a lot of time with us, trying to make up for the fact that my sister and I had lost our father." Again, he sounded defensive. "What are you getting at anyway?"

It was time to level with him as much as she could. "Our informant says that George Collins was actually responsible for your father's death."

His face darkened. "That's nonsense. It was an accident."

"What if it wasn't?" she challenged. "What if someone conspired with George Collins to suppress important evidence? Wouldn't your family be interested in finding out the truth?"

Michael McGrath shook his head. "I don't

know where you got your information, but I'd seriously question your source." He shoved his hands
into the pockets of his baggy trousers. "You've got
to understand—my family has accepted my father's
death as an accident. We've learned to live with it."

She tried to speak, but he stopped her. "If you
think you're helping us with this preposterous
story," McGrath said, his voice now an octave
lower, "you're wrong." Then, as if realizing that
his manner might be viewed as threatening, he continued on in a much softer tone. "We've been
through enough," he insisted solemnly. "My
mother's made a new life for herself. The past holds
a lot of pain. It would be best if you'd just let it
be."

"I understand where you're coming from. Unfortunately, if we believe someone may have covered up a crime, it's our job to check it out." She
stared at him, trying to assess his reaction to her
words. "Most families in such situations usually
encourage us to get to the bottom of what really
happened."

"We know what *really* happened," McGrath insisted again, his tone sharp. His eyes narrowed.
"Who did this tip come from anyway?"

"At the moment I'm afraid I can't tell you," she
said. "If any of the facts check out, we'll make a
full disclosure then." She paused again. "By the
way, are either of your father's parents still alive?"

"Yes. But they can't help you. My grandparents
are old and my grandmother's in ill health. They
don't even live in the L.A. area anymore."

"I see. What about your sister? I believe her name is Sally?"

"Leave her alone," he ordered. He must have caught the flash of surprise on Alexandra's face, because he changed his approach. "Look," he said, "my sister Sally is . . ." he hesitated, "well, let's just say she's unwell."

"I'm not sure I understand."

"Sally leads a very . . . secluded life," he replied. "Are we almost done?"

"Just a few more questions."

McGrath looked relieved.

"At the time of your father's death, were you questioned by anyone from the sheriff's department or the D.A.'s office?"

"Why would I have been questioned?"

"Any number of reasons. They might have wanted to ask what time your father left the house. Details like that to establish the sequence of events."

"I was a kid," he reminded her.

Alexandra was pensive. From his answers, it didn't appear he'd ever spoken to her father. She leaned forward and handed him her card. "I know this has been painful, but please call me if you remember anything more. I'd really appreciate it."

She stood up and held out her hand to shake his. At the touch of his strong, surprisingly warm hand against her skin, she felt a ripple of electricity course through her. Startled by her unexpected reaction, Alexandra glanced up quickly, hoping he hadn't noticed. She was unable to fathom his thoughts as he studied her from beneath long, dark lashes. An unwelcome flush spread up her neck and into her face. She quickly tugged her hand back, wanting to break the physical contact between them.

"Thank you again for seeing me," she said, heading for the door, her heart hammering in her chest.

Outside, Alexandra was shaken by her physical attraction to this man. It had been a long time since she'd felt that way. In New York she and Kyle had been more like roommates who shared a bed and good times.

Had she even felt this way when she first met her ex-husband? The answer was no. Richard Locke had been a corporate lawyer who didn't have Alexandra's same work ethic, or as he repeatedly pointed out, her single-minded dedication to her career. He'd complained that her compulsive work habits ruled out any quality time for a personal life. Then he used her absences as an excuse to cheat on her, thus confirming her basic belief that no man could be trusted—a belief that had just been painfully reinforced by Kyle.

Pushing aside her personal thoughts, she focused again on the man she'd just met. Michael McGrath had seemed overly defensive, especially for someone who supposedly had nothing to hide and no information to provide on the subject of his father's death. What had he been so afraid of having her find out?

                    *   *   *

Shortly after Alexandra left, Michael McGrath made some calls and postponed his shoot. He then hopped into his black Porsche convertible and sped toward the 101 Ventura Freeway to the 405 San Diego Freeway North. After he exited, he took surface streets to a modest California ranch house in Northridge, a suburb in the San Fernando Valley close to the epicenter of the devastating 1994 earthquake.

After ringing the bell, Michael stood on the porch, impatiently shifting from foot to foot, waiting for his brother-in-law to let him in.

"What's wrong?" Arnold Potter asked, a look of concern on his sallow face.

Arnold, a sociology professor at California State University at Northridge, was a lot older than Michael's sister, but he approved of their marriage because Arnold seemed to exert a stabilizing influence on Sally.

"Where's my sister?" Michael wanted to know, glancing around at the cluttered living room. One of the back bedrooms had been made into an office for Arnold, but he always seemed to have his paperwork spread out over the rest of the house.

Arnold gestured toward the hallway and the master bedroom. "She's resting."

Michael sighed with relief. "Good. I don't want her to overhear us." He proceeded to tell Arnold about the visit he'd had from deputy D.A. Alexandra Locke.

When he was through, it was Arnold's turn to look alarmed. "They're thinking of reopening the case?"

"That's what it sounds like to me."

"That's terrible," moaned Arnold, scratching his balding head.

"We have to derail her investigation before it can go any further," Michael stated firmly. "Ms. Locke also mentioned she wanted to talk to my grandparents as well as to Sally. I think I discouraged her about Lester and Frances, though I doubt she could find them anyway. It's Sally I'm the most worried about."

Arnold was unconsciously pulling on his full, almost totally gray beard. "I'd hate for that woman to show up and upset Sally."

"That's why I'm here. We both know how irrational Sally can be when it comes to George. She'll say things about him that Ms. Locke will definitely misconstrue." Michael gave Arnold a meaningful glance. "Sally's got to understand that she can't talk to the prosecutor. In fact, if the woman comes here, Sally shouldn't even answer the door."

"Don't worry," Arnold assured him. "I'll warn Sally that if she speaks to her she might have to testify in court. The thought of taking the witness stand in front of all those people will terrify her."

There was a worried frown on Michael's brow. "Can't you discourage her from speaking to the woman without resorting to scare tactics?"

"I know some of my methods sound cruel to you, but in many ways Sally's like a child," Arnold replied in a patronizing tone of voice. "She needs to be told that something can hurt her before she understands the danger."

Michael scowled. "I just don't want you to overdo it."

"I won't," Arnold assured him again. "You can trust me."

In her bedroom, with its white canopied bed, Sally McGrath Potter pressed her ear against the closed door and listened to her husband and brother as they spoke about her.

She resented the way everyone treated her like she was a child. They all thought there was something wrong with her because she still hadn't gotten over the death of her father. As far as she was concerned, the real problem was the way everyone in her family protected her stepfather, George.

Sally adored her brother, Michael, but she couldn't understand how he could have switched his allegiance to George. She'd never betray her father's memory that way.

Opening the top drawer of her dresser, she searched for a pencil. Then on a corner of a magazine cover, she scribbled down Alexandra Locke's name before she could forget it.

It was difficult for her to go against either her husband's or her brother's wishes, but she was twenty-nine years old, and she'd been waiting a long time for God to answer her prayers.

The next morning Alexandra was leaving her office for a pretrial hearing when Geena hurried in.

"There's a woman on the phone," Geena said with a perplexed look on her face. "She won't give her name, but she insists you're expecting her call. She sounds scared."

Glancing at her watch and realizing that if she showed up late for court she'd incur the wrath of Judge Clemens, who was scheduled to hear her motion, Alexandra started to tell Geena to get a number, then abruptly changed her mind and lifted the receiver. "Alexandra Locke speaking."

A hoarse whisper came across the line. "This is Sally Potter. My maiden name was McGrath."

Pulse racing, Alexandra motioned for Geena to close the door, then spoke to Sally. "Is something wrong? I can barely hear you."

"I can't let them know I'm talking to you," the woman explained in a low voice. "I just wanted to tell you that George Collins is a murderer. He killed my father." The whisper had turned into an angry hiss.

Startled, Alexandra heard a male voice in the background shouting, *"Sally, are you in there? What are you doing?"*

There was a loud pounding like someone rapping on a door or a wall.

"Do you need help?" asked Alexandra, concerned that this woman was in some kind of danger.

"Just remember what I said," the woman blurted out. Then there was a click, and the line went dead.

Alexandra sat in stunned silence. Should she call the police? But what could she tell them? She didn't even know where this woman had been calling from. Confused, she shook her head. Michael Mc-

Grath had been adamant that George Collins could never have harmed Jeffrey McGrath. But Michael's sister had just insisted that Collins was a killer. As she rubbed her sore neck, Alexandra wondered which one of Jeffrey's offspring she was supposed to believe. And where did her own father fit into the picture?

5

———— ∼ ————

EARLY SATURDAY morning, as Alexandra headed for the desert, she punched the button on her CD player and let the music from Whitney Houston's latest album waft over her. Her one splurge since coming to L.A. had been leasing this sporty blue BMW coupe. After living in New York City, where the most practical mode of transportation was a cab or subway, it was relaxing to be once more at the wheel of a car on the open highway.

After the call from Sally McGrath Potter, Alexandra hadn't been able to get the woman's frightened voice out of her mind. Unable to locate her, she'd considered asking Michael McGrath, but decided against it—he'd been adamant that she stay away from both his sister and his grandparents.

In spite of Michael's admonition, however, Alexandra felt it was important to find out how the elder McGraths viewed their son's death. Michael had indicated that they were in poor health, retired and no longer living in the L.A. area. Taking a chance that they hadn't left the state, Alexandra checked out some of the more desirable retirement locations. She finally found them residing in Rancho Mirage, an affluent desert community lying beyond Palm Springs, California, where most of the residences were enclosed enclaves.

After the guard pointed Alexandra in the right direction, she followed the winding road to the McGrath place. The beautifully landscaped homes in this gated community were all built around a large golf course with an artificial lake at its center. Keeping the grounds looking so lush and green in this arid desert climate had to be expensive, thought Alexandra, especially in the summer when temperatures here could easily soar up into the one hundred twenties.

Frances McGrath kept rubbing her cold, stiff hands in an effort to increase her circulation. Getting old was so bothersome, she thought, as she sat in her wheelchair and gazed out at the purple-hued San Gorgonio mountains.

"She'll be here any minute now," Lester said, glancing at his gold wristwatch.

"I'm ready," Frances replied.

"Let me tuck the blanket around your legs," he offered.

She watched as her seventy-nine-year-old husband knelt down in front of her. The two of them had been married fifty-six years. Although his skin was now weathered and wrinkled, Lester had once been very handsome. In fact, Jeffrey had looked just like him. Sally too had the same fair coloring and silvery blond hair. Only her grandson, Michael, resembled his mother—dark and mysterious, with large, melancholy eyes that rarely let one know what he was really thinking.

Frances patted down her short silver-gray hair. "Does my hair look okay?"

"Yes. It's fine."

It had been traumatic having to cut her long hair, but after she'd gotten sick it became too difficult to manage.

"When the doorbell rings, I'll answer," he said. "Then I'll come back for you."

"All right." Taking a deep breath, she decided to mention what was on her mind. "I've been thinking, Lester, that it could be time to tell what we know."

Lester looked at her askance. "And have everybody's nose in our business again?" He shook his head vigorously. "Never!"

Ever since Lester had mentioned the call from the deputy D.A., Frances had been in turmoil. All of the pain surrounding her son's death had come flooding back to haunt her as if it had happened yesterday. Not that a day went by when she didn't think about her darling son, Jeffrey. Mercifully she'd learned how to separate her memory of him from the gory details of his death. "Don't we owe it to Jeffrey?" she asked, gazing up at her husband.

"We honor our son more by keeping our mouths shut," Lester countered.

"I disagree," Frances told him. "I'd like to see Lorna and George forced to acknowledge their sins."

"Be patient," he advised, checking his own appearance in the mirror and straightening the collar of his shirt. "They'll have to account for everything when they meet their Maker."

"That's not soon enough for me."

"It will have to do for now," he said, his lips pulled back into a grim line.

Just then the doorbell rang. "That must be her," Lester said as he started for the doorway. He turned and looked again at Frances. "Remember—whatever this woman has to say, we'll just listen politely." His watery brown eyes focused sternly on his wife. "I don't want Miss Locke leaving here knowing one more thing than when she came."

"Mr. McGrath? I'm Alexandra Locke." She extended her hand and smiled warmly at the elderly man in white pants and melon-colored shirt who greeted her. Although his silvery hair was sparse, there was still an uncanny likeness between him and the pictures of Jeffrey McGrath she'd seen in the newspaper articles.

The house was deliciously cool as Alexandra followed Lester McGrath into a sunken living room that was done in dusty pastel shades. The color scheme reminded her of those tall, frothy tropical drinks that were served around the pool in the Ba-

hamas, where she'd gone on her ill-fated honey-
moon.

"Before I get my wife," he said, "I just want you
to know that Frances has a heart condition. It's not
good for her to get too worked up."

"Then it might be wiser for her not to sit in on
our discussion," Alexandra replied, scanning
Lester's face for his reaction.

"That's what I told her," he asserted grimly.
"But she insists on being here. I'll be right back."

Lester soon returned, wheeling Frances into the
living room to meet Alexandra. The elderly Mrs.
McGrath was diminutive, with prominent cheekbones and opaque gray eyes.

"This is my wife, Frances," said Lester, rather
formally.

A faint smell of jasmine had entered the room
with the woman. Alexandra smiled. "I'm pleased
to meet you."

Frances smiled back, her hands folded primly in
the lap of a blue cotton dressing gown. Around her
legs was a multicolored pastel afghan.

After exchanging small talk about the weather,
Alexandra explained her reason for asking to see
them. "Someone has come forward who claims
that your son Jeffrey's death wasn't an accident,
but a murder."

Alexandra caught the unmistakably triumphant
look on Frances McGrath's face as she glanced over
at her husband. It seemed to say, *I told you so.*

In response, he shook his head. "There were
only two people there that day, and one of them is

dead." He squinted at Alexandra and said, "George Collins didn't tell you this, did he?"

"No," Alexandra admitted.

"Well, if someone wasn't there they can't know what happened," he said stubbornly.

"At the moment, I can't respond to that because I can't reveal my source. Not until I've checked out all the facts." Feeling that the wife might be more cooperative, Alexandra focused on her. "Were both of you convinced that your son's death was an accident? Or did you have some doubts?"

"My son was too smart to run with a loaded—" Frances started to say when Lester interrupted her with a wave of his wrist.

"What Frances means is that Jeffrey was around guns most of his life. But we all know accidents still can happen. The police were satisfied with George's story and we had no reason to question it."

It sounded to Alexandra like a rehearsed statement. "How did you feel when your son's widow married George?"

There was a flash of anger in Frances's eyes. "I for one thought it came a mite too soon."

"Now, Frances, how long one mourns is not important," Lester said, before directing his comments toward Alexandra. "Women are funny about things like that. But the marriage was really best for our grandkids. A few months after Jeffrey's death, our grandson, Michael, had a nice relationship going with George. The boy needed a father. I was close to sixty, but George was still a young man." He cleared his throat. "A boy needs someone he can go camping with and play ball with. You know, someone to show him what it is to be a man."

Alexandra wanted to say that there were a lot more things to teach a child of either sex besides how to camp or play ball, but she held her tongue. "And how about Sally?" she asked instead. "Was George and Lorna's marriage good for her too?"

Lester walked over to the large window facing the golf course, while Frances glanced down at her hands. Alexandra, knowing the value of silence, waited for one of them to speak.

"Sally's one of those girls who are born high-strung and delicate, if you get what I mean," Lester explained solemnly. "She took the death of her father real hard. We were all worried about her at the time."

"We still worry about her," Frances admitted, pointedly meeting Alexandra's gaze. In spite of her frail appearance and her husband constantly contradicting her, Alexandra sensed that this woman had inner strength.

"I wish you could have met my Jeffrey," Frances said. "He was such a wonderful son and father."

Alexandra noted that neither Lester nor Frances had answered her question about Sally. Frances also had failed to mention that Jeffrey was a good husband. Was that omission a mistake or was it deliberate? "I understand how much you loved your son and I know this must have been very difficult for both of you," Alexandra said, picking and choosing her words as carefully as if she were tiptoeing her way through a meadow filled with land mines. "But now that your grandchildren are both adults, if there's evidence Jeffrey was in fact murdered, wouldn't you want your son's killer or killers brought to justice?"

There was a glimmer of hatred in the older woman's eyes before her husband silenced her with a shake of his head. "Too late for that," Lester insisted.

"It's never too late," Alexandra said. "There's no statute of limitations on murder."

He exhaled loudly. "I mean Jeffrey's dead. He's not ever coming back—no matter what we do."

"True. But it's still against the law to kill someone. Whether or not there is enough evidence to prove it is for a trial court to hear and a jury to decide."

"A trial means a scandal. It'd only hurt Michael and Sally more." In spite of his reasonable tone of voice, the way he clenched and unclenched his fists communicated a hidden anger. Alexandra wondered at whom it was directed.

She debated telling them about their granddaughter's call to her. Mindful of Frances McGrath's heart condition, she decided against it. Instead, she concentrated on finding out what part her father might have played in the aftermath of Jeffrey's death.

"At the time of your son's death, did you speak

to anyone at the L.A. County Sheriff's Department?"

"Don't think so," Lester stated.

Swallowing hard, she asked her next question. "What about the D.A.'s office? Did you speak to anyone there?"

"Nope."

"Yes you did," Frances reminded him.

Catching the look the woman had given her husband, Alexandra said, "Who was that?"

Lester McGrath's gaze hardened. "Afraid I don't remember. Frances doesn't remember either."

Alexandra knew better than to let them see her frustration. She tried another tack. "Are there any papers you still might have, or documents I might provide that would help refresh your memory?"

"Nope," he said.

She still didn't believe him, but kept her voice light and casual. "Why don't I mention a few names and see if you can recall anything?"

"Don't bother," he said. "Hell, I'm seventy-nine years old. No court is going to say an old man like me is perjuring himself 'cause he can't remember."

He was lying. Why else point out that he couldn't be punished for refusing to talk? She needed to find a way to get through to him. "No one can *make* you remember," she agreed, a slight smile at the corners of her mouth. "But we're both on the same side here. I'm sure you agree that it's wrong to take someone's life?"

Frances was nodding as Alexandra spoke.

"Of course," said Lester. "But we mind our own

business. We expect others to do the same." His chin was set in a firm line as he added, "We won't go along with any reinvestigation of our son's death."

There it was—he was stonewalling her. Still, there had to be a way to get through to them. Alexandra walked over to the baby grand piano in the corner. "What a beautiful piano," she said, admiring it. She shifted her attention to the pictures in antique frames that sat along its top. "Is this Sally?" she asked, gesturing to the photograph of an ethereal-looking woman in her twenties with silvery blond hair.

Frances McGrath maneuvered her wheelchair over to where Alexandra was standing. "Yes," she replied proudly. "And that's our grandson, Michael."

"She's lovely. He's handsome, too." Even more so in person, she thought to herself.

The woman pointed out another picture of her two grandchildren. "That one was taken when Michael was a little boy and Sally was just a baby."

Out of the corner of her eye Alexandra spotted a photograph of the two children with their father, Jeffrey. It was toward the back and wedged in between several others so that it was almost hidden from view. She lifted it forward and noticed part of a woman's arm and hand around Michael. The fourth finger also had a diamond ring on it. Whoever the woman was, she'd been artfully cut out of the picture. She pointed to the arm. "Was this Sally and Michael's mother?"

There was a sharp intake of breath from

Frances, and Alexandra caught the angry look Lester gave his wife as he hurried forward. "Nope. It was just a friend." He took the frame away from her and put it facedown on the piano. "I think we've overtired my wife. It'd be best for you to go now, Miss Locke."

Hoping to change his mind, Alexandra took a step forward. "If you want I could wait while you tend to your wife. Perhaps then you and I could continue our talk?"

"No need," he countered, shaking his head. "I've told you everything there is. We've got nothing more to say." His jaw remained set.

She'd obviously stepped over some boundary he didn't want her to cross, and he wasn't going to change his mind. "I appreciate you both taking the time to see me." She took out a card and put it on the piano. "I'll just let myself out."

In the entry hall, Alexandra opened the door and paused briefly when she heard voices coming from the other room.

"We should have told her," Frances said.

"Never," Lester responded in a harsh voice. "We don't need that woman nosing around in our private affairs."

It seemed obvious that Lester and Frances Mc-Grath didn't care for their former daughter-in-law, Alexandra mused, as she closed the door softly behind her. But how did that tie into Jeffrey McGrath's death? And what else had the elderly couple been hiding?

6

ERICA COLLINS'S deadline was approaching, and Alexandra had nothing substantive to report. She was still no closer to finding any definitive answers as to how Jeffrey McGrath had died, or if her father had been involved in some kind of cover-up. She was also troubled by the inconsistencies and half-truths she had encountered so far in her investigation of the case. Whether or not it was a murder, she couldn't say, but it certainly appeared that people were hiding something, and the more she learned, the more suspicious she became.

As she drove toward the City of Hope, she tried to figure out what she was going to tell Erica. Somehow she'd have to convince the woman that she needed more time. She glanced over at her purse. Inside was her tape recorder. Alexandra intended to question Erica more thoroughly and to record her statement.

Over the last several days, as Alexandra had

split her time between her work, her mother and this investigation, she'd realized how important it was to assess Erica's credibility by doing a background check on her.

So far, Alexandra had determined that Erica had no record with the police. After her divorce from George Collins, she'd gone back to school at USC, where she'd obtained a degree in education. Then, for a number of years, Erica had taught at one of L.A.'s junior high schools, and she was now on disability leave.

As for Erica's personal life, Roberta had been right. No remarriage—no children. Not even any close relatives. It seemed like a very lonely existence.

At the City of Hope, Alexandra found the hallways busy. No one paid her much notice as she made her way to Erica's room.

Once there, she slipped quietly inside. The room was dark and very cold. Why hadn't they left the light on in the bathroom like they usually did in her mother's room? Alexandra couldn't see anything, so she stood still and waited for her eyes to adjust.

When the room finally came into focus, she blinked in confusion. Had she somehow entered the wrong room? Groping toward the wall, she found the light switch and flicked it on. The bed was empty.

With a wave of panic she tried to figure out what had happened. Had Erica been moved to another room?

Alexandra made her way down the busy hall to the nurses' desk. "Excuse me," she said to a nurse she didn't recognize. "I'm looking for Erica Collins. Her room is empty. Has she been moved?"

The young woman glanced up and eyed her curiously. "Are you a relative?"

"Not exactly," Alexandra said. "My mother is another patient here." She reminded herself to smile. "She wanted me to see how Erica is doing."

"Who is your mother?" the nurse asked, a suspicious look on her oval face.

"Roberta Kendell."

The nurse's features relaxed. "Oh yes."

Alexandra put her hands on the counter, her patience wearing thin. "So where's Erica?"

The young nurse cleared her throat, her eyes filled with sadness. "I'm sorry to be the one to tell you this," she said, "but Mrs. Collins died early this afternoon."

Dazed by the news of Erica's death, Alexandra had hurried to the cafeteria, where she bought a cup of coffee and then took a seat by herself. She realized that she was filled with both sadness and relief. Had Erica's ultimatum died with her? she wondered, contemplating her choices. If she did nothing further, who would know? Certainly Thomas wasn't going to complain. Nor would Roberta. As for the McGrath family, only Sally and Frances seemed eager to have this investigation pursued. But Frances had been silenced by Lester. And since Sally had been too afraid to leave a return phone number, it was doubtful she'd be willing to testify in court.

She thought about New York and her work in the political corruption unit there. If anyone other than her father had been implicated in a cover-up, would Alexandra forget about it because the main accuser was dead? And if George Collins really was a murderer, should Erica's death allow him to escape punishment?

Alexandra wanted to believe that her father had nothing to do with any cover-up. She certainly didn't want to be the one to derail his career. She'd been hoping that Erica would give her additional facts—facts that would help exonerate her father.

Not knowing yet what she intended to do, Alexandra tried to compose herself before visiting her mother. She would have to be careful, because Roberta had an uncanny way of knowing when something was troubling her daughter.

"Did you hear about Erica Collins?" Roberta asked.

"Yes," Alexandra nodded. "One of the nurses told me." She gazed at her mother. "Wasn't it rather sudden?"

"She'd been sick a long time," Roberta pointed out, her voice dropping.

"I wasn't aware of that." Sensing her mother's unspoken thoughts, Alexandra added, "It must be hard on you when one of the other patients dies."

"Yes. It's scary," Roberta admitted. Her voice held a slight tremor as she raised her chin. "But I also feel guilty because with another death the odds against my being one of the lucky ones to beat ovarian cancer go down."

"It's only natural to think like that," Alexandra said, trying to reassure Roberta as she squeezed her hand.

There was a knock at the door and one of the hospital's many volunteers came in carrying a large wicker basket covered with transparent wrap. She smiled at Alexandra and Roberta, then placed the gift on the bed and left.

"Oh how beautiful," Roberta said, reaching eagerly for the card.

Alexandra was glad to see her mother's thoughts of death pushed from her mind, if only for a short time. "Who's it from?" she asked.

"Patrick Ross," Roberta replied, admiring the basket filled with soaps and lotions and other bath items. "Wasn't that sweet of him?"

At the mention of her old boyfriend's name, Alexandra's stomach did a small flip. "Yes." She nodded again, not knowing what else to say.

Roberta removed the plastic wrap and reached for some soap, which she held up to her nose. "Mmm. Smells delicious."

"That was nice of him to think of you," Alexandra remarked, watching as her mother continued to dig around in the basket.

"We've kept in touch," Roberta said as she next removed a beautiful picture frame from the basket. "You know, Alexandra, I've never been the kind of mother to say 'I told you so'—but you really missed the boat when you let Patrick slip through your fingers."

"Yeah, I guess." Alexandra fell quiet, thoughtful. Sometimes she wondered how differently her life might have turned out if she hadn't been so pigheaded, so stubborn about starting a new life in New York. Because of her inflexibility, Patrick and she had gone their separate ways. He had tried to reason with her, to convince her to stay with him, but she had been adamant. In the end their parting had been angry and bitter.

"Alexandra?"

She turned to find her mother staring at her. "I was thinking about Patrick," she admitted with a slight catch in her throat. "I guess we were young and stubborn. Anyway, we both eventually married other people."

"True. But when I wrote you that he was getting a divorce, why didn't you contact him?"

Alexandra gave a nonchalant shrug as she sat there sorting through her own emotions. Two years ago, when Patrick had been profiled in the *Daily Journal,* a legal newspaper widely read by the legal community in L.A., Roberta had cut out the article and sent it to Alexandra in New York with a note that said he was getting a divorce and that Alexandra should call him.

She remembered reading the laudatory comments about Patrick and the unexpected joy she had felt. She'd dashed off a letter congratulating him on achieving his dreams of becoming one of the most sought-after criminal defense lawyers in

L.A. In return, she'd received a one-line thank-you note. Hurt by the curtness of his reply, she'd been too embarrassed to tell her mother—one of the only times she hadn't confided in Roberta, who had always been like her best friend.

"The last time I spoke to Patrick, he mentioned that he'd run into you at court," said Roberta, eyeing her daughter curiously.

"Yes," Alexandra conceded, her voice matter-of-fact. "We chatted for a few minutes. I got the definite feeling he was involved with someone."

"It's his law partner, Nancy something. I don't think they are officially engaged," Roberta explained with a knowing smile. "But they might have an understanding. Want me to find out?"

"No thanks," Alexandra said, shaking her head. She had strong feelings about staying away from men who were married or in committed relationships. To her they were strictly off limits.

Roberta looked at her daughter and frowned. "You know you need to start dating again," she said.

Alexandra was not ready for this conversation. "One thing at a time, Mom, okay? Let's get you well first."

As Alexandra left her mother's room, she spotted Ms. Stevens coming toward her. When she was close enough she said, "I just heard that Erica Collins died."

"Yes," the nurse responded with a sad shake of her head. "She went in her sleep."

"At least it's good that she didn't suffer at the end," Alexandra said, wondering how best to approach the subject on her mind. "Do you remember last week when you asked me to talk to Erica?"

"Yes."

"I was planning on taking her statement tonight," Alexandra explained, pointing to the tape recorder in her purse. "I was wondering if Erica said anything to you about it?"

The nurse assessed Alexandra frankly, as if making a decision about something. "Yes. Mrs. Collins said that if you came back to see her, I was to give you an envelope. Let me go get my bag," she said, rushing off.

When the nurse returned she suggested that they go into Erica's empty room. Once inside, she handed Alexandra a bulky manila envelope. As Alexandra turned it over in her hands she noted that it looked like the same one Erica had showed her.

"Erica also gave me some precise instructions," Ms. Stevens said with a note of authority in her voice. "She told me that if she passed away before you could visit her again, I should give you this envelope. But *only*," she emphasized, "if I was absolutely positive that you had come back to see her and not just your mother."

"Did she also tell you what to do if I didn't return to see her?"

"Oh yes," Ms. Stevens replied. "Mrs. Collins said to wait a few days. If by then you hadn't shown up, she wanted me to mail the envelope to someone else." She reached into her tote bag and pulled out a scrap of paper. "To a man named Frank Sanchez. Supposedly he's a deputy district attorney in downtown L.A."

Alexandra felt a jolt of surprise. So Erica apparently had been serious about her time limit. If she hadn't tried to see Erica again, the matter would have been out of her hands. She considered that possibility for several seconds. Maybe it would have been better that way. Then the burden of deciding what to do would have been removed from her shoulders. "Did she say anything else?"

"Just that it was very important for me to follow her wishes explicitly."

Recognizing the curiosity on the nurse's face, Alexandra debated opening the envelope in her presence. At some later date she might be glad she'd had a witness. Of course, the opposite might also be true. Taking a deep breath, she decided to chance it. She pried open the flap and peered inside. There was a key and a note.

She flipped open the note. *"To Alexandra Locke,"* it began. The words were scribbled and difficult to read, as if Erica's hand had been shaking when she wrote it.

It's up to you now to prove that George Collins murdered Jeffrey McGrath and that he escaped prosecution by bribing a deputy D.A. I'm leaving you the key to my storage locker, which contains things that will make your search easier. I trust you to see that justice is done.

It was dated and signed simply, *Erica Collins*.

The nurse was gazing at the letter. "What does it say?" she asked.

Alexandra decided to level with her as much as possible. "Erica believed a crime had been committed twenty years ago and wanted me to look into it." She watched for the woman's reaction. "Did she ever speak to you about it?"

The nurse shook her head. "No."

"I see," Alexandra muttered, absently turning the key over in her hand.

"I've got to get back to my patients," Nurse Stevens informed her, smiling apologetically. As she turned to go, she suddenly stopped. "Oh, I forgot to mention one thing."

"What's that?" Alexandra asked.

"Erica had a visitor shortly before she died."

Surprised, Alexandra focused her eyes on the nurse. "Do you know who it was?"

"Oh yes," Nurse Stevens replied with a quick smile. "It was your father."

7

EVER SINCE Ms. Stevens had mentioned that
Thomas visited Erica before she died, Alexandra
had been on edge. Why had he done that? she kept
asking herself. Wasn't that proof that Erica's accusations had been more worrisome than he'd admitted to his daughter? If he'd truly believed that Erica
was crazy, he wouldn't have bothered.

Taking one hand off the steering wheel,
Alexandra rubbed her throbbing temples. She was
exhausted. Trying to investigate the Collins/Mc-
Grath case while carrying her full workload, as
well as making sure she still had quality time to
spend with her mother, was leaving her no time to
sleep.

She was so mired in her own thoughts that when
she came to a dead end, Alexandra realized she was
lost. After consulting her map, and making two
more wrong turns, Alexandra finally located the
storage facility Erica had used. It was not in the best

part of Glendale, she noted, as she parked in front
of the run-down gray concrete building.

Inside, a pimple-faced young woman sat behind
a counter, reading a magazine.

"I'd like to get into a locker," Alexandra explained, smiling.

The woman appeared annoyed by the interrup-
tion as she pushed a large ledger toward Alexandra, mumbling that she should sign it.

Alexandra scribbled Erica's name and hers underneath it as well as the number of the unit. Holding up the key, she asked, "Which way do I go?"

Glancing down at the register, the woman then
looked back up at Alexandra. "Number 122 is
down that hall," she finally said, gesturing to the
left.

Relieved that she hadn't run into any bureau-
cratic red tape, Alexandra headed in what she
hoped was the right direction.

After locating the locker and inserting the key,
she removed the padlock and began rolling the gal-
vanized metal door up into the ceiling.

Her heart sank when she saw that the entire
storage space was crammed to the ceiling with
cartons of all sizes and shapes. It could take her
weeks to go through everything. Remembering
the mess she'd had to go through in the archives,
she was beginning to think storage boxes were her
nemesis.

Alexandra removed one of the brown cardboard file boxes from the nearest stack. It was
covered with grime. Blowing the dirt off the top,

she surmised that Erica hadn't been to this place in years.

The box was stuffed with papers that looked like they had been tossed in without any regard for order. She revised her original time estimate. It could take months to go through these boxes and to organize the material. And what if after she'd expended all that time and energy she turned up nothing of any evidentiary value?

She couldn't work here. There was no place to spread out except on the cold cement floor of the hallway, where she'd be in the way of other people going to their lockers. Alexandra could see that her only option was to sort through this mess at home, a few boxes at a time. With a groan, she lifted one of the larger boxes and headed for her car.

"It's nice to have my two favorite people here at the same time," Roberta said, smiling from her hospital bed as she gazed from Alexandra to Thomas.

Alexandra nodded at her father and then went to the sink and washed her hands before she gave her mother a kiss. She hadn't seen Thomas since their confrontation in his office and she felt ill-at-ease. She wanted to ask Thomas several questions, including why he had visited Erica, but she couldn't say anything in front of her mother.

"Have you eaten dinner?" Roberta asked.

"Not yet," Alexandra admitted.

"You must be hungry then?"

"I'll eat when I get home. In fact, I can't stay too long because I have a huge trial brief to read tonight."

"You're working our daughter too hard," Roberta chided her husband.

"It isn't just me, Mom," Alexandra said, scraping off a smudge of dirt on her forearm that she hadn't noticed. Erica's locker had been filthy. "Everyone in the office puts in the same long hours."

"That's because we can't get the damn Board of Supervisors to loosen their purse strings," griped Thomas. For the next five minutes he complained nonstop about the budgetary problems he dealt with on a daily basis.

"You must be hungry too, dear," said Roberta, looking at Thomas. "Why don't you and Alexandra get something to eat together?"

"I can't," Alexandra hurried to say. "I wanted to spend an hour here with you, then I have to go home. Like I said, I've got a lot of work waiting for me."

Her father fixed his gaze on her for an uncomfortably long time before he spoke. "I'd like it if you'd join me for dinner, Alexandra."

Surprised by his unexpected invitation, she quickly contemplated the pros and cons of sitting across the table from him. It would give her a chance to ask her questions, but she'd have to be careful not to let him know that she was continuing her investigation. She was still undecided when he addressed her again.

"We both have to eat." Thomas's tone of voice was conciliatory as he flashed his daughter a brief smile. "We'll just grab a quick sandwich. Thirty minutes at the most."

"All right. But first I want to visit with Mom." To her embarrassment, her voice came out sounding high and squeaky, like a child's.

"I'm tired tonight, darling. Really I am," Roberta chimed in as if on cue. "Stay a few minutes more, then go with your father," she urged. "I'll feel better knowing you both have company for dinner."

They had gone to Mitzi's Café, a colorful chain restaurant with a large menu, located not too far from the hospital.

"I shouldn't have been so short with you the other day," Thomas said apologetically, smiling at Alexandra as she sat across the table from him.

She chose not to reply, waiting instead to see what else he had to say.

He took the white paper napkin in front of him and put it on his lap. "I'm sure you appreciated my reasons for being upset. With the primary so close, I just don't need any more headaches. Anyway," he shrugged his broad shoulders, "Erica Collins is dead. So let's just forget about the entire incident, okay?"

Alexandra was stunned that he actually expected her to do that without more of an explanation. She took a sip of water to avoid answering him directly. Then, putting the glass down, she leaned forward with her elbows on the table. "I understand that you visited Erica before she died?"

Thomas glanced up, his surprise registering on his face. "Who told you?"

"One of the nurses," she responded. "Did you go see Erica to confront her about her accusations?"

"No, no," he said smiling and shaking his head as if that thought had never entered his head. As usual, he'd quickly recovered his aplomb. "I was just seeing how she was doing." He paused, then added, "Your mother had asked me to check on her."

"And you never spoke to Erica about anything having to do with the Collins/McGrath case?" she queried, struggling to keep the cynicism out of her voice.

"No," he said, shaking his head again. "We actually never spoke. When I got there she was sleeping."

Alexandra looked at him, unsure whether to believe him. Even though his words sounded reasonable, at an emotional level she remained unconvinced. "Have you given any more thought to why Erica might have accused you of participating in a cover-up?"

"No." The lines around his mouth became tense. "Like I said, let's just forget about it."

She stiffened. Gazing at her father, she wondered what was the truth. Could he have taken a bribe and let a murderer go free? She didn't want to believe it, but his actions and his attitude toward the entire situation only made her question him more. For a moment, she considered mentioning Erica's letter as well as her instructions to the nurse about turning everything over to Frank Sanchez. Then she decided against it. Thomas might demand the key to Erica's storage locker; it was a situation she didn't want to face.

As if oblivious to his daughter's reaction, Thomas changed the subject. As he talked about the upcoming primary, he unconsciously organized the silverware on the table so that soon all the knives, forks and spoons were facing the same way in a precise line.

She had long ago determined that her father had a need for orderliness. It was almost as if he felt that by controlling these small things, he could avert the larger, more threatening situations in his life.

Thomas then went to another familiar subject— how the press was not treating him fairly. For years the media and Thomas had shared a fabulous relationship, as story after story lauded his skills as a prosecutor and his savvy at running the D.A.'s office. Then his office suffered two high-profile losses that embarrassed him and threatened his future in the job.

When the waitress appeared with his hamburger and Alexandra's salad, Thomas bantered lightly with her. Alexandra envied the ease with which her father could communicate with anyone on virtually any subject. She often felt awkward with small talk. It was only in her capacity as a deputy district attorney that she truly exhibited a poise that reflected self-confidence.

Peering at the food, Alexandra realized she wasn't very hungry. Lately she barely had an appetite. She pushed her food around with her fork while Thomas devoured his burger.

Afterward, he neatly piled all of the dirty dishes off to the side. Then he settled back in his seat. "How does your mother look to you?"

"Her color isn't good, and she's way too thin," Alexandra replied honestly.

"She may be a little pale, but her spirits are excellent." He tapped the table for emphasis. "She's fighting like a real trooper."

"There's no denying that," she agreed. "I just don't like the way the cancer cells are still showing up in spite of the treatments she's been getting."

He frowned. "Really? Whenever I ask, your mother insists that she's responding well."

Alexandra wondered at the apparent lack of communication between her parents on the subject of Roberta's illness. "What she means to say, Dad, is that she's responding about as well as can be expected. We've got to remember that ovarian cancer, especially like hers, is one of the worst kinds to get."

"We must stay positive, Alexandra," he insisted, shaking his head again as if he could rid himself of all unpleasant, unwelcome thoughts.

"I think it's good to be hopeful," she agreed with a sigh. "But it's also important to give Mom a chance to talk about the downside. She shouldn't be afraid of sharing her feelings with us." She regarded him. "What she's going through is very scary."

"There's nothing to be afraid of if she stays focused on getting well."

His refusal to acknowledge that Roberta had a right to her fears frustrated Alexandra. She'd had this conversation with him before and didn't relish going through it again. "What's important," she said instead, "is for us to spend as much time as possible with her."

His brow furrowed. "I can't do any more than I'm doing, Alexandra. I'm in the middle of an election. Your mother understands."

"Mother always seems to understand," she said, tilting her head. "That's one of her problems."

Thomas straightened his shoulders. "What's that supposed to mean?"

"That Mother has trouble asking for what she wants." She paused, trying to figure how to get through to him. "Listen, Dad, Mom adores you. You realize that by now, don't you?"

Reddening slightly, he nodded.

"Would it be possible for you to take a leave of absence for a month or so and spend it by her side? Your wife is fighting for her life," she said softly. "It could be the last time you'll have together."

Eyes narrowing, Thomas leaned forward. "That isn't a good idea. Without my work—the election—I'd go crazy. I can't just sit around doing nothing. And I'd only end up being more of a burden to her than a help."

Her father's inability to understand how much

this would mean to Roberta upset Alexandra, and she spoke more harshly than she'd intended. "Is that how you rationalize not coming to the hospital more often?"

"I think how often I visit my wife is between your mother and me," he shot back, the veins in his neck pulsating. Then his anger seemed to deflate. He took a deep breath. "I know you still blame me for what happened that spring . . ." His words trailed off as he stopped to clear his throat. "If your mother and I have managed to work things out, don't you think it's time you and I did, too?"

Alexandra realized he was referring to her discovery of his affair and her parents' consequent separation. "I know that Mom forgave you," she said. "I just have my own opinion on the price she may have paid for it."

"So . . . it's obvious you think she made the wrong choice."

"No. If that's what she wanted, it was okay with me. But it's not that simple." Alexandra searched for the words to describe her feelings. "I think she loved you unconditionally and what happened wounded her deeply. Mom never really understood how you had lived a lie for five years without her even guessing at the truth."

"But I explained all that," Thomas protested. "It had nothing to do with not loving your mother. There was just something . . . something missing for me."

"And that made it all right?"

"No. Of course not," he muttered quickly. "I know what I did was wrong. That's why I asked for her forgiveness. During the time your mother and I were separated, I came to realize how much I had lost."

"Have you ever thought about how much *she* lost?"

He appeared confused. "She didn't *lose*. We're still together."

It was clear to Alexandra that she wasn't doing a good job of explaining to her father what she meant. She lowered her voice and tried again. "Like I said, she forgave you. But the two of you never really talked it out; Mom didn't go for any counseling. She never got the chance to express her anger and get beyond it. That's not your fault. But that's why I wonder if she has ever been able to forget."

Thomas's blue eyes bored through her. "Are you implying that I'm responsible for her getting *cancer?*"

"No. I'm not blaming you. But I believe there's a connection between the mind and the body. When the mind suffers a terrible trauma, sometimes the body breaks down."

"You don't know what you're talking about!" he sputtered. Waving for the waitress, Thomas added, "For an intelligent grown woman, you sometimes act remarkably like a child."

It was painful to have him dismiss her feelings

as being childish. He hadn't really listened to her or tried to understand. Instead, he'd just lost his temper.

She stood, too, and took out some bills and left them on the table. "I'll pay my own way, thanks." Then, slinging her purse over her shoulder without another word, she walked out of the restaurant.

8

So far, Alexandra's closing argument had been one of the best she'd ever given, probably because she'd been speaking directly from her heart. It was fortunate, considering how little time she'd had to prepare.

When she turned to face the courtroom she saw that the defendant was glaring at her. He was angry because she'd fought to bring him to trial even though everyone, from her supervisor at the D.A.'s office to the judge, had tried to convince her to accept a plea bargain. Alexandra really hadn't given a damn that the court system was overcrowded. In spite of the pressure, she'd remained firm about her strategy, feeling that only a prison term and a rehabilitation program would fully serve both justice and the victim.

Taking a deep breath, she pointed to the defendant. "This man can't even admit he might have *unintentionally* hurt his wife. He's six feet six and over two hundred pounds. She's five feet nothing, one hundred-five pounds. She ends up in the hospital with multiple injuries, including knife wounds from which she almost dies, while he sustains a few fingernail scratches. Who's he fooling? Not me. I hope not you." She paused to let her implication of juror responsibility sink in as she faced them.

"Ladies and gentlemen of the jury, don't let the next stop for this terrified woman be the morgue." Her voice rose dramatically as she paced in front of them. "You have the evidence before you. Do the right thing. Find this defendant guilty of attempted murder." Feeling good about her argument, she thanked the jury and sat down.

After the judge recessed for the day, Alexandra gathered her papers and headed for the back of the courtroom. For the first time, she noticed a man watching her. As she got closer, she realized with a mixture of anxiety and curiosity that it was Michael McGrath. How long had he been standing there? she wondered.

He moved toward her. "That was an unbelievable closing argument," he said, his eyes boring into hers. "I wish I could have captured it on film."

"Thanks," she said, feeling slightly flustered. "What are you doing here?"

"I went upstairs to your office and they said you were in court today. I wanted to apologize," he said. The sheepish grin on his face made him look like a completely different person from the one she had encountered at the studio. "I was rude the day you came to see me, and I was hoping you'd let me make it up to you over dinner."

His invitation caught her off guard. A part of her wanted to say yes, but she hastily calculated that it wasn't a good idea. "Thanks, but I've got too much work to do." She kept her voice professional. "Why don't we go up to my office and chat there instead?"

"I don't blame you for declining. I was definitely out of line the other day." He lowered his head and swallowed several times as though he were nervous. "Is it possible we could start again?"

He seemed so sincere that Alexandra was rethinking her attitude toward him. "I guess my news did come as quite a shock . . ." she conceded.

As if sensing a weakening in her defenses, Michael rushed to speak. "I was completely overwhelmed by the things you said—I couldn't think straight. Look, I understand your reluctance to see me, but I promise to be on my best behavior. I was on the set all day, then drove directly here so as not to miss you. I haven't had anything to eat since five this morning. So please have dinner with me."

His words poured out so rapidly and with such earnestness that again Alexandra found herself wavering. It was already after five, and she'd missed lunch too. One hour—a quick sandwich—and then she'd go to the hospital to visit Roberta.

"Okay," she agreed. "I'll meet you at—" she hesitated, trying to think of a place.

"How about the New Otani?" McGrath said eagerly, referring to a nearby hotel. "They've got a lounge where you can get a drink and something to eat."

"Fine," she nodded in a detached manner that belied her actual nervousness. "See you there in twenty minutes."

His deep green eyes reflected glimmers of light as he smiled. "Thanks for the second chance."

The restaurant at the New Otani Hotel was bathed in a warm glow, and as she ate her sandwich, Alexandra found herself wishing that she could sit back, relax and let the problems of the day slip away.

She sneaked a quick glance at Michael McGrath. He was dressed casually in a brown suede jacket, brown cords and a forest-green sweater. Now that he'd abandoned the angry persona she'd encountered at their first meeting, she found him even more physically attractive.

As if sensing that she was judging his appearance, he glanced at the other men in the room, all of whom were wearing suits and ties. "I don't think there are too many industry people in this crowd," he teased.

"No. Just lots of uptight lawyers and bankers." She smiled at him as if they were sharing a private joke. "Downtown L.A. is stuffy."

"I like what you're wearing." His gaze traveled the length of her, and she felt butterflies in her stomach. "Wardrobe would recommend that color suit for a TV interview scene. So subtle, so classic . . ." he was gesturing grandly as he joked with her.

"Thanks, I think . . ." she replied. "I often wish I didn't have to dress up every day, but that's what jurors expect, and we don't want to risk upsetting them."

"Then become a filmmaker like me. We get to wear anything we want."

Alexandra smiled and sipped her coffee. She felt surprisingly at ease with him. "How did you become a director?"

He settled back in his chair. "As a kid I used to go to the movies and figure out how I would have shot a scene to make it better or what I could have done to give the story more impact." His hands moved for emphasis as he spoke, and she could clearly imagine him on a movie set, directing his cast and crew. "I also knew I would never be a corporate kind of a guy."

"Did your family encourage you?"

The same dark shadow she'd seen that day at the studio momentarily flickered over his features. "Not at first. My dad, my real dad, that is," he clarified, "wanted me to get a degree in business or law—things he felt would be more useful."

She had read that Jeffrey McGrath was a businessman, but couldn't remember what kind. "What exactly did your father do?"

"He ran an automobile parts company."

"And how did your mother feel about your ambitions?"

Michael's face broke into a wide smile. What a

handsome man he was when his face lost its melancholic expression, she thought. Even the deep color of his eyes lightened. "She fully accepted that her kid was a dreamer," he replied.

It wasn't hard to see that he adored his mother. It made Alexandra think about his grandparents and her suspicion that it was Lorna whom Frances McGrath had cut out of the family picture. "Did your mother have a career, too?"

"No," Michael replied, then paused as though considering whether or not to say more. Instead he changed the subject. "How about you? Always want to be a prosecutor?"

"Absolutely. Before I was eight I was firmly convinced that it was the most important job in the world."

"I suppose the fact that your father was a D.A. helped?"

Alexandra nodded. So he had figured out who she was. She remembered the way he'd responded to her questions about his being interviewed by the sheriff's department or the D.A.'s office. If he'd been honest with her then, she doubted he had any inkling of her father's possible involvement in the aftermath of Jeffrey McGrath's death.

Wanting to steer him back to talking about himself, Alexandra looked at him and said, "It must have been hard losing your father when you were so young. What was he like?"

Michael rubbed his stubble. "Strict . . . with definite opinions on most everything. Not very flexible." He paused before adding, "He wanted things to be done in an orderly way."

"And your mother?"

"She always went along with Dad. She'd be sympathetic, but she'd never interfere. His word was law." There was an edge to his tone.

Alexandra surmised that his father must have been a very exacting, very controlling man. "And George Collins kind of stepped into the void when your dad died?"

His jaw relaxed. "Yeah. George felt responsible, like maybe he could have prevented what happened. Maybe he should have yelled out to my dad not to run—or stop—or something like that." He seemed to be gauging her reaction. "Of course, none of us believed it was his fault."

She chose not to go down that road for the moment. "What type of man is George?"

"Kind. Patient." His eyes changed color again, becoming even lighter, friendlier. "He's always been there for me."

Alexandra smiled. "Did George get along well with your sister, too?"

He rubbed his glass with his long fingertips. "No," he admitted. "But it wasn't George's fault."

She wondered then whose fault it was. "Do you think your sister somehow blamed George for your father's death?"

He grimaced slightly as he shook his head. "Sally may never have liked George, but she didn't blame him. She feels as we all do, that my father's death was an accident."

If the woman who had called Alexandra had indeed been Sally McGrath, then Michael didn't know his sister that well. She regarded him. "Are you sure about that?"

"Of course." For the first time, his eyes didn't meet hers. "You have to understand, Sally worshiped my father and that made it hard for her to accept George. But he was always kind to her."

Thinking again about the phone call she'd received from Sally, Alexandra wondered if it had been Michael whom she'd heard shouting in the background. Talking with him now made her think that unlikely. She debated bringing up the subject, then she decided to move on rather than make him defensive. "When your father died, wasn't George already married?"

"Yes. But it wasn't a good marriage."

Her eyes were questioning. "Why is that?"

"I'm not sure." He shrugged his shoulders. "I only know George was wonderful to my family." He lifted his glass again, and Alexandra found herself noticing his lean, supple hands.

"It helps to see things in context," Michael explained, almost as an afterthought. "Here was this nice guy who had a lousy marriage and who loved kids. But for some reason, he and his wife never had any. In the meantime our house had two kids who desperately needed a father. And then there was our mother, who was a beautiful and lonely woman."

Alexandra found herself nodding again. To hear Michael tell the story, it made perfect sense that George and Lorna had ended up together.

"Mom was also struggling to cope financially," he said solemnly. "She had no idea how much money Dad owed until after he died. For a while, she had to take two jobs to make ends meet."

Her ears perked up. Whether or not his mother had a financial motive for wanting Jeffrey dead was a subject Alexandra definitely wanted to know more about. "Didn't your dad have any life insurance?"

"No. My grandparents, on the other hand, were loaded, but it didn't do us much good." He frowned. "Grandpa Lester is just like my father, very exacting—very controlling. So whatever they'd do for us always had strings attached."

Alexandra knew that now was the time to tell him she'd met his grandparents, but she was afraid he would react by clamming up. "What kinds of strings?"

"We'll give you the money, but we have to approve of how you spend it."

She remembered her visit to Rancho Mirage. The grandparents had acted as if Michael and Sally were more important to them than anything else in the world. Was that not true? "So you're saying that George eased some of the family's money problems?"

"He was very generous—to all of us."

She played with the spoon on the table. "It sounds like you didn't object when George and your mother became romantically involved."

"Actually, I was glad. George's presence seemed to give my mother something vital—something she needed. She became happy." He smiled. "One of these days you'll have to meet my mother. Like I said, she's a beautiful woman. Smart too." Michael's face shone with love. "No one could expect her to be alone for long. After all, she was only thirty-two when my dad died. That's still so young."

"I'm thirty-two and lately I feel really old," Alexandra admitted aloud without even thinking.

His eyes filled with concern. "Maybe you're working too hard."

She hesitated, surprised at her own unexpected personal confession. "Probably," she said, glancing at her watch.

"Do you have another engagement?" he asked, not bothering to hide his disappointment.

"My mother's at the City of Hope. I try to visit her every evening if I can. It's a long drive."

"That's a cancer hospital and research facility, isn't it?"

"Yes."

He reached out and took her hand. "I'm sorry. That's rough."

Her skin tingled from his touch. And he sounded so genuinely caring that without warning, tears sprang to her eyes. Embarrassed, Alexandra pulled back and bit her lip to keep from crying. It was so unlike her to allow her emotions to overcome her that way. "Sorry. Sometimes it just gets to me."

"There's nothing to be sorry for." His voice was full of empathy. "What kind of cancer does she have?"

"Ovarian."

Michael exhaled loudly. "No wonder you're so down. One of our production assistants had it." He shook his head sadly, but didn't elaborate.

Alexandra couldn't help herself from asking the obvious question. "She died, didn't she?"

"Yes," he admitted, his gaze direct.

She appreciated his blunt honesty. The dance people typically did around the subject of death was wearying. "They say her chances are slim, but I keep on hoping."

"Of course you do. And you should," he added firmly. "Without hope what else is there?"

"Nothing," she agreed. It was nice to have someone truly understand. "It's getting late. I really have to go."

He leaned forward. "Can you just answer one question? Are you planning to continue your investigation into my father's death?"

She carefully measured her words. "I'm not sure. I need to check a few more things." Aware that it was becoming difficult for her to remain objective in his presence, Alexandra motioned for the bill.

Michael shook his head. "My treat. Please. It's the least I can do."

Alexandra decided to let it pass this one time.

Outside, while waiting for their cars, an awkwardness settled in between them. He was standing so close to her that Alexandra could smell his cologne. She wanted to move away but feared if she did it would only underscore her unease.

Suddenly he reached for her hand. "I'm sorry," he said with a look of chagrin as he held it in both of his. "I know I have no right, but you seem so sad . . . so . . . vulnerable. I wish there was something I could do to help." His gaze was intense.

For a brief second Alexandra wanted to toss caution to the wind, throw herself into his arms and be held. She was lonely—starved for affection and physical closeness. Kyle's rejection of her had been an added blow on top of her other troubles. Astounded by her own need, she realized how crazy her thoughts were and forced herself to pull away.

When the headlights of her BMW appeared from the underground garage, Alexandra was relieved. "Thanks. Bye," was all she managed to get out before running to her car.

Turning onto the street from the hotel driveway, Alexandra headed for the freeway, tears now streaming down her face. After a few blocks, she had to pull over to the side of the road. Then she sobbed for what seemed like a long time as all the fears about her mother's possible death and her own loneliness washed over her.

9

ALEXANDRA HAD just stepped out of the shower when the phone rang. Dripping wet, she grabbed a towel and ignored the puddles forming on her floor as she rushed to answer it. Her mother's sobs on the other end of the line terrified her. "Whatever it is, I'm here for you," Alexandra said, feeling utterly helpless, not yet knowing what the tears were about.

Finally the sobbing subsided as Roberta seemed to regain her composure. "I'm . . . so . . . sorry," were the first words she uttered. "You have . . . to go to work . . . I shouldn't be bothering you."

"You're not bothering me," Alexandra insisted, her heart in her throat. "Did something show up on the bone scan?"

Roberta remained silent, but Alexandra had to know the truth. "It wasn't good, was it?" she finally managed to say.

"No—it wasn't," admitted Roberta, sniffling some more.

Her stomach churning, Alexandra felt like she might be sick. "Oh Mom, I'm so sorry."

"Me too." There was a long pause. "God, it gets so lonely here sometimes."

"I thought your friends were visiting a lot?"

"They did at the beginning. And I'm always getting lots of calls, presents and notes. But I think my illness has lost its novelty for the lunching ladies. And it's such a long drive."

Alexandra was surprised. Her mother's friends had seemed so supportive. "I'm sorry," she muttered, having a hard time getting beyond the terror that Roberta's cancer was still so aggressive. "Did you tell Dad about these new results?"

"Not yet. I'm waiting for the right opportunity."

Would that opportunity ever come? Alexandra wondered.

"Anyway, I told the doctor how blue I was feeling," Roberta explained with another sniffle. "He thought it would be okay if I came home."

The doctor wouldn't allow that if he was overly concerned, would he? thought Alexandra. "For how long?"

"He wasn't sure. It could be a few days or maybe even a week, depending on how I do."

"That's great, Mom! Aren't you excited?"

"Yes and no," Roberta said. "I think my being home makes things harder for your father. He needs his sleep, and I'm up a lot."

"Then stay with me," Alexandra suggested without even thinking.

Roberta sighed. "Thanks for the offer," she said softly. "But your place really isn't big enough."

"I'll sleep on the couch and give you my bedroom," promised Alexandra, glancing around and immediately figuring out how she could rearrange things in her apartment. "I'd love to have you."

"You're a darling," Roberta said. Then she was quiet for a moment as if thinking. "No. Your father would be upset. I better go home."

As they talked, Alexandra finished drying off and started getting together her outfit for the day. "Can Dad pick you up?"

"He's got a breakfast speaking engagement. I'm sure he'll be able to get me later."

Knowing that her mother would never ask Thomas to change his plans, Alexandra mentally reviewed her commitments. She didn't have any court appearances today. If she left within the hour, she could beat some of the traffic, take her mother home and get to the office by noon.

"Listen, Mom, I'm getting dressed and coming for you right now."

There was a relieved sigh. "Are you sure?"

"Yes," Alexandra replied enthusiastically, having heard the hopeful tone in her mother's voice. "Just call Dad and tell him what's going on."

Several hours later, Alexandra had tucked Roberta into her own bed at her parents' house, fixed her some lunch and gone to work.

"There's a surprise for you on your desk," Geena said.

Wondering what it could be, Alexandra walked into her office and saw a gorgeous bouquet of vibrant pink roses in a big vase. "Wow!" she said, truly astonished.

Geena grinned at her. "Got a secret admirer?"

"I have no idea," Alexandra admitted, putting her things down to search for a card. Her hands were shaking as she tore the envelope open.

The sorrow on your face when you spoke about your mother was heartbreaking. Hope these cheer you up.

Michael

What a nice thing to do, Alexandra thought.

"So?" Geena was standing there with her hands on her hips, waiting for information.

Flustered, Alexandra groped for a plausible explanation. She really liked Geena, but she was afraid to confide in anyone at this office, where anything she said might easily become grist for the gossip mill. "It's from a friend in New York," was the best she could do.

As the afternoon wore on and Alexandra tried to catch up on her paperwork, she kept glancing at the flowers and smiling to herself. She loved pink roses.

She was concentrating on reading a brief when she heard someone call her name. Glancing up, she saw her father standing in the open doorway to her office.

"I wanted to thank you for taking your mother home from the hospital this morning and for getting her settled," he said, looking uncomfortable.

"That's okay." She shrugged to let him know it was no big deal.

To her surprise Thomas walked in and slumped down in one of her chairs. He'd never visited her office before. She'd assumed it was because he didn't want the other deputies to feel as if she were being treated any differently.

"I appreciate your help," he said, straightening the crease in his immaculately pressed slacks.

"You're welcome." Suddenly, she noticed how tired her father looked. Older too. Alexandra spent so much of her time and energy worrying about her mother's condition that she hadn't stopped to consider how Roberta's illness must be affecting him. "You look exhausted. If it becomes too difficult for you at home, Mom can come to my place."

He seemed startled by the offer. "No, no. I want her home with me." Thomas suddenly noticed the roses. "Nice. Anyone I know?"

"I don't think so." She kept her voice deliberately evasive, not wanting to explain.

After an awkward moment of silence, Thomas seemed to regain his stamina. "Well," he said, standing up. "I'll be going home. Your mother has been alone for hours." He cleared his throat and fixed his blue eyes on her before adding, "Are you coming over tonight to see her?"

"No. I didn't get here until noon, and I've got a heavy schedule tomorrow. I'll call her. I'm sure she'll understand that I need a good night's sleep."

"Of course," he said quickly.

She tried to think of something else to say. She wished they had more of a father-daughter relationship, but she didn't seem to know how to go about it. At the moment, she'd settle for a genial relationship between colleagues, but that didn't seem likely either, at least not until she could put her mind to rest about the Collins/McGrath case.

After he was gone, Geena came into Alexandra's office with a message. "A Michael McGrath called. I didn't want to bother you while your father was here." There was a curious expression on Geena's face.

Alexandra thanked her. She then waited somewhat anxiously for Geena to leave, hoping that her secretary hadn't recognized the name.

"My mother would like to meet you," Michael said when Alexandra returned the call. "Can we get together at the same place we had dinner last night?"

She was about to tell him it was impossible, but then changed her mind. Her curiosity was piqued. What would Lorna McGrath Collins want to see her about?

"Michael told me someone is claiming my late husband was murdered," Lorna Collins said, as she fingered her huge diamond and emerald ring. "But that's ridiculous. There wasn't anyone who had a reason to kill Jeffrey."

The resemblance between Lorna and her son was remarkable, thought Alexandra, as she waited politely for the woman to continue. They had the same green eyes and fine features, and the same dark hair too. Yet there was a sadness to Michael that his mother didn't seem to have.

"The day it happened started out just like any other Saturday. My husband and George had decided to go hunting in the Santa Monica mountains. Of course, hunting wasn't legal there, but everyone did it because the chances of getting caught were so slim." A smile played around Lorna's mouth, which was painted a vivid red.

Alexandra leaned forward. "Please go on."

"Well, I wasn't expecting the two of them back until late in the afternoon, so I didn't think too much about it when the doorbell rang about one o'clock. It was a sheriff's deputy. He said there had been an accident and that my husband had been taken to the hospital." Lorna's eyes filled with tears. "I'd naturally assumed he'd meant a car accident. When he told me it was an accidental shooting and that Jeffrey was dead, I just . . . couldn't believe it."

Her face became drawn, the red mouth grim. "I asked how it had happened. The deputy explained Jeffrey had run after an animal, tripped and fallen—and that somehow the gun had gone off." Lorna's voice cracked.

Michael leaned over and took his mother's

hand. As Lorna fought to regain her composure, Alexandra realized that something about her performance didn't ring true, although she couldn't quite figure out what it was. At the same time, she was convinced that the agony displayed on Michael's face was real.

"Are you up to continuing?" Alexandra asked.

Lorna's hand went to her throat. "Yes. I want to tell you everything I can remember."

"Did the deputy sheriff ask you any questions?"

"He wanted to know what the men had been hunting for and I told him deer."

Alexandra was surprised. She'd heard of people illegally shooting rabbits and other small animals in the Santa Monica mountains, but not deer. "That's uncommon game, don't you think?"

"They usually went out for rabbits," Lorna conceded, nodding her head. "It was actually Jeffrey's idea to go after deer. He'd heard that they had been spotted, and he wanted to try and get one."

Knowing that the buckshot used to kill a deer was usually much heavier and more deadly than the kind used to shoot rabbits, Alexandra wondered if it could have been George, not Jeffrey, who decided to go after the deer that day. If it had been George's idea, that could be used as evidence to show premeditation on his part.

"If only they hadn't gone," said Lorna, her voice filled with sadness.

"Did you know that the gun which fired the fatal shot belonged to George—not Jeffrey?" Alexandra asked.

The other woman glanced hurriedly at her son. "We didn't know that right away. We heard about it later," Lorna explained. "In fact, the deputy who came to the door didn't say anything about which gun Jeffrey had been carrying while running after the animal."

Alexandra brushed her hair back off her face. "Do you recall the deputy's name?"

Lorna's brow was furrowed as if she were trying hard to remember. "Actually, I was questioned by two different deputies at separate times. One said he was a detective. Unfortunately I don't remember either name."

Taking a deep breath, Alexandra said, "Did anyone from the D.A.'s office ever contact you or ask you to come in for an interview?"

There was a flash of recognition in Lorna's eyes, quickly replaced by a blank expression. "I don't think so. It was such a long time ago. It was all a nightmare," she continued. "The children and I were in shock." Lorna turned to glance at Michael for affirmation. "The next days were a total blur. The funeral, people coming over all the time. Afterward things were rough. My husband didn't leave any life insurance and we were in debt."

So Michael had been right, Alexandra mused. There didn't appear to be any financial motive for Lorna to get rid of her husband. "Michael said George was quite a help those first terrible months?"

"Oh God, yes. I don't know how we would have managed without him. Poor George felt horrible.

That's the kind of man he is, always taking on other people's problems. Since George was the only one there when Jeffrey shot himself, he felt responsible and wanted to take care of us."

What Lorna was saying seemed to make perfect sense, yet Alexandra knew there was an entirely different way to look at the same events. "Is there any possibility that George could have wanted Jeffrey out of the way because of you?"

The other woman's eyes grew large. "Oh no. George knew that Jeffrey and I had a wonderful marriage and that we were very much in love."

"What about George's relationship with his wife? Were they a loving couple too?" Alexandra asked, watching Lorna's face.

"No. George's wife was impossible. One of those self-involved women, totally wrapped up in her own problems. It was embarrassing the way she belittled George." She gazed knowingly at Alexandra as she stopped to catch her breath. "Jeffrey would have told her more than once to shut up if I hadn't stopped him." Suddenly Lorna's eyes narrowed. "Wait a minute. I think I understand what's going on here. Your informant is Erica Collins, isn't it?"

Lorna was using the present tense. That meant she didn't know yet that Erica had died. Alexandra didn't want to give anything away, so she kept her voice neutral. "What makes you think that?"

Mother and son were both eyeing each other again. "Because it all makes sense now," Lorna exclaimed, giving a small, cynical laugh. "That

woman hated George for leaving her. She'd do anything, say anything to get back at him."

"Why?" Alexandra asked. "Were you the cause
of their divorce?"

"Oh heavens, no," Lorna replied, her hands gesturing in the air. "George's main reason for coming
to the house was to spend time with the children."
She looked at Michael for confirmation, and he
nodded slightly.

"It was all very innocent," she said. "George
wasn't the type to have ulterior motives." She absently twisted the ring on her finger. "It was a long
time after Jeffrey's death before anything happened
between the two of us." Lorna leaned closer and
held her hand over her heart. "I loved my husband.
I didn't want him to die." She focused on Alexandra. "If Erica Collins told you differently, it's a lie.
That woman has always wanted only one thing—
revenge."

10

~

As ALEXANDRA SAT with Michael McGrath in the restaurant, watching the rain pelt the windows, she felt pensive. A few minutes earlier Lorna Collins had announced that she had to leave to meet some friends for dinner and then go on to a play at the Mark Taper Forum. It would have been prudent for Alexandra to leave when Lorna did, yet she hadn't wanted to.

"Would you join me in a glass of wine now?" he asked with a smile as he leaned toward her. "It's officially after working hours."

She considered it. "Okay, but just one," she finally said.

Michael's face lit up. "Good." He signaled to the waiter, then turned back to her.

"Thank you again for the flowers."

"You're welcome." He fingered his water glass, silent for a moment before speaking. "I'm really glad you got to meet my mother."

"Yes," Alexandra nodded as she thought about her conversation with Lorna Collins. Maybe Michael and his mother were right. Jeffrey McGrath's death had been an accident and Erica Collins had merely been seeking revenge against her ex-husband for leaving her. And no murder meant no bribe.

"My mother's a beautiful woman, both inside and out," he stated emphatically, before taking a sip of water. "Anyway, now that she's gone, let's not discuss my father's death anymore tonight. It's a painful subject," he added, the scars of its memory clearly etched on his face.

She knew it had to be awful to lose a parent at any age, but especially at fifteen. It made her think about her own mother. When she glanced up a few seconds later, she found Michael gazing at her with a questioning look. "I'm sorry," she said, realizing she'd been lost in her own thoughts. "When you were speaking about the pain, it started me thinking about my mother . . ." The words caught in her throat and she couldn't go on.

He reached out and patted her arm as if to say things would be okay.

Alexandra didn't understand what was happening. She wasn't used to being this emotional, this fragile, especially in front of someone she barely knew. At the same time, she was very much aware of his hand against her skin, and she found herself imagining what his lips would feel like on hers. Afraid he could read her thoughts, she glanced quickly away.

Get a grip, she told herself, forcing her mind to focus elsewhere. It would be better if they stuck strictly to talking business. Last night she should have told Michael that she'd seen his grandparents. In spite of his not wanting to discuss his father's death, she had to explain. "There's one more thing I must mention to you about your father's—"

He put a finger to his lips in a shushing gesture. "Please. Not tonight."

For a moment she thought about protesting, but then backed off. Michael still had his hand on her arm, his fingers rubbing gently against her skin.

"You're uncomfortable about the two of us being here like this, aren't you?"

"A little," she admitted.

"It would have been nice if we could have met some other way."

Alexandra nodded, surprised at herself for acknowledging that thought.

"Well, we can't change that." There was a wistful quality to his voice. When she didn't respond he added, "You may find this hard to believe, but I seldom get a chance to meet a *normal* woman."

"Should I take that as a compliment?" she said with a laugh.

He flashed a devastating smile that changed his entire face from gloomy to handsome. "Please do. What I meant is that most of the women in my industry are more into their looks and themselves. They're completely self-absorbed and phony. It sometimes takes all of my willpower to deal with them."

"Rough life," she teased.

"You're as pretty as any of them—and smart, too. As a matter of fact, after seeing your courtroom performance yesterday, I'm really quite impressed."

His compliments were intoxicating, and she knew her resolve to remain professional was getting weaker by the second. In an effort to keep the conversation less personal, she started asking him questions about the movie he was making. From there they started discussing other movies, then books. Alexandra was pleasantly surprised to discover how well-read he was.

"It's amazing," Michael said, as if voicing her thoughts aloud. "Our tastes are so similar. We both read three books at a time. One fiction, one nonfiction and one slated to improve our minds—but hard to get through and *boring*."

Alexandra chimed in on the word *boring*, and they both started laughing. He was right. If only they could have met under different circumstances, she mused. Michael was sophisticated and world traveled, not the kind of man who could be easily fooled. It was hard to believe that he'd defend George Collins—no matter how grateful he was— if he had the slightest doubt the man might be guilty of murdering his father.

As Alexandra drove home she glanced in her rearview mirror, making sure that Michael's car was still behind her. When they had come out of the New Otani, it had been raining hard and

Michael had asked where she lived. It turned out that they didn't live very far apart—less than a mile. Because of the dangerous road conditions during a torrential downpour like the one tonight, Michael had insisted on following her home.

It entered her mind that she should wave him off before she pulled into her driveway. After all, she barely knew the man. Then she told herself she was being silly. This man was a respected movie director—not a rapist. She slowed down and motioned for him to come alongside her car. "I live back there," she called out, pointing to her small apartment atop the garage behind her landlord's house.

He smiled and waved his hand. "Good night."

She pulled into the driveway, then jumped out and ran to the back and up the stairs. By the time she got her key in the lock, she was drenched.

Inside, she threw her coat off and stepped out of her wet clothes. Then, wearing only her bra and pantyhose, she padded into the bathroom to get a towel to wrap around her wet head. A sudden knock at the door startled her.

"Who's there?" she called, not opening the door. She wished she had a peephole.

"Michael. You left your parking lights on. I wanted to turn them off, but your car was locked."

"Damn," she muttered under her breath. Opening the door a fraction of an inch, she peered out at him. "Thanks. I'm just getting out of my wet things. I'll go down in a minute."

"Give me your keys, and I'll do it for you."

"No, that's okay. I don't want to put you to all that trouble."

"Nonsense. I insist."

"Okay. Hold on a second." She closed the door and went for her keys. Before handing them to him, she hurriedly put on a robe.

When he came back, she opened the door a little wider. Now he was the one who was sopping wet. "That was really nice of you," she said, smiling.

He smiled back. "No problem." Gesturing with his hand, he murmured, "Well, good night again."

"Good night."

Michael started to walk away, then turned around and gazed longingly at her. When she saw the desire in his eyes, all her good intentions slipped away.

Suddenly he had her in his arms and his mouth was pressed hard against hers. She felt rivulets of water from his hair falling on her face, but she didn't care as she pushed herself closer to him, luxuriating in the hardness of his body. Her entire being was suffused with longing. An alarm in her brain warned her to stop this before it was too late, but she ignored it as he kicked the door closed behind him.

"No! No! Stop!" Sally cried out, throwing off the bedcovers as she thrashed about wildly.

"Sally, wake up. Wake up!"

From far away, Sally heard a voice calling to her, but she couldn't open her mouth to respond. Feeling like she was drowning in a bottomless pit, she panicked as she struggled to find her way out of the pitch-black darkness surrounding her. Her heart was beating erratically. As her mind battled toward lucidity, she still couldn't see anything.

"It's okay," the voice said. "I'm here now. Wake up."

Bright lights came on, causing Sally to blink. She didn't know where she was. Slowly she became aware that she was being held in someone's arms as the room swayed around her. She was so disoriented she could barely speak, and when she did, her voice came out ragged. "What's . . . going on?"

"I'm here, Sally. It's me, Arnold—your husband."

She felt one of her hands being lifted and then rubbed against his beard.

"What happened?" she asked again, trying to catch her breath.

"You've had a bad nightmare, that's all," he told her, his tone reassuring.

"A nightmare?" She tried to remember what it had been about. It still floated on the edge of her consciousness, but she couldn't grasp it. All she remembered was that she'd been filled with fear, a horrible, overwhelming sense of terror. She put her hands between her breasts and felt the dampness. "I can't stop shaking," she said between chattering teeth.

"I know. Come with me. I'll make you some hot tea." Helping her stand, her husband tied the belt of her robe around her as if she were a child.

A few minutes later, Arnold put a steaming cup

into her trembling hands. The warmth of the cup made her aware of her fingers, her body. She tried to make sense out of it all. "I can't remember anything except that I was frightened."

There was a worried look in her husband's eyes as he gazed at her. "Was it one of the nightmares like you used to have?"

Sally knew what Arnold meant—the terrible dreams she'd been having on and off since she was a young girl. A long time had passed since her last bad dream, and she'd been praying that they were finally gone.

"Did you hear me?" he asked.

She nodded.

"Was it like the bad dreams you had before?"

"Yes," she admitted.

He exhaled loudly. "Sally, it's time for you to go back to the hospital and Doctor Winters."

"No," she said, shaking her head.

"Doctor Winters can help you, Sally, but you have to give him a chance," Arnold told her.

"No!" she said again, her thin shoulders shuddering with dread. She disliked Doctor Winters. The way he looked at her wasn't right, nor were the questions he was always asking. "He makes me nervous. And I hate being hypnotized."

Arnold crossed his arms across his chest. "I'm afraid I'm going to have to insist."

Sally hated it when Arnold spoke to her in that stern voice. "Why can't we find another doctor?"

His posture only stiffened further. "Doctor Winters *is* the best. Most of the doctors out there today

haven't the faintest idea of what they're doing."
His voice dropped. "Sally, don't I always know
what's right for you?"

As he spoke, she could feel herself shrinking, becoming smaller and weaker with each passing second. It made her angry and she wanted to hurt him
back. "Sometimes I hate you!" she shouted, starting to cry.

"Statements like that only show how unstable
you are, so I'm just going to ignore it," Arnold said
disapprovingly.

"You're supposed to love me." She shook her
head. "So why can't you understand how I feel?"

"I do love you. But I've got years of experience
on you and that's why I know what's best."

Frustration welled up in her as her tears continued to flow. No one really understood how she felt.
No one.

11

ALEXANDRA AWOKE in a tangle of sheets and blankets and feeling disoriented. It was several seconds before it registered why she was sleeping in the nude. Sometime before dawn, Michael had whispered that he had to be on the set of the movie he was shooting by 6:00 A.M. After he'd kissed her good-bye and she'd heard his footsteps on the stairs, she must have fallen back to sleep.

Getting out of bed, she padded barefoot to the bathroom, suddenly aware that her body was sore. This morning, the cracked and peeling paint on the baseboards and doors was irritating to her eyes. Had this been New York, before her mother was ill, she already would have stripped, sanded and repainted her tiny rooms in bright, cheerful colors, but in the six months she'd been in L.A. she hadn't yet had time.

She wondered what Michael had thought of her simple abode. He'd probably felt sorry for her, slaving her life away in the thankless, low-paying world of a civil servant. It was easy to imagine him living in luxury.

As she went into the kitchen she discovered that he'd already made the coffee. There was also a note he'd scribbled on paper torn from the yellow legal pad she kept on the counter.

Last night was wonderful. Sorry I've got to hurry off, but I've got a crew and cast waiting for me. I'll call you later.

She showered, then dried her hair. Gazing at her reflection in the mirror, Alexandra began to have serious doubts about her impulsive actions of the night before.

As a prosecutor she represented the people of California, and consequently she was expected to treat anyone who was a victim or a potential witness in a case as a client—off limits for anything other than a strictly professional relationship. This policy was based on the fact that when people became emotionally involved it tended to cloud their judgment. Ignoring the rule meant she could find herself in an uncomfortable and compromising, not to mention legally conflicted, situation.

She mentally argued that Michael hadn't been a witness to anything. He'd been merely a fifteen-year-old boy who remembered nothing about the day his father had died except for how badly he'd been traumatized. At the moment there wasn't even an official investigation into Jeffrey McGrath's death. The case wouldn't be reopened if more evidence wasn't found to back up Erica Collins's accusations.

Still, Alexandra knew that falling into bed with someone connected to a potential case hadn't been a smart move. The more she thought about it, the more her conduct baffled her. It wasn't like her to discard her professionalism this way. Her only excuse was that she'd been desperately in need of human warmth and comfort.

In her office on the seventeenth floor of the Criminal Courts Building, deputy D.A. Elizabeth Nathan shoved aside a stack of unread memos, subpoenas and unanswered correspondence. She had to make room for the transcripts she needed to read. She found her workload daunting, and felt that her talents were often wasted because she wasn't given the kinds of cases she deserved. Yet, she wouldn't trade being a prosecutor for any other job in the world. She just wanted to secure her future here.

The other night she and Frank had discussed some of her ideas for getting him more name recognition. Despite her suggestions, he'd been stubborn about using the nepotism issue any more than he had already. But they were running out of time. The primary was now less than five weeks away, and he still was far behind. He'd have to be more ruthless.

That was why she'd been searching for information on the cases she'd overheard Thomas and

Alexandra arguing about. From the angry tone of voice Thomas had used with his daughter, and from the way he'd ordered her to stop whatever she was doing, Elizabeth was willing to bet there had to be something involved with one of those cases that Frank could use against Thomas. So far, however, she hadn't found either name on the active case list.

Picking up her phone, she called one of the courtroom clerks downstairs. "Hi. It's Elizabeth Nathan. Is Alexandra Locke in trial now?"

"Yes. Do you need me to get a message to her?"

"No. That's okay. I'll leave it with her secretary."

Elizabeth approached Geena with a smile on her face. "I'm looking for two case files, and I think Alexandra might be handling them."

Geena glanced up from her computer. Removing her glasses, she seemed to appraise Elizabeth. "What are their names?"

"One is McGrath. The other one is Collins."

The secretary frowned and shook her head. "Those names don't ring a bell. Let me look." Geena checked a list on her desk. "I don't see either name," she finally said.

"They both might have just come in," Elizabeth explained with a nod of her head. "I'm sure you've got more than enough to do." She gestured toward Alexandra's office and smiled. "I'll just take a look myself."

She was hurriedly flipping through the files on Alexandra's desk when she realized that Geena had followed her into the office. Trying not to show her irritation, Elizabeth flashed another smile. "That's okay. I don't want to take you away from your work. I can do it."

Geena didn't look happy about Elizabeth's suggestion. "Why don't I write down the names and ask Alexandra when she comes back?" She folded her arms across her chest. "Then I'll call you and let you know."

Realizing Geena wasn't about to leave, and anxious that she not become suspicious of her motives, Elizabeth backtracked. "Tell you what, I'll just go downstairs and talk to Alexandra myself. That way you don't have to be bothered. In fact, don't give it another thought." With a wave of her hand, she turned and left.

Of course, Elizabeth had no intention of asking Alexandra about the cases. Yet she headed for the elevators anyway and pushed the down button, just in case Geena was watching. She hoped her performance was convincing. The last thing she needed was to have Geena mentioning her visit to Alexandra.

Lorna Collins brushed her hair vigorously, eyeing her reflection in the mirror of her dressing table. She was proud of the great shape she was in. She didn't look anywhere near her age, which was fifty-five. People who didn't know that she had a son of thirty-five and a daughter of twenty-nine guessed that she was only in her early forties. Lorna intended to do everything possible to keep looking young and beautiful for as long as she could. Of course that took money—lots of money. Fortunately, George did very well financially.

Picking up the phone, Lorna dialed her son's office, careful not to harm her freshly manicured fingernails. "How do you think it went last night?" she asked when he finally came on the line. "Did Ms. Locke say anything more about your father's death after I left?"

"Not really. We actually stopped talking about it."

That was odd, thought Lorna, frowning to herself. She pictured Alexandra Locke, remembering her surprise that she was so attractive. Michael had described her as being strong and tenacious, leading Lorna to envision someone harder and older. Of course, no one knew better than Lorna herself how deceiving appearances could be. Hadn't her late husband, Jeffrey, been one of the handsomest men she'd ever seen? "So what *did* you talk about?" she asked, beginning to feel uneasy.

"Books, movies, that kind of thing."

His answers disturbed her even more. "How much longer did you stay at the restaurant?"

"About another forty minutes."

That's a long time, she thought, piqued that he wasn't being more forthcoming with her. "Surely Ms. Locke must have given you some idea if she's going to proceed?"

"I think she's leaning our way."

"I hope so." She tapped her fingernails on the phone. "You know, Michael, I could see that you were attracted to her. But it would be a big mistake to underestimate her just because she's pretty."

He exhaled loudly. "I'm aware of how dangerous she could be," he replied. "Listen, I've got to get back to my meeting. I'll call you later."

She wasn't going to let Michael hang up without answering her questions. "I called you several times last night, but there was no answer."

"My machine must have been broken," he responded.

Lorna wondered why her son was hedging. Before their meeting with Alexandra Locke, Michael had been confident that the two of them together, by being cooperative to a point, could convince the deputy D.A. not to reopen the investigation into Jeffrey's death. Now his focus seemed to have changed. Could Michael be romantically interested in the prosecutor?

"I know you too well, Michael," she finally said. "You've never been able to resist a good-looking face. You went back to her place, didn't you?"

"I followed her home because it was raining so hard. And since when is that any of your business, Mom?"

"Sleeping with Ms. Locke could be more than dangerous," she pointed out. "There's way too much at stake."

"I know that," he said. "Anyway, I've really got to get back to my meeting."

After Michael had hung up, Lorna continued to view her reflection. She had been counting on

Michael to put a halt to any further investigation into her late husband's death. Now she wasn't so sure. Perhaps, Lorna decided, she needed to find another way to abort Alexandra Locke's probe.

Dr. George Collins watched carefully as the seventeen-year-old boy walked back and forth for him in the large examining room.

"See, there's no limp at all," the boy assured him.

"Looks great," George agreed, feeling a surge of pride at what his skill had accomplished. Three years ago this boy had hobbled into his office, one leg shorter than the other. George had operated on him seven times. Now, finally, the limp had been eliminated.

A tall, broad-shouldered man with a ruddy complexion and light brown hair turning white at the temples, George Collins was headed toward the next examining room when he saw Doris Zimmer approaching him with a frown on her usually cheerful face. She was his nurse assistant and had been with him for over twenty years.

"Your wife says she needs to talk to you immediately," Doris whispered. "She's waiting for you in your office."

"Tell my next patient I'll be a few more minutes," he said. Alarmed, he went into his private office and closed the door behind him. Glancing over, he saw the worried look on his wife's beautiful face. "What's wrong?"

"I was hoping I could handle this without your

knowing, but I can't," Lorna said, her brows furrowing. "So I guess it's time to tell you." As Lorna spoke, she kept twisting her large ring.

She wasn't making sense. "What are you talking about?" he asked, becoming more concerned with each passing second.

"There's a deputy D.A. by the name of Alexandra Locke who claims that she has some new information regarding Jeffrey's death."

George felt his pulse start to race as he took a step forward. "What kind of information? And what prompted this?"

"Apparently the D.A.'s office received a tip. Someone is claiming that Jeffrey's death wasn't an accident, but a murder." She gazed directly into his eyes as if measuring his reaction before going on. "They're also saying that you're the murderer."

George suddenly felt faint. With a sense of foreboding he sat down in his chair, aware that his heart was beating rapidly. "Who did this tip come from?"

"The prosecutor wouldn't say, but I just know it had to be Erica." Her eyes narrowed. "Have you heard from her lately?"

Numb, he shook his head in dismay. After all these years this couldn't be happening. He studied his wife's face. "You're just guessing that it's Erica—you don't really know for sure, do you?"

"No. But don't be so blind, George," she exclaimed, her voice rising an octave, which was a sure sign that she was upset. "Who else would want to hurt us this way? It's got to be Erica."

He took a deep breath and exhaled loudly. Was it possible that even after all this time his ex-wife still wanted to punish him? "Let me call my lawyer."

George went over to his desk and dialed the phone. When the man came on the line, he got right to the point, "Has my ex-wife, Erica Collins, been in touch with you lately?" As George listened, he could feel the color draining from his face. After hanging up, he gazed at Lorna. "He said he was going to call me. Erica died last week."

"Then she can't hurt us anymore," Lorna said, with a look of relief. Suddenly she frowned.

"What now?" he asked, in a daze. Between Lorna's startling news and hearing of Erica's death, George's head was spinning.

Lorna squared her shoulders as if trying to regain her control. "Before she died, Erica could have spoken to Alexandra Locke. Just in case, we've got to find a way to stop this D.A. before she can ruin our lives."

"Maybe we're overreacting," he cautioned. "It happened so long ago. Who would believe it anyway?"

"George, if this hits the papers, it won't matter if people believe it or not. It will hurt your reputation—our reputation. Our standing in the community." Her eyes were turning stormy. "Even if we manage to stay out of prison, we'll be ostracized."

George pictured the scenario she was describing in his mind. The mere mention of prison had him shaking in fear. "You could be right," he finally admitted.

"That's why we have to do something. And quick." She stared at him, her gaze unblinking. "Think of all we've accomplished, George. We've come too far to risk losing it all."

Michael McGrath was standing in the middle of a circle of bright lights and cameras, waiting for the makeup people to pat his star's face dry with powder, when he saw his personal assistant heading toward him. He was annoyed. His assistant knew better than to interrupt Michael in the middle of a take. They had reshot this one scene fifteen times and the actors still hadn't given him what he was looking for. He waved the assistant off. "Not now."

Instead of turning back, his assistant leaned over close enough so that Michael smelled peppermint on his breath. "Your grandfather is on the telephone. He sounds really upset."

"Hold it," Michael ordered the crew. Then he grabbed the cell phone his assistant was carrying and held it up to his ear. "I'm in the middle of a shoot, Gramps. Can it wait a bit?"

He listened grimly while Lester McGrath explained how he was at the Eisenhower Medical Center in Rancho Mirage because Frances had had another heart attack. This news was so disturbing to Michael that he waved his hands at his crew and cast. "Take a break," he mouthed. Back on the phone he asked some questions. "When did this happen?"

"About an hour ago."

"What do the doctors say?"

There was a large sigh before the other man responded. "With your grandmother's prior history and weakened condition, they're worried." Lester's voice cracked. "I am, too."

Hearing the fear in his grandfather's voice, Michael asked, "Is there anyone at the hospital with you?"

"Nope."

"Have you called my mother yet?"

There was a moment of silence. "No," Lester finally said. "Don't think your grandmother would want her here."

It bothered Michael that his grandmother didn't like Lorna, but there wasn't anything he could do about it now. "Listen, Gramps, I'm shooting a scene with dozens of extras, which I have to wrap today. As soon as it's done, I'll catch a plane and meet you at the hospital tonight, about seven. Is that okay?"

"That's fine," Lester told him.

Shifting the phone to his other ear, Michael continued his probe. "Do they know what brought this attack on?"

"They say it was probably stress."

"I thought you were monitoring her," Michael chided softly.

"I was, but something unexpected came up. I was going to tell you when you got down here." The older man coughed. "You see, we got a call from a deputy D.A. saying they might be looking into your father's death again."

Michael stiffened. "What was this deputy D.A.'s name?"

"Alexandra Locke."

"Alexandra Locke?" he repeated, disbelieving. "When did she call?"

"Last week. And right after that, she drove down here to see us."

Michael was so unnerved by his grandfather's words that he almost dropped the phone. "She's already been there to see you?" he sputtered, shaking his head in dismay.

"Yep," Lester responded. "What's wrong, son? You hear from her, too?"

"Yes," Michael admitted. His mind was racing. Why on earth hadn't Alexandra told him she'd been to Rancho Mirage to visit his grandparents? His surprise quickly turned to rage. What kind of a game was she playing? "Why didn't you call me the minute you heard from her?"

There was another sigh on the other end of the line. "I didn't want to bother you," said Lester. "You're a busy, important man. Plus, I figured it might not be a bad idea for me to hear what the lady had to say."

"You should have called me," Michael repeated numbly, still trying to evaluate what all this meant.

"I suppose. But I just didn't count on your grandmother being so stubborn." Lester coughed once more before going on. "She wanted to be in the room while we talked about your father's death. Course, she'd promised not to get upset, but . . . well, you see, things got out of control."

Michael was growing more indignant by the minute. There was no excuse for Alexandra not telling him about this.

"Can we do anything about this woman?" Lester asked. "I mean, it would be terrible to have the case reopened."

That was an understatement, thought Michael. "Don't worry, Gramps," he found himself saying. "We'll come up with some way to stop her." He paused. "Let me get things squared away here, and I'll be down there as soon as I can."

"Good," said Lester.

After hanging up, Michael stood there mute, totally unaware of the people milling around him. He was stunned. What a damn fool he had been.

It was after five in the afternoon when Alexandra walked out of the Criminal Courts Building and headed for the parking lot. She was planning to stop and pick up dinner before going to visit her mother. It was cold and windy, and she buttoned her sweater up around her neck. As she hurried along, figuring out what to order from the Chinese restaurant near her parents' home, she thought she heard someone shouting her name.

"Alexandra!"

She turned around. Her heart started racing when she saw Michael McGrath rushing toward her. How quixotic of him to show up here and surprise her this way. Although Alexandra knew she'd let her body rule her mind last night, she still hadn't been able to stop thinking about him all day. In fact, she'd found herself becoming distressed as the hours passed and he hadn't called.

Thinking about their lovemaking, she blushed. It was getting dark. Hopefully, he wouldn't notice the effect he was having on her. As soon as he came abreast of her, she saw the strained expression on his face. Something terrible had happened.

"What's wrong?" she asked, a trickle of dread in her gut.

"Let's go over here, and I'll tell you." Grabbing her arm, he guided her away from the other people on the street.

Alarmed now by his angry tone and abrupt manner, she tried to pull free of his grasp. "You're hurting me," she said firmly.

Michael didn't respond. He just kept moving until they had crossed the street. Finally, he stopped and released her arm. Facing her, his eyes blazing, he almost spat out the words. "Why the hell didn't you tell me you had gone to Rancho Mirage to see my grandparents?"

Her throat became dry. "I tried to tell you last night, but you didn't want to talk any more about your father, remember?" As she spoke she rubbed the spot where his fingers had dug into her arm.

Stormy eyes glared back at her. "You started giving me some long explanation, so I figured whatever it was could wait. But not this. For God's sake—all you had to say was four lousy words: *I met your grandparents.*" His sarcasm echoed sharply and he was practically shouting at her now.

It had been wrong for her not to tell him about

her visit, but she hadn't committed a crime. He had no right to talk to her like this.

Without giving her a chance to respond, he blasted her again. "And what's your excuse for not telling me the night we had dinner after I came to apologize?"

Alexandra shook her head. "I'm sorry, Michael, I had no choice. I had a job to do," she finally explained. Then she repeated her earlier words, "I'm sorry."

"Sorry?" A mocking smile twisted his mouth. "I'm afraid sorry won't do," he added bitterly. Then jabbing a finger at her, he blurted out, "My grandmother's in the hospital. She's had another heart attack, brought on by you!"

Horrified by this news, Alexandra stood in stunned silence. Had she really caused Frances Mc-Grath to become sick?

"Didn't I tell you they were old and ill—and to leave them alone?" he shouted.

"Yes, but—"

Michael interrupted her again. "I'm late. I have a plane to catch. But I wanted you to know what you've done. I hope you're satisfied!" He gave her a withering stare. Then without another word he swung around and stalked off.

12

≈

ROBERTA HAD WANTED Chinese food for dinner as well, so Alexandra had stopped at the Twin Dragon on Pico Boulevard near La Cienega to get it for both of them. The family-owned restaurant had been in the area for years and had always been one of Alexandra's favorite places. Now, as she sat watching her mother eat, her mind kept wandering back to the earlier scene with Michael. She thought of all the things she might have said to break through his wall of anger.

"Aren't you going to eat?" asked Roberta, looking concerned.

"I'm really not hungry—I had a big lunch," Alexandra lied.

"In between bouts of nausea at the hospital I was absolutely craving this," Roberta told her daughter, smiling and pointing with her chopsticks to a dish called Buddha's Feast—one of the Twin Dragon's specialties. "Unfortunately, your father doesn't like it very much."

Thomas wasn't home. He'd had another speaking engagement tonight, so it was just the two of them. Alexandra focused her concentration on her mother. "It's nice to see you have an appetite for a change."

"It's nice for me, too," Roberta admitted. Putting down her chopsticks, she gazed at her daughter with a worried frown. "What's wrong, Alexandra? You don't seem yourself tonight."

"I'm fine, Mom," she said with a forced smile. "I've just got a difficult case, and I'm trying to decide how to handle it."

"Why not discuss it with me? That's what your father used to do. He claimed I really helped him." Her mother's voice had a wistful quality.

"I didn't know that." Alexandra tried to picture her father taking Roberta's advice. It was a difficult concept, since Thomas wasn't the type to seek advice from anybody, not even from one of his most experienced deputies.

Roberta smiled. "He felt my common sense was a good barometer of how a jury would react to certain evidence."

"I'm sure he was right," Alexandra responded, happy to see her mother eating. "Speaking of Dad, did you send him to see Erica Collins before she died?"

Her mother looked puzzled. "Not that I recall. Why?"

"He said you asked him to check up on how Erica was doing."

"I may have," Roberta said hastily, suddenly cagey. "To be honest, I just don't remember." She raised one eyebrow. "Memory loss is one of the side effects of chemotherapy. Why do you ask? Is something wrong?"

Alexandra wasn't going to drag her mother into the situation between her and her father. "No. I was just curious." She quickly changed the topic. "Tell me—have you talked to the doctor yet about that new experimental chemotherapy?"

"Yes," Roberta nodded, her brow furrowed. "I'm just not sure. It sounds really terrible." She proceeded to tell Alexandra about the process, the projected side effects, and the chances of a full or partial remission.

Listening to her mother talk about the difficult decisions she was facing, Alexandra pushed Michael's angry face out of her mind. She did the same with her thoughts about her father and Erica. Roberta's health was her major concern. She couldn't afford to let anyone or anything get in the way of that.

"I know you have some hard choices to make," Alexandra stated, giving her mother a big hug. "I just wish I knew how best to advise you."

"You can't, darling. No one can. Every person facing this awful disease must find their own way."

* * *

All morning Alexandra had performed in court as if on automatic pilot, bartering with lawyers as cases were called out, and, in many of them, striking plea bargains. Finally the calendar was over, and she could escape to her office.

She stopped in the ladies' room. Appraising her tired face in the cracked mirror, Alexandra wondered how much longer she could continue to function without enough sleep. Worried about her mother, and thinking of all the problems associated with the Collins/McGrath matter, she'd spent another miserable night.

If only she had someone in Los Angeles to confide in, even a close friend she could talk to. But after she'd gone away to school, she'd gradually lost contact with her old friends. Now the only friend she had left here was her mother. In spite of the distance between them, they had managed to remain wonderfully close. In fact, Alexandra had always considered her mother her best friend. But at the moment, she not only couldn't burden Roberta with any of her problems, she also had to be extra careful that her mother didn't suspect all that was going on.

As for Alexandra's friends in New York, they'd mostly been the people she worked with in the political corruption unit and at the various law enforcement agencies. She missed the sharing of insider gossip and the barhopping they sometimes did together, but she couldn't ask any of them now for advice about her current difficulties; she'd somehow have to muddle through them on her own.

Back at her desk, Alexandra sifted through the stack of folders, looking for the Collins/McGrath file but unable to find it. That's funny, she thought. She was sure she'd left it at the bottom of the pile.

She stood up and checked the old, battered credenza behind her, also stacked with files. It wasn't there, either. In a panic, she frantically pawed through the folders on the floor. By now her heart was racing. No one but her father knew about it. Had he had the audacity to remove the file from her office?

When she found Geena at her desk, Alexandra asked, "Did you take any of the files from my office?"

Geena, intent on a document she was proofing on her computer, shook her head no.

Alexandra went back into her office and closed the door. Gazing out the window past the brightly colored pagodas of Chinatown below, she became increasingly angry. She couldn't allow Thomas to treat her this way. She was a prosecutor who'd received a tip on a crime that apparently had been covered up twenty years ago. He'd been the deputy D.A. in charge at the time. He couldn't avoid responsibility for his past misdeeds just because he was now the head of the D.A.'s office. And she couldn't let the matter drop just because he was her father.

Making a decision, she marched up one flight of stairs to the eighteenth floor. Seeing the guard outside Thomas's office, she didn't bother to slow down. It wasn't like her to act this way, but she was too upset to care about protocol. Instead she headed straight for his door and angrily flung it open. To her dismay, Thomas wasn't there.

She turned around to ask his assistant a question only to realize that the woman was right behind her. "Where is he?" Alexandra demanded to know.

"Your father's a very busy man, Alexandra," Carol Eberhardt said in a patronizing voice. "He had several appointments this afternoon—all of them out of the office." She spoke formally, precisely, pronouncing every syllable as if Alexandra were deaf.

"Fine," Alexandra replied through gritted teeth. "But I want to be notified the minute he gets back. Is that understood?"

The other woman—obviously not accustomed to being treated this way by anyone other than her boss—looked startled. Knowing she should apologize, but finding herself unable to do so, Alexandra strode off.

Los Angeles sheriff's deputy T. J. Garret hung up the phone and looked over at his partner, Eddie Zacharias. "Guess what? I just got a tip involving Alexandra Locke and a shitload of drugs." He waved his pen in a circular motion. "What do you think?"

Zacharias lifted one blond eyebrow in surprise. "Deputy D.A. Alexandra Locke—like in the D.A.'s daughter?" There was a note of incredulity in his voice.

"Yep. That's the one."

"Take it to the captain," Zacharias suggested, shaking his head. "We don't need to risk our jobs."

A few minutes later they were both seated in Captain Ned Taylor's office. The captain had his hands clasped and folded behind his head as he listened to the story. "And this snitch identified the apartment where he saw the stuff and the sales going on as belonging to Alexandra Locke?"

"That's what he said," T.J. repeated, scratching his balding head. "Think we should contact her old man first? Just to be on the safe side?"

"Tell this to Thomas Kendell?" Captain Taylor's pasty complexion reddened in disbelief as he sat forward. "You've got to be kidding. We don't owe him shit. And if it turns out to be true, it would serve the bastard right."

T.J. remembered hearing that there were hard feelings between Kendell and the captain. Supposedly Captain Taylor believed that Kendell had gone over his head several years ago to complain about Taylor's handling of a case. It sounded as if the captain was still carrying a grudge. But T.J. didn't really care. As long as the current situation had been cleared with the captain, it would be Taylor's ass on the line and not his if this whole thing blew up.

Captain Taylor swiveled around in his chair as if thinking. "Doubt we're going to get a judge to sign a warrant on a tip like this."

"The drug hotline is set up so that people don't have to give their name if they don't want to," T.J. reminded him.

"Yeah. But a judge might not find enough probable cause," Captain Taylor said, frowning. "Shit!"

"Want me to set up a 'buy' situation?" asked T.J.

"If we go to all that trouble and expense and it's nothing, we'll look like fools. Not to mention the time involved." Taylor scratched his chin as he swiveled around in his chair. "Tell you what," he finally said. "Try a knock-and-talk. Might catch the lady off guard. And if she lets you in to look and that stuff happens to be there—" Captain Taylor rolled his eyes and allowed himself a smile. "Shit, I can just see Kendell's face now."

By that evening, Alexandra still hadn't spoken with her father, nor had he returned to the office. She figured that Carol Eberhardt had warned him that his daughter was on the warpath and was looking for him.

Before she'd left the office, Alexandra had written down everything that had happened in the Collins/McGrath matter, including all the facts she'd gleaned from her research since that first night she'd spoken to Erica Collins. Then she put the notes in a file marked PERSONAL, and stuck it far back in her bottom drawer.

Although she was anxious to discuss the missing file with her father, she couldn't confront him at home and risk upsetting her mother. In two days, Roberta was going back to the City of Hope. She'd decided to start the new experimental chemotherapy, and Alexandra wanted her to be in the best possible frame of mind going in. Any showdown with Thomas would just have to wait.

The wind outside her small apartment was howling and it set Alexandra's nerves even more on edge. She hoped that the large fir tree in the side yard was sturdier than it looked. It was frightening to think of it falling across the roof and into her apartment. She was also uneasy because she'd found the window in her bedroom ajar when she came home. It wasn't like her to go off to work and leave that window open, but she didn't have any recollection of closing it, either.

It was nearly ten o'clock when she heard noisy footsteps on the stairway outside her apartment, followed by a loud knock. Who could it be so late? she wondered. Maybe it was Michael coming to apologize for the way he'd behaved, she thought hopefully. She ran to the door and threw it open.

Two sheriff's deputies were standing there. "Evening, ma'am. I'm Deputy T. J. Garret," one of them said. He then gestured toward the second man. "And this is my partner, Eddie Zacharias."

Zacharias smiled.

"Windy night, isn't it?" Garret commented.

"Yes," she replied, glancing from one face to the other. "Is there some sort of problem, officer?"

"Well," said Garret, looking embarrassed and clearing his throat. "I'm sure you'll think this is crazy, but we got a tip that you're selling drugs from your apartment here."

At first Alexandra thought it was some kind of a

joke. "You've got to be kidding. I'm a D.A., for God's sake. I don't do drugs."

"Yeah, that's what we figured too. Still, we gotta check these things out," Garret said, with an apologetic smile. "Mind if we just take a quick look around to make sure?"

Alexandra shook her head in disbelief. They obviously had the wrong address. "Go ahead. Just don't make a mess."

T. J. Garret, who had a thick, dark mustache, disappeared first into her bedroom. A few minutes later, he went into her bathroom.

In the meantime, Eddie Zacharias checked the living room and kitchen.

Soon she heard Garret pulling out drawers and rifling her medicine cabinet. From the clatter of bottles and the creak of opened wooden doors, she surmised that he was searching underneath the tiny sink.

Was this a prank or just a mistake? she wondered. They certainly were being thorough. Suddenly, Alexandra decided to put an end to it, and was just about to tell them to stop, when Garret shouted out from the bathroom.

"Hey, Zacharias, check this out." He came into the living room, carrying an armload of stuff. There was a big smile on his square-jawed face.

Her mouth agape, Alexandra watched as he showed his partner a pile of small plastic bags, a few large bags of some kind of white substance and a scale. Alexandra had been around enough drug busts in her career to recognize immediately what they'd found. It sent shivers of fear up her spine. How had those things gotten into her apartment?

"Looks like our snitch was right," Garret said. "The lady here not only uses, but deals as well."

Alexandra swayed unsteadily on her feet. Someone must have broken into her apartment and planted this stuff. But why? She felt violated and angry. "I've never seen any of that before in my life," she protested, her voice rising.

"Hey, T.J., don't all dopers say the same thing?"

"Yep," T.J. responded.

"You guys are making a terrible mistake," she insisted. "Maybe you didn't understand what I said before." Her heart pounding, she ran over to the table where her wallet was and held out her badge. "Look," she said. "I'm one of you. I'm a deputy D.A."

"So we've been told," said the younger of the two men with a smirk. The fact that she was a D.A. didn't seem to faze him at all.

"Honestly," she insisted again, "I don't do drugs. I never have. I have no idea where this stuff came from."

"Is this your apartment?" asked T. J. Garret.

"Yes," she replied. "But can't you see this is some kind of a setup?"

T.J. turned to his partner. "You ever heard anyone confess to the stuff being theirs?"

Zacharias gazed at her and shook his head.

Alexandra stood with her hands clenched. She tried to quell her rising panic so that she could think clearly. It was time to use her trump card. It was demeaning, but she had been backed into a corner and had run out of options.

"Look," she said, trying to get their attention again. "My father is Thomas Kendell, the D.A. Can we just call him? I'm positive that a short conversation between him and your boss will settle everything."

The younger cop had his arms folded across his chest. "You'll get your one phone call down at the jail just like all the rest of them," he said. He now had stationed himself as if to guard her while the other cop finished the search.

"Please," she begged. "Let me make just one short call?" To her embarrassment, her voice cracked.

"Later," he snapped.

Alexandra tried to calm herself, but her nerves were taut and her insides felt like a bowl of Jell-O.

The older cop came out of her bedroom. "Ma'am, we're going to have to place you under arrest." He reached into his pocket, removed a plastic card and began reading. "You have the right to remain silent . . ."

Alexandra tuned out the words. They couldn't really be serious, could they? When he finished, she began again. "Look, this is crazy and I—"

Interrupting, T. J. Garret issued a warning. "Get your coat if you want, because we're taking you in."

"I'm a deputy D.A.," she protested one more time, a feeling of unreality taking over. "Surely your boss will let me surrender voluntarily tomorrow morning?"

He shook his head. "Afraid not. We've got strict orders. Find anything—bring her in."

"I can't believe this." Her mind was reeling, searching for a way to make them see they were wrong. "I swear to you, I've never seen any of this stuff before." Her voice cracked again as she gestured toward the drugs they were holding. "In fact, when I got home tonight I noticed that the window in my bedroom was open. Someone must have broken in here before I got home and planted the drugs."

"Yeah, yeah," said T.J., smoothing down his mustache with his hand. "That's what they all say." His dark brown eyes gave her a once-over. "Now you gonna get your things, or you gonna go as you are?"

With a deep sigh she reached for her jacket, then started putting on her socks and shoes. Maybe at the station she'd have better luck.

When she saw the handcuffs come out, she blanched. Her mouth went dry, and her pulse started racing. She gazed from one cop to the other. "There are two of you. I'm not a flight risk. I don't need those."

"I think she's got a point," Zacharias said. "What do you say?"

"Yeah, sure," the other cop agreed.

Grateful for small favors, Alexandra mumbled a weak thanks. Taking her keys from her purse, she locked up. Then the three of them made their way down the stairway and over to the police car that was parked on the street.

The younger deputy opened the back door of the vehicle. At least it was late, she thought, and none of her neighbors were standing around watching. As she got in and Zacharias slid in beside her, the taste of bile rose in her throat. She felt like a common criminal. "Where are you taking me?"

"Sybil Brand," replied T.J.

As they headed for the women's jail, Alexandra tried to figure out what had happened. It was obvious that she'd been set up, but she didn't have the faintest idea by whom—or why. All she knew was that she'd never felt so helpless or so frightened in her entire life.

Patrick Ross had just come out of the bathroom in Nancy Breslaw's condo when he heard the phone ringing.

Nancy was waiting for him in bed. "Don't answer it," she said, smiling at him. "The machine will pick it up."

"I'm on call. I told our service to forward them to me." As he reached for the receiver he gestured for something to write with. She rolled over toward her chrome-and-glass nightstand and threw him a pen.

Patrick turned his attention back to the telephone. It was Alexandra Locke calling him, and from Sybil Brand. He couldn't believe it. As she related her story, Patrick shook his head. "Sounds pretty inconceivable to me, too," he finally said.

Clearing his throat, he contemplated how best to handle a situation like this. "Tell you what, let me find out what it's going to take to get you out of there. In the meantime, try not to worry."

When he hung up, Nancy blurted out, "Who's in jail?"

"Alexandra Locke."

Her green eyes widened in surprise. "Your old girlfriend? The D.A.'s daughter?"

"Yep."

"What was she arrested for?"

"Possession for sale. Drugs."

"Marijuana?"

"No. Much worse than that. Methamphetamine to be exact."

Nancy looked puzzled. "Speed?"

"Yes." He nodded.

She frowned. "Of all the defense lawyers in this city, why do you suppose she's calling you?"

"I'd like to think it's because of my reputation." He flashed her a wry smile. "In case you haven't noticed, I'm damn good at what I do."

"Oh, I've noticed," she remarked, smiling back. "But it still sounds fishy to me."

Patrick heard the hint of jealousy in her voice and could have kicked himself. Once, when Patrick had had too much to drink, he'd confessed to Nancy that his one true love had been Alexandra Locke. This had been before he and Nancy had become law partners and long before they'd formed a personal relationship. But he could see that wasn't going to matter now.

"Honestly, Nancy, I've barely spoken to Alexandra in years." Glancing at the crystal clock in her armoire, he saw it was almost one. "It's late. Let's do this another night, okay?"

She ran her fingers through her short red hair. "But I wanted to be with you."

"And I wanted to be with you, too. You know this isn't the kind of thing I usually do." He gave her a peck on the cheek.

"Are you going home?" There was another frown on her pretty face.

"After I visit the jail." He got up and started to dress.

"You can't do anything for Alexandra at this hour," she insisted. "I want you to spend the night. It's silly to go over there now."

"Alexandra sounded really shaken up. And you know I don't like to leave Jenny alone all night."

"She's not alone. Your housekeeper's there."

"It's not the same thing." He pictured his six-year-old little girl asleep with her menagerie of stuffed teddy bears lined up along the wall. Luckily, he had a wonderful housekeeper who stayed with Jenny when he wasn't there. But no matter how late it was—unless he was out of town—he always managed to get home.

Patrick gazed into the mirror and patted down his curly black hair. Lately, the fine lines at the corners of his brown eyes were becoming more pronounced. At thirty-three, he'd finally begun to look his age after years of being called a kid. Hurriedly, he buttoned his shirt, then slung his tie around his neck.

Still in bed, Nancy gazed at him, her eyes searching his face as if trying to read his thoughts. "I've never seen you do this before. Why don't you just send someone to bail her out?"

Patrick wished again he'd never told Nancy about Alexandra. That had been so long ago, and he had absolutely no romantic interest in Alexandra anymore. Once burned was enough.

Smiling, Patrick leaned over and planted a kiss on Nancy's lips. Then he tilted her chin toward him. "There's no reason for you to be jealous," he promised.

13

~

THE DEPUTIES had brought Alexandra to Sybil Brand Detention Center, the L.A. County jail for women located in East L.A. Although she'd been to this facility before, she had never had the experience of actually being behind the bars, looking out. She felt humiliated and angry as they booked her. She cringed when they took her mug shot and fingerprints. The worst part came when she was forced to hand over all of her personal effects.

"The watch, too," the deputy said.

Unfastening it, Alexandra remembered how Roberta had come to New York and given it to her when she'd graduated from law school. Tears of rage and helplessness stung her eyes, but she held them back. She would not let them see her cry.

"We also need your badge."

Handing it over was traumatic. Until this moment, she hadn't realized how much she relied on certain external trappings for her identity. Her badge announced to the world that she was one of the people in charge—one of those who could be trusted. Now she was experiencing what it felt like to have no rights whatsoever. It was shameful and degrading.

Alexandra knew what could happen to a deputy D.A. locked up with drug pushers, addicts, thieves and murderers. No doubt there were many disgruntled detainees at this jail who would like nothing better than to beat her up—maybe even kill her. Just thinking about it made her sick with fear.

"Will I be put in a cell by myself?" she asked.

The deputy nodded, and Alexandra breathed a sigh of relief, grateful to get this tiny bit of good news.

Her cell had a high window with bars. When the door clanged shut behind her, the horror of her confinement became real. She wanted to scream out that she didn't belong here—that her arrest was all a terrible mistake. Knowing it would be futile, she slumped down on the bench.

Earlier, when they had notified Alexandra that she could make her one call, she'd been stymied. If her father had been forthcoming instead of evasive about the Collins/McGrath case, she would have used her call to ask him to find her a good lawyer.

Instead, Alexandra had tried to think of every defense lawyer she'd met since returning to California. With each face, a fresh wave of humiliation washed over her. In only five short minutes—the time it took for the deputies to search her home—she'd gone from being a proud D.A. to being a suspected criminal. There was no way she could face any of those same defense lawyers.

Finally she'd focused on her onetime boyfriend, Patrick Ross. Since she'd been back in L.A., they had run into each other in court and chatted a few times. He hadn't been overly friendly, but he had a solid reputation as a criminal defense lawyer. She also remembered the gift basket he'd sent her mother. Not knowing whom else to trust, she'd placed her one call from the jail to him.

Without her watch she had to keep glancing at the clock on the outside wall, counting the hours until the bail bondsman Patrick had promised to send could get her out of here.

Gazing around the barren cell, Alexandra felt both powerless and exhausted. Yet, she knew she'd never be able to sleep in this awful place. The terror she was experiencing kept rising like acid in her throat. To keep her fear at bay, she concentrated on trying to figure out who had set her up this way. At the moment, she didn't know. But when she found the answer, she'd personally see to it that the guilty party spent a very long time in prison.

By the time Alexandra was brought to the visiting area, she was a nervous wreck. During her long wait, she'd reverted to a childhood habit and had chewed her fingernails down until there was nothing left but raw flesh. As she was escorted into a small conference room, she hid her hands behind her back.

Seeing Patrick Ross standing there, she froze.

She hadn't expected him to show up himself—not in the middle of the night. Unconsciously, she let her hands fly to her hair in an attempt to make herself more presentable.

His short, curly black hair gave him a youthful appearance. But as she had noticed the first time she saw him after being back in L.A., Patrick's face had matured into that of an extremely handsome and self-confident man. His strong jaw had become more pronounced, and with his olive skin and full mouth, the overall effect was striking.

"Hello, Alex," he said.

Patrick had been the only person she'd ever allowed to call her Alex. Hearing him say it now gave her a funny feeling in the pit of her stomach. A small sigh escaped her lips and she realized she'd been holding her breath. "Thank you for coming." She smiled sheepishly, not sure of what else to say in such awkward circumstances.

He nodded. "That's all right."

"Were you able to find out anything?"

"No," he said, shaking his head. "Everyone's being unusually close-mouthed."

"When they searched my apartment and found the drugs, I heard one of the deputies say to his partner that their snitch had been right."

Patrick frowned.

"Someone has gone to a lot of trouble to frame me," she said.

His eyes narrowed, and there was an instant where she thought he looked skeptical. Her body tensed, then she realized that if the situation had been reversed, she probably would have had that reaction too. *I was framed,* was an excuse often heard after an arrest.

"Do you have anything to back that up with?" he asked, his gaze focused on her.

"No," she acknowledged. "At this point I'm not sure who is involved. But they had to know there's a presumption that the stuff belongs to me if it's found in my place." She then told him about coming home and noticing the open window in her bedroom.

While she spoke, Patrick had started to pace the room. Now he turned to face her. "Tell you what, let's talk about how to get you out of here first. Then we'll see about the rest."

His voice was polite, but there was no mistaking the fact that his tone was strictly professional. She wondered if it had been a mistake to call him. "What do you think it's going to take?" she asked.

"Do you have any real property we can get a bond on?"

"I have a co-op in New York." She glanced up at him. "I think that will take time to arrange, won't it?"

"Yes." He ran a hand through his hair as if trying to make a decision. "Any cash?"

"I have about twenty thousand dollars. But it's tied up in retirement funds in New York. It will take me time to arrange that, too."

"How about your folks?"

She panicked at the thought of asking them for help. "I can't go to them," she admitted.

Patrick stared wordlessly at her, but she was grateful that he didn't ask her to explain. "Okay, tell you what," he finally said. "I'll post the bond for you. But it will be morning before I can arrange it. Then we'll get all the information and figure it out."

His offer was totally unexpected. Touched, she didn't know what to say. "Thank you, Patrick," she said softly. "That's very kind of you."

He merely nodded again, his face impassive. "I'll see you in the morning." At the door, he turned and added, "Try not to worry."

As soon as he left, and she was back in her cell, Alexandra felt the walls closing in on her again. *Hurry, Patrick, hurry*, she silently prayed.

Captain Ned Taylor finished signing the papers that had been put in front of him. "I want to look at this one again," he said, giving all but one of the documents to the deputy standing by the side of his desk.

As the young woman walked away, he yelled, "Close my door on the way out."

When he was alone, Taylor quickly read over the arrest report in his hand and smiled to himself. Then he picked up the phone and placed a call.

"I think I've got something you can use," he said, chuckling when the other person came on the line. "Alexandra Locke, the D.A.'s daughter, was arrested for possession of drugs with intent to sell. Methamphetamine. No," he said shaking his head, "I'm not pulling your leg."

The captain leaned back in his chair and put his feet up on his desk. "Yeah, I thought it might make your day."

He listened for a minute, then gave a hearty laugh. "You're right. It totally screws up her credibility. Thomas Kendell is going to have a fucking heart attack when he finds out."

Mentally and physically drained from being up all night, Alexandra, escorted by Patrick Ross, headed toward the jail exit, eager to breathe fresh air. Suddenly she stopped in her tracks. A swarm of reporters and television cameras was stationed outside. *Please, dear God,* she thought, *don't let them be waiting for me.*

Patrick reached for her arm and squeezed it gently. "Take it easy," he cautioned in a soothing tone. "Just keep your eyes down and let me answer their questions. Okay?"

Her mouth was dry and she felt herself tremble. Where was her customary courage? Alexandra was used to being the one in charge, the one who met with the reporters and made the statements. Feeling intimidated by this scene was as shattering to her as the nightmare swirling around her.

"Are you ready?" Patrick asked.

She nodded, afraid that if she tried to speak her voice would betray her terror.

The door opened and they stepped outside and into the glare of lights and the rush of reporters and photographers.

"Are you planning on resigning from the D.A.'s

office, Ms. Locke?" a young male reporter called out.

"No comment," Patrick responded in a confident, take-charge voice.

The question shook Alexandra. It was something she hadn't even let herself think about. She'd been arrested on suspicion of a felony, and if she were tried and convicted, they'd take away her license to practice law. She wouldn't be allowed to be a prosecutor. Dread clutched at her stomach as the very real possibility sank in.

A woman reporter shoved her microphone directly in Alexandra's face. "What do you think your arrest will do to your father's hopes for reelection?"

Patrick again said, "No comment."

Perspiration formed at the back of Alexandra's neck while at the same time she was shivering from the chill of the morning.

"Have you spoken to your father yet?" yelled another reporter.

With a sudden flash of clarity, Alexandra realized her father must have already been called for his reaction to her arrest. Her poor mother had to be so worried. She had to telephone Roberta as soon as she could and reassure her that she was all right.

"What kind of drugs did they find?"

"Yeah. What were you on?"

Alexandra just kept shaking her head as every few steps another microphone was thrust in her face and people tried to impede her progress through the parking lot.

"No comment," Patrick repeated several more times, waving the media away with one hand while with the other he guided Alexandra through the melee.

It seemed to take hours instead of minutes to arrive at his car. After they were safely inside the vehicle with the doors locked, Patrick attempted to back out of his parking space only to find a number of reporters blocking their way.

"They're like a swarm of killer bees," he muttered under his breath. He honked his horn and gunned the motor. This scared most of them off. But as he wheeled the automobile out of the lot, a few of the more ambitious reporters kept running after them. One or two of them even pounded their fists on the car.

"Don't worry, you're going to be fine," Patrick assured her, as he deftly maneuvered the car in jerks and stops.

When they broke free and he drove away from the jail lot, Alexandra took several large breaths of air. "My God," she exclaimed, dabbing at her upper lip with the back of her hand. Her entire body felt wet and clammy.

He glanced over at her, a worried frown on his face. "Are you okay?"

"Yes. I think so." It was a lie. The ordeal had been one of the most frightening experiences of her life.

"I'm going to drive you home, so you'll need to tell me where you live," he said. "I want you to take the phone off the hook and try to get an hour or two of rest. Then come to my office so we can go over everything. Grab a cab from a neighbor's home if there are reporters around." He took a hand off the wheel long enough to pull a card from his pocket and give it to her.

She glanced at it briefly. "What about my job?"

Patrick's face was grim. "I'll handle it. Usually, in these types of cases they put you on administrative leave."

"God," she groaned, as the enormity of her predicament hit her again. "If I can't be a prosecutor, my life might as well be over."

After Patrick had dropped her off, and she was safely behind the closed door in her apartment, Alexandra totally lost it. There were several minutes of uncontrolled crying before she pulled herself together and went to take a shower.

While the steaming water ran over her, she soaped her scalp and her body, then began scrubbing hard. Head back, she let the water cascade over her face and down her torso, sweeping the suds away. Taking another handful of shampoo, she started washing her hair again, repeating the entire process. She had no idea how many times it would take to wash away all the dirt—all the shame.

When she finally came out of the bathroom the phone was ringing. Alexandra cringed. Could it be a reporter? Worried that it might be important, she picked up the receiver. "Hello?"

"Alexandra, are you all right?" It was her mother and she sounded panicked.

With a sigh, Alexandra slumped down on the edge of her bed. "I'm fine, Mom. Don't worry."

"What happened?"

"I don't really know," she admitted with a calm she did not feel. "Two cops just showed up at my front door. They said they'd heard I was selling drugs, and like a dummy I let them in without a search warrant. They found the stuff in the bathroom. I asked for a chance to make one call, but they wouldn't listen. They just read me my rights and dragged me off to jail."

"I know that any drugs they found weren't yours."

"They weren't," Alexandra said, grateful for her mother's vote of confidence. "How did you find out about my arrest?"

"Some reporters called here for your father; they told him."

"I'm so sorry. You've got enough to worry about."

"That's okay, darling," Roberta replied. "I'm just relieved to hear your voice. I was so afraid for you."

"I'm fine. Really I am." Alexandra hesitated, then acknowledged, "I'm just a little shaken up."

"How did you get out?"

Using one hand to dry her hair with the towel, Alexandra explained. "I called Patrick Ross. He came down to see me last night, and this morning he bailed me out himself."

"That was kind of him," Roberta said. "Please tell Patrick I said thank you."

"I will." Although Alexandra hated to ask the next question, she had to know the answer. She took a deep breath. "How's Dad handling it?"

There was a large sigh on the other end of the phone. "He's in the den with Dale Jensen, talking to some people on the phone. Naturally, he's upset, but then that's to be expected under the circumstances."

Alexandra wanted to ask if Thomas was upset because she was in trouble or because of the potential damage to his own career, but she bit her tongue. It bothered her that once he had knowledge of her arrest, he'd done nothing to try to reach her. "That's really all I know for now, Mom," she finally said. "I'm going to get some rest. I have to meet Patrick at his office in a little while. He should know more by then."

"All right, dear." There was a slight pause before Roberta whispered, "Alexandra, promise me you won't let anything your father says upset you, okay?"

With a pain in the pit of her gut, Alexandra grasped the underlying message. Without even hearing her side, her father was already blaming her for what had happened.

14

---～---

LATER THAT MORNING, as Frank Sanchez was standing by his desk talking to two other deputies, Elizabeth Nathan hurried into his office.

"Did you hear about Alexandra Locke's arrest last night?" she asked, sounding as breathless as if she'd run up a flight of stairs.

"Yep," Frank replied, nodding his head.

"This is exactly what you need to beat Thomas," she told him excitedly, her dark eyes flashing. "His daughter's arrest makes the D.A. vulnerable."

"I still find it hard to believe that Alexandra would be so stupid as to deal drugs. Especially out of her own apartment," one of the other deputies remarked.

"Who knows. Maybe she did the same thing back in New York," Elizabeth suggested, shrugging her small shoulders. "In the meantime what's important is that her arrest reflects badly on all the rest of us." She turned to Frank. "You need to seize the initiative and schedule a press conference right away."

Frank frowned. She was asking him to get involved in a sticky situation. "Since Alexandra's a prosecutor with our office, the Sheriff's Department can choose to go directly to the Attorney General's office." He fingered his tie. "I'm not sure it's right for me to comment on an arrest when no one has brought us the case yet. I also think Thomas will have to bow out."

"Forget what's right," she said in that brittle tone of hers that he found so irritating. "If you want to be the next D.A. you're going to have to speak out on her arrest."

"We were just discussing the matter when you came in," he said in a firm voice, letting her know that he wasn't about to go off half-cocked. "There's a lot to consider."

The corners of her mouth turned downward. "You thought it was wrong when Thomas hired Alexandra, didn't you?"

"Yes," he admitted, shifting his weight to his other foot and adjusting the collar of his shirt. "I felt then and I still do that nepotism gives the appearance of favoritism."

"So what's your problem?" Her eyes were questioning. "Just use that same premise, but go further."

Frank looked at her askance. "What do you mean?"

Elizabeth gave an exasperated sigh. Leaning

over his desk, she grabbed a yellow legal pad and a pen. After hurriedly writing a few lines, she handed it back to him. "This is what you need to say," she told him, pointing to her notes.

Meanwhile, on the eighteenth floor, Thomas sat in his office with three of his most trusted advisers, including Dale Jensen, his campaign manager. They'd been arguing over how to handle his daughter's arrest when his intercom buzzed. "Yes?" he muttered, irritated at being interrupted.

He listened to his assistant, then said, "I'll have to call him back. I'm tied up in a meeting." Putting down the phone, he explained the call to the others. "That was Patrick Ross on the line. Seems he's going to be representing my daughter."

Dale spoke up. "I'll bet you anything that they're cheering downstairs in Frank Sanchez's office." He looked sullen. "That bastard knew the only hope he had of climbing up in the polls was to discredit you, Thomas. I think this situation with Alexandra will give him the ammunition he needs, unless I can think of something brilliant."

"He's right, Thomas," agreed one of the other men. "For Frank, Alexandra's arrest has to be like a gift from God. Only your being caught in a whorehouse with your pants down around your ankles could have been worse."

There were loud guffaws from the other men as Thomas shot the speaker a dirty look.

"Your daughter was never into drugs before, was she?" one of the men asked.

"As far as I know she wasn't," Thomas said, straightening his shoulders and letting them know that he clearly resented questions like that.

"It doesn't really matter," Dale interposed with a grim expression on his face. "If the voters believe it, then we've got problems."

Thomas nodded glumly. His head throbbed as he reluctantly acknowledged to himself that Alexandra's arrest could very well derail his reelection bid.

After getting away from the reporters staking out her house and then fighting heavy crosstown traffic from West Hollywood to Century City, Alexandra was running late when she finally turned onto Avenue of the Stars.

Century City wasn't really a city, just the name for several blocks of prime real estate. The property had been the back lot of the Twentieth Century–Fox Film Studios before the land had been sold off to a large company for hotel, office and retail development.

Located between Beverly Hills and Westwood, the area was known for its towering skyscrapers peopled with an upscale assortment of lawyers, accountants, investment bankers, business managers and other types of professionals who charged large fees in order to cover their exorbitant rents. There was also an open-air shopping mall filled with expensive department stores and pricey boutiques. First-run theaters and a variety of restaurants and take-out places all added to the mall's appeal.

Alexandra pulled into the underground parking

lot in the building where Patrick's law office was located. Exiting the elevator on the fortieth floor of the high-rise building, she found herself standing in a stunning entry. The walls were paneled in rich teak while the couches and chairs were upholstered in cream, beige and tangerine. Accents of jungle-print pillows and abstract art dotted the room. It was sleek, stylish—and obviously costly. It was also intimidating. A brass plaque on the wall read BRES-LAW & ROSS. She had known that Patrick had done well for himself, but she hadn't been expecting anything quite so plush.

When Alexandra was ushered into a large corner office, Patrick stood up and came around a massive, high-gloss, burl-veneered desk. "How're you doing?"

"Not great."

He turned to his secretary. "Could you bring us some coffee, please? Come, sit down," he said to Alexandra as he motioned to a beautifully carved ebony chair.

Patrick returned to his desk, and while they waited for the coffee, Alexandra forced herself to make small talk. Again, she was aware that he was behaving in a polite but strictly professional manner. "I wanted to thank you for the lovely gift basket you sent my mother. It really cheered her up."

"I'm glad." The corners of his eyes crinkled as he smiled back at her. It was the first break she'd seen in his reserve. "How is she feeling?"

"Her spirits are good although we still don't have a favorable prognosis."

"I'm sorry."

She was spared the necessity of responding when Patrick's secretary reappeared with the coffee. It scalded Alexandra's tongue as it went down, but she knew the caffeine would help her focus.

As soon as the woman had closed the door, Patrick gestured toward Alexandra with his hand. "Okay, start at the beginning and tell me every detail of what happened last night."

While she filled him in, he scribbled notes on a legal pad. Suddenly he stopped and looked up at her with an astonished expression on his face. "You let them in without a search warrant?" His voice was incredulous.

"I know it was stupid," she admitted, feeling her cheeks flush. "But the way they just showed up talking about drugs was so far out in left field that I figured they merely had the wrong place. I thought they'd be gone in five minutes at the most."

"Unbelievable," he said, shaking his head.

"I wasn't thinking very clearly," she conceded in self-defense.

After a few seconds, he said, "Okay. Let's go on." In spite of his words, Patrick's face continued to communicate that he couldn't comprehend what she'd done. Finally, he glanced down at his legal pad. "And you still have no idea how that stuff got into your apartment?"

"Absolutely none," she stated. "Like I told you last night, someone obviously planted everything that was found."

"You also mentioned they could have entered through a window."

"Right. I always close the bedroom window before I leave for work in the morning. But when I got home last night it was slightly ajar."

"I better get someone up there to dust for fingerprints." He twirled his pen in his fingers. "Any other way someone could have gotten in, like say with a key?"

"I haven't given a key to anyone."

"What about visitors?"

"I haven't had any visitors since I've been back."

Patrick eyed her curiously as he raised one eyebrow. "None?"

Briefly, she reflected on her interlude with Michael. He couldn't have had anything with him that night, because she clearly remembered the way they'd hurriedly removed their clothes on the floor of the living room before making love. If he had been concealing anything she would have been sure to notice.

"No," she said again, too embarrassed to admit that she'd had a one-night stand with someone she barely knew. "Have you been able to find out anything more from the Sheriff's Department?"

"Just that they're planning to take what they have to the D.A.'s office."

"Have you spoken to them yet?"

"Your father is tied up in a meeting, or so they tell me. No one seemed to know if you'll be charged or not. I left a message that you wouldn't be in and asked for the D.A. to call as soon as possible."

She peered down at her fingers wrapped tightly around the mug, wondering how her arrest was being viewed at the D.A.'s office.

Patrick took a few gulps of his coffee. "So let's try and figure this out. Is there anyone that you've recently put in jail who's threatened you?"

"No."

"Anyone you've dealt with in the last six months that's been vicious or menacing in any way?"

"I haven't been threatened. I mean there are the usual protests that I've got the wrong person, but nothing more than that."

He jotted down some more notes and then glanced up at her. "Look, Alexandra," he finally said, "no one goes to the trouble—not to mention the danger—of framing a deputy D.A. without a damn good reason. Something must have triggered this mess."

Alexandra played with her cup. "There is something going on. Whether it's behind this situation or not, I really don't know."

Standing under the Spanish-style porte cochere at the entrance to the Kingsway Country Club in Brentwood—a tony, upscale area in West Los Angeles where many people connected to the movie industry resided—George Collins tried to quell his anxiety.

As soon as Michael drove up in his Porsche,

George quickly took his arm and led him inside. "Thanks for meeting me, Michael. I know how busy you are, but I wanted a chance to talk—alone."

"No problem," Michael told him.

George deftly guided his stepson out onto the terrace, where he'd already reserved a table.

After they had ordered their lunch, George leaned forward. "I'm worried about your mother," he said in a low voice. "Since she learned about the possible reinvestigation into your father's death, she hasn't been sleeping."

"Yeah," Michael said, raising one eyebrow as if to commiserate. "I haven't slept myself since I heard the news. And then Grandma Frances having a heart attack hasn't helped. How are you doing?"

"I'm up all night, too," George admitted. "I'm just hoping that those drugs that were found in Alexandra Locke's apartment will squelch any move to reopen the case." He gave Michael a meaningful look.

"I hope so too." Michael took a sip of his water, and George saw a muscle working in his stepson's jaw. "Unless someone else picks up where she left off."

"The way I see it, our biggest problem was Erica and whatever she said to Ms. Locke before she died. With Locke busted for drugs, her credibility is shot," George stated. "So even if she claims Erica accused me of being a murderer, no one will believe her."

"You know I'll do whatever I can to make sure

you don't have any problems," Michael promised somberly.

George smiled at his stepson. He loved him as if he were his own, he thought. Gazing out over the rolling green lawns dotted with golfers, he added, "There's something else bothering your mother."

"What's that?" asked Michael.

"She feels there's more than a business relationship between you and the prosecutor." George tried to judge what effect his words were having on Michael, but it was hard. His stepson had sunglasses on. Even when he wasn't hiding behind the dark glasses, it was difficult, if not impossible, to read the younger man's thoughts.

Michael shoved his salad around the plate with his fork. "I found her to be extremely bright and totally unaware of her beauty—quite a change from the majority of women I come in contact with."

"I can sympathize with that, but still we must remember—"

Before George could finish, Michael interrupted him. "Don't worry. Nothing's going to come of it."

Eyes narrowed, George asked, "Are you sure about that?" He gave Michael a few seconds to think about his statement. "Your mother's convinced that you're having an affair with her."

His stepson put his fork down. "I spent one night there. It meant nothing. I'm smart enough to watch my step. You can tell Mom not to worry."

"That's good," George said with a sigh of relief. Having heard what he wanted, he could now go on to something else. "How's your grandmother doing?"

"I saw her when she arrived at the UCLA Medical Center by ambulance a few days ago, from the hospital in Rancho Mirage. She seems better, just tired." Michael glanced at his watch. "I'm picking Gramps up at two o'clock and taking him to the hospital to visit her."

"Is Lester staying with you?"

"No. I got him a suite at the Westwood Hills. It's within walking distance of the hospital. That way he doesn't have to drive or worry about cabs. I've got a heavy shooting schedule, so I thought it was best."

"Sounds like you made a good choice," George said, motioning to the waiter for the check.

"Have you spoken to Sally or Arnold?" Michael asked.

"No, I haven't," George responded. "Your mother may have, but she didn't say anything about it to me. Why?"

"If you hear from either one of them, mention that Grandma's been asking for Sally." Michael adjusted his sunglasses as he continued. "I've left several messages at their house, but I haven't heard back."

"That's not like Arnold," George said. "Usually he tells your mother if they are going to be away . . . or if . . . well, you know what I mean."

"Yes," said Michael. "That's why I'm worried too."

15

TIME PASSED QUICKLY as Alexandra told Patrick about the series of events that had occurred since she spoke with Erica Collins. She'd even mentioned how Michael McGrath had followed her home because of the rain. The only detail she left out was the fact that Michael had spent the night in her apartment.

When she was through, he gave her a forthright glance. "Do you believe that your father participated in a cover-up twenty years ago?"

"I don't want to," she stated emphatically. "But to be honest, I'm not sure. Too many things about Jeffrey McGrath's death don't add up."

"The mere fact that Thomas rejected the case doesn't mean criminal charges could never be brought against George Collins," Patrick remarked, looking as if he was thinking the situation over. "There's no statute of limitations on murder.

It could be there just wasn't enough evidence at the time."

"I thought of that too," she said. "But going through the file I became suspicious. The cops would never have brought the case to the D.A.'s office without more evidence than what I found. Besides, if my father's reason had been something as simple as lack of evidence, he would have said so. But as I've already mentioned, when I questioned him, his attitude was baffling." She shook her head. "Instead of telling me anything about the case, he tried to charm me, and when that didn't work he ordered me to stop investigating the matter and even threatened to fire me."

Patrick tapped the pen on his desk. "That's not the behavior of a person with nothing to hide."

"Right. Anyway, I feel that someone connected with the Collins/McGrath case has to be responsible for planting the drugs. They're the only ones who have a motive for wanting to discredit me. It's too coincidental that a little more than two weeks after I first hear about the case, I'm set up."

"What about a political motive?" he asked.

She was surprised by his question. "You mean someone trying to ruin my father by discrediting me?"

"Yes."

"I suppose that's a possibility." She took a quick sharp breath. "But why not go after my father himself? Doesn't that make more sense?"

Before Patrick could reply, his secretary stuck her head in the door. "Jenny's on the phone."

Patrick smiled. "That's my daughter. I've a standing rule: No matter what I'm doing, if she calls and says it's important it's okay to interrupt me." He nodded at his secretary, who closed the door before he picked up his phone. "Hi, sweetheart. What's the matter?"

Listening to him reminded Alexandra of all the times she'd longed for her father's attention when she was a little girl and how he'd usually been too busy. Attempting to shake off the sad memories, she glanced around Patrick's office. Behind his desk on the credenza was a picture of an adorable little girl with dimples. It had to be Jenny.

After promising to be home early, Patrick hung up. "Sorry. She fell and wanted me to hear all the gory details."

"It's wonderful that you stop what you're doing for her. It must make her feel special."

He probably heard the note of wistfulness in her voice, because he gave her a curious look.

"How old is she?" she asked.

"Six going on forty." Patrick grinned.

Alexandra gestured toward the picture. "Is that her?"

"Yes," he said, nodding.

"She looks like you. Do you have joint custody?"

"No. I have full custody," he replied. Then, glancing down at his legal pad, he said, "Now where were we?"

It was clear that Patrick intended on keeping their relationship purely professional. Alexandra was disappointed. She had been hoping they could also be friends. "We were looking for a motive behind the planted drugs," she reminded him.

"Right. Okay. Let's start with the grandparents. What would they have to gain by framing you?"

"Lester McGrath, the grandfather, was opposed to any reopening of the case. He said their primary concern was protecting their grandchildren, especially Sally, from any more pain or scandal. I had a feeling that his wife, Frances, wanted to say more, but Lester wouldn't let her. She's also got a heart condition. In fact, she had another heart attack after I visited. It could be that Lester wants to make sure I can't harm any of them."

"It's hard to conceive that he'd go so far as to plant drugs on a deputy D.A. How would an elderly man even go about doing something like that?" He tapped his desk with the end of his pen.

"He could have hired someone."

"I suppose," he agreed. "And the son?"

She wondered if Michael's ulterior purpose in following her home that night had been to find out where she lived. If so, their lovemaking hadn't been a moment of passion, as she'd thought, but a setup.

"Alexandra?"

She glanced up. "I'm sorry. My mind was wandering. Michael McGrath said his family had been through a lot and asked me to leave them alone." She bit her lower lip. "I think he can't face the fact that his stepfather could be a murderer. I believe he's trying to protect George Collins out of a misguided feeling of loyalty."

"And this need to protect George means he'd go so far as to frame you?"

"I don't know," she replied honestly.

"This Michael knew where you lived," Patrick pointed out, his brow furrowed. "I think that's significant."

"Yes, it is," she acknowledged, rubbing her fingers over the rim of her coffee mug. What she didn't say was that the possibility Michael had been involved bothered her more than she could admit, even to herself.

"And the sister, Sally McGrath Potter, she told you on the telephone that George was a murderer, right?" Patrick asked.

"Yes. She specifically stated that he'd killed her father. Like I said, I heard loud noises in the background, as if someone was banging on a door. Maybe Sally's husband found out that she called me and planted the drugs to keep her from becoming involved."

His eyes bored into her. "But why?"

"I'm not sure. Everyone says Sally's not well."

"I think we need to find her."

"Easier said than done. I've been trying but with no luck."

"We'll put an investigator on it." He paused for a moment before adding, "You never spoke to George Collins, did you?"

"No. Just his wife. Lorna Collins didn't strike me as being totally truthful. My questions might have panicked her, so she went to George and together they decided to stop me." Alexandra leaned forward in her chair. "George could be terrified of standing trial for a crime he thought he got away with. With both his freedom and his financial future in jeopardy, he might have become desperate."

Patrick stood up and went over to the window. "Of all the scenarios," he eventually said, "that last one makes the most sense. As a prominent doctor with a flourishing career, George has a lot to lose. And if he's guilty, he certainly wouldn't want anyone digging up the past." He turned to face her. "Did any of these people mention your father by name?"

"No. When I asked if they had spoken to anyone at the D.A.'s office at the time of Jeffrey's death, they all managed to evade the subject. But if Jeffrey McGrath *was* murdered by George, isn't it more than likely he got away with it because someone in law enforcement helped him?"

"Good point." He paused for another moment. "Okay. Since you haven't been charged yet, I'll call the sheriff's department, ask for a meeting and see what I can find out."

She took another deep breath. "Patrick, my whole life is wrapped up in being a prosecutor. If I can't do that anymore—" Her voice broke and she found she could not go on.

"Don't think the worst yet," he cautioned. "We are a long way from defeat. Didn't you say that Erica left you a key to her storage locker?"

"Yes. I've been going through all of those boxes one at a time, but so far I've found nothing but old financial records."

His hand gripped the back of a chair. "It's an impossible job for one person. You'll need investigators to help you." He stopped momentarily as if thinking again. "Of course, that runs into a lot of money."

Alexandra put her coffee mug on his desk. "I neglected to ask about your fees. What's your usual retainer?"

He seemed hesitant.

"Go ahead, tell me."

"Twenty thousand dollars," he said, his face coloring slightly.

"Wow! I guess I'm really on the wrong side of the courtroom," she said in a feeble attempt to make a joke. "And I owe you the twenty thousand dollars in cash you put up for my bail. That's no problem. I'll cash in my retirement savings to cover the bail. But the retainer . . ."

"Don't worry, we'll work something out. The investigators are more important. That can run another five to ten thousand dollars."

She shook her head. "I don't have that kind of money, Patrick. I'm just going to have to do as much snooping around on my own as I can."

"How about your folks? Can you ask them for the money?"

"I'd rather not," she said. "With the possibility that my father might be implicated in a cover-up, I'm not sure that's a good idea."

"You're right." He ran his hand through his hair. "Well, we'll think of something."

"Just give me a little time and I'll manage it," she promised.

"No problem."

"Thanks." She picked her purse up off the floor, getting ready to leave, then she remembered something else. "There are two more facts I've neglected to mention."

He considered her. "What are they?"

"I learned that my father visited Erica shortly before she died. When I asked him about it, he said my mother had sent him. But I don't think it's the truth."

His expression was now watchful. "And the other thing?"

She faced him directly. "Right before I was arrested, I discovered that the Collins/McGrath file had disappeared from my office."

Patrick's eyebrows arched and his mouth compressed as he looked across his desk at her. "Who had access to those files?"

Alexandra shrugged her shoulders. "I guess all the people who work down at the D.A.'s office."

"Like who?" he prodded, his eyes still focused intently on her.

"Like my father," she conceded.

Gazing through the window of the firm's conference room, Nancy Breslaw watched anxiously as Patrick escorted out a beautiful woman with thick blond hair and a stunning figure. She assumed it was Alexandra Locke. She wasn't sure she liked the way his hand was resting on the woman's shoulder. With his warm, sympathetic nature, Patrick's friendly manner could be easily misinterpreted.

Nancy said good-bye to her own client and then she followed Patrick back to his office.

He glanced up when she came in. "How'd your meeting with Phil go?"

"I had him eating out of my hand," she stated proudly. "My negotiations on those contracts will be good for at least twenty thousand dollars more in fees, not to mention the retainer."

"Nice." He grinned. "You really think you'll be able to bill that much time on it?"

"Absolutely," she said firmly. "But even better than that, down the line my work will save Phil three times that much."

"That man's lucky to have you on his side," he said, offering her a mock salute.

She smiled. "How did it go with Alexandra Locke?"

"It's complicated," he said, filling her in on the high points of his meeting.

As she listened, Nancy kept shaking her head. "Sounds like she's in a terrible bind. If she explains to the authorities why she thinks she was framed, she has to turn over what she knows about her father."

"Right. And it becomes even more difficult because her mother's so ill."

"Seems to me she'd better find out if the D.A.

was involved, and then try to save herself. If not, they both could lose," Nancy pointed out.

"That's a clear-headed appraisal," he said. "Unfortunately, when one's emotions are involved, it's not always easy to see things that objectively."

"Did you get the twenty-thousand-dollar retainer?"

"No."

She was surprised. "Why not?"

He had picked up the brass paperweight on his desk and was turning it over in his hand. "She doesn't have it at the moment," he said in a matter-of-fact tone.

Nancy was disappointed. "We had a deal, Patrick. You promised not to take any more criminal cases unless you got the agreed retainer up front."

He sighed. "Sometimes it's just not possible."

"There are a million other lawyers out there who will work for less," she reminded him. "You're too good. If a client can't pay you what you're worth, then you have to show him or her to the door."

"I can't do that to an old friend."

She stifled the retort on the tip of her tongue. She had learned that it was far better to use patience with him. "It takes a lot of money to run a firm like ours."

"That's why I say if we ran a smaller, more limited operation it would be better." His gaze held hers. "And we wouldn't need such fancy offices."

Taking a deep breath, Nancy let it out slowly.

Patrick put the paperweight down. From the expression on his face it appeared that he was trying to make a decision. "You know that client—Pittman—the one you wanted me to see on his insurance claim? I'll meet with him, okay?"

Finding herself speechless after his concession, Nancy walked over to the window and looked out. She and Patrick had been having a running argument for months. She wanted him to take over more of the firm's civil trial work but he'd refused, insisting that he'd become a lawyer to practice criminal law—period. They had been at an impasse.

When she finally turned around she waited several moments before speaking. "I've begged you for weeks to see Pittman," she pointed out. "And now an old girlfriend shows up, and suddenly you're willing to do it? I'm afraid I don't understand."

"I'm just trying to effect a compromise," he said softly.

She stared at him for a moment, then said, "Well, just be careful you aren't compromised in the process."

After Alexandra had left Patrick's office she'd wanted to visit her mother, but when she'd called the house there was no answer. Had the news of Alexandra's arrest sent Roberta back to the hospital early? Or had the doctor decided it was time to start the new treatment? Worried, she dialed the now familiar number.

"City of Hope," answered the operator.

"Yes. Can you please connect me with Roberta Kendell's room?"

"I'm sorry. There's a 'do not disturb' on that line," the operator stated. "Would you like to talk to the floor nurse?"

"No, thanks."

Forty minutes later, Alexandra walked into her mother's hospital room and found Roberta lying in her bed, watching television. Before Alexandra could even say hello, the newscaster mentioned her name. Gazing at the screen, Alexandra saw her own frightened face staring back at her. The footage had obviously been shot this morning as she left Sybil Brand with Patrick. She felt the impact of her arrest again like a swift kick to the stomach.

When Roberta caught sight of her daughter, she smiled, then put her finger over her mouth in a shushing gesture. "Your father's about to speak."

With a disquieting feeling in her gut, Alexandra walked over to sit by her mother.

An announcer stood in front of a microphone. "We now take you to the office of the D.A., Thomas Kendell, who we understand has a statement for our viewers."

The cameras panned the outside of the Criminal Courts Building, where minicam vans complete with rooftop radar dishes were parked. Then the picture shifted to a room inside the building where the D.A. and his deputies usually met with the press.

Thomas looked dapper but tired as he stepped in

front of the microphones and read from a sheet of paper. "While it's usually the policy of the D.A.'s office not to comment on arrests before concerned law enforcement has presented us with the facts, the arrest last night of my daughter, Alexandra Locke, has raised certain concerns in the media that I feel I should address."

Heart racing, Alexandra steeled herself for what might be coming.

"Since Ms. Locke is a deputy D.A. with this office," Thomas continued on, "we have a conflict of interest that precludes our reviewing the matter. Therefore, we must recuse ourselves." He cleared his throat. "I'm hereby asking the Attorney General of the State of California to take over Ms. Locke's case. Further, because the prosecutors in my office must avoid all vestiges of impropriety, we're putting Ms. Locke on administrative leave while the allegations against her are being investigated."

Thomas folded the paper he had been holding and glanced out at the cameras. "That's all I have to say at the present time. Thank you."

Alexandra swallowed hard several times as the full import of his message sank in. Up until now, the threat of losing her job had seemed temporary. She kept thinking that in a few days she'd be back at work. But she could see that wasn't going to happen.

"Mr. District Attorney, will you answer a few questions?" called out one of the reporters.

"I'll try," Thomas replied.

"What effect will your daughter's arrest have on your running for a fourth term?"

Straightening his shoulders, Thomas gazed unflinchingly forward. "None. I plan to continue my campaign. I feel positive about the job I'm doing and that I'm the best person to serve this county for the next four years. I trust the public to judge me on my proven record and not on what a member of my family may have done."

Alexandra was devastated. Why hadn't Thomas said that he was sure that there had been some kind of a mistake? That his daughter would be found innocent of all charges. Suddenly it dawned on her that while her arrest was going to hurt him, maybe the alternative in his mind had been worse. Thomas could have decided that his daughter's credibility had to be destroyed in order for *him* to remain beyond reproach.

He waved at the cameras, and then he was gone. The picture suddenly clicked off, and Alexandra realized that her mother had used the television's remote control by the side of her bed.

As she leaned down and planted a kiss on Roberta's cheek, a cold, clammy hand grabbed hers and squeezed hard. "Try not to be too angry," her mother cautioned in a tired voice. "He's in a difficult position."

"I'm not exactly having the time of my life," Alexandra replied with more force than she'd intended.

Roberta stroked her daughter's hand with her own. "I know, and I'm sorry, darling."

"He hasn't even tried to reach me," Alexandra complained, not bothering to hide her hurt feelings. "Shouldn't he be my father first and the D.A. second?"

"He's trying to stay impartial. This is very embarrassing for him, too."

"You knew I couldn't have done it," Alexandra insisted, shaking her head. "Why doesn't he have the same confidence in me?"

"He does. But your father also has a responsibility to the people of this county. He's always been tough on crime. It wouldn't look right if he suddenly turned around and said that because his daughter is involved, the rules shouldn't be followed." With a tired sigh, Roberta leaned back against her pillow.

A pang of guilt shot through Alexandra. Her problems were taking a toll on her mother, who didn't have the strength to fight anything other than her illness. She forced herself to swallow both her anger and her hurt. Smoothing her mother's forehead with her hand, she asked, "How are you feeling?"

"Very weak," Roberta admitted with a wan smile. "They start the new chemo in the morning, and I'm dreading it."

"I'm sorry. I know this situation is making things worse for you."

Her mother nodded and again took Alexandra's hand. Then she looked up at her daughter, her love for her clearly showing. "I'm sure that this is some kind of a horrible mistake, Alexandra. But I have faith in our justice system. I know you'll be found innocent. In the meantime, try to be strong, and try to understand how hard this is for your father, too."

Alexandra didn't know how to respond. She was worried about her mother, angry at Thomas, and frightened by what she herself was facing. And right now she didn't have Roberta's faith in the justice system. After all, if her own father didn't believe her, why should anyone else?

16

CLIFFORD WOLSEY, the stately Attorney General of California, glanced at his friend Frank Sanchez, who was sharing the backseat of a long, dark limousine with him. He and Frank had gone to college and then law school together, and had remained good friends ever since.

"Glad you could get away on such short notice," Clifford said with a wide grin on his patrician face. "When I found out I was coming to L.A. just for the day, I was hoping we'd have time for a chat."

Frank smiled back. "Luckily I got the judge to recess early for lunch." He seemed to be appraising his friend. "You're looking great, Cliff. Sacramento must agree with you."

Clifford straightened his wide shoulders. He'd been the captain of the football team at UC Berkeley and still prided himself on keeping his large frame in shape by vigorous daily exercise. "It does.

But I'll like Sacramento even better after I've been elected governor," he added somewhat smugly.

"How are your chances looking?" Frank asked.

"Good," Clifford replied. For a moment, he focused on the differences between Frank and himself. He had grown up in San Francisco with every luxury money could buy. In contrast, Frank had been born in the U.S. to illegal immigrant parents and had gone to college and law school on scholarships.

He smiled inwardly when he recalled the way his other buddies in law school had been amused by his friendship with Frank, because of the difference in their backgrounds. But Clifford had wisely anticipated that a bond with a smart, clearly up-and-coming Latino would prove useful someday. On top of that, he really liked the man.

"But I'll need the support of the Latino community here in L.A. if I'm going to make it." He shot Frank a purposeful glance. "That's where I'm hoping you can help."

"You can count on me, Cliff," Frank said, nodding his head. "You know I'll do whatever I can."

"You're a good buddy." The Attorney General gave his friend a pat on the shoulder. "How's your battle against Thomas Kendell going?"

Frank shrugged. "I'm not sure. I got a lot of play out of the nepotism thing, but it's a negative message. I need positive media exposure for my ideas and the changes I'd like to see, but I don't get much chance to be in front of the cameras."

"Are the other prosecutors supporting you?"

"Lots of them say they will, but who knows? They may grumble to me in private about the boss, but very few will actually put their ass on the line."

"That's politics for you," said Clifford. He offered the other man an encouraging smile. "Anyway, I think you'll make a great D.A."

"Thanks," Frank said.

The Attorney General nodded. He'd meant what he'd just said, even though he had his own reasons for wanting Frank to win. Clifford had been hearing rumors that if Thomas won another term as D.A., he was planning on challenging Clifford for the California governorship in a few years. If Thomas lost, however, it was presumed that he'd go into private practice. The good thing about Frank was that he didn't have any ambitions beyond becoming the next District Attorney of Los Angeles County, so he didn't pose any future threat to Clifford.

"Did you see the D.A.'s press conference?" asked Frank.

"Yep." The Attorney General leaned forward and dropped his voice. "What do you make of the arrest of his daughter?"

"Well," Frank said, pausing as if mulling over his words. "Cops don't have the time to go around planting evidence. If the stuff was found in Alexandra's apartment, it's hers or some guy's she's gotten mixed up with."

"That's how I feel," Clifford responded, clearing his throat and carefully eyeing his friend. "Got any ideas on how my office should handle it?"

Frank frowned as he stroked his chin. "I can't tell you how to run things," he finally pointed out. "But, I think it's bad to have people believing that prosecutors are above the law. That's not a good message to send in a city that's waging a nasty war against drugs."

"Do you want a bow around these?" asked the woman behind the counter at the hospital gift shop, holding the flowers Alexandra had picked out.

"Yes. That would be nice," Alexandra replied.

Troubled that Frances McGrath might have had a heart attack because of her visit, Alexandra wanted to apologize. She'd learned that Frances had been at the Eisenhower Medical Center in Rancho Mirage, but had been transferred to the UCLA Medical Center, located on the campus of the University of California in Westwood, just west of Beverly Hills.

Clutching the flowers in one hand, Alexandra took an elevator up to the ninth floor of the hospital. As she exited, she ran into a crowd of people waiting for the down elevator. She was debating in which direction to go when she heard her name.

Turning around, she was surprised to see Michael McGrath standing there with his grandfather, Lester.

"What are you doing here?" Michael asked. His voice resonated with anger.

It looked to her like he'd lost weight since the

last time she'd seen him. His fine-boned face was also lined with fatigue. She wished that he wasn't with his grandfather, because it made the situation between them even more uncomfortable. "I'm visiting a patient," she replied, purposely evasive.

"Well, it better not be my wife, young lady," warned Lester, a frown on his weathered face.

Not wanting to lie, Alexandra gestured toward the flowers she was carrying. "I wanted to give Mrs. McGrath these, and tell her how sorry I was about her heart attack."

Lester took a menacing step forward, his finger pointed at Alexandra. "Now see here, you stay away from my wife. Is that clear?"

"I just—"

Michael interrupted, "My grandfather feels your visit was the cause of my grandmother's heart attack."

Before she could respond, Lester jumped back into the fray. "I've been hearing a lot about you. Why, you're nothing but a drug addict and a pusher." There was a drop of spittle forming at the corner of his mouth. "I was a fool to let you visit us. I don't trust you or anything you have to say. Just stay out of our lives."

Their raised voices were causing people to stare at the three of them. It made Alexandra wish she could just disappear. "I'm neither of those things," she protested quietly, glancing carefully from Michael's face to Lester's, trying to see if she could pick up any trace of guilt or knowledge on their part regarding the drugs.

A muscle in Michael's jaw was moving. Lester's weathered face was flushed with righteous anger. Neither of them appeared interested in hearing her side of things.

She thrust the flowers at Michael. "Please, give these to your grandmother, and tell her I hope she feels better." Then she turned on her heel and pushed the DOWN button.

"We better not find you here again," Lester barked after her. His voice was still ringing in her ears as the elevator doors closed.

Her face flushed with humiliation, Alexandra lowered her eyes, not wanting to meet the curious gazes of the people sharing the car with her. As soon as it stopped on the main floor she rushed down the corridor, then headed through the long lobby toward the parking garage.

When she felt a hand on her shoulder she whirled around, her heart pounding loudly in her ears. It was Michael. He had obviously followed her.

"It shook my grandfather up to see you here," he explained. "But he shouldn't have made such a scene."

It was probably the closest thing to an apology she was going to get, thought Alexandra.

"Could we grab a cup of coffee in the cafeteria?" he asked. "I'd like to talk to you."

Her throat was dry, but she managed a quick nod.

A few minutes later they were seated at a table by the window in the clean but dreary cafeteria.

Outside the plate-glass window, the large courtyard was filled with people.

Alexandra blew on her coffee as she waited nervously for Michael to break the silence.

"I'd like to know why you went to see my grandparents when I asked you not to," he said, his eyes boring into hers. "And why didn't you at least tell me about your visit afterward?"

She decided to level with him. "I know it's hard for you to understand, Michael, but I had an obligation to check out the tip I got. And for reasons having to do with my investigation, I thought it best not to say anything at first about meeting your grandparents. Later, if you remember, when I tried to tell you, you stopped me from talking about your father's death." She paused. "But I should have said something anyway."

His eyes were now hooded, making it impossible to guess what he was thinking. "I'm sure it never entered your mind that Erica Collins was a vengeful, miserable woman who would say anything, do anything, to get back at her ex-husband."

It was more of a statement than a question, and Alexandra realized he was giving her a graceful way out, but she couldn't take it. "Actually, I did consider that. But it's been my honest experience that people who are dying generally speak the truth."

"Maybe the majority of them do," he conceded, glancing over at her. "But Erica Collins was a conniving, hostile woman."

She met his direct gaze with a challenge of her

own. "Why didn't you tell me that the first time we spoke about her?"

It was Michael's turn to be embarrassed as his face colored. "I didn't realize then that it was Erica who had accused George of being a murderer. It wasn't until my mother figured out that the informant had to be Erica that it all made sense."

Alexandra considered his words. Could this man, who had made such passionate love to her, have set her up for a drug bust? It was painful to think that he'd slept with her merely to find out where she lived and how best to break into her apartment.

He ran his fingers along the top of the yellow-and-green spotted Formica table. "I read about your troubles with the law. Were the drugs yours?"

The question was unexpected and she immediately wondered if it was sincere or if it was meant to throw her off guard. "No. I've got no idea how they got into my apartment. But I'm assuming that they were planted by someone who wanted to discredit me."

Michael's jaw muscles tensed. "Aren't there a lot of criminals who'd like to get back at you as a prosecutor, for putting them away?"

"I've had my share of threats," she admitted. "But this was different. I believe that this situation was a setup by someone who wanted to stop me from investigating your father's death."

His green eyes darkened and his face turned grim. "Surely you don't suspect that my family was involved?"

"It's more than entered my mind," she told him, her chin held at a defiant angle. "After all, you did manage to find out where I lived. It's an old building. You saw for yourself that it wouldn't be hard to break in."

He shook his head. "I can't believe you'd think that of me."

Alexandra regarded him. Was his response indignation, fear, or a masterful performance? she wondered. "I may have slept with you, Michael," she conceded, her voice suddenly becoming hoarse, "but in truth, I barely know you."

It was after ten and eerily quiet in Beverlywood—a lovely residential area situated adjacent to Beverly Hills—where Alexandra's parents lived. Using the key her mother had given her when she'd first returned to California, Alexandra let herself into the house.

Silently, she walked through the darkened rooms, remembering all the wonderful times she'd spent here as a young girl growing up.

In the kitchen her eyes were immediately drawn to the hand-painted pot sitting on the windowsill. She smiled to herself, recalling how she'd made that piece of pottery at summer camp when she was only ten years old. She wasn't sure why her mother had kept it in such a prominent place, and for so many years, but it made her feel loved.

She couldn't remember her father ever attending a visiting day at camp. It seemed as if he'd always had a last-minute emergency that kept him from driving up to the mountains. Did he ever look at that same flowerpot and recall who had made it? she wondered.

Feeling utterly exhausted, Alexandra sat down in the darkened living room to wait for her father. She must have dozed off, because she awoke with a start when she heard a key turning in the lock.

Thomas flipped on the lights, but didn't notice Alexandra.

"Hello, Dad."

"What the . . ." Thomas sputtered, a startled look on his face. After a moment, he appeared to regain his equilibrium. "Why are you sitting here in the dark?"

"I was tired and resting my eyes."

"Well, you scared the hell out of me."

"I needed to talk to you, and I knew eventually you'd come home."

"Did something happen with your mother?"

"The two of us listened to your press conference together."

Thomas cleared his throat. "I'm sure you realize that your arrest has forced me into the uncomfortable position of having to defend myself."

His comment hit a raw nerve. "I'm sorry about that. If you'll just answer a few questions, I'll be out of here."

He glanced at her warily. "What questions?"

"Did you remove the Collins/McGrath file from my office?"

"No," he said, shaking his head. "Of course not. Why would I?"

"You were the only one in the entire office who knew that I was looking into Jeffrey McGrath's death."

"I told you I didn't take it," he replied stubbornly.

Alexandra stood up, looking directly into her father's eyes. "Were you so afraid of what I might dig up that you decided to silence me?"

"It would help if you'd remember that I'm your father and that you owe me some respect."

"In case you forgot," she said, taking another step closer to him so that they were less than a foot apart, "I'm your daughter and I'm facing a felony conviction and the loss of my license to practice law—not to mention having to spend a few years in prison."

He paled as if her words had finally had an impact on him. "I'm very upset about that too, Alexandra. I keep telling myself that you must have gotten mixed up with the wrong friends and the drugs belonged to one of them."

She was speechless. "Is that what you think happened?"

"What else could it be?"

"Did it ever enter your mind that I'm innocent? That someone planted that stuff because they wanted to discredit me?"

"Well, I . . ." his voice faltered.

Alexandra pressed her advantage. "Why haven't you even offered to help me?"

He took a deep breath and seemed to regroup. "You know I can't legally use the taxpayers' money that way. You're a deputy D.A. with my office and you've been arrested. I've got to remain strictly impartial."

"No, that's not it at all. You're just worried about your political future," she said, flinging her words at him angrily.

Thomas flinched but he didn't deny her allegation. "What would anyone hope to gain by planting that stuff, anyway?"

"I believe it has to do with Jeffrey McGrath's death and the subsequent cover-up. Someone was so terrified of my investigating the matter that they went to a lot of trouble to destroy my credibility."

"That sounds like paranoia," he sputtered.

"I don't think so," she countered, shaking her head vehemently. "And I don't believe that you really do, either."

17

SALLY MCGRATH POTTER was upset as she sat across from her doctor in her hospital room and begged him to let her go home. "Please. I want to get out of here."

"It's not advisable," Doctor Winters said, his hands stuffed into the pockets of his jacket. "We haven't found out what's causing your nightmares."

"But I've tried," Sally insisted, her voice trembling with anger and frustration. "You can't say I haven't."

"You haven't tried hard enough," he replied, giving her that look that meant he knew best.

She felt like she was beating her head against a wall when she talked to him. He just didn't listen. Still, she had to try. "I don't want to be hypnotized anymore," she stated, shaking her head. "It scares me."

"How can you be frightened when I'm right there with you?" he said, smiling at her.

"I don't care." She wrapped her arms around her body and hugged herself. "I don't want to do it."

His eyebrows arched as he considered her. "Now Sally, am I going to have to call Arnold?"

Glancing over at Doctor Winters, she shuddered at the warning in his voice. The way he was looking at her wasn't as innocent as he tried to pretend. He wanted to hypnotize her for his own selfish reasons. God only knew what he did to her once she was under his spell. That's why she wasn't going to give him another chance.

Sally stood up and made her way to the small, shatterproof window. Below her in the parking lot, people were free to come and go as they wanted. They weren't locked up in a loony bin like she was. It wasn't fair and it made her even more angry. She turned around to face the doctor, squaring her shoulders. "I've been here almost seventy-two hours," she pointed out with a slight tilt to her chin. "You can't keep me here after that without a court order."

"That's not true," he countered, his fingers drumming on the chart he was holding. "If, in my opinion, you're still a threat to yourself or to others, I can easily convince the hospital commitment review committee to keep you for another fourteen days." He gave her a knowing glance as the corners of his mouth curved upward. "According to Arnold, you tried to commit suicide." He shrugged. "Which one of you am I supposed to believe?"

Her stomach clenched into an angry knot. She knew who he'd believe. Doctor Winters always sided with Arnold. Chewing on the inside of her cheek, she resolved not to give in. "I'm twenty-nine years old," she asserted. "I didn't try to hurt myself this time. I want to leave."

The doctor abruptly stood up and gestured toward her with his hand. "Sally, I'm a respected doctor in this community. I think I know when someone is having problems." He paused to let the implication of his words sink in. Then he lowered his voice to a more reasonable tone. "I also want to try you on another medication—something new on the market." His smile was condescending. "It's best to be under observation for a few days when you're taking a new drug."

"I don't want to change pills," she stated firmly. "I like the ones I'm on."

Doctor Winters exhaled loudly. "When Arnold brought you here, he said he hadn't slept in a week because of your nightmares. That poor man can't teach his classes when he's so exhausted." His voice had now taken on a scolding tone. "A few more days of rest would be good for him. And I think if you cared for him, like you say you do, you'd agree."

Sally tried to work up the nerve to say she was sick of being manipulated for everyone else's benefit. Doctor Winters was an expert at it. He knew she hated to upset Arnold and he was using it against her. She cleared her throat. "I—"

Before Sally could speak, a nurse raced into the room, a troubled expression on her flushed face. "You better come right away, Doctor Winters!" she said, a note of panic in her voice. "We've got an emergency in the dining hall!"

"We'll finish our little talk later," the doctor said to Sally in a patronizing manner as he hurried out the door.

Slouched down in the backseat, his long legs thrust out in front of him, Thomas was being driven back to his office from a speaking engagement. He was morose and barely listening to his campaign manager as their car approached the downtown Criminal Courts Building. The attendance at the Chamber of Commerce luncheon had been poor, which had put Thomas in a foul mood.

"Look at that crowd!" Dale said, pointing his finger at the front of the building.

Thomas's stomach lurched as he leaned forward. Frank Sanchez and some of the other deputies from his office were facing a slew of reporters and television cameras. "How dare they hold a press conference on my turf!" he fumed, ordering his driver to turn on the car's radio. A few seconds later, the voices filled the interior of the sedan.

A reporter was talking. "Mr. Sanchez, how do you and some of the other rank-and-file members of the D.A.'s office feel about the arrest of the D.A.'s daughter?"

Frank cleared his throat. "Morale in the office has been low, and Alexandra Locke's arrest is one more blow. As I've said before, Thomas Kendell was wrong to hire his daughter. I just hope the public doesn't allow her arrest to reflect poorly on the rest of us. Most of the prosecutors here are honest and decent people."

"That bastard is milking the situation for everything he can," Thomas complained through clenched teeth, his pulse racing.

"If you were elected, Mr. Sanchez, what would you do differently?"

"I'd do everything I could to show my respect for our prosecutors, our justice system and our laws. And I'd also make sure that the poor people in L.A. County got a fair shake."

"I can't believe this," Thomas seethed. "He's making it sound like I don't do any of those things."

"It's an election and you're a public official," Dale reminded him as the driver pulled into the underground parking structure. "But we've clearly got us some planning to do."

Alexandra had been worrying about all the cases she'd been handling at the time she'd been put on administrative leave. Her supervisor at the D.A.'s office hadn't even given her a chance to write up summaries. Two cases especially had her concerned, so she picked up the telephone and called Geena.

"How are you doing?" Geena asked.

"So-so," Alexandra admitted.

Geena's voice lowered to almost a whisper. "I sure hope things work out for you."

"Thanks," Alexandra replied, finding herself genuinely moved by the empathy she'd heard in her secretary's voice. "Listen Geena, do you know who's handling my cases?"

"Yes. Elizabeth Nathan," Geena answered. "By the way, what do you want me to do with your personal things?"

Alexandra had been hoping that this nightmare would end quickly and she'd soon be back at work. But she also needed some items she'd left at her office.

Geena must have anticipated Alexandra's thoughts. "Want me to pack them up for you?"

"That would be great," Alexandra said, relieved. "Could you take them home, and I'll pick them up at your place?"

"No problem," Geena said. "I'm sometimes in your neighborhood, too. Maybe I can drop them off. If I can, I'll call first."

"Thank you, Geena. I appreciate your help more than you could ever know."

"That's okay. Hold on and I'll transfer you to Elizabeth Nathan."

"Thanks." While she waited, Alexandra tried to picture Elizabeth Nathan. She vaguely remembered a rather small, intense woman with a brittle way of speaking.

"Elizabeth Nathan here."

Alexandra explained why she was calling. "I'd

be happy to write up summaries of each case and my plans for handling them."

"No, thank you," Elizabeth countered in a clipped tone. "I've been a prosecutor a long time. I know what I'm doing."

"I didn't mean to imply you didn't," Alexandra said as nicely as possible, wondering why this woman was acting as if she'd insulted her. "I merely figured it had to be a burden taking over my cases on top of your existing caseload, and I wanted to help."

"That won't be necessary. Now if you'll excuse me, I've got to get back to work."

After Elizabeth hung up, Alexandra found herself trembling with rage and humiliation. How dare the woman speak to her that way? She barely knew her. If Elizabeth's attitude reflected the views of the rest of her former colleagues at the D.A.'s office, then Alexandra had already been found guilty. So much for a presumption of innocence.

A short time later, Alexandra was on her way to Patrick's office when she flicked on her car radio and caught deputy district attorney Frank Sanchez's press conference. For a brief moment she was so upset by Frank's comments that she contemplated doing something crazy—like driving off a bridge.

Then it dawned on Alexandra that Frank was using her predicament to make a lot of points for himself. She recalled Patrick asking her about a political motive. Could she be wrong about the McGrath family's involvement in her problems? Could the drugs have been planted by someone looking to hurt her father by discrediting her?

After Geena had gotten off the phone with Alexandra, she'd suddenly remembered that day a while back when Elizabeth Nathan had been looking for some files in Alexandra's office. Geena hadn't told Alexandra about it because she'd seen Elizabeth leave the office empty-handed.

Geena wondered if after she had gone home Elizabeth had returned and removed some files. For a moment, Geena debated whether or not to call Alexandra back and tell her about the incident. Then she changed her mind. Elizabeth was now handling all of Alexandra's cases, so what difference could it possibly make?

When Alexandra had told Patrick about Erica's overflowing storage locker and her own tiny apartment, he'd offered her the use of an extra file room in the Breslaw & Ross suite. Now, as Patrick's secretary turned on the lights, Alexandra glanced around the room. It had a vinyl floor, gray walls and contained two chipped metal folding tables, an assortment of mismatched, broken-down chairs, a green steel filing cabinet and several stacks of file boxes. There were no windows, but she didn't care. She was just grateful to have a place to work.

As Alexandra was setting up, a petite woman with short red hair and a serious look on her pretty face breezed in the door.

"I'm Nancy Breslaw," she said rather stiffly.

Realizing she must be Patrick's partner, Alexandra smiled warmly and held out her hand. "Alexandra Locke. I can't thank you enough for letting me use this extra room."

Nancy's return smile was brief as she shook Alexandra's hand. "I only learned about it myself a short time ago. But I want to make a few things clear," she stated in a firm voice. "That way there won't be any misunderstandings."

"Of course." Alexandra nodded.

"Since you're being hooked up through our system, we'll answer your phone," Nancy explained. "And we'll set you up with your own voice mail. But please don't expect my staff to place your calls or to take messages."

"No problem," Alexandra responded quickly.

"What are you doing for a computer?"

"To be honest," Alexandra told her, "I hadn't thought that far ahead yet. I suppose—"

Before Alexandra could finish her sentence, Nancy interrupted. "I'm sure you understand that I must protect the privacy of our clients, so I can't have you hooked up to our network. You'll have to bring in your own computer and your own software as well as office supplies."

Puzzled by the other woman's tone of voice, Alexandra nodded her head again. "That's fine."

"Any questions?"

"One." Alexandra gave Nancy an uneasy smile. "May I use your copy machine? Naturally, I'll pay you whatever you want for the copies."

The other woman hesitated. "I don't know. I'd have to give you a client number," she muttered, as if thinking the matter through.

"She already has a client number," Patrick said, entering the room. "You can use that one."

"Of course. Don't worry about a thing, Patrick, it's all been settled," Nancy said, smiling brightly at him.

Watching the instant change in Nancy's attitude and the way she gazed at Patrick with an air of possessiveness, Alexandra could see that they were more than partners. It was also clear that Nancy perceived her as some kind of a threat. But why?

"If you need to ask me anything else," said Nancy in a more conciliatory tone of voice, "just call my secretary and let her know. She'll look at my schedule and arrange a time." With a nod of her head, she excused herself from the room.

Alexandra turned to Patrick. "It seems you didn't clear my coming here with your partner."

"Don't mind her," he said with an apologetic smile. "Nancy's a wonderful woman and a fabulous lawyer. In fact, I couldn't ask for a better partner. She just likes to be in charge." He walked around the room, running his fingers across the tops of the dusty boxes. "It was my fault. I shouldn't have sprung this on her without any warning, but after I made the offer to you I got busy preparing for my hearing this morning and it slipped my mind."

"If she doesn't want me here . . ."

"No . . . don't worry," he said. "It just takes Nancy a little time to adjust to new situations. It'll be fine." Glancing around, he asked, "How many more boxes are there?"

"All together, I think I counted something like sixty."

"Jesus!"

"It's a lot," she agreed. "By the way, did you happen to hear the press conference from the courthouse?"

"I saw the news vans gathering outside as I was leaving." There was a curious expression on his face. "What was it all about?"

"Reporters were questioning Frank Sanchez and some of the other deputies about my arrest." She paused briefly before going on. "You asked me the other day if anyone could be trying to get at my father through me."

"Right."

"Well, at the time I didn't think so. But after listening today, I'm not so sure."

He flashed her a look of concern. "What do you know about Frank and the other challengers?"

"Two are lawyers in private practice and a third one is a City Attorney. I don't know any of them personally. As for Frank, I've spoken to him about a case, that's all. From everything I've read and the polls I've seen, Frank is the only real threat my father is facing in the primary."

"What kind of a man is he?"

"He seems to be respected by the other deputies." She stared off into space for a moment.

"There was this one incident that I've been thinking about."

Patrick glanced up at her, waiting for her to continue.

"I was in the ladies' room one day when I heard two women talking about the race. Of course, they had no idea I was there. One said my father was more interested in the pressroom than the courtroom. The other said Frank was a novice, running an underfunded campaign and taking on an incumbent with both name recognition and cash. It was her last statement, however, that got my attention—especially in retrospect."

"And what was that?"

"That Frank better think of a way to get some more publicity, and *fast*, or he could forget about forcing Thomas into a runoff."

Patrick frowned. "Do you think Frank would do something as devious as planting drugs in the apartment of another prosecutor to bring down your father?"

"I hope not. It would make him a dirty law enforcement official, just like those I used to prosecute in New York." She paused again to take a breath. "When you work in the political corruption unit, you develop a sixth sense about that kind of person, and Frank doesn't fit the profile."

"Are you ruling him out?" Patrick asked.

"No," she said glumly, shaking her head. "Someone is profiting from my arrest. And if we don't figure out who it is, and soon, I'm not sure what I'm going to do."

*   *   *

Elizabeth left her Acura with the parking attendant and rode the elevator to the fourth floor. Once there, she walked down a long corridor before she reached her two-bedroom condominium.

Inside the entry she threw her keys onto the table. Then, unbuttoning her jacket, she made her way to the bedroom. She tried not to think about the large house filled with sunshine that she'd shared with her husband and little boy in Cheviot Hills. She'd adored that area of hilly streets and lovely homes by Roxbury Park and Century City.

After Peter had left her and then her child died, she couldn't stand being alone in the home they had all shared. The memories were just too painful. So she sold the house and every piece of furniture in it. She'd even left behind her bedding and matching towels for the new owners to enjoy.

It had been an especially difficult time for her to decide where she should move. While her house was still in escrow, Elizabeth had been accosted in the driveway one day by a man she'd prosecuted for armed robbery. He'd started pistol-whipping her. Luckily, her screams had attracted the attention of a neighbor, who called the police.

From that day on she'd carried a firearm. The incident had shown her how vulnerable she was living alone. So, opting for safety, she'd purchased this small condo in a nondescript high-rise building on Wilshire Boulevard. Every time Elizabeth came home, she convinced herself that it was better to live in a place where she couldn't open the win-

dows because of the noise and soot, but where she
had a modicum of protection.

Shaking her head to clear it, she checked her machine and noticed she had a message.

"Hi, Elizabeth. Frank here. Give me a call when
you get in." He'd left a number, which she quickly
dialed.

"Hello." A woman with a slight accent and a
soft voice answered the phone.

"Frank, please."

"Who's calling?"

"Elizabeth Nathan."

"Oh yes. Just a moment."

Elizabeth heard the sound of a TV in the background and the voices of several others as the
woman asked someone, probably one of Frank's
daughters, to get her father.

"Hold on a sec," Frank said before she heard
him call out, "I've got it, you can hang up now."
Coming back on the line, he said, "I'm glad you
called back."

"Sure. What's up?"

"The press conference went well today."

"So I heard," she said. "Congratulations."

"Thanks. Anyway, I'm having a small get-
together here Saturday evening for a strategy session. I thought you might like to join us."

"I believe I can manage that," she replied, trying
not to sound too eager. She wanted him to think
that she had a million invitations to choose from.

"Great," he said. "Bianca's going to make her

famous tamales. They're wonderful. Be here at seven."

After getting directions to his house, Elizabeth said good-bye and hung up. As she sat there staring at the phone, there was a small flutter in her chest. What a nice feeling it was to have somewhere to go on a Saturday evening.

18

—— ≈ ——

READING HIS DAUGHTER a story while he stroked
her silky dark-brown curls, Patrick felt a surge of
love. Jenny was a wonderful child with an enor-
mous curiosity about people and places. She was
the light of his life.

"The end," he said, kissing her on the top of the
head as he closed the book.

"One more story, Daddy, please."

Smiling, he shook his head. "You've already gotten two more out of me and it's thirty minutes past
your bedtime."

Jenny smiled, and the gap where she'd lost her
front tooth was clearly visible. "I know. But I love
when you read to me." She snuggled up to him.

Hearing her words melted his heart. At six years
old, she was an expert at getting whatever she
wanted from him. What chance was he going to
have in the future?

They compromised on a story he made up and

told in less than five minutes. After he tucked her in for the night, with her teddy bear clutched to her chest, he went into his own room.

Patrick was still wearing his work clothes, having only removed his jacket and loosened his tie before putting her to bed. He was getting home later and later, and yet he couldn't catch up on all his work. It wasn't fair to Jenny.

Stripping to his boxer shorts, he flopped down on his bed and then opened his briefcase and removed some papers. When the telephone rang he reached over to grab it. "Hello."

"It's me," said Nancy. "I hope you don't think that I was rude to Alexandra. I was just setting guidelines."

Patrick sensed that she was apologizing for her earlier behavior. Nancy had so many good qualities that he was usually able to ignore the little quirks that sometimes made her seem inflexible. "That's okay. I should have told you I offered to let her use our spare file room."

"I'm glad you understand." Her voice became husky. "We're still on for Saturday evening, aren't we?"

"I wouldn't miss it."

"I'm glad."

They hung up and Patrick went back to his work. After several minutes, he realized that his mind had been wandering. He'd been thinking about Alexandra and the way she was always on guard, as if afraid to let anyone get too close. Yet underneath the independent attitude she pro-

jected, he sensed an extremely vulnerable woman.
Was that because of the terrible stress she was
under now? If he'd run into her in New York,
would she have been more like the wonderful girl
he remembered—so open, so warm, so full of
laughter?

Earlier, his forensic expert had called to tell him
they hadn't found any fingerprints on the window
of Alexandra's apartment, except hers. Of course,
the person who broke in—if there had been such a
person—could have worn gloves.

Patrick didn't have to believe a client innocent in
order to defend him or her. He'd made his peace
with that issue years ago. Every defendant was entitled to a presumption of innocence and a lawyer
for their defense. What he did insist upon was that
his clients level with him so that he could do the
best job possible. And this was where he felt uneasy. Something told him that Alexandra had not
yet spilled all the proverbial beans.

The next day, Alexandra spent a long time visiting with her mother. Roberta was having a very
bad reaction to the experimental chemotherapy
and was sicker than Alexandra could remember
ever seeing her.

Driving home from the hospital, she called the
D.A.'s office. Even though she was on administrative leave, every few days she still checked in for
her messages. A Vince Donovan had telephoned,
and Alexandra recalled that he was the retired
sheriff's deputy whose report she'd read in the

Collins/McGrath file. She'd been trying to reach him.

"Twenty years is a long time," Donovan said when she called him in Colorado, where he was now living. "But I remember a few things about that case. A guy claimed his friend heard an animal of some kind and ran after it with a shotgun."

"Right. Do you recall anything else?"

The retired deputy cleared his throat. "Yeah. The guy chasing the animal supposedly tripped, his gun went off and he got hit. Isn't that the case you mean?"

"Yes," she said, surprised. "That's pretty good."

He laughed. "Sometimes at night when I can't sleep, the crap I used to see as a cop plays back in my mind like a movie. That one just stuck." She could hear him taking a swallow and the clink of ice in a glass.

"Just having a drink and looking at the sunset," he said by way of explanation, as if he had all the time in the world.

"Any reason why this particular case has stayed in your mind?"

"It wasn't any one thing," he admitted freely. "But lots of stuff just didn't seem right, if you know what I mean. That's why I called the Homicide boys to check it out."

That was surprising news. "I found an old case file but yours was the only police report. I didn't know Homicide had been involved."

"Those other reports shoulda been there," he said with a slight drawl. "Two detectives came out to the scene. I remember the first detective's name. It was Barton. Joe Barton. He retired awhile back, too. Don't recall the name of his partner, but I'm pretty sure he died."

"Do you know how I can reach Joe Barton?"

"No, ma'am."

She sighed. Twenty-year-old cases were difficult if not impossible to investigate. Witnesses died or moved away. People forgot. Evidence disappeared. "What were some of the things that bothered you about the scene?"

"Let's see now," he said, and Alexandra heard the clink of the glass again. Impatient to glean as many facts as possible, she wished there was a polite way to hurry him up.

"Well, to begin with," he finally said, "the shotgun that caused McGrath's death had been smashed."

She wasn't sure she understood what he meant. "Jeffrey McGrath shot himself with a smashed gun?"

"Nope. According to the friend . . ." he paused. "I'm trying to recall the other guy's name."

"Does George Collins ring a bell?"

"Yep. That sounds right. A doctor, wasn't he?"

"Yes," Alexandra replied. "What did he tell you?"

"If I remember, Collins said that when he realized his friend was dead he got upset, picked up the shotgun McGrath had used and smashed it against a tree. I saw the gouge myself in the big pine."

"My God," she exclaimed, wondering why such

significant information hadn't been in the file. "Sounds like George Collins was trying to destroy evidence."

"I thought so too. Course, since Collins handled the gun after his friend shot himself, it meant that the scene was contaminated."

Alexandra figured that was exactly what George had intended. "The file also lacked records of any tests done on that weapon. Would the damaged gun explain why I didn't find any additional reports?"

She heard him taking another sip before he responded. "Nope. Even if they couldn't run all the tests there shoulda been some they could do. Those shoulda been in the file."

"They weren't," she retorted, wondering who could have removed them. "What else looked wrong to you?" Waiting for his answer, she readjusted the pillow behind her back.

"The way that Doctor Collins said he threw pieces of the damaged shotgun into a nearby stream."

Alexandra sat up straight, jarred by this latest detail. "That definitely sounds like George Collins was trying to destroy evidence. Did you retrieve the pieces from the water?"

"Nope. Figured it was something the detectives would want to do."

The way Donovan wouldn't expand on any of his answers was frustrating. Still, she didn't dare complain. It was important just to keep him talking any way she could. "What else didn't seem right?"

"The metal on the stock looked like it had been wiped clean." He clinked his glass again. "But Collins claimed both he and the deceased had been wearing gloves."

"Do you remember what the weather was like?"

"Cold."

"You were the first deputy on the scene, weren't you?"

"Yes."

"Was Collins wearing gloves when you first saw him?"

"No."

"Did you ask him about it?"

"Yeah. I remember he said he took them off to check on his buddy."

"What about the deceased. Was he wearing gloves?"

"Yeah. I think so."

"Did Collins ever explain how Jeffrey ended up with his gun?"

"Yeah. Said they got mixed up when they sat down earlier to rest."

"Did you believe him?"

"Since he didn't tell me that right off the bat, I thought it was fishy."

"I see." Alexandra quickly processed these new facts. "Was an autopsy performed on the deceased?"

"Shoulda been. Is that missing from the file too?"

"Yes, it is."

"Hmm," he muttered. "Maybe when they decided not to prosecute the case they misplaced some of the reports."

She was sure there was a more sinister reason for the missing reports but didn't let on. "Do you remember anything about the autopsy itself?"

"Nope. Can't say that I do."

"Did Collins indicate how long his friend lived after he was shot? Or if McGrath was killed instantly?"

"Let's see," the retired sheriff's deputy mumbled. "Think Collins mentioned he'd tried CPR on his buddy, but when he couldn't revive him, he realized McGrath was dead. The guy was a doctor, so I figured he ought to know." He clinked his glass again. "That's when he supposedly took his car and went to call us. He said he came back and stayed with the body until I arrived." There was a long pause before he added, "I recall how surprised I was when I heard the D.A.'s office had rejected the case."

Her heartbeat quickened. "Did you ever speak to the deputy D.A. handling the matter?"

"Not that I can remember. Don't think they ever called me. I figured the detectives gave them what they needed."

Taking a deep breath, she nervously asked her next question. "Do you recall who the deputy D.A. was?"

"Yeah. The guy that rejected the case is now the big honcho himself. Thomas Kendell."

At the mention of her father's name, Alexandra felt a chill of apprehension. "But you say you never spoke to Mr. Kendell yourself?"

"Right. I never did."

After thanking him for his help, she hung up. It had been a lucky break to find a witness who could recall events from twenty years ago and especially in such detail. Although he hadn't spoken to Thomas himself, Vince Donovan had confirmed that her father had definitely played a role in the case. She sorted through all of the facts in her mind. It seemed as if the more she learned about Jeffrey McGrath's death, the less it looked like an accident.

When Sally heard that Doctor Winters had been hospitalized with a shattered arm, she felt a surge of relief. A patient had become violent and thrown a chair at the doctor and he'd tried to stop it with his arm. Sally also knew she should feel sorry for him, but she didn't. In fact, she was rather glad. She only wished she'd had the courage to throw the chair at the doctor herself.

Feeling nervous, Sally hesitantly entered the small office of the doctor taking Winters's place. She found a thin woman with a pleasant face, short brown hair and kind-looking eyes behind tortoise shell glasses.

"Hello, Sally. I'm Doctor Abbott." The woman gestured with her hand. "Please sit down."

"Thanks," Sally said, taken aback by the woman's friendly attitude. Doctor Winters was so cold and calculating.

"How are you feeling?" asked the new doctor, smiling at her warmly.

"I'm okay," Sally replied with a tentative smile. "My only problem is that I sometimes have nightmares. But not all the time, just once in a while." She inhaled deeply before going on, "I don't want to be here at this hospital. And I really don't want to be hypnotized anymore."

Doctor Abbott's eyes widened in surprise. "Give me a moment to read your chart," she said, looking puzzled. After a short time, she glanced up. "It says here that you've signed up for hypnosis treatment. Is that not so?"

"I signed for it only once," Sally explained. "But it was a long time ago. And I never signed for it again. I keep telling Doctor Winters that being hypnotized scares me." She suddenly felt tears welling up in her eyes. "Please don't make me do it," she pleaded in a childlike voice.

"Well," Doctor Abbott stated, with a shrug of her shoulders and a shake of her head, "if it frightens you and you don't want it, then you don't have to do it."

"Just like that?" Sally asked, shocked by the doctor's answer. She hadn't expected her to give in—and so fast.

"Of course," Doctor Abbott said in a reassuring tone of voice. "No one can force you to do something against your will." She paused before adding, "Didn't you know that?"

Sally looked skeptically at the doctor. "I thought when they locked you up like this you lost all your rights."

"Absolutely not," Doctor Abbott said firmly.

"Let me check your chart again." As the woman reviewed the papers there was a worried frown between her brows. After a short time, she spoke. "It says that your husband, Arnold, brought you in because you tried to kill yourself."

"But I didn't," Sally protested, feeling frustrated as she thrust both of her arms out for the doctor to see. "Look, there are no scars on my wrists. They didn't pump my stomach out. There were no drugs in my system." Her voice started to rise in indignation. "If I tried to kill myself, then how did I do it?"

Doctor Abbott had a deeply troubled expression on her face as she looked at Sally, then read the notes in the file for a third time. "That's odd," she said. "This admittance report doesn't specify how the suicide attempt was made."

"That's because it's a lie."

"Help me out here for a minute, Sally," Doctor Abbott urged, leaning forward across the desk and speaking in a forthright manner. "Why do you think your husband would say that you tried to kill yourself if it wasn't true?"

"It's a long story," Sally said, her voice filled with sadness.

"That's okay. I've got plenty of time," Doctor Abbott responded with a nod of her head.

Encouraged by the woman's genuine sympathy and comforting presence, Sally unexpectedly found herself telling Doctor Abbott why she'd been so troubled lately.

*　　*　　*

From what Alexandra could ascertain, if George had in fact murdered Jeffrey, his motive was his love for Jeffrey's wife. Whether or not Lorna had known about George's intent, or had assisted him in any way, was something that remained to be seen.

She knew from experience that it wasn't unusual for someone like George to live an exemplary life after committing murder. Curious, she ran a litigation check and uncovered several malpractice suits against him. That wasn't unusual either, she reasoned, especially since he'd been practicing for such a long time.

The key to George's character would more likely be found in his earlier years. While going through Erica's boxes, Alexandra had discovered an old medical school yearbook belonging to George. She decided it might be helpful to talk to some of the people who had known him back then.

So far, she'd managed to contact several of George Collins's classmates. He was remembered as bright, hardworking and very ambitious.

Alexandra had also located a nurse who had worked in the same clinic where George had started out as a young doctor. After playing phone tag, they finally arranged to meet at a small restaurant in Sherman Oaks.

The woman had just come from her exercise class and was still wearing her black tights and a pink tee shirt. "George was a good doctor," she said in response to Alexandra's question.

"Did he ever lose his temper?"

"Yeah. But all doctors and nurses get overtired and overworked. It doesn't mean anything."

"Did he have any other faults?"

"Let me think." The woman scrunched up her face. "Well, I recall the way he was always complaining about money."

"How do you mean?" Alexandra asked.

"He acted like it was the most important thing in the world to him. George had lots of student loans to pay off. He used to grumble about how unfair it was to start out practicing medicine owing so much money. He called it his 'ball and chain.' "

"Were his circumstances that unusual?"

"Oh no. Lots of doctors and nurses got through school on loans. George just seemed to resent it more. He was in a big hurry to be a success." The woman gave Alexandra a curious glance. "What's this background check about anyway?"

"Something that happened twenty years ago," Alexandra explained. "Did you know much about his personal life back then?"

"Just that he was married to a woman he didn't seem to love."

This news caused Alexandra to sit forward. "Did he tell you that?"

"Not exactly. It was just obvious. He never talked about her or brought her to our parties or anything."

"Did you ever meet his first wife, Erica?"

"Once. She wasn't pretty at all. He's a good-looking guy. None of us could figure out what he saw in her."

Maybe a meal ticket, thought Alexandra, remembering what her mother had said about Erica slaving to put George through medical school. "Do you know his current wife, Lorna Collins?"

"Not personally. I'd heard she was a widow with two kids. Supposedly George fell for her really hard." She lifted one eyebrow. "Anyway, it seemed that as soon as George started making really big bucks, he and his new wife began traveling in another social world." She gave Alexandra a meaningful look. "It was like all of his old friends just weren't good enough anymore."

19

~

Lester McGrath sat across the room from his wife, Frances, who was resting comfortably in her hospital bed at the UCLA Medical Center in Westwood. It was late afternoon. The bright sunlight, which only a few minutes before had been streaming in through the window, was now fading. He'd just started to nod off himself when he heard someone come into the room.

Looking up he was surprised to see his former daughter-in-law, Lorna. She was carrying a large white box with a lavender bow. "What are you doing here?" he asked her under his breath, glancing over quickly to see if Frances was still asleep. She was. He put his fingers over his mouth and shook his head, warning Lorna not to talk. Then he guided her out to the hallway.

"Frances had a restless morning. She needs her sleep. Why don't you just leave that box with me, and I'll tell her you were here?"

"Lester?" Frances called out from her room.

"I'll just say a quick hello," Lorna announced, sidestepping him and slipping into the room. Lester tried to stop her but it was too late.

"Hello, Mother Frances. How are you feeling?" Lorna asked, throwing her a kiss.

"Better," Frances replied, her thin lips pressed together in displeasure.

If Lorna noticed, she chose to ignore the older woman's sour reaction to her. "I brought you something to cheer you up," she exclaimed brightly as she started opening the box.

"Do it over there," Frances pointed toward the chair next to her. "You're jostling the bed."

Undeterred, Lorna balanced the box on the chair and removed the bow. Then reaching inside, she brought out something silver and satiny and held it up to her body. "It's a lounging robe. I thought the silver color would be beautiful on you."

"A little too flashy for my taste," Frances said, shaking her head.

The other woman colored slightly but quickly recovered. "When you feel better, you'll try it on. And if you still don't like it, I'll take it back."

"Where's Sally?" Frances said, abruptly changing the subject.

Lester jumped in before Lorna could respond. "I told Frances how Sally and Arnold were away for a few days." He hoped Lorna got the message not to mention that Sally had been hospitalized. It would only upset Frances, and he was afraid to risk the consequences.

Frances focused her shrewd eyes on Lorna. "Where did they go?"

"Up the coast," Lorna told her, smiling. "I'm sure that as soon as they get back, Arnold will bring her to visit you."

"Even if they were on a trip they could have called me on the telephone," Frances said, shaking her head again. "Something is wrong. I can feel it."

Lester reached over and took his wife's hand. Her skin was dry, but still soft. "Don't be silly, Frances," he chided. "The medications they're giving you must be making you anxious, that's all. Sally's fine."

"Then why hasn't she called me?"

"We had your phone shut off until today," he hurried to explain, hoping she'd buy his little white lie.

"Oh, I didn't realize." She sounded relieved. "Will you get word to her that it's been turned back on?"

"Sure thing." Lester brushed a few wisps of gray hair off her face. She was pale, but not the deathly white she had been after her heart attack. He'd been frightened, convinced that Frances was going to die. Now he had hope again that she'd pull through.

Lorna stepped closer to the bed. "I understand that a deputy D.A. by the name of Alexandra Locke visited the two of you in Rancho Mirage?"

Lester shot Lorna a dirty look. How dare she bring that subject up now?

Either she didn't catch his warning or she chose to ignore it as she went on. "What did the two of you tell her?"

"Nothing," Lester grumbled, glaring at Lorna.

Frances struggled to sit up. "I didn't mention how you tricked my precious Jeffrey into marrying you if that's what you're worried about."

Her former daughter-in-law stiffened. "That's not true, Mother Frances. Jeffrey was very much in love with me and you know it."

"No. Jeffrey just wanted to do the right thing after you told him you were pregnant," Frances alleged, reaching for Lester's hand and motioning for him to fluff up her pillows.

"I didn't come here to rehash the past," Lorna said. "I was very worried when I heard about your heart attack, and I wanted to see how you were doing."

"I wasn't born yesterday. You came here because you're afraid we'll tell that deputy D.A. how you tricked George into doing your dirty work." Frances's eyes had narrowed as she scowled at Lorna.

"You don't know what you're talking about," countered Lorna, angrily.

Frances pointed her finger at her. "You're fortunate that, because of Sally, we've kept our mouths shut all these years."

"I don't think any of us want to see Jeffrey's death reinvestigated." Lorna's posture had become rigid and there was an edge to her tone of voice.

By now Lester was furious. "That's enough," he ordered loudly, glaring at Lorna again. "We've already made it clear we don't want the case reopened. I'm not going to see our family's business spread across the news. As for that young deputy

D.A. who started this whole mess, she won't be doing any more snooping around." His chin jutted out at a defiant angle. "She's going to jail instead."

Patrick was frustrated. He hadn't been able to pry any details out of the sheriff's office with regard to Alexandra's case. As for the Attorney General's office, they were playing hardball, telling him he'd have to make a formal discovery motion before they'd divulge any information. That meant waiting until after Alexandra was formally arraigned, at which time she'd plead innocent or guilty to the charges in front of a judge. Even though the arraignment was coming up soon, he didn't want to wait.

He thought about his friend Tricia Yardley, who worked as a deputy attorney general in the L.A. office. They had gone to law school together and had remained friends. Over the years he'd done Tricia a few favors. She'd always reciprocated. Now he needed to call in one of his markers.

A few minutes later, he had her on the phone. "Listen, Tricia, I need a favor."

"Sure," she said, her voice as friendly as always.

"It's about my client Alexandra Locke. Do you know anything about the case?"

"Not really."

Patrick immediately sensed that her tone had become guarded. "Can you find out for me if the sheriff's department has presented your office with their evidence yet?"

"I'm not sure I can help you on this one, Patrick."

He'd been right. She was hesitant. "Look, I don't want to put you in a difficult position, Tricia. But I've known Alexandra Locke since she was fifteen years old. She's a dedicated prosecutor, just like you are. There's absolutely no way she'd be mixed up with drugs!"

"I can appreciate how you feel," she stated evenly. "But like I said, I don't think I can do you much good this time."

Although Patrick hated to beg, for Alexandra's sake he had to get Tricia to change her mind. "Between you and me, I'm sure my client was framed. I just need to know something about the snitch so that I'm not flying blind." He took a deep breath while he decided how far to push her. "After she's charged," he finally said, "it's something I'll be entitled to anyway."

She didn't respond.

"Please, Tricia," he said, throwing himself on her mercy.

There was a large sigh on the other end of the phone. "Let me think about it," she told him before hanging up.

Alexandra looked at her dirty hands. She'd been through ten of Erica's boxes. Except for the medical school yearbook, she'd discovered nothing else of importance. If she didn't find something useful soon—something that would help to extricate her from the mess she was in—she was going to explode.

Frustrated, she yanked the lid off another box and pulled out a large pile of checks. Most of them looked like they went back years. She found the same thing in two more boxes. It was puzzling. Why had Erica bothered to keep so many old checks? Reaching for another box, she turned it over and dumped the contents on the floor. Several large medical textbooks landed on top of the pile.

She picked one up. George Collins's name was scribbled inside the front cover. As she was putting the book on the table next to her, a pale blue envelope fell out. Alexandra noted that it was addressed to a Bunny Lovett at a post office box in Beverly Hills. The stamp on it hadn't been canceled and the envelope was still sealed. She wondered if Erica had even known of its existence. These old textbooks might have been packed away and inadvertently left by George when he and Erica divorced.

Anxious to read what was inside, she carefully slit open the flap with a letter opener and pulled out the thin sheets of paper. At the top, the letterhead said, *The Oaks Inn*. Hotel stationery, she surmised.

> *Dear Bunny,*
> *All I can think about is how your naked body felt in my arms yesterday afternoon. Your skin is like velvet, smooth and soft, yet firm. I love your breasts, especially the dark, puckered skin around your nipples and the*

way they harden when I suck them. I love
how wet you are when I put myself inside.
Just writing this is giving me a hard-on. If
you were here now I'd show you how much I
care. You know I'd do anything in the world
for you. Anything. Don't be sad or fright-
ened. Very soon we'll be together forever. I
promise.

Love, Teddy

The person who had written this letter must
have planned to mail it, then either changed his
mind or forgot. Her breath caught in her throat
when she realized that it had been written exactly
one week before Jeffrey McGrath's death.

Alexandra sat back in her chair, still holding the
letter. Who were Teddy and Bunny, and what was
this letter doing in a book belonging to George
Collins?

When Patrick strode into Alexandra's messy office, she saw that his expression was grim. He put
down his briefcase, then slumped into a chair and
thrust out his feet in front of him.

"I found an old love letter in one of Erica's
boxes, in a medical book belonging to George,"
she told him eagerly. "It was written a week before
Jeffrey's death. I believe there's a good chance it
was written by George to Lorna."

He read it quickly and then shrugged his broad
shoulders. "At most, it means the doctor was an un-
faithful husband. Hardly evidence of murder."

She was surprised to hear him dismiss the letter so lightly. "I think you're wrong. If George wrote to Lorna promising they'd be together forever—and soon—it could prove premeditation on his part. And how about where he says he'd do anything for her?"

"I suppose it's a possibility," he replied in a brusque, clipped tone of voice.

His demeanor was disturbing. He was usually so cheerful and upbeat. "Did something happen?" she asked, warily.

Patrick eyed her carefully before responding. "Yes," he nodded. "I went to see Michael McGrath today."

A flicker of apprehension coursed through her. "Why did you do that?"

"I was hoping he'd be less reticent with me about his father's death than he'd been with you. And I also wanted to judge for myself if this man could have planted the drugs in your apartment." A frown settled over his handsome features. "I found him to be very angry—*especially* at you."

"Oh?" She stirred uneasily in her chair, waiting for him to go on.

"He feels you abused your position as a deputy D.A. In fact, he accused you of strong-arming his family."

"That's not true," she protested. "I merely told them that Jeffrey might have been murdered. It was a possibility they all had a right to know."

"It's strange, but I got the feeling there was something more personal about this man's anger toward you." Patrick paused, his mouth taking on an unpleasant twist. "Any idea why?"

Struggling to maintain her composure, she pushed some papers around on the table. "No. I can't imagine why he'd be angry at me." She tried to sound convincing, but her voice wavered.

"Why do I have the feeling you're not leveling with me?" He faced her squarely, his gaze pinning her down. "Was there something going on between the two of you?"

Her throat tightened and she found herself unable to speak. The awkward silence between them grew.

Finally, he said, "If you lie to your own lawyer, Alexandra, you're a fool."

An unwelcome blush crept into her cheeks. "Things sometimes happen," she admitted, wishing at the moment that she could simply disappear.

Patrick regarded her. "Do you think that was a wise decision?" His tone held more than a hint of sarcasm. "After all, you say someone planted drugs in your apartment to stop you from investigating Jeffrey McGrath's death. I'd think that sleeping with one of the possible suspects wasn't a very prudent thing to do." He paused again. "Wouldn't you agree?"

"It was before the drug incident," she said, unable to meet his eyes. "And anyway, it's over."

"Already?"

"It happened only once."

Eyebrows raised, Patrick looked shocked. "You and McGrath had a one-night stand?"

She resented the way he was making it sound cheap and ugly. "Something like that. I didn't do anything wrong," she rushed to explain. "I was never *officially* investigating Jeffrey McGrath's death."

"Weren't you going to turn over to the authorities any incriminating evidence you happened to find?"

"Yes," she conceded, feeling like she was being cross-examined by him.

"Then it might not have been legally wrong to sleep with the man, but how about professionally?"

Being called unprofessional bothered Alexandra more than being ridiculed for having a one-night stand.

There was another awkward silence as Patrick stood up and began pacing back and forth. "After you were arrested, I specifically asked you if anyone had access to your apartment. You said no." He was glaring openly at her now.

"I said that Michael McGrath had followed me home because of the weather." She looked down at her hands. "It was too . . . embarrassing to explain the rest."

"Embarrassing or not, I'm your lawyer," he said, his voice harsh. "Remember, you picked me, not the other way around. I've committed myself to defending you. Not telling me everything is a luxury you can't afford. This man could be the culprit we've been looking for."

Alexandra exhaled loudly before nodding. "I know."

"Did McGrath bring anything in with him . . . like an overnight case or a duffel bag?"

She shook her head. "No. It wasn't like that."

His face was somber. "Why don't you tell me what it *was* like."

"I merely meant it wasn't planned." She gazed at the papers in front of her as she spoke. "After I waved his car off, I ran upstairs and into my apartment. A minute or two later, there was a knock on my door. It was Michael. He said I'd left my car lights on and offered to turn them off if I gave him the keys."

"Do you think you had really left your lights on, or was it merely a ruse? A way for him to get into your apartment?"

Alexandra had considered the possibility that Michael had been interested in finding out where she lived. But until this moment, she'd never doubted his story about the lights. "I'm not sure," she acknowledged. "At the time, I believed it to be the truth. It seemed entirely plausible that I might have left them on."

He rolled his eyes at her.

She was beginning to feel that Patrick was enjoying watching her squirm. If she didn't know better, it almost sounded like he was jealous. Could that be possible after all these years? No. She was misreading the situation. Patrick was involved with his partner, Nancy. He was just upset because she hadn't been entirely straight with him.

"Can you imagine how this is going to look if it comes out during your trial?"

She wanted to say that he didn't know what it felt like to be so lonely, so terribly bereft that you opened like a floodgate to the smallest kindness by another human being. The person she loved most in the world was fighting a terminal illness, and Alexandra had needed to be held, to be loved. But she said none of these things. "I guess it was pretty stupid."

He tensed and she had a feeling he was about to say something else. Then he seemed to change his mind as he suddenly leaned over and picked up his briefcase. "I've got some calls to make," he muttered.

After he was gone, Alexandra stood there furious with herself. Now Patrick not only thought that she was a fool, but that she was a liar, too.

20

─── ～ ───

EXITING THE 405 San Diego Freeway at Nordoff, Alexandra headed for Northridge, a suburb in the San Fernando Valley area of Los Angeles County.

Patrick's investigator had turned up the fact that Sally McGrath Potter was married to a professor of sociology at Cal State University at Northridge, or CSUN, as it was more commonly known. Now, as Alexandra passed the first buildings belonging to the university, she hoped that the professor was at school and not at home with his wife.

She'd only had time to do a brief probe on Professor Arnold Potter. But what she'd turned up was interesting—the man was rumored to have indulged in a number of affairs with his female students. Not exactly the kind of recommendation most parents were looking for when they sent their daughters to college.

After locating the street and the nondescript house, she rang the bell several times. A neighbor peeked her head around the side of the house next door.

"Do you know if Sally Potter is home?" Alexandra called out in a friendly voice.

The neighbor shrugged her shoulders and disappeared. Giving it one more try, Alexandra rang again, and this time she saw a face peering out at her from behind the blinds.

"Who's there?" asked a woman in a high-pitched voice.

"Alexandra Locke. I believe you telephoned me at the D.A.'s office not too long ago."

The door opened slowly to reveal a pale, thin young woman. Her face matched the image Alexandra had seen in the photos on Lester and Frances McGrath's piano. There was also a definite resemblance to Jeffrey McGrath. With her silvery blond hair tied back in a ponytail, Sally looked no more than thirteen or fourteen years old.

"I don't let anyone in when I'm home alone," Sally explained, her voice trembling slightly.

"Then how about if you come out on the porch? Would that be all right?"

"I guess so." The screen door squeaked as if it hadn't been oiled in years.

Alexandra put her hand out. "Glad to meet you," she said, with a wide smile.

Sally looked hesitant as she returned the handshake. "My family doesn't want me talking to you."

"I'm sorry to hear that," Alexandra replied, trying to make eye contact with Sally, who kept glancing around. "I've been worried about you ever since you called me."

"Really?" Sally appeared surprised, but still very nervous.

"Please don't be afraid of me, Sally," Alexandra said gently. "I only want to talk to you." She pointed to the steps. "How about if we just sit there?"

"Okay." The young woman sat neatly down on the top step, her hands folded tightly in her lap. Alexandra settled down next to her. "Were you telling the truth, Sally, when you said George Collins was a murderer? That he killed your father?"

Sally nodded.

"Are you aware that no one else in your family thinks that George is a murderer?"

"That's because George has them all fooled. He's this big, successful doctor making tons of money." Sally's tone of voice became derisive. "They're all a bunch of hypocrites."

"Do you have any evidence to back up your claims?"

A puzzled look appeared on Sally's pretty face. "I'm not sure what you mean."

Alexandra smiled again, trying to put her at ease. "I mean something that would help me prove in a court of law that your father was in fact murdered by George?"

There was a loud noise as a car screeched to a stop at the curb. Next to Alexandra, Sally became taut. A thin, middle-aged man with stooped shoulders and a graying beard got out of a dirty white Honda Accord, and hurried toward them. He was balding. The hair remaining on his head was a mousy brown and also turning gray. Thick glasses and an ill-fitting suit rounded out his appearance.

"Is that your husband?" asked Alexandra, thinking to herself that he looked old enough to be Sally's father.

"Yes," Sally muttered miserably.

"Are you afraid of him?" Alexandra quickly whispered under her breath.

"I'm . . ." Sally's voice trailed off.

"Who are you and what are you doing here talking to my wife?" Arnold Potter demanded.

Alexandra had prosecuted enough men who had physically or verbally abused their wives to recognize one of them. Regardless of this man's harmless appearance, he clearly belonged on that list.

"This is Alexandra Locke," Sally said, as if suddenly finding her voice. "She's a deputy D.A."

"I know exactly who she is. I'll handle this." He wiped his hands on his trousers as if they were a towel.

"But I want . . . to . . . talk to her," Sally insisted, her words sounding choked.

"That's not advisable," he said, as disapproval darkened his face. "Go in the house, Sally."

The young woman shook her head. "We're talking about my daddy's death and it's really important to me." Her lower lip started to tremble.

"Sally," he said again, a note of warning creeping into his demeanor. "Go into the house or . . .

I'll . . ." He didn't finish, just left an unspoken threat hanging in the air.

Shoulders slumped, Sally reluctantly got up. At the door, she hesitated.

"Go inside and close the door!" he ordered.

When Sally finally did so, he turned his attention back to Alexandra. "I'm afraid you'll have to leave. My wife's not well."

She saw the sweat glistening on his forehead. "I only have a few questions," she started to say before he forcibly took her arm.

"If you don't go," Professor Potter lashed out, moving inches from her face, "I'm going to call the police."

"That's not necessary," Alexandra replied, yanking her arm out of his slick grasp and pushing him away from her. Not willing to give up, she tried one more time. "Why are you so afraid of letting me talk to your wife?"

"Go," he said firmly, ignoring her question.

Alexandra pictured what would happen if the cops came. She had no legitimate reason for being here on private property. She was also worried that if they checked, they might find out that she was on leave from the D.A.'s office. It could be embarrassing.

Driving away, Alexandra thought about the sheen of perspiration on the professor's forehead. Her presence had definitely made the man nervous. But why? Could Arnold Potter have been the one who planted the drugs? She didn't know the answers to her questions, but she was coming to the conclusion that everyone associated with the Collins/McGrath case seemed to have an unusual number of secrets.

The Thai restaurant was crowded and Patrick was squeezed against the wooden bar, trying to hear his friend Tricia Yardley above the din.

"I'm not sure I understand," he finally said. "Are you telling me that the case against Alexandra Locke is being treated like some sort of state secret?"

"Yes," she nodded, her dark eyes scanning the room as if she was worried that she might be overheard.

Tricia had insisted on meeting him in this small restaurant on Olympic Boulevard in the heart of what was referred to as Korea-town on the outskirts of downtown L.A.

"All I can tell you is that a good friend of mine works directly under Karen Hunter. You know who she is, don't you?"

"Of course," he replied. "She's the Senior Assistant Attorney General of the Criminal Division here in L.A."

"Right. Well, my friend, who will remain nameless, felt it wouldn't be in my best interests if Karen found out I was asking questions." Tricia glanced quickly around again before continuing. "I've got to go. I just wanted you to know I got a warning to back off for the sake of my career."

He was dumbfounded.

After Tricia had left, Patrick sat alone at the bar trying to figure out what was going on. In his experience there could only be one reason why people would be afraid to talk—politics. Someone was using Alexandra and the case against her to further their own career or agenda. What he didn't know yet, but needed to learn as soon as possible, was who that someone was.

Taking the letter she'd found in Erica's belongings, Alexandra quickly determined that the P.O. box location no longer existed. So she decided to try something else.

"Doctor Collins's office," said a woman on the other end of the line.

"Doctor Collins ordered some flowers for his wife, Lorna," Alexandra explained. "And I'm having trouble making out the nickname my assistant wrote down. Does the doctor ever call his wife Bunny?"

"Which florist is this?"

Alexandra blurted out the first name that came into her mind. "Brent Hills Florists."

"That's strange," remarked the woman. "I usually order the flowers for Doctor Collins, and from another florist."

"Well, I don't know about that, but I'd like to get this right," Alexandra said. "Does Bunny ring a bell?"

"I've never heard him use it," the woman told her. "But let me get his nurse, Dora. She may know. What's your name again?"

"Gladys," Alexandra said, her heart pounding in her ears.

"Just a second."

Biting her fingernails, Alexandra waited impatiently. If her ruse failed at least she could hang up the phone and no one would be the wiser.

"Hello, this is Dora," said a cheery voice.

Alexandra repeated her story.

"I've heard him call her Bunny once or twice," Dora admitted. "But it was a long time ago. Do you want to hold on while I ask the doctor what name he asked for on the card?"

"No, that's okay. I'm sure it's correct. Sorry to have bothered you." Before the nurse could reply, Alexandra hung up.

So—her hunch had proved correct. These love letters were in fact written to Lorna McGrath, alias Bunny. Therefore, it only seemed logical that George Collins had to be Teddy. Alexandra drummed her fingers on the tabletop. She would have to prove her hypothesis. But if she was right, given the date on the letter, then Lorna had lied about when her affair with the doctor had started. What else had that woman lied about?

Pulling into the parking structure of a medical building in Beverly Hills, Alexandra turned her car over to an attendant.

Upstairs, she found the waiting room crowded with people. It was definitely a notch or two above the usual doctor's office decor. In fact, it looked more like an expensively decorated living room. There was plush forest green carpeting on the floor, and the couches and chairs were covered in a rich-looking chenille that picked up the hue of the carpet. Lamps with fabric shades rested on dark walnut end tables and bathed the room in a soft glow.

She dutifully filled out the forms with bogus information, then explained to the woman at the front desk that she had no health insurance and would be paying in cash. Finally, after a long wait, she was shown into an examining room and told to change into a dressing gown.

George Collins turned out to be a strapping man with a ruddy complexion, sandy hair turning white at the edges and inquisitive blue eyes. He smiled when he introduced himself before glancing down at the chart he was holding. "So what's the problem?"

"My left leg has been bothering me." She stuck out her leg and pointed. "I was doing some exercises and I felt something pull. Since then, I've been limping a little bit. But not all the time."

He focused his eyes on her. "How long does the limp last?"

"A few minutes or so," she said, hoping that sounded right for her symptoms.

Doctor Collins wrote something into the chart. Then he took out an instrument and used it to examine her leg, touching it in several places and asking how it felt. He also tested her reflexes. "Everything looks good. But let's take an X-ray to be sure."

When that was done, he came back in. "Nothing showed up. I believe you've merely strained a mus-

cle. I'm going to give you a prescription for a mild
anti-inflammatory."

After he wrote it out, she tucked it away in her
purse.

"Why don't you get dressed," he said. "Then
we'll talk for a few minutes in my office."

As soon as he was gone, she compared the prescription Doctor Collins had written to the copy of
the letter she was carrying in her purse. Even with
her untrained eye, she saw a few similarities. While
she wasn't a handwriting expert, she was willing to
bet that the two samples were written by the same
person.

Alexandra was shown into his office a few minutes later and took the seat opposite his desk.
Glancing around, she noticed all the degrees hanging on the walls. He'd spent a lot of years qualifying as a medical specialist.

He came in with her chart. Sitting down at his
desk, he made a few more notes before glancing
over at her. "I want you to use ice on the area. If
the pain persists after two weeks, give us a call and
I'll probably want to see you again."

"Fine."

"Any questions?" he asked politely.

It was time to tell him the real purpose of her
visit. "Doctor Collins, did you ever use the nickname Teddy when you were younger?"

There was a startled expression on his face.
"What are you talking about?"

"I'm investigating an old crime. I believe a handwriting expert will be able to testify that the pre-

scription you've just given me was written by the same person as some letters I've found addressed to a Ms. Bunny Lovett and signed by Teddy."

The doctor looked confused. To convince him that she was serious, she pulled the copy of the letter from her purse and began reading.

"All I can think about is how your naked body felt in my arms yesterday afternoon. Your skin is like velvet, smooth and soft, yet firm. I love your—"

"I'm afraid I don't understand what's going on," said Doctor Collins, interrupting her. "Who are you? And where did you get that letter?"

"My name is Alexandra Locke," she said simply. "Your ex-wife gave it to me."

He immediately became wary. "What is it you want, Ms. Locke?"

"The truth. Were you and Lorna McGrath lovers before her husband died?"

"I really don't think that's any of your business. Now I . . ."

"Your ex-wife claimed you murdered Jeffrey McGrath and that she helped you get away with it by paying a bribe."

All of the color drained from the doctor's face. "You can't believe anything Erica told you. She supported me while I went to medical school. Subsequently, she felt entitled to half of everything I earned after becoming a doctor. When I asked for a divorce, she became a bitter, angry woman." He shook his head as if remembering. "Actually, Erica was always emotionally unstable. She lied to me, told me she wanted children when she secretly didn't. Our marriage was doomed long before I met Lorna."

"How convenient for you then when Lorna's husband died."

"It was an accident," he mumbled, shaking his head again. "A terrible, tragic, but unforeseeable . . . accident." He had a far-off look in his eyes before he pulled himself together. "What are you planning to do with that letter?"

"This one is only a copy," she said. "The original is in a safe place, ready to be turned over to the authorities. It's evidence that should have come out at the time of Jeffrey McGrath's death."

"If you do that it could end my career."

"I can't help that," she said.

Taking a deep breath, he straightened his shoulders. "Yes you can." His features became rigid. "I've got money. If word of this leaks out, I'll sue the county, you and everyone else personally."

As his voice got louder, it wasn't hard for Alexandra to picture him becoming physically violent. "I'll hire the best lawyers in town, and I'll drag everyone through the courts until you're all ruined."

She had no choice but to call his bluff. "I guess we both have to do what we feel is right."

"You're not even at the D.A.'s office anymore," he said.

"I'm on administrative leave," she admitted with a nod of her head. "Tell me, how much did you pay Thomas Kendell to stay out of prison?"

His neck reddened and he couldn't meet her gaze. "I don't know what you're talking about."

"I'm referring to the bribe you paid to a deputy D.A. The one that kept you from going to prison for killing Jeffrey McGrath."

"I didn't kill him!" His face was now turning red also. "I'll give you the names of people who will swear to it that Erica was a vindictive woman. Do you know what she said to me the last time I saw her?"

She shook her head.

"That because I left her, she'd make sure I spent the rest of my life in prison."

He sounded so convincing that for a moment Alexandra considered the likelihood of it being the truth. Then she remembered the unexplained things she'd uncovered along with the fact that someone had wanted to stop her investigation badly enough to plant those drugs in her apartment. The real question here was whether or not George Collins had been that person.

21

SHIFTING FROM FOOT to foot, Sally tried to bolster her courage as she waited for a teenage boy in a red baseball cap to finish his conversation on the pay phone in front of her. She was standing outside a small convenience store two blocks from her house. In the parking lot, three rough-looking men were lounging against a beat-up old Chevy. They made Sally nervous, but she forced herself to ignore them. She didn't dare make this call from home.

The boy finally hung up. Her body was trembling as Sally took a deep breath, picked up the receiver, dropped in her coins and dialed the number she had memorized.

"District Attorney's office."

Wiping her clammy hands against the cool fabric of her pants, Sally's voice came out in a squeak. "I'd like to speak to Alexandra Locke."

"Ms. Locke's away on leave. Can someone else help you?"

Sally's heart was beating erratically and when she heard that Alexandra wasn't there, she felt momentarily paralyzed. Two nights ago Sally had told Doctor Abbott about Alexandra Locke's visit and how her husband Arnold had reacted to it. The doctor had been very encouraging when Sally said she wanted to tell the truth.

"Can someone else help you?" asked the receptionist.

"Uh-uh . . . well I'm not sure. It's something I talked to Ms. Locke about . . . before."

"Is this in reference to a case Ms. Locke was handling?"

"Uh . . . I guess so."

"What's the name of the case?"

"I'm not sure."

"Another deputy D.A., Elizabeth Nathan, has taken over most of the matters Ms. Locke was handling. I'll connect you with her."

As she waited, Sally thought about her family. They would be furious with her for telling what she knew. But the book the doctor had loaned Sally said that getting rid of troubling secrets was one of the best ways to get well.

"Elizabeth Nathan," said a clipped female voice.

"Uh . . . well . . ." Sally couldn't seem to find the words to explain why she was calling. Alexandra Locke had acted a lot nicer.

"Is there something I can help you with, Ms. . . . ?" Elizabeth Nathan's question hung in the air.

"Yes . . . I mean I don't know. You see I talked

to Ms. Locke before and I was . . . expecting to talk to her again."

"I'm sure I can help you if you'll tell me your name and what this is about."

"Sally McGrath Potter and it's about . . . an old case she was looking into. I want her to know I'm ready to answer her—I mean Ms. Locke's—questions about it."

"I see," Elizabeth Nathan said. "Tell you what. Would you like to come down and see me in person?"

"I think so. I mean yes."

"Good," the woman deputy replied. "Let's say next Thursday at four-thirty. I should be back from court by then."

"Okay."

"Do you know how to get here?"

"Uh . . . no, not . . . really."

After the woman gave her directions, Sally hung up. Downtown Los Angeles was far. It would cost a lot of money for a cab. Somehow, she was going to have to come up with a really good story to get that much cash away from Arnold.

Alexandra sat in the third row of the spectators' section in the Santa Monica courtroom, trying to be as inconspicuous as possible as she watched Patrick cross-examine one of the prosecution's experts. She had to admit that she was impressed with his handling of the witness. He was articulate, conscientious, quick on his feet and seemed to be putting on the best defense possible. Patrick was also very personable, and she could see that the jury liked him.

Earlier, when Patrick's secretary had mentioned that he was in trial and needed some files, Alexandra had volunteered to take them. She and Patrick hadn't spoken since their unpleasant exchange over Michael McGrath. She knew it was up to her to get their professional relationship back onto a firm footing.

As soon as the judge recessed court for lunch, she walked up to Patrick in the hallway. "Care to join me for a sandwich?"

"I've got some notes I want to go over," he hedged, looking distracted.

"Please," she said, trying to convey with her eyes that it was important to her.

Reluctantly he agreed, and they walked from the courthouse over to a small Italian restaurant a few blocks away.

After they were seated, an uncomfortable silence seemed to fall between them. Alexandra took a quick sip of water and then leaned forward across the table. "I just wanted to tell you, Patrick, that I was wrong. I know you can't defend me unless you have all the facts. Will you accept my apology?"

He stared at her for several anxious moments, then he nodded. His lips, however, remained compressed.

She'd been hoping they could talk things out, but it didn't seem as if he wanted to belabor the subject, so she searched for something else to say. "Your

cross-examination of that witness was very skillful."

"Thanks." He reached for his water and took a
few gulps.

"You like being a defense lawyer, don't you?"

"Yes," he admitted, "I've definitely found my
niche." He paused before going on. "How about
you? Have you ever considered switching sides?"

"No." She shook her head and smiled. "I was
born wanting to be a prosecutor and I've never
changed my mind."

"One of the things that really makes defense
work satisfying for me is the pro bono stuff I do.
Unfortunately, it drives my partner crazy." Patrick
gave a half smile. "Nancy firmly believes that people don't appreciate what they don't pay for." He
said it like it was a joke, but she sensed an under-
current of conflict beneath the words.

Alexandra studied him. "And you?"

"I think they do. Especially when a lawyer is all
that is standing between them and the death
penalty or years in prison."

"I'm sure in capital cases what you're saying is
very true." She played with the fork in her hand.
Since he'd mentioned his partner, Alexandra
wanted to ask him about his relationship but didn't
want to step over the line. She tried to make her
voice sound casual. "Are you and Nancy planning
to get married?"

"Probably," he said with a shrug. "We've been
together for over a year. We've just never gotten
around to making any definite plans."

She lifted her coffee to her lips and waited patiently for him to explain.

"Our relationship just kind of happened," he went on to say. "We've been partners for three years—and I couldn't ask for a more competent partner. I hate all those administrative chores it takes to run a practice and Nancy genuinely thrives on them." He stopped as if he'd said more than he wanted to. Breaking off a piece of the Italian bread the waiter had put on the table, he said, "How's your mother doing?"

"We're waiting for the test results on the experimental chemotherapy they've been giving her." She put the cup down. "But it's been making her really sick."

"I'm sorry. I hope the news is good at least."

"Me too," she replied.

Another awkward silence settled in between them. She took a deep breath. "I've been wondering what would happen if I went to the Attorney General's office and told them everything I know. Do you think they would make a deal with me?"

Patrick looked surprised. "You mean like pleading guilty to a lesser offense regarding the drugs?"

"No," she stated emphatically. "I mean asking them to do a full investigation into who could have planted the drugs in exchange for my cooperation regarding Jeffrey McGrath's death."

He frowned and shook his head. "Want to hear the pros and cons of doing something like that?"

The waiter came and took their order. As soon as he left, she answered Patrick's question. "You're going to say that I don't have anything to negotiate with yet."

"You don't."

"Let's say I did have something, could I tell them what I know about the murder but remain mum on the bribery issue?"

"What are you getting at?" he asked.

"Telling them everything means mentioning the part my father might have played in covering up the crime. And I don't think I can do that—at least not yet."

Lifting his cup, he sipped his coffee and gave her a chance to sort out her thoughts.

"It's bad enough seeing what my arrest has done to my mother. Can you imagine what will happen if my father is accused of participating in a cover-up? It could kill her." She gave a small shudder. "And yet I keep asking myself, if it wasn't my mother and my father involved, what would I do?"

He seemed to be considering her words. "Do you know the answer to that?"

"Yes. While I might feel sorry for a critically ill spouse, parent or child, I wouldn't let it stop me from going after the perpetrator of a crime." She paused for several seconds before meeting his eyes. "What would you do?"

Patrick leaned back in his chair. "I've actually thought about it a lot. Of course, prosecutors tend to see things as more black or white than defense lawyers do." He exhaled loudly. "But to be honest, I don't know."

She appreciated his sincerity. "I'm still hoping

that my father is innocent. But if he did participate in a cover-up, is it my fault if it comes to light?"

"Go on," he urged.

"Isn't it really a clear-cut case of cause and effect? He knew the rules going in." She ran her finger over the checkered tablecloth. "But then he's still my father. I may not like certain things about him, but I love him." She sighed. "I don't want to be the one to ruin his career or his life. I also can't bear the thought of my mother having to deal with that now. She loves him very much."

"Yes," he nodded. "She does."

Alexandra was pensive as she tried to frame her next words. "Do you remember that bed-and-breakfast place up the coast where we went for our ... first weekend?" There was a note of uncertainty in her voice.

"I've never forgotten it," he said softly.

She tried to read the expression in his eyes, but couldn't. Her heart was pounding. She wanted to ask him what he'd meant, but she was too afraid to know. Instead, she concentrated on the Cobb salad the waiter had just put in front of her.

"Finding your father with another woman was traumatic for you," Patrick said, gazing at her intently. "And it changed the course of our lives, too."

Was he offering her an opportunity to talk about the past? she wondered. About what she had done? Her haste in leaving L.A. Her stubbornness in ending their relationship. Her inability to deal with the fallout from that weekend. She felt suddenly ill-

equipped to undertake such a task. The words she
needed to convey her feelings seemed to be stuck in
her throat. She recalled the old saying that there
was no going back. "Yes, it did change our lives,"
she finally acknowledged in a faint voice.

After giving her another long, measuring glance,
he fingered his coffee cup. "So, back to the problem."

Alexandra knew that she had lost a chance to
make amends for the past, and felt sad. Taking a
deep breath, she tried to regain her poise and focus
on the present. "I've got to prove I was framed,
Patrick. But I can't figure out how I'm supposed to
do that without hurting the people I love the
most."

Standing with her father by Roberta's bed,
Alexandra listened as the doctor brought them up
to date.

"As I said, Mrs. Kendell's CA level is extremely
high and her last CAT scan confirms that there's a
significant mass in the same area as before." He
was a lanky, balding man in his early forties, with a
low voice that made it difficult to hear him at
times.

Thomas leaned forward. "Can you operate and
remove it?"

"No. I'm afraid it's metastasized."

"Can we try another round of the experimental
chemotherapy she just finished?" Alexandra asked.

The doctor shook his head. "We've found that
repeating that same course of treatment doesn't do

much good unless the first round was minimally successful."

"Then there has to be some other course of therapy we haven't tried," Thomas insisted.

"We've performed all of the conventional treatments appropriate for this classification of cancer," the doctor advised them. "As for other approaches, there's nothing right now. The experimental chemotherapy she just had is the only new treatment on the horizon. We've simply run out of options."

Roberta sat up straighter in her bed, pulling her robe around her as if chilled. Then she asked the one question they had all been avoiding. "Without any further treatments, doctor, how long do I have?"

"It's hard to say," the doctor replied. "Some people live two months or more. Some don't survive longer than two weeks."

His words were devastating. Alexandra struggled to keep herself under control, her thoughts filled with doubts and fears. As she leaned over and rubbed Roberta's bony shoulder, she wished there was a way to transfer her physical strength to her mother's failing body.

A picture of Roberta as she'd looked when Alexandra had been a young child came flashing into her mind. Her parents had been going to a charity ball. Roberta had looked absolutely glamorous in a gold strapless taffeta gown with small diamond studs glittering on her ears, her hair piled up in a mass of chestnut curls. Thomas had been dashing in his black tuxedo, white pleated shirt and gold cufflinks.

Alexandra remembered being jealous because she had to stay home with the baby-sitter while her parents went out dancing. Roberta had been so full of vitality—so full of laughter.

Thomas's voice broke her reverie. "There must be other things we can try," he insisted again, unable to accept the doctor's prognosis as the final word.

"I'm afraid we've done all we can," the doctor reiterated, giving a sympathetic nod.

"But if others have had a second round of the experimental chemotherapy," Thomas argued, "shouldn't Roberta get the same chance?"

"It's not that simple. I must caution you that Mrs. Kendell is in a very weakened condition." The doctor's mouth was grim. "It might be more than her body can take."

Thomas continued to push for a better answer. "Can we build her body up in any way?"

"There's always the option of giving her transfusions," the doctor responded.

"What can that do for me besides keeping me alive a little longer?" Roberta said, looking suddenly small and frail as she gazed up at the doctor.

He hedged. "It's complex—everyone's different."

Thomas kept shaking his head as if that could somehow change the diagnosis. "I've read about spontaneous remissions—surely that can still happen, can't it?" There was a desperate, false hopefulness to his voice.

Clearing his throat, the doctor looked ready to bolt from the room. "I guess anything is possible," he finally said rather lamely.

Roberta glanced at Alexandra as if to convey that she didn't want to talk about miracles. Alexandra got the message and took the conversation in another direction. "Doctor, how long do we have to make these decisions?"

"That's difficult to say. As I told you, if Mrs. Kendell wants to try another round of the drugs, we may have to first build up her immune system. There are no hard and fast rules in cancer treatment. It varies significantly from patient to patient."

Alexandra thanked him for his honesty, and after promising to let him know their decision, walked him to the door.

"I say we've got to give it one more run," Thomas stated, his jaw set in a stubborn line.

Like a rag doll, Roberta had collapsed against her pillows. "I'm tired," she admitted with a large sigh. "I don't think I can go through another round of that chemo." There was an expression of resignation on her face.

Alexandra couldn't remember ever hearing her mother sound so discouraged. But then the drugs had made Roberta very ill.

"Of course you can," Thomas blustered. "We'll help you, won't we, Alexandra?" He gave his daughter a nudge along with a sharp glance.

"It's Mom's choice," she said quietly, even though she knew that wasn't what he wanted to hear. Turning to Roberta, she patted her mother's shoulder again. "Want to talk about it now? Or would you rather have some time?"

Before his wife could answer, Thomas spoke for her. "We're going forward, Roberta. You can't just give up. Where's your fighting spirit? I can't be- lieve—" There was a catch in his gruff voice and he abruptly stopped, unable to go on.

Reaching out for his hand, Roberta shushed him. "Thomas, I need time to absorb this," she said weakly.

Feeling that her parents wanted to be alone, Alexandra picked up her purse and quietly excused herself from the room.

Deeply in need of some spiritual guidance, Alexandra headed for the hospital's garden chapel. The area was empty. She sat down on one of the benches and inhaled the fragrant smell of the roses.

The entire time her mother had been battling this terrible illness, Roberta had remained so confi- dent that she would win that Alexandra, too, had tried to believe her mother could beat the odds. Now it no longer seemed possible, and she didn't know what to do.

Would it be better to talk with Roberta about death? To cry with her mother over how unfair life was? Or would it be wiser to deny the reality of the doctor's words and act as if a miracle could still happen? Not knowing the answers to her questions, she finally bowed her head and wept.

A few minutes later, she heard someone approach.

"Your mother wants to see you," her father said quietly.

"All right." Alexandra stood up to go, but Thomas was blocking her passage.

"I know we don't agree," Thomas said, his voice hoarse. "But I'd be extremely grateful if you'd convince your mother to give it one more shot." There were tears in his eyes and his shoulders were slumped forward.

Alexandra was struck by the realization that her father wasn't prepared to accept that Roberta could die. Her own eyes welled with tears again, and she swiped them away with her hand. "I understand how you feel. It's hard for me to let go of Mom, too," she said softly. "But this is one decision we can't make for her."

"You're wrong," he said shaking his head, his voice growing louder. "Can't you see that she isn't in the right frame of mind to make such a decision?"

"It's her life. She has to tell us what she wants."

"No!" His face was now turning red. It seemed to be much easier for Thomas to get angry than allow himself to feel his sorrow. "We're her family. It's up to us to *make* her give it one more try."

22

~

ON THE DAY OF her arraignment, Alexandra's stomach was in knots. After passing through a gauntlet of reporters and spectators, Patrick and she finally made it to the courtroom doors. Once inside, her heart sank. It was packed. Spectators were standing in the aisle and along the walls and she recognized several of the reporters who were seated in the front rows. She was mortified. All these people had come to witness her disgrace.

At a desk next to the judge's bench, a telephone receiver wedged between her ear and her shoulder, the court clerk looked harried as she spoke to the attorneys surrounding her.

Before long, the bailiff came to the front of the room. In a loud voice he called out, "Division 5 of the Municipal Court of California, in and for the County of Los Angeles, is now in session, The Honorable Mary Yamaguchi, presiding."

The judge stepped quickly into the courtroom,

went up the three steps to the bench and sat down. A stack of files waited in front of her.

Judge Yamaguchi had been a prosecutor before being appointed to the bench several years ago and was known as a capable, if not particularly innovative, judge. Alexandra was aware that former prosecutors often bent over backward to be fair to the defense so as not to give the impression that they were biased in favor of the prosecution. She wondered if that would be true with this judge but doubted it. If anything, a former prosecutor might be appalled by the idea of a law enforcement officer gone bad.

"People v. Locke," said the judge, her eyes scanning the municipal courtroom.

Hearing Judge Yamaguchi call her case, Alexandra flinched. It didn't seem possible that this arraignment was actually happening to her. Usually when a case was called, Alexandra jumped to her feet, eager to address the court. But the cold, harsh truth overwhelmed her today; she wasn't the prosecutor—she was the defendant.

Her lawyer stood for her instead. "Patrick Ross, Your Honor," he said in a strong voice. "I'm making a general appearance for Ms. Locke. We waive formal arraignment and waive reading of the complaint. We'll enter a plea of not guilty."

Alexandra felt the gaze of the other people in the courtroom focusing on her. How many of her former colleagues had shown up to view her humiliation? she wondered. She gave a small shiver, feeling the impact of unfriendly eyes on her back.

At the adjacent table was Enrique Vasquez, the state deputy attorney general, who'd be prosecuting the case against her. Alexandra didn't know him personally, but Patrick said that Vasquez had a reputation for being tough but fair. From her vantage point, he seemed to have an air of self-importance, as if her downfall had been engineered by him. Clearly, he was enjoying the publicity her case attracted.

The next thing on the agenda was setting a date for her preliminary hearing. At that time the prosecutor would only have to put on enough evidence to hold Alexandra over for trial. But that wouldn't be hard to do because of the drugs that were found in her apartment and the presumption that they belonged to her. So she'd asked Patrick to delay the preliminary hearing for as long as possible. She didn't want the public to hear the evidence against her without some kind of a defense. For that, she needed evidence to support her position that the drugs were planted in her apartment.

"Your Honor, my client is aware that she has a right to a preliminary hearing within ten court days, but she is waiving that right. I'd like to ask the Court to set this matter for a preliminary hearing in one month so as to accommodate my trial schedule. I have a murder trial starting next week that is supposed to last four weeks."

The judge looked over at her clerk, who gave her an available date in four weeks, and she set Alexandra's preliminary hearing for that time.

"Thank you, Your Honor." Patrick cleared his

throat. "I'd also like to ask that my client be released on her own recognizance and that cash bail be exonerated."

The judge glanced at the prosecutor.

"Your Honor, the People object to defendant's release on her own recognizance," Vasquez said. "We feel she poses a flight risk."

The ball was back in Patrick's court as Judge Yamaguchi switched her gaze to him.

Patrick took a step forward before addressing the court. "Your Honor, we don't see where Ms. Locke poses any flight risk. She has no prior convictions. Up until now, Ms. Locke has been working as a deputy district attorney on behalf of the people."

It was the prosecutor's turn. "Your Honor, the defendant has resided outside the state of California for the last fourteen years and that has us very concerned."

Alexandra noted the way Vasquez kept emphasizing the word *defendant,* while Patrick kept humanizing her by saying "my client" or "Ms. Locke." It was the usual courtroom shenanigans, only this time it was happening to her and she didn't like it. She prayed that the judge wasn't falling for the prosecutor's attempt to label her as a dirty deputy D.A.

Patrick again jumped to Alexandra's defense. "Your Honor, Ms. Locke has worked as a deputy D.A. in Los Angeles County for the last seven and one-half months. It is in her best interest to have this matter adjudicated as soon as possible so that she can get back to her job. She would have absolutely nothing to gain by fleeing this jurisdiction."

Alexandra touched his arm and Patrick leaned down to listen. Then he stood up straighter. "Also, Your Honor, Ms. Locke's mother is gravely ill. That is why she came back to L.A. in the first place. She has no intention of leaving the jurisdiction of this court."

Judge Yamaguchi toyed with her pen, her gaze narrowing as she appraised Alexandra. "I'm going to release the defendant on her own recognizance. Cash bail is exonerated," said the judge with a nod of her head.

Thank God, thought Alexandra, as she breathed a sigh of relief and smiled gratefully at the judge. Having her bail exonerated would lessen her cash crunch. She had already reimbursed Patrick for putting up her bail money by cashing out her retirement funds. When she got this bail money back she could then give it to Patrick toward the rest of his fees and costs.

Her knees were shaking as Patrick guided her to the back of the courtroom.

"I need a few minutes to talk to the deputy A.G.," he whispered. "Might be a good idea to stay here. The hallway is crowded with reporters."

Alexandra counted the minutes until Patrick returned. Being in the courtroom reminded her that a trial wasn't always a search for truth or justice, but a battleground where two gladiators fought it out. And like any shoot-out, victory didn't always go to the one who was right, but to the one who had the best gun.

At least she had an excellent lawyer, she told herself. Yet, how was Patrick going to dispute the actual physical evidence—the drugs that were found in her apartment—unless she uncovered the culprit who'd planted it? The terrifying reality was that she could very well be convicted and sent to prison.

When Patrick returned he leaned over and whispered again in her ear. "Vasquez isn't going to release any information regarding the informant unless I make a formal discovery motion. And even then, I have a feeling they're going to maintain they can't."

More games, she thought, feeling a rush of despair.

"Are you ready?" he asked somberly, indicating with his head the crowd waiting for them out in the hallway.

She nodded. Together they walked into a corridor crowded with cameras, lights and microphones. Her cheeks flushed with embarrassment.

"No comment. No comment," Patrick kept saying as he steered her toward the elevators.

One of the reporters called out, "How will your arraignment affect the primary on Tuesday?"

Again Patrick said, "No comment."

The question had unnerved Alexandra even further. If her father lost the primary he'd probably blame it on her.

Patrick stopped in front of the elevators. "I've

got to see a deputy D.A. on another case. Want to come upstairs with me?"

Alexandra couldn't face the stares of the other people on the seventeenth and eighteenth floors, where the D.A.'s offices were located. "No. I'm going to see my mother."

"Then I better walk you to your car."

With a small, grateful smile, she nodded again. After getting through the rest of the crowd and the reporters outside, they crossed the street to the parking lot. "How is Roberta doing?" he asked.

"Not well, I'm afraid. They told us there is nothing more they can do." She felt the tears pushing at the back of her eyes. Biting down hard on her lip, she ordered herself not to cry.

There was a stricken look on Patrick's face. "Why don't you wait for me. I'll drive out to the City of Hope with you."

Taken aback by his offer, she said the first thing that entered her head. "I'm not sure Mom's up to visitors."

"I can at least give you some moral support."

She wavered. Although their lunch the other day had bridged some of the awkwardness between them, Patrick had still been reserved around her. Now he was being kind and she wasn't sure how to handle it. "Maybe another time," she finally said.

"Sure. Tell Roberta I send my best."

"I will." Before she could change her mind, she walked quickly toward her car, ignoring the empty feeling in her gut.

* * *

Michael McGrath was in the middle of a budget fight with the producer of the movie he was working on when he was told he had an urgent call.

"Sally wants to do what?" he said loudly, his mind reeling as he listened to his brother-in-law.

Arnold Potter explained how he'd discovered Sally's plans to go to the authorities regarding her father's death, after she'd asked him for one hundred dollars. Reluctant at first to give a reason for needing so much cash, she'd finally admitted that it was for cab fare downtown. At his first break, Arnold had called Michael from the university.

After informing the producer and other executives that he had an emergency, Michael tore out of the parking lot at the studio and raced across the San Fernando Valley to his sister's home. He had no alternative but to convince Sally not to do this.

"Michael? What's wrong?" Sally said, when she opened the door. "Did Grandma get worse?"

"She's the same. Although she's been asking about you. You need to have Arnold drive you over to visit her."

Sally was dressed in blue jeans and a white tee shirt. With her long hair and no makeup, she looked like a child. "I've had a few problems," she said. "That's why I haven't gone."

"Arnold told me that your nightmares had gotten really bad again and that you'd been in the hospital."

She nodded. "Do you want something to drink?"

"Got any coffee left from this morning?"

"No. But I've got some instant. Come on, I'll make it for you."

He followed her through the living room and dining room to the kitchen. A small wooden table and three chairs sat squeezed in front of a window that looked out across a tiny side yard to an identical house next door.

Watching his sister get down a cup and fill it with water before putting it into the microwave, Michael wondered about her life. As far as he knew, she seldom ventured out of the house alone. "What do you do with yourself when Arnold is teaching?"

"Oh, I read—magazines and romance novels mostly." She gave him a hesitant smile. "I've got some television shows I like. If it's a nice day, I like to sit in the backyard, too." She gazed up at him, her blue eyes guileless.

"And how did things go at the hospital?" he asked.

She shrugged her thin shoulders again. "Okay, I guess. The good thing is I've got a new doctor, and I really like her." Sally's face lit up. "Doctor Abbott's real understanding. Kind of like a mother, if you know what I mean. Anyway, she's trying to help me find out what causes my nightmares."

"Arnold said you'd recently remembered something about Dad's death—something you wanted to tell the district attorney's office about?"

Her mouth turned downward. "Is that why you're here?"

Michael felt like kicking himself. He hadn't wanted her to become guarded. "I meant to visit you in the hospital, but I'm editing my last movie at the moment and fighting with my producer over the budget for the next one."

Sally's blue eyes lit up again. "What's the new movie about?"

As he explained the basic plot to her, she smiled and kept nodding. Sally enjoyed watching movies, and he frequently shared his Academy Award voting tapes with her.

"That sounds neat," she said. "I'd like to see it."

"You will, I promise." He gave her a big smile. Michael felt guilty that he didn't spend more time with Sally. He truly loved his sister, and he also worried about her. In recent years, however, he'd depended more and more on Arnold to take care of her.

After she handed him the coffee, she took the seat across from him. He took her small fingers in his hands. "I'm curious as to what it is you remember. I mean, you were so young."

"Everyone thinks I was too young to understand anything when Daddy died, but that's not true."

"Tell me," he urged.

"Well . . . , one night, a few weeks after Daddy's death, we were both supposed to be sleeping. It was a couple of days before Christmas and I wanted to see if I could find out what gifts I'd be getting. So I snuck out of my bed, went downstairs and hid behind the couch." She paused to take a deep breath. "From there I saw

Mommy and George on the living room floor . . ."

As he listened to the rest of her story, Michael's stomach roiled. He couldn't believe she'd kept this a secret for so many years. Somehow, he had to discourage her. "You don't really know for sure if that's what they were doing," he chided.

"But I do. I heard them," she insisted stubbornly.

"Then you misunderstood."

"I didn't."

He sat there shaking his head. "You were only nine years old, Sally. A child. No one will believe you."

"Maybe," she conceded. "But I've kept these secrets for a long time. I never said anything 'cause I didn't want to hurt Mommy. But Doctor Abbott says if you keep things locked up, it can make you sick. That's why I've got to tell now."

"But you could be causing a lot of damage. How will you feel if they put George in prison because of what you say?"

"I'll feel good. He killed Daddy. I'm sure of it."

"Don't be silly! You weren't there. Think about how wonderful George has been to us all these years."

"Wonderful to you maybe, but not to me," she stated firmly. "I can't stand him. He's a murderer." She'd begun to cry as they argued, and now the tears were falling unchecked.

"And what about Mom? Do you want her to go to jail?"

"No."

"Then you better think about it," he said sharply. "If Mom helped George, she could be found guilty, too. How would you feel if you were responsible for that?"

Sally looked crestfallen. "I don't want anything to happen to her. But it's not my fault she married a murderer."

"God, Sally, just listen to what you're saying."

"You don't understand, Michael," she said sadly, her eyes searching his. "When I first heard you and Arnold talking about a D.A. who was investigating Daddy's death, I felt like God was finally answering my prayers. That he had sent someone to make right a terrible wrong. I've got to help."

He took a deep breath. It was important to stay calm if he was going to dissuade her. "First of all, that deputy D.A. we were talking about has been arrested herself—on drug charges."

Sally's eyebrows raised in surprise. "Arrested?"

"Yes. So there isn't even an ongoing investigation at the moment."

"I didn't know about that. But she isn't the only D.A. down there . . ." She stopped in midstream, as if she'd said more than she'd intended.

Michael didn't want to hurt his sister, but her stubbornness was forcing him into a corner. He took another deep breath and exhaled. "The real problem, Sally, is that once you tell the D.A. or the cops about what you think you saw or heard, there will be a trial and you'll have to take the witness stand."

"I know. I'm trying not to be scared."

"That's not all. Although it's not your fault, you've been hospitalized a number of times. When you're on the stand, the other side will bring up everything. They'll make it look like you're crazy." He reached for her hand. "Please Sal, don't do it. I couldn't stand to watch them hurt you that way."

Her eyes had grown large and fearful. "They can ask me about those kinds of things?"

"Yes," he said, nodding. "Before they finish with you it will look like you made up this story about George and Mother—or worse, that you're hallucinating. It will only cause everyone in the family more pain." He squeezed her hand. "Please. I'm your brother, I love you. I couldn't stand to watch them rip you apart. Don't do this."

She wiped her tears away with the back of her hand. "It isn't right for George to get away with Daddy's murder."

"Look at me, Sally," Michael said.

Reluctantly, she looked up at him.

"Your father loved you, Sally. He wouldn't want people to make fun of you."

"I don't know . . ." she mumbled, shaking her head.

He could see that she was beginning to have second thoughts. As bad as he felt about making her cry, he had to keep on pressing his advantage. "Save yourself all that pain and embarrassment, Sally, or you'll end up miserable and sorry."

"I guess I've got to think some more about it," she finally conceded, unable to meet his gaze.

23

≈

DURING THE WEEK prior to the local primary there had been a flurry of last-minute campaign appearances for Thomas. It seemed as if his campaign manager, Dale Jensen, had scheduled him back-to-back all over the city. But Thomas had no choice since the most recent polls showed that Frank Sanchez was doing better than anyone had expected. Thomas needed to get a 50.1 percent majority to win and avoid a runoff, and that wasn't an easy task when there were four challengers siphoning off his votes.

Now, on the day of the primary, the thought of having to wait until the general election in November to have his future decided was too awful to contemplate. Usually, Thomas loved campaigning. But with Roberta so sick and all the other problems on his mind, he really couldn't face another five months of constant appearances and back-slapping.

It was after eight o'clock and the first returns would soon be coming in. Thomas felt bad for not being at the hospital with Roberta, but she had insisted that he wait at his campaign headquarters with all the people who had worked so diligently for him over the last year.

Thomas finally broke away from a crowd of well-wishers and made his way to the hotel suite they had taken on an upper floor. Then he sat down on the bed and called the hospital.

His daughter answered the phone. Although he was glad that Roberta was not alone, the fact that Alexandra was at the hospital made him feel even worse. It seemed that lately she was always there for her mother, while he wasn't. "How's she doing?"

"She's sleeping. I've been here several hours, but she hasn't woken up."

A feeling of dread lay heavy in Thomas's stomach. "What does the doctor say?"

"That she's worn out."

"Has she made any decisions yet about the transfusions or another round of chemotherapy?" he asked.

"No. She's still thinking about it."

Thomas exhaled loudly. Somehow, he had to convince Roberta to keep trying. "Listen, the polls just closed a few minutes ago, and I broke away to call your mother." He rubbed his tired eyes. "If she wakes up, beep me, okay?"

"I will."

After he hung up, Thomas massaged his throbbing temples. He prayed that he'd won the primary. If not, he wasn't sure he'd know how to cope.

Alexandra came awake with a start and realized she'd fallen asleep in the chair next to her mother's bed. The television was on low. A nurse was in the room, and her mother was also awake. Glancing quickly at her watch, Alexandra couldn't believe that almost two hours had passed. "Hi, Mom. How are you doing?" she asked.

"So-so." Roberta inclined her head toward the television set. "Are there any returns yet?"

It was unbelievable, thought Alexandra. Here her mother was facing her own death, and yet her first concern was whether or not Thomas was winning in the primary. "I'm not sure. Let me turn the volume up. Dad called. He wanted me to page him the moment you awoke."

"Would you do that for me?" her mother asked. Her voice was very weak.

Nodding, Alexandra punched in the numbers. After the beep, she punched in more numbers and then hung up.

A few minutes later the phone rang. Alexandra answered it and handed the phone to her mother.

"Hello, darling. How's it going?" There was a big smile on Roberta's face as if from somewhere deep inside herself she had summoned all her strength to sound upbeat for her husband. It was an amazing transformation, thought Alexandra.

Roberta's smile quickly faded as if she'd heard

some bad news. "Oh Thomas, I'm so sorry. Well, it's early yet. Maybe the tide will turn."

They spoke a few minutes more, then Roberta wished him good luck, told him she loved him and hung up. She took a tissue and wiped her brow before reaching over for her daughter's hand. "The news isn't good. Your father is well ahead, but it doesn't look as if he's going to get the majority he needs. The other candidates are taking away too many votes and Sanchez is doing better than anticipated." She paused. "Your father will be devastated if he has to face Frank Sanchez in the general election."

"He'll get over it," Alexandra said, with a reassuring smile. "You know Dad. He'll come back fighting."

"No," Roberta said, shaking her head. "I don't think you understand, Alexandra. Your father's only human. He won't be able to handle so much loss at one time."

Realizing that her mother was referring to her own death, Alexandra fell quiet. "Have you made any decisions on transfusions or another round of the experimental chemotherapy?"

"Not yet," said Roberta, focusing her gaze on her daughter. "What do you think?"

The question was one Alexandra had been expecting, but it still took her breath away. "Honestly, Mom, I don't know what I would do if I were in your place. I want you to live more than anything in the world, but . . ." Her words trailed off as she was suddenly overwhelmed with emotion.

"I know, darling." Roberta smiled sadly. "This is going to be really rough on you, too."

"Don't worry about me or Dad. For God's sake, worry about yourself and what you're facing. That's more than enough for any human being to handle."

"I can't help it. I love you. I love your father. It breaks my heart to see you both so upset."

"Aren't you angry, Mom? Don't you feel that life's unfair? I mean, you're only fifty-three years old. That's so young!" The words pouring out of Alexandra's mouth were laced with bitterness. Knowing that it wasn't fair to vent all of her own feelings in front of her mother, she clenched her fists by her sides.

"No. I'm not angry," Roberta replied with a placid expression on her face. "What good would that do?"

Alexandra wanted to scream, *Get angry! It will be good for you,* but she didn't. "You know, Dad wants me to convince you to try another round of chemotherapy. He'd really like you to give it one more chance."

"Yes. He's told me. It's just that I was so sick last time, I barely got through it. I don't want to feel that horrible again. And the doctor wasn't very encouraging." Roberta stopped to rest for a few seconds. "I want to be coherent in my last . . . weeks or . . . months." Her eyes were clear as they met those of her daughter. "And I want to be home."

"Is that your decision then?"

"I'm not sure," Roberta said. "I need some more time."

"Sure, Mom. Take as long as you need." Alexandra patted her mother's shoulder. "Whatever you decide, I'm behind you one hundred percent. And if you just want to talk about it some more, that's okay, too."

"That means . . . a lot to me." Roberta sighed and seemed to shrink back even farther into the pillows. "I'm very tired. I think I'm going to sleep now. Why don't you go home and get a good night's rest yourself? I'll see you tomorrow."

The next morning, wearing her silk lounging pajamas and sitting on the edge of her large king-size bed, Lorna listened to her son Michael on the telephone.

"How can my own daughter want to see me in prison?" Lorna said in dismay when he was through explaining that Sally wanted to go to the authorities.

"Now, Mom," Michael responded, "you know that will never happen."

Lorna was so upset she barely heard him. She ran her hand over her cream-colored satin spread. "How can Sally even contemplate betraying us this way?"

"Try and see it from her point of view," Michael suggested in a soothing voice. "Sally feels that you betrayed her by marrying George."

"That's not fair," Lorna complained, picking up the phone as she began pacing her bedroom. "She's been saying that for years. Wasn't I entitled to some happiness after your father died?"

"Of course you were," he replied. "Look, Mom, I told you because I felt you should know, but I've already spoken to Sally myself. Hopefully I've convinced her not to do it. So don't say anything, because she'll feel like we're all ganging up on her."

"How can I keep quiet?" Lorna said, her voice becoming shrill, "when my future and George's future are both threatened."

"I know. But I've also been in close contact with Arnold. He's doing his best to discourage Sally from going forward with her plans."

"Tell Arnold he must be *firm.*"

"He knows, Mom. Don't worry. I'm sure he'll handle it. Let's give him a little time."

The moment Lorna hung up with Michael, she dialed George. "Please get my husband on the phone right now," she said to the receptionist. Told that he was with a patient, Lorna became insistent. "Tell him it's an emergency. I must speak to him."

When George finally came on the line, she explained what had happened. "If Michael and Arnold are talking to Sally," George counseled, "let's give her a day or two to come to her senses. I'm sure when she thinks things over she'll change her mind."

Lorna was in no mood for a reasonable approach. "How can you be so calm when our entire lives are hanging in the balance?"

"Because worrying and wringing our hands won't do any good," he said. "You know your daughter, Lorna, she sometimes gets hysterical, throws tantrums—then she calms down. Didn't you say that she was just in the hospital again?"

"Yes. Arnold put her there because she was having those nightmares of hers, and he was afraid she'd hurt herself. But Sally insisted on being released."

"She's just having a bad time of it. The best thing for all of us to do is to ignore her when she gets like this," he advised.

After she had finished talking with her husband, Lorna realized she was shaking. Quickly, she rummaged through her drawers until she found an old, crushed pack of cigarettes. She couldn't even remember how many times now she'd tried to give up the habit. But under circumstances like this, she had to have something to steady her nerves.

Taking several deep drags, she felt the smoke travel down into her lungs and then flow into her body. The cigarette acted like a sedative and soon she could feel herself relaxing.

She couldn't make up her mind what to do. Was George right this time? It was so hard for Lorna to sit by and wait for others to take care of things. Flushing the remains of her cigarette down the toilet, she strode to her closet and began dressing.

There was a surprised look on Sally's face when she saw Lorna standing at her front door. "Hello, Mommy," she said, taking a step backward into the house.

Lorna nodded at her daughter and walked into

the small living room, where she glanced around. "You've rearranged the furniture?"

"Yes," Sally said. "Do you like it?"

From her daughter's eager expression, Lorna surmised that it had been Sally's idea to change things. "Very much," she said, smiling. "Maybe you should take some decorating classes at the junior college. You seem to have a talent for it."

Sally's whole face lit up with pleasure. "Can I get you something?"

Lorna would have relished a real drink but didn't say so. "Something cold would be nice." She reached into her alligator bag to remove her cigarettes.

"Arnold doesn't allow smoking in our house," Sally advised timidly.

"Very well, then let's go outside," Lorna suggested, heading for the sliding glass doors to the patio.

"Sure. Give me a minute and I'll be right back with the drinks," said Sally.

Dusting off one of the patio chairs with her hand, Lorna then sat down and lit her cigarette. This house depressed her. When her daughter had been born, she'd had high hopes for her. Such a pretty child. But Sally had been difficult and highstrung from the time she was a little girl.

The first time she met Arnold, Lorna had shuddered at the thought of Sally married to a man so much older than herself. Then Lorna saw what a calming influence he seemed to have on her daughter, and slowly became accustomed to the idea. It wasn't actually a bad arrangement. Arnold was a lot easier to handle than Sally.

Sally came back carrying two cans of diet soda. She handed one to her mother and then sat down in the chair next to her. "It's nice to see you. If you had told me you were coming, I could have gotten us something for lunch."

"That sounds lovely. Maybe another time. I can't stay long today," Lorna said. She took a deep drag on her cigarette and blew out the smoke. "I've actually come to talk to you about something important."

"Oh?" Sally tensed.

"Michael says you're planning on going to the D.A. with some story of what you *think* you saw between George and me after your father's death. Is that true?"

"I'm not sure yet," Sally admitted. "But I don't want to talk about it."

Her daughter jutted her chin out in the same stubborn way she'd done since she was a child. It made Lorna angry, but she cautioned herself to stay cool and composed. "Sally, you just can't do this. It will cause terrible problems for both George and me."

"I have to do . . . what I feel is right," Sally said, beginning to stutter.

"Be reasonable, Sally. You know George is a very wealthy man. And I've always intended to leave most of our money to you because Michael does well enough on his own." Lorna took several more long drags of her cigarette before she pointed to the house and the cluttered backyard. "You and Arnold have been struggling for years, and we've always helped out, haven't we?"

"Yes. But this doesn't have anything to do with money."

"That's very naive of you," Lorna said, shaking her head. "Families do things for one another. We help out as much as we can. In return, we ask for nothing but kindness and consideration. Surely you can understand that if you tell that crazy story of yours it would be like a slap across our faces?"

"I don't want to hurt you, Mommy. But I've been sick for a long time and—"

"Yes," Lorna said, interrupting her. "That's another reason you shouldn't do this. You have no idea what they'll do to you if you're forced to testify. It will only make you sicker, Sally, I can promise you that."

"Try to understand," Sally pleaded, her voice becoming high pitched. "I want to get better. And the only way to do that is to get rid of the secrets I've been carrying around. Can't you see that?"

"No, I can't," Lorna said, finally losing her patience. Her daughter's refusal to listen to reason infuriated her. She reached out and took Sally's arm, forcing Sally to look her in the eye. "You're being foolish. Listen to me and you can have anything you want. Anything your heart desires."

Sally flinched. "I don't care about your money, Mommy," she asserted, standing her ground.

"Your husband cares about money," snapped

Lorna. "That's for sure. If I didn't subsidize Arnold on a regular basis, do you think he'd stay here?"

"Arnold . . . loves me," Sally said, her voice wavering. "And I don't want George's money. It's dirty money. He's a murderer!"

"Don't say that," Lorna ordered in a harsh voice. "You don't remember what you saw. You couldn't. You were only a child."

Unable to argue with her mother, Sally started to cry. "I do remember!" she lashed out. "And maybe you deserve to be punished, too. You're an . . . an . . . unfit mother." Sobbing harder now, Sally buried her face in her hands.

Lorna gazed at her daughter. If this had been Michael, she would have been down on her hands and knees kissing him—begging him to forgive her. She couldn't bear for him to be angry with her. But with Sally, she never seemed to know what to do. No matter how hard she tried she couldn't communicate with her.

"I'm going to the bathroom," she said. "In the meantime, try and pull yourself together." Lorna stubbed out her cigarette and went inside.

As she passed through her daughter's bedroom, Lorna saw a picture of Jeffrey next to the bed. It was amazing how much Sally looked like her father. Jeffrey had never listened to her either. In many ways it had always seemed as if Sally was much more Jeffrey's child than hers.

24

THOMAS HAD WATCHED all night as the returns trickled in, hoping against hope that the tide would turn in his favor. Dale, in the meantime, had muttered under his breath every time more results were posted. Even though there was only a slim chance of getting the 50.1 percent majority Thomas needed to preclude a runoff in the general election in November, he'd waited most of the next day too, before making any kind of a statement.

Finally, he was forced to face the inevitable conclusion. Frank Sanchez had garnered enough votes to deny Thomas an outright victory in the primary and to ensure that there would be a runoff between the two men. For Thomas, it was a humiliating turn of events.

"What's done is done," Dale said, trying to put the best spin possible on the results. "Remember, the other three candidates got votes that rightfully belonged to you. They'll never switch over to

Sanchez. The election in November will be only a
formality. We'll knock him dead."

Too upset to assess the situation clearly, Thomas
felt bitter. "All I know," he said, "is that when we
started this campaign, no one had ever heard of
Sanchez or the other candidates. Somehow Sanchez
managed to turn that around."

"There are only two reasons Sanchez got his
name in the papers and both of them fall squarely
on the shoulders of your daughter," Dale said,
scowling.

Thomas shot his campaign manager a disgruntled look. He didn't like being reminded of how his
daughter's hiring and subsequent arrest had under-
mined his position.

"What do you want to do?" Dale asked.

"I sure as hell don't feel like making any kind of
a concession speech," Thomas said. "Frank didn't
garner more votes than I did. All he got were
enough to keep me from having a clear majority."

Dale handed Thomas a sheet of paper. "I've
written a script for you. I think you should follow
it."

A short time later, Thomas stood in front of the
newspeople who had gathered at the D.A.'s office.
"I'm disappointed by the results," he grudgingly
admitted. "Sometimes when there are choices between too many qualified candidates, a runoff is inevitable."

He straightened his shoulders and forced himself to sound positive and upbeat. "I'm confident
that when the race is narrowed down to only two

people—Sanchez and myself—the people will re-elect me with a resounding majority." Then, smiling and waving as if he'd just won, he left the room.

"Sally," Arnold Potter said, trying not to lose his patience. "Stop being so difficult, and look at this from your mother's point of view."

"I don't want to," she protested.

Arnold didn't know what to do about his wife's behavior. Although she had cried for hours after her mother's visit, Sally was still intractable. Lorna had called Arnold at the university and threatened to cut off all financial aid if he didn't stop Sally from going to the authorities and talking to them about her father's death.

"I want you to tell Mommy that we don't want their damn money," Sally insisted, her voice becoming shrill.

"You know that's not a good idea."

"Why do we take money from them anyway?" she asked.

He sighed. His wife didn't know the first thing about finances. Arnold had never been at one school long enough to get tenure. Almost sixty, he had to provide for his own retirement. And then there was his mother. Without Arnold's help, she'd never be able to live in her own small home a few miles from them. Arnold's father had been a drunk and had died penniless, leaving his wife and child destitute. George and Lorna had been very generous. He couldn't risk alienating them.

"You know I have to help my mother, Sally," he

said, sternly. "You're only thinking of yourself. You're being very selfish."

"I'm not. Besides, I can always get a job," she announced, her eyes brightening. "Doctor Abbott said there's no reason why I can't work."

Arnold didn't like the things that this new doctor was telling his wife. Doctor Abbott obviously couldn't see that Sally was manipulating her. "It's too soon to talk about working yet," he cautioned, a frown furrowing his brow. "And I spoke to Doctor Winters. He's feeling much better and he's starting to see his private patients again. He has a Tuesday and Thursday night opening for you and I told him we'd take it."

"No," she said, shaking her head stubbornly. "I'm not going back to him. I really like Doctor Abbott; she makes me feel good about myself."

"I don't believe Doctor Abbott is experienced enough. Your emotional problems are very deep— very complicated. You can't simply put a bandage on them and then pretend that they don't exist."

"That's not what she does. Come with me one time." Sally's face became animated as she looked up at her husband. "You'll see how smart she is. Nice too. I feel really comfortable with her."

"Well, you won't be able to see anyone without your mother and George's help. These therapy sessions cost a ton of money, you know."

"I already said I'll get a job."

Arnold debated whether or not to become even tougher. "Sally, you're being very unreasonable." He put his hand on his heart and a worried expression on his face. "I haven't been feeling well. You don't want me to have a heart attack now, do you?"

She exhaled loudly, her shoulders slumping. "No."

"Then listen," he said softly, smiling at her. "I know what's best for you. Forget telling anyone what you remember about your father's death. It's a foolish idea."

"It's not. George is a murderer."

He wasn't sure if that was true or not. Nor did he really care. He had more important things on his mind. "It was twenty years ago," he reminded her. "Let it be."

"I can't," she said simply, her eyes pleading for his understanding.

Sally was pushing him too far. Like a child, she just didn't comprehend the consequences of her actions. He suddenly sat down in a chair, sweat breaking out on his forehead. "I don't feel good. I think something's wrong."

Instead of becoming contrite as she usually did when he played on her sympathy, she looked even more determined. "Then call the doctor," she said firmly, as she squared her small shoulders. "Seeing that my Daddy's killer goes to jail means a lot to me. You know that. Why can't you just, one time, be on my side and stand up to Mommy?"

Arnold could see he'd have to change tactics again. "I am on your side. You know that. I don't think your mother should have made you cry or have threatened to cut you out of her will."

"Then do something about it."

"I will," he promised in a soothing voice. "Just let things cool down a bit, okay?"

Her eyes wouldn't meet his but he could feel her resolve weakening. Standing up, Arnold drew Sally's rigid body close to his own and patted her head. "That's my good girl. I knew you'd listen to reason."

George Collins drove through the gates of his English Tudor residence in San Marino. He then pulled his Bentley into the large four-car garage, where he took a deep breath before turning off the motor.

Back in Texas, where George had grown up, his father had periodically labored in the oil fields, although he spent most of his life out of work and on welfare. George's beautiful but unstable mother had deserted her family when he was only ten years old. He'd worked hard to get where he was today, and living in this exclusive area of the San Gabriel Valley was proof to him that he had made it. The idea of losing everything was terrifying.

He went directly to his den, where he poured himself a large Crown Royal on the rocks. After a few gulps, he felt the liquor take the edge off his worries.

Upstairs, he walked through a sitting room decorated in pale yellows with accents of light blue and into Lorna's cream-colored bedroom. A few years before, Lorna had decided that because he snored too loudly they should sleep in separate bedrooms connected by a shared sitting room. So she'd spent hundreds of thousands of dollars, first gutting and then redoing the entire upstairs of their house, including adding on several thousand square feet.

"Lorna?" he called out.

"I'm in the bath," she responded.

In the huge marble bathroom he found his wife soaking in a bubble bath. The air smelled like gardenias. A bottle of chilled white wine was perched on the ledge next to her, along with several different colorful jars of lotions and oils.

Lorna's dark hair was pinned up on top of her head. Her face was flushed from the heat of the water. As she lay submerged under a thick layer of bubbles, he pictured every inch of her still-lovely body. She smiled and tilted her wineglass toward him.

He held up his own glass in response before bending over to kiss her cheek. "How was your day?"

Her face clouded over. "Not one of my best. I had words with Sally."

"We agreed you were going to leave Sally alone for a few days."

"I know. But the more I thought about it, the more I couldn't wait." She lifted her other arm and swept a lock of hair from her forehead. "I had to tell her how I felt. I just hope I got through to her. Stubborn little fool." She took a sip of her wine.

George thought about Alexandra Locke's visit to his office the other day. He still hadn't told Lorna. Now might be a good time. He removed his jacket, undid his tie and positioned his broad back against the wall. "I've got some upsetting news of my own."

Her clear green eyes gazed up at him. "What's that?"

As George described the prosecutor's visit to his office, he saw the look of incredulity on Lorna's face.

"I can't believe that woman found a letter you meant to mail to me all those years ago," she muttered, shaking her head.

"It's spooky," he agreed. "When I heard those words I had written back then, I almost had a stroke."

Lorna's mouth tightened as he explained what had happened during the rest of Alexandra Locke's visit. "You actually *admitted* you wrote that letter?" she said, disbelieving.

"No. But I didn't deny it either."

Lorna's shoulders stiffened as she sat up straighter in the tub so that her breasts were now above the waterline. "You have to be more careful, George," she scolded. "We're talking about a murder charge, not something trivial like what you had for lunch."

"I know. Yet the more I think about it, the more I feel we don't have to worry."

She raised one of her dark eyebrows. "Why is that?"

"Since Alexandra Locke's arrest, no one is going to believe what she says. Remember, I've spent the last twenty years building both my practice and my reputation. I don't think people will be so quick to assume I'm a murderer."

"I hope that's true," she retorted. "But we have to look at this realistically. What if the worst happens, and they charge you with Jeffrey's murder?"

He tried to sound casual. "I'll hire myself the best lawyers that money can buy. There isn't a shred of physical evidence against me, Lorna. They'll have no choice but to acquit me."

"Don't you think—"

"Stop," he cut in, waving his hand to ward off her words. "I already told you, you don't have to worry."

Her brow was creased. "And what about me?"

"You were home at the time. There isn't any evidence to connect you to Jeffrey's death."

"But if Sally tells them that she saw and heard the two of us . . ." her voice trailed off.

"She was nine years old," he countered, shaking his head. "She's not sure about any of it." He kept his voice upbeat and full of confidence. "As a precaution, I called Walter Underhill. He said Ms. Locke would have a hell of a time getting anything I'd said into evidence. She didn't come to visit me in any official capacity. And there were no witnesses, so she can't even prove that our conversation took place."

Lorna didn't look convinced. "What if she taperecorded you?"

"I don't think that she did, but that would be inadmissible, too. Most likely it would be my word against hers, and I'll insist that she made the whole thing up."

"What else did Walter say?"

"That smart people never talk to the cops without their lawyer present." He gave her a meaningful glance before he took a few swallows of his drink.

"That makes a lot of sense." For a moment, Lorna was thoughtful. "And what did he say about the letter?"

"That's not going to be a problem either," he stated, exhaling loudly. "Walter explained that we would hire our own handwriting experts to contradict what the prosecution's experts say. It then becomes a battle of our experts against theirs. In that case, it will be easy for the jury to find reasonable doubt, and I'll get off."

Lorna's dark eyebrows slanted downward in a frown. "Let's just hope it turns out to be that simple."

25

~

"LOOK, DADDY," JENNY giggled. "I'm doing it all by myself."

Patrick smiled. It was a Sunday afternoon, and he was working on the couch in Nancy's condominium in Santa Monica. Over the top of his briefcase, he could see Jenny and Nancy in the open kitchen. His daughter, wearing a frilly apron, was standing on a chair, cutting slices of cookie dough and putting them onto a greased baking sheet.

Nancy, meanwhile, was busy wiping the granite countertop with a sponge. It would be so much simpler if she just waited until they were all through before cleaning, but Nancy was compulsive when it came to tidying up. Because of that, Patrick never felt at home in Nancy's apartment. It was also too modern for his taste. The glass, chrome and polished surfaces made it very sterile, especially for a child. He preferred lots of big comfortable pieces of furniture that he could put his feet on, and that children could jump on and not ruin.

"Daddy, look!" Jenny's excited voice demanded his attention.

She was holding a cookie in the shape of a large animal.

"An elephant?"

"No, silly," she said with mock disapproval. "Guess again."

"A gorilla?"

"Right!" she squealed. "I'm making giraffes and lions, too. Want to see?" Before he could respond, she scooped them up in her hands and started running toward him.

"Don't take those into the living room," Nancy yelled. "I don't want food everywhere."

His daughter looked crestfallen as she stopped midway between the two rooms.

"I'll come there," Patrick suggested, getting up quickly and escorting his daughter back to the kitchen.

Nancy was already on her hands and knees, scooping up the sprinkles and powdered sugar that had fallen on her charcoal carpet.

After exclaiming how beautiful all of her cookies were, Patrick removed Jenny's soiled apron and lifted her up onto the sink to wash her hands and face. With the wet edge of a dishtowel, he also wiped down her corduroy pants and shirt.

He appreciated Nancy's efforts. She'd been in the kitchen for over an hour, patiently helping Jenny mix the ingredients and place the shapes onto the cookie sheets before putting them into the oven to bake. Yet Nancy didn't look like she was enjoying herself. Her laugh seemed forced and the lines around her mouth were tense. It was almost as if she were trying too hard. Nancy said she wanted to be a mother, but he sometimes felt it was more the idea she liked, rather than the reality.

Patrick had a hard time trying to picture the three of them living together as a family. Maybe he was just being overprotective where Jenny was concerned. He'd always envisioned finding a woman who would be calm and loving with his daughter—not one who would cause his stomach muscles to tighten every time Jenny's voice became a high-pitched squeal. It just seemed that whenever they were all together, he didn't relax.

Jenny's mother hadn't been a control freak like Nancy—just restless and totally uninterested in raising a child. Later, Patrick had realized that he'd ignored all the signs. Julie had been a wanderer who didn't want to put down roots and have a family. That was one of the reasons why Nancy had been so attractive to him. Not only was she extremely bright, capable and pretty too, she was also someone you could count on.

While Jenny was in the bathroom, Nancy saw her chance. She went over to Patrick and put her arms around his neck, inhaling the fragrance of his cologne. "Why don't we put a video on for Jenny so that you and I can take a little 'nap.' "

"I don't think that's a good idea." Untangling

her arms, he smiled as if to lessen the impact of his refusal.

She tried to make light of the situation. "Surely adults are allowed to sleep together, aren't they?"

Instead of answering her right away, he took a deep breath.

"Well . . . aren't they?" she asked again.

"Of course. And if we were married, that would be different. I just don't want to confuse her."

Nancy crossed her arms over her chest and looked him squarely in the eye. "Patrick, I'm getting tired of this. I want an answer. We either get engaged and set a wedding date, or we stop seeing each other."

"Please don't do this, Nancy," he said quietly. "I'm just not ready to make that decision."

She felt a stab of hurt. "Is it because you're still in love with your old girlfriend?"

His eyes widened in surprise. "Alexandra?"

"What other old girlfriend is there?"

"This has nothing to do with her," he protested, shaking his head.

Gazing at him with narrowed eyes, she wondered if he was telling her the truth. She'd never known Patrick to lie, but then they'd never been faced with someone from the past before.

The door to the bathroom opened and Jenny came skipping out.

"I'm hungry," she said, with a shy smile. "Aren't we going to CPK like you promised, Daddy?"

He glanced up at Nancy with an apologetic smile. "I told Jenny I'd take her to California Pizza

Kitchen for dinner. Can we finish our conversation later?"

Nancy nodded, although she wasn't happy about it. What choice did she really have? Forcing him to fight with her in front of his child would only push him further away.

"Would you like to join us?" Patrick's brown eyes were fixed on her.

Eating dinner at a noisy pizza joint wasn't appealing to her. Nancy preferred soft lights, fine wine and a more sophisticated atmosphere. But she knew Patrick would never go back on a promise he'd made to his daughter. "No," she said, shaking her head. "I've got work to do. Tomorrow's an early day. The two of you go ahead."

"What will you do for dinner?" he asked.

Although Patrick looked genuinely concerned, Nancy was sure his daughter's sigh was one of relief. "Don't worry. I've got stuff in the refrigerator."

He gave Nancy a peck on the cheek, then turned to his daughter. "C'mon, Cookie Monster," he teased. "Let's scram. I'm starving."

Something was going to have to give, Nancy fumed to herself as she watched Patrick and Jenny leave. She didn't care whether she was pushing him before he was ready. She wanted a commitment, and she wasn't about to let some girlfriend from the past mess up all her plans.

Sally was terribly disappointed when Arnold refused to stand up to Lorna about the way she'd treated her. First Arnold had put Sally in the hospital against her will and now this. In the past, she had always given in to Arnold's demands, but this time she couldn't.

During her mother's visit, while Lorna had been in the bathroom, Sally had seized the opportunity to pilfer some money out of her mother's purse.

When Thursday came, she dressed carefully in her best skirt and sweater, and even put on a pair of low-heeled shoes. After tucking her mother's hundred-dollar bill into her bra, Sally walked to the small grocery store a few blocks from her house and used the pay phone to call for a cab.

By the time the cab arrived fifteen minutes later, Sally had chewed the inside of her cheek raw. She gave the driver the address, and settled back into the uncomfortable seat for the forty-minute freeway ride to downtown L.A.

Elizabeth had been happy with the way things were going. The dinner at Frank's house on that Saturday evening had been a success. She'd been accepted by everyone there as a valuable member of Frank's support team. And then Frank had done really well in the primary, forcing Thomas to face him in a runoff. She was beginning to be more confident that Frank could actually win in November, and equally sure that if that happened, Frank would reward her with a top spot in his administration.

Now, as Elizabeth sat in her office, she tried to be objective about the pale, extremely nervous

young woman facing her—Sally McGrath Potter—
and the story that she had just related.

"You're saying that about two months ago, after
hearing that Alexandra Locke was reinvestigating
your father's death, you called her here at the
D.A.'s offices?"

"Yes," Sally nodded.

"Are you absolutely sure it was Ms. Locke you
spoke to?"

"Yes," Sally said again. "I asked for her and
when she picked up the phone she gave her name."

Elizabeth gazed down at the legal pad in front of
her. "And you told Ms. Locke what you've just told
me?"

"Not all of it," Sally explained. "I told her that
my daddy, I mean my father, Jeffrey McGrath,
didn't die in an accident like everyone says. But
that my stepfather, George Collins, really killed
him." Sudden anger lit her eyes. "But I had to hang
up before I could tell her why George had never
been arrested."

"I see." Elizabeth wrote down a few more notes.

"Ms. Locke also came to see me one day at my
house."

The prosecutor's eyebrows rose. "She did?"

"Yes." Sally twisted her hands in her lap as she
spoke. "But my husband came home while she was
there, and he wouldn't let me talk to her."

"And the rest of your family has also discouraged you from coming forward about what you remember?"

"Right." Sally looked like she might be on the

verge of tears as she stared directly at Elizabeth.
"But I just couldn't keep my mouth shut any
longer," she said, her lower lip quivering. "My father was murdered. George killed him and he
should be punished for it."

Tapping her fingers on the legal pad, Elizabeth
looked for discrepancies in Sally's story. "And you
never spoke to your mother about what you saw?"

Sally shook her head. "No."

"Why not?"

"I was afraid," the young woman replied in a
small frightened voice.

"Of whom?" Elizabeth prodded, scanning
Sally's face for clues.

"I'm not sure," Sally admitted, with a large sigh.
"My mother was marrying George. I tried to stop
her, but she wouldn't listen." Looking miserable,
Sally started to cry. "I guess I was afraid of him."

Elizabeth sat there waiting for the young woman
to regain her control. "You said you had a close relationship with your brother. Why didn't you tell
him?"

"I couldn't," Sally said, her voice sounding
choked. "Michael would have told my mother."

Elizabeth recalled the argument she'd overheard
between Alexandra and her father. At the time, she
had thought they were talking about two separate
cases. One called McGrath and another one called
Collins. But as hard as she'd tried, she hadn't been
able to find out anything on either matter.

This young woman's maiden name was Mc-
Grath and her stepfather, whom she kept insisting

had actually murdered her father, was named Collins. The case had to be one and the same. What Elizabeth had heard Thomas and Alexandra arguing about had to be this case.

"Are you going to arrest George?" asked Sally, with a hopeful look on her tear-stained face.

"If your story checks out, your stepfather is going to be one sorry man," Elizabeth promised, feeling her skin tingling with excitement. If Sally had told her the truth, and if her own hunches were correct, Elizabeth might have found the means for assuring not only Thomas Kendell's downfall, but her own future at this office as well.

As soon as Sally McGrath Potter left, Elizabeth had done some more investigating on her own. Then, too impatient to wait until tomorrow to tell Frank what she'd found out, she'd convinced him to meet her at a deli in West Los Angeles.

It was nice to have the company. Elizabeth usually ate dinner in a restaurant alone or picked something up and took it home to eat while she worked. She skewered a piece of liver, smothering it in grilled onions before putting the fork into her mouth. "Sure you don't want anything more than pie and coffee?"

"No thanks," Frank said. "I just finished a huge dinner at home." He patted his stomach.

Elizabeth dipped one of her french fries in ketchup and popped it into her mouth. Frank had been married to the same woman for over twenty years and had four children. Now that she'd been there, it was easy for her to picture him going home every night to a loving family and a home-cooked meal. *Not like me,* she mused.

"Let me get this straight," Frank muttered, as he put his coffee cup down on the Formica table. "You heard an argument between the D.A. and his daughter regarding an old case? Then a young lady shows up at your office and tells you about the very same case?"

"I know it sounds like a coincidence," she admitted. "But it's really very simple. This Sally McGrath Potter heard Alexandra Locke was reinvestigating her father's death, so she called her and told her that George Collins was a murderer. When Alexandra went to see her, Sally's husband showed up and ordered her off his premises. When Sally finally worked up the courage to contact her again, she discovered Alexandra was on leave, so the receptionist turned her over to me." Elizabeth didn't mention that she had actually been looking for the two cases for quite a while—although she hadn't yet found them at that point—before her meeting with Sally. "Are you following?"

"Yeah. But wasn't this Sally just a kid at the time of her father's death?"

"Yes. But Sally was very clear about what she had seen and heard." *Even clearer after I finished with her,* thought Elizabeth. She gestured with her fork. "After Sally left my office, I went over to the Hall of Records and checked the archives. A couple of months ago, Alexandra signed out a case called

Collins which has never been returned." She raised her eyebrows for emphasis. "And it wasn't in the files that were turned over to me. So I searched Alexandra's entire office, from top to bottom. Nothing."

"How did you happen to hear this argument between Alexandra and her father?" Frank asked, a suspicious look on his face.

Something told her to slightly alter the facts. "They were in the hallway and didn't see me."

"Okay. Go on."

"When I couldn't find the file, I figured Alexandra might have made some notes." Elizabeth decided to veer from the truth again. "When I told her secretary that I was looking for notes on a case of Alexandra's I was handling, Geena gave me some boxes of stuff she'd packed up."

He frowned. "Are you sure those weren't Alexandra's personal papers?"

Knowing that Frank would be livid if he discovered she'd removed Alexandra's personal things from Geena's car by promising to drop the boxes off at Alexandra's house, she lied. "No. It was all work-related stuff."

Frank's hesitancy made Elizabeth uncomfortable as she went on with her story. But she couldn't stop now. "What I found is dynamite, Frank. It's the ammunition you need to beat Thomas."

He still appeared unsure. It was maddening. Elizabeth could see that Frank wasn't going to become the next D.A. without a push from his friends. "Let me tell you the substance of what

I've found. Then you can decide what to do about it."

"Go on," he said, taking another gulp of his coffee.

She proceeded to give him the details of Erica Collins's confession and subsequent events as contained in Alexandra's handwritten notes.

When she was finished, he seemed stunned. "Erica told Alexandra that Thomas Kendell took a bribe to cover up a murder?"

Her eyes glistened. "Right."

"And you're sure that this Potter woman also mentioned Kendell specifically?"

She nodded. It was a small lie. Sally hadn't known the name of the prosecutor in charge of the case, just that a deputy D.A. had been bribed. But Erica had clearly said it was Thomas. And then there was the argument between Thomas and Alexandra that Elizabeth had overheard. The D.A. wouldn't have ordered his daughter to forget about the case unless he, or someone on his watch, had been somehow implicated. All of the evidence pointed to it being Thomas.

"It will take more than Sally's recollections and Erica's statements to convict George Collins of murder and Thomas Kendell of accepting a bribe. And I'm not sure any of it would even be admissible in court."

"A lot of it should be," she countered. "And this is just the beginning. Obviously, there has to be a further investigation to turn up more evidence."

He still appeared unconvinced.

Her frustration was growing. "You forced our illustrious leader into a runoff when the chances of that happening were nil. I heard the press conference. I noticed that you didn't hesitate to use the issue of Thomas's daughter to help you." She exhaled loudly. "So what's the problem with using *this* stuff against Thomas?"

He looked offended by her suggestion that he had used Alexandra's legal problems to beat Thomas. "I've said from the beginning it was wrong for the D.A. to hire his daughter. As for Alexandra's arrest, a reporter asked me a question, and I replied. I didn't even set up the press conference. The reporters called us."

Elizabeth swallowed her annoyance. She wasn't about to tell him her part in arranging that press conference.

"I just don't want to get into something that might backfire," he added.

She decided to try another approach. "Look Frank, I admire you." She stopped and smiled at him warmly. "But again, I think you're missing the point here. Alexandra came into possession of some evidence relating to a crime and a cover-up that happened twenty years ago involving her father. She looked up the case and did some investigating—and then what did she do?"

He remained quiet as if waiting for her to finish.

"Did she take this information to some disinterested third party, like the Attorney General?" Elizabeth shook her head. "No. Even though she had evidence of a possible murder and cover-up involv-

ing our very own D.A., Alexandra told her father
instead, and he *ordered* her to forget about it." She
gazed at him directly. "Now, does that seem right
to you?"

"When you put it that way," Frank finally said,
"I think I see what you mean."

26

"MORE FINANCIAL documents!" Alexandra said out loud as her frustration reached a boiling point. Grabbing some papers from the pile, she went looking for Patrick.

He was working in the law library where he had told her he often did some of his best thinking. He'd removed his suit jacket and hung it over the back of a chair. His tie was undone and the sleeves of his white shirt were rolled up.

"Look," she said, tossing the stuff onto the polished walnut burl table in front of him. "Tax returns, checks, registers, loan applications, financing agreements and receipts, dating back over twenty years. Even the IRS says you can throw most things away after three years. I don't understand why Erica paid for a storage facility just to house all this old junk."

Pushing his reading glasses up over his dark curly hair, Patrick sat back in the chair and stretched his long legs out in front of him. "Some people are just packrats," he said, shaking his head.

"But packrats save *everything*," she pointed out impatiently. "They hoard pieces of wrapping paper, string, old coupons, magazines, newspapers. This woman only kept financial documents. That's all I'm finding in every one of the boxes." Unable to conceal her frustration, she exhaled loudly. "Who knows, maybe I'm just missing the relevance. But at this rate, I'm going to spend the next ten years in prison."

"Let me take a look," Patrick suggested with a patient smile. He began shuffling through the papers until he came to a document that he seemed to find interesting. He quickly scanned it, then reached for another one. After going through several more records, he glanced over at Alexandra with a quizzical expression. "Sure looks like George borrowed a lot of money."

"I saw that. I figured as a doctor he had to buy an assortment of equipment and other things to open his own practice."

He was pensive. "When did he do that?"

"Not long after Jeffrey's death." She raised one eyebrow. "Do you think that's significant?"

"It's an angle we might not have considered before." He rubbed his chin and stared off into space. "We've been going on the assumption that George killed Jeffrey to marry his wife—but why? Couldn't they each have just divorced their spouses?"

"George did divorce Erica not long after Jeffrey's death," she reminded him. "As for Lorna, I don't know. Maybe she was worried that Jeffrey would fight her for custody of the children."

"That could be. But I was thinking of something that might have involved money. That nurse you met with, didn't she say that George had an insatiable drive to get ahead?"

"Yes." She gave him a long, level look.

"And didn't you also say that at the time of his death Jeffrey had been having some financial problems?"

"Both Michael McGrath and his mother told me that."

"What about George? Was there any change in his financial condition either before or after Jeffrey's death?"

Suddenly it dawned on her what she might have missed. Her face flushed with excitement. "You've given me an idea." She started picking up the documents. "I'm going to analyze all this information from a totally different perspective."

As she headed back to the room she was using for her office, her mind started considering the possibilities. Maybe Erica had in fact left a trail for Alexandra to follow. She just hadn't been reading the signs properly.

"Sure you don't want a beer?" Joe Barton asked, fingering the graying stubble on his cheeks.

"No thanks," Alexandra replied, smiling politely at the retired sheriff. Barton was the detective

who had investigated Jeffrey McGrath's death
twenty years ago after the first deputy on the scene,
Vince Donovan, requested someone from Homicide.

Patrick's investigators had finally tracked Barton
down and arranged for both Patrick and Alexandra
to visit him at his home in Long Beach.

In faded jeans worn low on his hips to compen-
sate for his large belly, Barton was on his third beer.
He had confirmed Vince Donovan's memories surrounding McGrath's demise, and said they'd re-
trieved the pieces of shotgun thrown into the
stream.

"You explained why you were suspicious of
George Collins's story," she said. "What I'd like to
know is this," she paused to gather her thoughts
before going on, "at what point did you feel sure
you were dealing with a murder?"

Barton sat back in his La-Z-Boy recliner, which
had been positioned so that it was facing a small
television set. "I think it was the autopsy report
that cinched it for me."

"The file I found in the archives didn't have an
autopsy report in it," Alexandra told him. "That's
why I'm interested in what you can remember."

"I can't say why the darn report wasn't in the
file," Barton said, shaking his head. "But I recall
there was some question in the medical examiner's
mind regarding the angle at which the buckshot hit
the body."

Alexandra and Patrick exchanged glances as her
heart started racing. "Are you saying there was

medical evidence that the accident couldn't have happened the way George Collins described?"

"Yes. I'm sure that's why I took the case to the D.A.'s office."

She sat forward. She'd been right. There had been more evidence. "Was the deputy D.A. you met with Thomas Kendell?"

"No."

His response was so unexpected that her head snapped up. As if sensing that she was momentarily speechless, Patrick took over. "It wasn't Thomas Kendell you saw?"

"Not that first time. I think I might have spoken to Kendell later on in the case. But at the beginning, there was another deputy D.A. handling the matter."

"Who?" she blurted out.

"I don't recall," Barton admitted. "Started with an F. But I remember that it was Kendell who sent the rejection letter. He claimed that there wasn't enough evidence to prosecute George Collins. So Kendell's name is the one that has stuck in my mind."

"Do you know how it happened that Kendell took over the case?" asked Patrick.

"Sorry, no. Can't say that I do."

Trying to digest this news, Alexandra was vaguely aware that Barton was staring at her.

Patrick gestured with his hand. "Is there anything else you can add?"

"Not really." Barton shrugged his hefty shoulders. "One of the reasons I'm a little fuzzy is that I got transferred right about then." He gave a little chuckle. "You know how it is, you get a whole new load of cases to worry about. No time to follow up on the ones you left behind."

"Was this transfer something you had previously asked for?"

"No," Barton replied. "It came out of left field."

More startling news, thought Alexandra, wondering how it fit into the overall picture. Her throat constricted. This new fact made her father's machinations seem even more ominous.

"What about your partner on the case?" she asked.

"Poor guy had a heart attack right about the time I got transferred," Barton said. Gazing from Alexandra to Patrick, he added, "I'm going to have another beer. Anyone else want anything?"

They both shook their heads. While he was gone, Alexandra looked over at Patrick. "Only the heart attack looks like a coincidence."

"Let's wait and talk in the car," he cautioned, motioning with his head toward the other room.

She busied herself checking her notes. As soon as Barton came back from the kitchen, Alexandra asked him another question. "I've been trying to locate the shotgun that was involved in McGrath's death. Even though it was smashed, Donovan said some tests still should have been done on it. Do you have any idea where it would be?"

"Not exactly, but smashed or not, I'm sure we would have taken any test results in as evidence along with the pieces." Barton scratched his chin.

"Since there are all those missing reports as well as the missing gun, want me to ask some of my old buddies to check a few of these things out?"

There was a moment of silence before Alexandra realized he was waiting for her to speak. "That would be great," she said, nodding her head.

On the way home, Alexandra turned toward Patrick. "I've been thinking about the missing reports. At one time there must have been duplicate reports in the files of the other various agencies, like the medical examiner's office and the sheriff's department."

"I'm sure there were," he agreed. "The only problem is that twenty years is a long time and they might have been destroyed."

"You're right." She nodded.

"Even though Barton promised he would check into it," Patrick said, "I'd like to get our own investigators going on it, too."

"Good idea." A few seconds passed before she spoke again. "The things Barton said make my father look worse. First he got the case away from the original deputy D.A. Then he arranged for Barton to be transferred. Then he took all the incriminating reports out of the file and destroyed them. For all we know, he arranged to have the duplicate reports eliminated too. He could have even paid someone else off. And he must have also destroyed any other evidence, like the pieces of the gun." She had been counting on her fingers. "After that, he could write his letter rejecting the case without any worries that at some later time the case would be reopened."

"And while there's no statute of limitations on murder, unless some startling new evidence appeared—he was home free," Patrick said grimly.

"It was a lot of work on his part, not to mention the danger of being caught," Alexandra continued. "So my father got one hundred thousand dollars, and Doctor George Collins got away with murder."

"It's beginning to look that way."

"Why did he do it?" she said, almost to herself. "I just can't believe my own father would sell justice. I keep hoping there's another explanation."

He didn't respond, as if he knew she was just voicing her thoughts aloud.

"You know what keeps going through my mind?"

Turning to look at her, he shook his head.

"I've been picturing the sentencing hearings I've attended over the years. I've watched the tears being shed by the parents, wives and children of those I've convicted, and felt sick. It's hard to be let down by a loved one and to watch as they're led off to prison."

"I've thought about that, too," he admitted. "It won't be easy on you if that happens to your father."

"No." She took a deep breath and exhaled loudly. "It's one of the worst things I can imagine."

He reached over and patted her hand. Touched by his gesture, she nodded. As she peered out the window, she noted that they were passing the off-ramps to the coast. "I've been back in Los Angeles almost eight months and I've yet to see the ocean," she suddenly remarked without even thinking.

"You're kidding!" Patrick swerved over to the right lane and a few seconds later they were exiting the freeway.

"Where are you going?" she asked.

"To the beach," he said, smiling.

"That's sweet of you, Patrick. But let's do that another time, okay? I've got too much on my mind to appreciate it."

"Don't be silly," he countered. "There's nothing like a walk by the ocean to clear a person's head."

Patrick had been right, Alexandra mused, standing near the water and looking out over the grayish-green ocean. It was wonderful to be on the beach. The day had been overcast, and while it was chilly, it was also incredibly beautiful. She wrapped her arms around herself and watched the seagulls land on the water.

He removed his suit jacket and put it around her shoulders.

"Thanks," she said with a grateful smile.

"Take off your shoes," he ordered, hopping around on one leg as he removed his.

When they were both barefoot and he had rolled up his pant legs, they started walking along the edge of the sand, allowing the water to splash up and over their feet.

"It's freezing," she laughed. "But the air smells delicious." She took in a deep breath and exhaled loudly.

"See," he said, "didn't I tell you you'd feel better?"

She nodded. "I really needed this." A large sigh escaped her lips. "I can't believe my life lately. It couldn't get any worse."

"You're facing a lot," he agreed. With a grimace, he added, "I hate the fact that Roberta is so sick."

"Me too. I appreciate all your concern for my mother," she said with a wan smile. "I hadn't realized you kept in such close contact with her over the years."

"I've always adored your mother. Even after you and I broke up, we continued to talk. Not often, but once in a while." He stopped to pick up a seashell. Rubbing the sand off of it, he put it in his pocket before going on. "Actually, Roberta's been an important influence in my life."

She was curious. "In what way?"

"My marriage was miserable, but I was willing to stay for Jenny's sake. Then one day I discussed it with your mother. She pointed out that if Julie had no interest in raising a child, why didn't I just do it myself."

"It was my mother's idea?"

"Yes. It was so simple I hadn't thought of it. Or maybe I had, but I wanted Jenny to have two parents. Roberta made me realize that if Julie would rather be off flying planes, then staying was only making her resentful and she was taking her frustration out on Jenny."

"You mentioned that Julie was a Navy pilot?"

"Yes. She was the daughter of a career Navy officer. She'd lived all over the world and attended at least twenty different schools while growing up. I found her worldliness, her fearlessness, appealing."

"But she obviously wanted to get married and settle down too, didn't she?"

"Not really. We'd been dating about six months. She was in Los Angeles on a temporary assignment." He shuffled the sand with his toe. "When Julie became pregnant she told me she intended to get an abortion." Patrick shook his head as if remembering. "I wanted my child and I begged her to reconsider. I thought once she had the baby she'd enjoy being a mother." He gave a bitter laugh. "I didn't realize how restless she was. Shortly after Jenny's birth, she signed up again for active duty."

"So what happened?"

"I told Julie I was willing to take over raising our child. Of course, she could visit anytime she wanted."

"Does she?"

"Since she has reenlisted, Julie hasn't come to L.A. even once to see her daughter. Instead, I've gotten on a plane with Jenny, flying all over the world so that Jenny could spend time with her mother. I keep hoping for Jenny's sake that Julie will change—but so far, she hasn't." Patrick paused. "We don't go much anymore."

Alexandra felt sorry for the little girl she'd never

even met. "How often does she hear from her mother?"

"Jenny gets a card and a present from Julie on her birthday. At Christmas there's usually a gift too. And that's it."

"Oh, how terrible."

He turned to gaze at her. "It's sad for Jenny. But she and I have a wonderful life together. I've never been sorry. She fills my life with love. And you'll never meet a happier child."

In spite of what he said, there was something about a mother turning her back on her child that tugged at Alexandra's heart. She thought of her own mother, and how empty her life would be when she was gone. Without warning, a tear rolled down her cheek.

Patrick pulled out a handkerchief, which he handed to her. "I was thinking about Jenny and my mother . . ." she tried to explain, but couldn't.

"That's okay." He put his arms around her, and with her head on his chest, she let out some of her bottled-up grief. After a few minutes, she took the handkerchief and dabbed at her eyes. Encircled in his warm arms, she gazed up at him.

The expression on his face was unreadable. Slowly, his face came down, and he brushed her lips with his. She knew she should pull away, but she didn't want to. She melted into his arms and their kiss became longer, more intense. A sensation of pure joy flooded her.

Heart pounding, she finally forced herself away. "I can't do this. I don't want to be the cause of problems in someone else's relationship." She touched her lip, still feeling the pressure of his mouth, as she searched for the right words. "As long as you're with Nancy, this can't happen again."

He studied her thoughtfully for a moment. Finally, he nodded. "You're right. It's also unprofessional. You're my client. I just wasn't thinking —I'm sorry." He paused before adding, "Forgive me?"

"There's nothing to forgive." She smiled sadly and held out her arms.

They hugged briefly, then side by side they walked back to the car.

27

ALEXANDRA LISTENED intently on the telephone as Joe Barton filled her in on what he'd been able to find out.

"I've spoken to my friends at the sheriff's department," he said. "What was left of George Collins's gun was disposed of a few years after the D.A.'s office rejected the case."

"I thought in a possible murder case they aren't supposed to dispose of the evidence," she said. "After all, there's no statute of limitations."

"Looks like the evidence clerk made a mistake. According to the papers my buddy found, the man thought the gun had to be destroyed because the case had been rejected by the D.A.'s office." He cleared his throat. "Of course, that's wrong. But stupid things like that sometimes happen."

Had it really been nothing more than a simple error, or had her father arranged for it? "What about the missing reports?"

"I've got better news there. They found the old sheriff's department case file and my report as well as the report of the other detective—the one who died. They also uncovered a copy of the missing autopsy report. It will back up a lot of the information I gave you."

"Can you send me copies of everything you found?"

"Sure thing."

Sitting behind her massive Art Deco desk, Nancy looked even more petite than she usually did, thought Alexandra, gazing around the room as she waited to find out why she'd been summoned.

It was a beautiful office. The Lalique conference table surrounded by four chairs upholstered in lush gray velvet was a work of art. On the opposite side of the room, the seating arrangement consisted of couches and chairs covered in shades of gray and maroon suede. But it was the two abstract paintings that hung on opposite walls that caught the eye the moment one stepped into the room.

Nancy pointed to some papers in front of her. "My accounting department tells me you've only managed to pay us part of our retainer."

Alexandra felt ill at ease when she wasn't asked to sit down, but she refused to give Nancy the satisfaction of knowing it bothered her. "I'm not sure if Patrick told you, but the judge exonerated my bail. When I get that twenty thousand dollars back, less whatever the court deducts for costs, I'll give it to you."

"Certainly you must have other funds?"

Uncomfortable about explaining the details of her life, Alexandra hedged. "I'm trying to arrange a loan on my co-op in New York. These things are harder to accomplish when the banks find out that I might lose my job."

"Sorry to hear that, but I have a law firm to run." Nancy cocked her head and gave Alexandra a level stare. "Has Patrick spoken to you about signing a personal note to guarantee our fees?"

"No," Alexandra replied, shaking her head. "He hasn't."

"He should have. Take a look at this." Nancy slid a document across the table.

Alexandra read it quickly before looking up. "I'd like to discuss it with Patrick."

"I run this law firm," Nancy informed her, squaring her shoulders. "I pay the bills. I do the hiring and firing. Patrick really doesn't get involved in these kinds of details."

"Still, Patrick is the lawyer I hired," Alexandra pointed out as evenly as possible. "And I intend to talk to him about this."

The color rose in Nancy's cheeks. "What exactly *is* the nature of your present relationship with Patrick?"

Several seconds passed while Alexandra stood there with her mouth open. Feeling guilty, she thought about the kiss on the beach, then promptly put it out of her mind. "I'm afraid I don't know what you mean," she finally said.

"You know exactly what I mean," Nancy countered. "From what I understand, the two of you were once an item. I'm getting the feeling that you're trying to turn the clock back and pick up where you left off."

"Our past relationship has been over for a long time. I married someone else . . . and so did he."

"I know all that," Nancy retorted with a quick wave of her hand. "What I want to hear is why you called him out of all the thousands of other attorneys in L.A."

It was a valid question and Alexandra wasn't sure she knew the answer to it herself. She cleared her throat before responding. "I'd hoped that since we were old friends, Patrick might be inclined to help me. I also knew he had an excellent reputation as a criminal defense lawyer, which I suddenly found myself in need of." She hesitated briefly before adding, "I think that's all very understandable."

"Maybe. But I'd like you to understand where I'm coming from. Patrick's the man I *intend* to marry." Nancy's voice dropped several notches. "If there's something other than a professional relationship between the two of you, then maybe Patrick is getting compensation I don't know about."

Alexandra couldn't believe her ears. How dare Nancy suggest that she was sleeping with Patrick to pay off her legal fees? For a brief second she allowed herself to imagine what making love with Patrick would be like after all these years. Coloring slightly when she realized what she'd been thinking, Alexandra hurried to reply. "There's nothing going on between us. Besides, do you really think Patrick would do something that unprofessional?"

Nancy frowned and actually seemed at a loss for words. Alexandra had managed to turn the tables on her.

After a few seconds, Nancy recovered. "Then I don't see any reason why you can't sign this note."

Infuriated by her smug attitude, Alexandra grabbed a pen from Nancy's desk and scribbled her name across the bottom of the document. "Here," she practically shouted. "Have your secretary make me a copy for my records."

When Patrick came back to the office later that evening, he was tired. If he didn't have an early appearance in the morning for which he needed a file, he would have gone straight home. He hated getting there after Jenny was asleep.

As he made his way down the deserted hallway, his thoughts were interrupted by sounds coming from behind a closed door. Glancing at his watch he saw that it was after ten. Who was still here? He opened the door and found Alexandra standing at the copy machine.

"Oh!" she said, looking up, startled. "I wasn't expecting anyone."

"What are you doing here so late?" he asked.

"I've prepared a spreadsheet outlining Erica and George's finances both before and after Jeffrey's death. I was making some copies to leave on your desk." Her eyes had dark circles under them, but she looked excited. "I think I found something. Got a minute?"

He hesitated, then decided it was already so late that a few more minutes wouldn't matter. "Let me just get my things for the morning."

When he came in, she motioned for him to sit at one of the long tables where she had her papers. Then she picked up the spreadsheet. "Look at this," she said, pointing to some columns. "This shows all the money that George borrowed during his years of schooling to become an orthopedic surgeon. And this one shows the amount of money he and Erica earned during that time." She glanced up. "As you can see, it was Erica's salary as a secretary that kept them fed and clothed. But the amount they owed was a lot. Easily a couple of hundred thousand dollars."

She flipped the sheet over. "When George was ready to start practicing, according to some rejection letters I found, he couldn't find a practice to join. Finally, he took a job at a clinic. While the pay wasn't great, they lived a lot better. But there wasn't enough money to pay off all the debts. That went on for a few years."

Alexandra rushed to the other table and brought another chart over. "Then Jeffrey died."

He gazed up at her expectantly.

"A week later, George and Erica went to a bank and borrowed another hundred thousand dollars."

"Okay," he said, waiting for her to explain the relevance.

"I can't find a record of that money ever being

deposited into any of their accounts. Not one penny was used for anything I can substantiate."

Patrick felt his curiosity mounting. "Are you saying what I think you're saying?"

"Yes." Her voice rose. "There's a good possibility that was the money used for the bribe."

"Do you have anything to back that up?"

"I think so." She put some more papers in front of him. "Look at this. A few months later, a lot of cash started rolling in. Different amounts every week. Eventually it adds up, but there's no source. George and Erica even started paying off all of their debts, including the hundred-thousand-dollar loan. Then he rents an office and spends hundreds of thousands of dollars outfitting it. Shortly after that, he opens his own practice and starts earning some really big bucks. But there's still no explanation for where all that previous money came from."

"Sounds like they won the lottery."

"I think it was more than that." She pulled a piece of paper out of the pile. "What does this look like to you?"

"A copy of an insurance check for one million dollars."

"And the payee?"

Patrick began to sense her excitement. "Lorna McGrath."

"Right. Now turn it over."

"Jesus!" he said, startled to find that underneath Lorna McGrath's endorsement was George Collins's name and a bank account number.

"Looks like she gave George the proceeds from an insurance policy on Jeffrey's death. Then he deposited it into another account—probably one that the two of them shared."

"That's what I figured. But I couldn't understand Erica's part in all this. Why would she help her husband when he was in love with another woman? Then I reviewed the terms of her dissolution agreement with George and it all made sense."

"What do you mean?"

"Erica got a lot of money. And it was to be paid to her every month for the rest of her life."

"So you figure her favorable divorce agreement was a payoff to keep quiet?" he asked.

"Exactly," Alexandra replied. "She must have realized that George was being investigated for Jeffrey's death. She knew about the bribe because she told me the exact amount—one hundred thousand dollars. That means she went with George to the bank to borrow the cash knowing precisely what it was going to be used for. I think that's why she felt so guilty. Why she wanted to die with a clear conscience."

Patrick was silent for a moment. All that could be heard were his fingers tapping on the table. "Alexandra, you're probably right. If George Collins murdered Jeffrey, then Lorna could have been either a co-conspirator or an accessory after the fact. Erica too."

"Now I just have to find out if George and Lorna were the ones who planted the drugs in my apartment." She stopped to gather her thoughts, and her face clouded with uneasiness. "And whether or not my father actually took that bribe."

"That's a hard one," Patrick agreed. Gazing at her, he saw how drawn her face looked. The stress of her mother's illness, added to the threat of losing her freedom and her license to practice law, was too much of a burden for anyone to handle. "Don't dwell on that until we find some additional evidence," he cautioned.

"I'll try." Putting the papers down on the table, Alexandra opened her briefcase. "By the way, Nancy called me into her office today. She asked me to sign this."

He glanced down at the document. It was a promissory note. Once in a great while they asked a client to sign one of these. He couldn't believe that Nancy had done this without consulting him. It made him both angry and embarrassed. "I'm sorry. She should have talked to me first. I know you're waiting for the court to give you back your bail money."

"I told her that, but she didn't seem to care." She fidgeted with the button on her suit. "I know Nancy isn't happy with me being here and all . . ." She paused. "If she's making your life miserable because of it, I'll find somewhere else to work. I don't want to cause any problems."

Her eyes didn't meet his, and he wondered if she was thinking about the kiss on the beach, too. "Don't be silly. You're staying right here. You shouldn't have signed this. Tomorrow I'll get the original and destroy it."

"No. Please don't do that. I'm going to pay the money whether I sign a note or not. It's just that I was caught off guard when she asked me today. Maybe I shouldn't have brought it up. Nancy told me she handles all the finances for the firm."

"Yes, she does," he admitted with a rueful grin. "But this is different. And I don't want a note signed by you." Realizing how late it was, Patrick stood up. "Listen, I've got to get home. I've got an early appearance in the morning. Don't give this note another thought. You've got enough on your mind."

The tension in Alexandra's face relaxed.

"You've done some amazing work here," he said. "I'm impressed. And I've got some ideas on how we can use it." Looking at her again, he suddenly felt awkward. "We'll talk about it tomorrow, okay?"

She nodded.

Riding the elevator to the basement, Patrick wondered what was happening to him. His thoughts drifted back to that first year in college when he and Alexandra had been so much in love. She'd been smart, funny, eager to experience life and positive about what she wanted to do with her future. Seeing her across the quad, he'd feel his pulse racing as he rushed to her side. At nineteen he'd been unable to imagine living life without her. But that had been a long time ago. Things changed. People changed.

Yet, upstairs he'd wanted to put his arms around Alexandra and comfort her. And he still couldn't understand why he'd kissed her on the beach. Was Nancy right? Could he still be in love with Alexandra after all these years?

28

SADDENED BY HER mother's worsening condition, Alexandra couldn't seem to shake the depression that enveloped her. Jerking open the door of the refrigerator, she took out the milk carton. As soon as she poured some milk into her coffee, it began to curdle. "Yuck," she said, tossing the entire contents into the sink.

She grabbed her purse and drove to one of the hillside areas of Hollywood near her home for some breakfast. It was a beautiful day. Yesterday's rain had pushed all of the smog out of the L.A. basin, and the sky overhead was blue with wisps of white clouds. The trees and green shrubbery on the hillsides and along the canyon reminded Alexandra of Central Park.

At the grocery store in the small shopping center she bought a newspaper and took it with her into the nearby diner, where she ordered coffee and whole wheat toast. On the patio she scanned the paper. What she saw made her gasp out loud. Under a picture of her father taken during a recent campaign speech, the bold headline said: D.A. KENDELL SUSPECTED IN COVER-UP.

Her pulse was racing as she read on. The article quoted informed sources as saying that D.A. Thomas Kendell was suspected of having accepted a bribe twenty years ago in exchange for letting a murderer go free. There were details about Jeffrey McGrath's death, and George Collins was named as the alleged killer. She gazed at the picture of George in a tuxedo standing next to Lorna in a beaded black gown at a recent charity function.

The article went on to explain that the long-ago incident came to light when the doctor's ex-wife told a deputy D.A. details of the crime—details that could only have been known by someone involved in the murder and subsequent cover-up. Further, that before the prosecutor, Alexandra Locke, had herself been arrested on a possession for sale charge, she'd been ordered by her father, the D.A., to stop her investigation into the allegations made by the ex-wife, Erica Collins.

At the end, the article stated it was incumbent on the Attorney General of California to order a full investigation as soon as possible to ascertain the truth before the fall election could take place between Thomas Kendell and Frank Sanchez.

In a state of disbelief, Alexandra tried to figure out who could have leaked this information to the press. Her stomach was in knots as she went over the possibilities. There was her father, but that made no sense. Frank Sanchez was another obvious culprit, but how could he have found out? There was the McGrath family and the Collins family. There were also the retired cops she'd spoken to. But none of those people knew all the facts that had been printed in the newspaper. Only Alexandra, Thomas and Patrick had knowledge of the argument between her father and herself, and Thomas had nothing to gain and everything to lose from this information being made public.

Could Patrick have leaked the details to the press in a misguided effort to help her? Or was someone else at his office responsible?

Turning the page for the rest of the story, Alexandra was suddenly confronted with a picture of herself. The caption identified her as D.A. Thomas Kendell's daughter, who had recently been arrested on drug charges. Her face flushed with shame, Alexandra snatched her things and hurried to her car.

As soon as she was ushered into Patrick's office in Century City, Alexandra pointed to the front page of her newspaper. "Did you see it?" she asked, her voice close to panic.

"Yes." He nodded, solemnly.

"Did you have anything to do with the leak?" She searched his face, trying to ascertain the truth.

Patrick's expression turned grim. "Jesus, Alexandra, I understand you're upset, but I'm your lawyer! I wouldn't divulge anything I've learned from a client in confidence." He gestured angrily with his hands. "Forget the fact that I consider you a friend—or did until this minute—I've no desire to be disbarred."

Shamefaced, she realized she'd overreacted and in the process she'd insulted the only person who was trying to help her. She collapsed into a chair. "I'm sorry, Patrick. I'm not thinking very clearly."

He nodded again, but the tight lines around his lips were evidence that he was still upset.

"Somehow that reporter learned things that only you, my father, and I know." She hesitated briefly before going on. "Is there a chance that someone here, a secretary or a law clerk, might have copied my file?"

"I suppose anything's possible," he acknowledged unhappily. "But it's highly unlikely. We're extremely careful about our hiring practices. We handle too many well-known clients to take any chances. Our files are locked up at night, and all references of our employees are checked and double-checked."

She knew he wasn't going to appreciate her next question but she had to ask it. "What about Nancy?"

"She might not like you, Alexandra," he conceded, "but Nancy would never jeopardize her career that way." He studied her for a moment. "If it will make you feel better, though, I'll check out every possibility."

"Thank you," she managed to say.

Reaching for the brass paperweight on his desk, he began tossing it from hand to hand as he paced his large office. "Whoever leaked this information to the press had to be an unimpeachable source. Newspapers don't like to be sued for libel." He turned toward her. "Any *other* ideas who it might be?"

Alexandra flinched at his tone of voice. Patrick was still smarting from her accusations and she couldn't blame him. "I thought of my father," she admitted, "but this is terrible for him. As for Frank Sanchez, I don't know how he could have found out." She shook her head in total bewilderment.

The buzz of the intercom interrupted their conversation. Patrick put the paperweight down and picked up the phone. Alexandra saw a worried frown cross his features as he said, "Put her on."

Patrick tried to follow what Tricia Yardley was saying, but it was difficult because she was talking in such a low voice.

"You can't tell anyone I've called you," Tricia whispered, "because it could ruin my career."

"I understand," he said, wondering what the hell was going on.

"I've just found out that my boss, Karen Hunter, is going to ask you to bring in your client Alexandra Locke."

"About her drug case?"

"No. She wants to ask her some questions about the death of Jeffrey McGrath."

He had to be circumspect. "Is that the person I just read about in the newspaper this morning?"

"Yes."

"Do you know how the media got hold of that story?"

"No, I don't," Tricia said. "Listen, I've got to go. I just wanted to warn you."

"Thanks, Tricia. I appreciate it."

As soon as Patrick hung up the phone he told Alexandra what he had learned.

"I'm not ready to talk to them yet," Alexandra stated firmly.

"I understand your concerns," he said, his gaze meeting hers. "Still, if the call comes, my advice is that we comply. Let's find out what they want and how much they know at the attorney general's office. Then we'll be in a better position to see if we can push for a deal."

"They'll want me to discuss my father's role in the matter. Can't we stall them until I know the truth about the bribe?"

"From the newspaper article it appears they've already learned about your father's involvement. We have to be careful not to lose our credibility with the same people who are handling the criminal case against you."

The buzzer rang again and Patrick answered. As soon as he heard who it was, he said, "Put the call through." Then he motioned to Alexandra to use the extension on the table next to the couch.

She picked up the phone and listened for a moment, then her face turned pale. "I'll be there as fast as I can," he heard her say, her voice shaking. When she looked at Patrick, there was a stricken expression in her eyes. "It's my mother. She's gotten worse. They said I should come."

Across town, Frank Sanchez held the morning paper in his hand. How could the facts surrounding Jeffrey McGrath's death be in the newspaper already when he'd just sent the information yesterday to the criminal division of the attorney general's office here in L.A.? He had expected them to investigate the entire matter before making any of the allegations public. Had someone leaked this to the press? He thought about Elizabeth. Could she have been responsible?

He found the prosecutor in her office loading her wheeling cart with boxes. "Did you read the morning paper?" Frank said.

"I don't have time to breathe, let alone read." Glancing at her watch, Elizabeth added, "I've got a trial starting in less than five minutes. Want to walk with me?"

"Okay," he said.

"Might as well make yourself useful then." She handed him one of her large briefcases filled with files and other documents. Turning her cart around so that she could drag it behind her, she led the way to the elevators. "What's up?"

When he told her about the article in the newspaper, her eyes widened as if she was genuinely surprised, but he couldn't be sure. "Did you talk to anyone about this?" he asked, observing her carefully.

"Nope." Peering at her watch again, she swore.

"Damn these elevators. If I'm late, Judge Waters will never let me hear the end of it." She looked at Frank. "Anyway, I didn't say a word to anyone. Who else did you tell besides me?"

"No one. I just sent the information by courier yesterday to the local attorney general's office."

Elizabeth shrugged. "Well then, it's obvious that someone there must have leaked the details to the press."

All the way to the City of Hope, Alexandra was plagued with worry. Had her mother's condition worsened because of the news accounts that morning saying that Thomas might have been involved in a cover-up? She stared glumly out the window while Patrick, who had insisted on driving her, raced through traffic to get them to the hospital.

At the room, they found Thomas already there. Roberta was being transfused with blood and appeared to be sleeping.

"How is she?" Alexandra whispered.

"They don't know yet," Thomas said in a low voice.

She wondered if her mother had agreed to the transfusion, or had Thomas—willing to do anything to keep Roberta alive, even if it meant more suffering—ordered it for her?

The doctor came in. "Can you please wait outside while I check her?"

Alexandra, along with her father, walked out into the hallway, where Patrick was standing. She quickly filled him in on her mother's condition.

"Jesus, I'm sorry," Patrick said to both of them. She gave him a brief smile and Thomas nodded.

There was an uncomfortable interval before Patrick turned to Thomas. "I'm also sorry about the primary," he said.

"I appreciate that," Thomas replied. "You know, up until this morning, I felt that while I might have lost the battle, I didn't intend to lose the war." His vexation was obvious as he frowned at Alexandra. "Thanks to my daughter, that's now changed."

"What do you mean?" Alexandra asked, offended by the angry tone in his voice.

"Don't play innocent with me," Thomas scoffed. "Who else but you could have leaked all that information to the newspapers?"

She stiffened. "It wasn't me."

The doctor came out of Roberta's room and joined them. "She woke up briefly when I examined her, but she's fallen back to sleep. It could be a while. The pain medication should last for hours."

"Is she any better?" Thomas asked. His eyes, now focused on the doctor, were filled with hope.

"Yes," the doctor said, looking from father to daughter. "You'll probably see an improvement by tomorrow. Just remember though, that the benefits from her last transfusion lasted less than a week. I doubt that this one will do much more."

Alexandra, Thomas, and Patrick had stayed at the hospital for hours waiting for Roberta to wake up. The tension between Alexandra and her father was palpable, and Thomas had chosen to spend most of the time outside the building, talking on his cellular telephone.

In the meantime, Alexandra and Patrick had sat in the waiting room and discussed her mother's choices if she pulled through this crisis, as well as her options for future treatments.

The one subject they purposefully avoided was the implications from the day's headlines. She would deal with her own problems only after she knew what was going to happen with her mother.

Finally the doctor came in and suggested that they all go home and get some rest.

Totally drained, Alexandra was grateful that Patrick remained quiet during the first part of their drive back to L.A. When he took one of the exits to downtown Pasadena, however, she was confused. "Where are you going?"

He smiled. "Just getting us a sandwich or something else that's quick."

"I'm not in the mood," she insisted.

"I know," he replied. "But you didn't eat all day. We'll just get something light. We won't even talk."

It suddenly dawned on Alexandra how in tune he was to her feelings. "I'm sorry you lost an entire day of work."

"No problem. Your mother is a special woman. I wanted to be there."

She saw the genuine compassion on his handsome face. "Thanks."

Inside the coffee shop, she sat quietly as Patrick ordered sandwiches for both of them. It was a strange feeling to have someone taking care of her, she thought. But she liked it.

"I'm sorry about this morning," she finally said. "I didn't mean to accuse you of the leak to the media."

"It was a shock," he admitted. "But I understand that acute stress can sometimes make us do and say things we don't mean." He paused for a moment, his gaze direct. "By the way, I spoke to Nancy. She has no idea how the information got out, and I believe her."

Alexandra nodded. How could she argue with him? He certainly knew his partner far better than she did.

"I've been thinking," he said. "Would you like me to talk to your father? Explain how much you've tried to protect him while searching for the truth?"

"Thanks for the offer," she said with a grateful smile, "but no. It wouldn't do any good. He's got it in his head that I'm responsible, and there's nothing you or I or anyone can say that will change his mind."

29

ALEXANDRA'S MOUTH was dry and she had a hard time swallowing as she gazed at the plaque on the door: CALIFORNIA DEPARTMENT OF JUSTICE, OFFICES OF THE ATTORNEY GENERAL, CRIMINAL DIVISION. It was an intimidating feeling to be entering these premises accused of a criminal act.

Before they went into the outer office, Patrick pulled her aside. "Remember," he cautioned, in a solemn tone of voice, "you have to forget for the next hour that you're an attorney. Forget you ever went to law school. Let me do the talking—for both of us."

She audibly exhaled. It was going to be difficult. Alexandra wasn't used to letting anyone speak for her. Filled with apprehension, she smoothed down the skirt of her navy-blue suit, took a deep breath and tried to calm her nervous stomach. "I'm ready," she finally said.

When they were brought into the office of

Karen Hunter, the Senior Assistant Attorney General of the Criminal Division for Los Angeles, the woman stood up to shake both Patrick's and Alexandra's hands.

Alexandra judged the prosecutor to be in her mid to late forties. She had a long, narrow face, ice-blue eyes and dirty-blond hair worn short, but stylish. In her tan suit she looked stern and in control—definitely someone who wasn't going to allow herself to be pushed around.

"Thank you for coming in," Ms. Hunter said, gazing first at Alexandra and then over at Patrick. With a polite smile, she gestured for them to take the two chairs in front of her desk.

The room was a typical government office with a long walnut desk, some bookcases, file cabinets and client chairs. Like most employees, noted Alexandra, the Senior Assistant A.G. had done her best to dress it up with artwork, plants and colorful accessories.

Karen Hunter got right down to business, addressing Patrick. "I assume you know why we're interested in talking to your client?"

"Why don't you clarify it for us," Patrick replied, smiling at her and sitting back as if he had all day.

"Very well," Ms. Hunter said, her voice tinged with a hint of annoyance. "We have reason to believe that a man by the name of Jeffrey McGrath was murdered twenty years ago by a Doctor George Collins. Collins then bribed a law enforcement official, quite possibly Thomas Kendell, to escape punishment."

"What makes you think my client has anything to say on that subject?"

"We have certain notes Ms. Locke wrote while working as a deputy D.A., detailing statements made to her by Erica Collins, the ex-wife of George Collins. These notes also mention a key and a storage locker that belonged to Erica Collins as well as bank records and other documents. We'd like to ask your client some questions on all of these things."

How on earth had they gotten hold of her notes? Alexandra wondered, her mind in a tailspin.

Patrick must have been thinking the same thing. "Just how did you obtain these notes that were supposedly written by my client?"

"They were found in Ms. Locke's files at her office," the Senior Assistant A.G. said with a confident half smile.

He looked quickly at Alexandra, and she inclined her head, trying to convey with her eyes how surprised she was.

There were several seconds of silence before Patrick asked his next question. "Are you planning to convene a grand jury to look into Mr. McGrath's death?"

The prosecutor gave him a withering glance. "Not unless we are forced to."

Without a grand jury they would have no subpoena power over her. However, they could still cause her a lot of problems, thought Alexandra unhappily. She studied Patrick's face and then Ms. Hunter's face. The two of them seemed to be sizing each other up, like two fighters in a boxing ring.

Alexandra felt like a third wheel. For the moment, she wasn't even a player in their little power struggle.

Ms. Hunter folded her hands together in front of her on the desk. "I must remind both of you that keeping information from us could be viewed as impeding a murder investigation." She paused. "Of course, if Ms. Locke doesn't intend to cooperate, I can also freeze her apartment while I get a search warrant for the premises."

Hearing these threats, Alexandra tensed.

"Excuse me for a moment," Patrick said politely, before he leaned over and whispered in Alexandra's ear. After a quick conversation, he took the initiative again. "My client insists that those notes you've mentioned were in with her personal papers. We've no idea how they've ended up in your possession, but there's a good possibility they were illegally obtained. If so, they would be inadmissible in a court of law."

Karen Hunter frowned as Patrick went on. "That means that any information you've obtained through the use of those papers would also be tainted."

"I know the law, Counsel," she retorted, her voice sharp. "And I'm equally convinced that these notes of Ms. Locke's do not constitute her personal papers in any way, shape or form." Her posture had become rigid. "It's my view that they constitute work product from a deputy D.A.'s office and that Ms. Locke wrote them on county time and on what appears to be an unsolved crime."

"You're entitled to your opinion, and I'm entitled to mine," he said with a slight shrug and a wide smile. "Of course I'd rather not, but if need be, we'll just have to let the courts decide the issue."

Alexandra guessed that the government wasn't going to relish a court fight over the admissibility of evidence already in their possession. In her opinion, neither one of them had an ironclad position. A reviewing court could conceivably rule either way.

The Senior Assistant A.G. shot Patrick an angry look. "Let me just remind both you and your client again, that if she refuses to cooperate with this office, she'll be impeding a murder investigation. It's also possible we'll have her on an obstruction of justice charge."

As Patrick and Karen Hunter battled each other, Alexandra's entire body was taut with anxiety.

Patrick held out his hands in a conciliatory gesture. "I think we're getting ahead of ourselves here. What we need to discuss first is some kind of a deal. I'd like to suggest that you drop the drug charges against my client in return for her cooperation in the Collins/McGrath matter."

"No way," the Senior Assistant A.G. said firmly, shaking her head to emphasize her point.

Patrick was nonplussed. "I sincerely hope you'll reconsider."

The lines around her mouth tightened. "I must tell you, Mr. Ross, that your client is not in any position to be asking for a deal. Not only that, she's risking a lot by refusing to cooperate."

The woman's attitude was galling and it took all of Alexandra's willpower not to jump into the fray and defend herself.

"My client is not refusing to cooperate," Patrick said smoothly. "Quite the opposite. All she's asking for is some cooperation from you in return." He looked at Alexandra and then back at the Senior Assistant A.G. "I think my client is going to need some time to think this matter over."

Signaling that this round was over, he stood up and motioned for Alexandra to do the same. "See what you can do about a deal for Ms. Locke, and I'll be back to you in a few days."

"Make sure it's no later than Friday," Karen Hunter warned him with a haughty expression on her face.

On the way back to the car, Alexandra lost her cool. "The two of you were talking about me like I didn't exist. This is my life, my freedom." She jabbed a finger into her chest. "I'm the one who could end up spending years in prison."

He put his hands on her shoulders. "Now you know why they say that the lawyer who represents herself has a fool for a client."

She realized he was trying to calm her down, but she was too upset. "I'm not in the mood for jokes," she snapped.

"I'm sorry," he said, smiling apologetically. "I know this is hard for you, but you handled yourself like a pro. In fact, I actually think our meeting with her went quite well."

"I didn't particularly care for the way she threatened to freeze my apartment and get a search warrant!" Alexandra said, her voice rising an octave.

"She was bluffing," he pointed out. "If Karen Hunter had really wanted to do that, she wouldn't have told us. I'm sure she's concluded that any information you have is already in my possession."

"You're probably right," Alexandra said, feeling suddenly deflated. "I just didn't like the way she was trying to intimidate me."

"It's all part of the game," he reminded her, before his expression became serious again. "Tell me more about these notes she seems to have."

"After I realized the file had disappeared, I sat down and made notes of everything I could remember. They were definitely in with my other personal papers. But then I was put on leave and I never went back to the office. Instead, I asked Geena to pack my things up for me. I was planning to either get them from her, or Geena was going to drop them off at my house."

"Did you ever get them?"

"Yes," she nodded. "One day several boxes unexpectedly arrived by UPS."

"Was everything there?"

"I thought so." She squared her shoulders. "In fact, I brought those notes to your office. They should be in your file."

His brows came together in a frown. "It looks like someone copied them first."

"I never thought of that," Alexandra admitted.

Still, she was puzzled. "But how did they even know to look for them in the first place?"

"That's a good question."

She took a deep breath and let it out slowly. "Only my father was aware of what I was doing. I can imagine him copying my things, but not turning them over to the A.G.'s office."

"I agree—that doesn't seem likely." Focusing on her, he added, "And those are the only notes they could have?"

"Until I actually see what the A.G.'s office has, I can't be positive. But those are the only ones that contain everything Karen Hunter mentioned."

Patrick looked pensive as Alexandra went on. "No matter how this all came to their attention, Ms. Hunter and the A.G.'s office must have other evidence against George Collins beside my notes." She raised her head and considered him. "As for the other things that I've learned, like the fact that Lorna gave George the life insurance money she collected, in my opinion they could also help to strengthen their case."

"You're thinking like a prosecutor," he cautioned.

"Maybe. But in my mind the copy of the insurance check is evidence that changes the underlying motivation from a crime of passion to cold-blooded murder for financial gain. That entitles them to seek the death penalty." She paused. "Even though I don't like Karen Hunter's attitude, I feel almost obligated to turn over to them what I've found."

"Alexandra," he said patiently, "you must remember you're a defendant here. Defendants have to protect themselves any way they can. I don't think you should give them *anything* unless you get something back." Patrick stopped, as if wanting to give his words a chance to sink in. "I'd rather push them into offering us some kind of a deal on the drug charges."

"I'd like that, too. But a deal also means I'll be forced to talk about my father." She bit her lip. "I don't want to do that until I know if he's guilty or not."

His solemn gaze met hers. "Then maybe it's time that you confronted him again."

When Alexandra got home, she saw that there was a call on her machine and she pressed the button to listen to the message.

"Joe Barton here. I just remembered the name of the first deputy D.A. on the Collins case. It was Bob Frazier, but he died some years back. Anyway, I saw on TV that the case was being reopened, so I gave the A.G.'s office copies of all the documents I found."

After erasing the message, Alexandra sat down on the couch. Once the attorney general's office received those additional documents, she knew that they would increase their pressure on her to cooperate. She needed to find out whether or not her father had taken a bribe—and quickly.

Alexandra did some on-line research and called

around for information until she had located Bob Frazier's widow. Then she made an appointment to see her the next morning.

Irene Frazier lived in Burbank, not far from the NBC Broadcasting Studio. When the door opened to her small but well-kept house, Alexandra found herself facing a short woman with protruding eyes and lips that were smudged with pink lipstick. The result was a startled look, as if the woman had awakened from a long sleep only to end up in the middle of a mad tea party.

"So you're Thomas Kendell's daughter," Mrs. Frazier said, after Alexandra had introduced herself.

"You know my father?" Alexandra asked, studying the other woman's face.

"Yes," she nodded. "But I haven't seen him in a number of years." She invited Alexandra into a musty-smelling living room. After giving her a glass of lemonade, Irene Frazier insisted that Alexandra sit on the couch while she took the wing chair for herself.

Alexandra cleared her throat. "What was my father like back then?"

The woman put her hand to her mouth before she slowly began to talk. "Ambitious. Self-confident. Charming. Probably very much like he is today. But I'm sure you didn't come here for that. Now, what can I really do for Thomas Kendell's daughter?" There was a coy smile on her face that seemed inappropriate for some reason.

"I believe that your husband worked as a deputy

D.A. with my father many years ago. Is that correct?"

"Yes."

"Did they know each other from school?"

"No. They met at the D.A.'s office. Thomas had been there for a number of years when my Bob was hired. Your father showed him the ropes." Mrs. Frazier reached over and lifted a picture frame from the small table next to her. "This is Bob," she said proudly. She handed Alexandra the tarnished silver frame that held the yellowing photo of a man with a large nose and a prominent jaw.

"Is this you?" Alexandra asked, pointing to the woman in the picture next to Bob.

"Yes. It was our wedding day." Mrs. Frazier reached inside her blouse and pulled out a handkerchief, which she used to dab at her eyes.

There was another picture on the table showing the two of them with a small boy. "Is that your son?" Alexandra inquired, smiling at her

Irene Frazier nodded again.

There was something odd about the child in the picture, thought Alexandra, unable to figure out just what it was. "How old is your son now?"

There was a faraway look in Irene Frazier's eyes as if she was mentally calculating the years. "He's twenty-six," she finally responded.

"Did he become a lawyer like his father?"

"No," the woman said in a sad voice.

"Does he live close by?"

As if uncomfortable with Alexandra's questions,

Mrs. Frazier shifted her position in the chair. "He doesn't live far," she said before changing the subject. "Now, how can I really help you?"

"Have you been reading the newspapers lately?"

The woman gave Alexandra a shrewd glance. "You mean about that old case? That Collins/McGrath business?"

It was apparent that Irene Frazier knew exactly why she was here, so Alexandra decided to be direct. "Yes. I spoke to a retired detective with the sheriff's department by the name of Joe Barton. Did you know him? Or have you ever heard his name mentioned before?"

"I don't believe so."

"I see." Alexandra stopped to collect her thoughts. "Well, Mr. Barton told me that your husband handled the Collins case for the D.A.'s office twenty years ago. In fact, he remembered having several conversations with your husband about it."

"If he says that, it's probably true."

Alexandra took a deep breath. "Are you aware of the accusations being leveled against my father, that he took a bribe from George Collins, and that's why Collins wasn't prosecuted for Jeffrey McGrath's murder?"

"Yes. I read that."

"Since your husband handled the case even before my father did, I was wondering what he might have told you about it."

The other woman sat forward stiffly. "If you're suggesting that my husband was involved in a bribe, you're wrong." She shook her head as if for emphasis. "Bob was the most decent, honest man that ever lived."

Why had Mrs. Frazier suddenly become so defensive? Alexandra wondered. "I wasn't suggesting that he did anything wrong," she assured the woman.

"Good. Because if he'd had anything to do with a bribe, I certainly wouldn't have been forced to work all these years as a legal secretary," she huffed.

"Are you still working?"

"Yes. I took the day off so that I could talk to you."

"Thank you," Alexandra said. In spite of the woman's growing reluctance to talk, she still had several more questions. "When did your husband die?" she asked softly.

"A long time ago." Irene sighed before abruptly standing up. "Is there anything else?"

Alexandra was forced to stand also. "Yes. I'd like to know how my father ended up with the Collins case if Bob had it first?"

"That's easy," said Irene, with a hint of anger in her voice. "One day Thomas just came into Bob's office and took the case away from him."

Alexandra tried not to show her surprise. "Did he give him any reason?"

"No," Irene replied firmly. "That wasn't Thomas Kendell's style. He was a man who just took what he wanted."

30

~

WANTING TO MEET her father someplace where they could talk away from prying eyes, Alexandra had chosen the Museum of Contemporary Art in downtown Los Angeles. It was a striking building—seven levels with skylights ascending up the sides like a pyramid—that housed a collection of international art going back to 1940.

Realizing that she was a few minutes early, Alexandra wandered over to the gift shop to wait for him. As she looked at the various postcards her mind went back to her conversation with Irene Frazier. How did Bob Frazier really figure into all this? she wondered.

She was nervous about seeing her father. Since his startling accusation that she had been responsible for the news leaks, they had barely spoken. And he was certainly not going to like what she had to say to him today.

When Thomas arrived, he motioned to his

daughter and together they went looking for a quiet place to talk.

"Did you see your mother today?" he asked.

"No. I'm going there after I leave here."

"Call me and let me know how she is. I probably won't be able to get to the hospital until late."

"Okay."

As soon as they were seated on a bench, she turned to him. "Do you remember Joe Barton?"

His brow crinkled. "Wasn't he a sheriff's deputy?"

"Actually he was a detective. He worked on the Collins/McGrath case."

Thomas frowned but said nothing more.

"Barton told me that you weren't the first D.A. to handle the case. He said that there was another deputy D.A. on it by the name of Bob Frazier?"

"That's right."

Taken aback that he'd admitted it so freely, she didn't bother to hide her chagrin. "Why didn't you mention that fact to me before?"

"I probably didn't think it was important," he said, fingering the crease in his pants.

Alexandra didn't appreciate his flippant excuse. Noticing that they were attracting stares, she lowered her voice. "I also spoke to Bob Frazier's widow. According to her, you arbitrarily took the case away from her husband."

"Come on now, Alexandra," he said, shaking his head and giving her a patronizing look. "Twenty years is a long time. Maybe Irene didn't remember that Bob asked me to take the case over because he had a conflict."

She drew in a quick breath. Finally, he was offering her a reason. "Is that how you ended up with it?"

"Yes. Of course, hindsight is a wonderful thing to have. I realize now that I should have checked into the case myself, instead of taking Bob's word for it that the shooting was an accident. But I had no basis for doubt at the time."

Her father's answer sounded so plausible that she briefly hesitated. Still, she wasn't convinced. "What happened to Bob?"

"He killed himself."

His response caught her by surprise. "When?"

"Actually, it was not long after I rejected the case for him." Thomas stopped, then added, "Bob blew his brains out with a Magnum."

It took her a moment to process this astonishing news. "Do you know why?"

"I assumed that it was because of his son. The boy was retarded."

Now she understood why Irene Frazier had been reticent to discuss her son.

"Bob felt responsible," Thomas said, continuing on, "because he'd recently discovered that he carried a defective gene." He shrugged. "But now I'm not so sure."

"Are you implying that Bob might have taken the bribe that Erica told me about?"

"Alexandra," he said, folding his arms across

his chest, "I've already said that I don't know anything about any bribe."

"But doesn't the fact that Bob killed himself so soon after you rejected the case look more than a little suspicious to you?"

"I'm not a shrink. I'm not sure what to believe. Who knows what happened twenty years ago?"

She tried to decipher this new data. So much still wasn't making any sense. If there was a possibility that Bob Frazier had taken the bribe, then why hadn't her father mentioned the man's involvement earlier? "Why did you order me to stop looking into the case?"

"I was merely trying to discourage you," he explained. "I'm sure you can understand, Alexandra, that no prosecutor needs an old case reopened and rehashed before a primary."

While that sounded logical on the surface, it didn't mesh with the fact that he'd also threatened to fire her if she continued to dig around for information. "And what about the file on the case? What happened to it?"

Thomas looked down at his hands. "I don't know."

Again, Alexandra was skeptical. "Did you have anything to do with Joe Barton's being transferred?"

"No." His eyes didn't meet hers.

It seemed to Alexandra that although her father was answering her questions, he was hiding more than he was saying. Leaning forward, she pushed on. "Listen, Dad, I'm being pressured by the attorney general's office to tell them everything I know about Jeffrey McGrath's death. They've managed to get hold of some notes I made on the case. While I don't want to cooperate, I'm not in any position to oppose them, either. They are also prosecuting me on the drug charges."

For the first time, he looked genuinely upset. "What was in those notes of yours?"

"Details of my conversation with Erica and other facts."

Frowning, Thomas appeared to be considering the implications for him. He exhaled loudly before he spoke. "Cold notes don't mean much, Alexandra. What's more important is how *you* relate the facts to them." He raised one eyebrow and shot his daughter a measured glance. "What *I'd* do is to paint Erica as a less than reliable witness. I'd emphasize that she was dying and taking mind-altering drugs. I'd also make it clear that she was an extremely bitter woman who wanted revenge on her ex-husband."

There was a momentary pause. "If you put the right spin on your testimony, Erica will come off sounding like a crazy woman. Which of course," he hurried to add, "she was."

He stopped again and regarded his daughter. "I'd act like the bribery issue was just some last-minute ploy on Erica's part to get your attention and that you never took it seriously. Just answer their questions as directly and simply as possible, and *never* volunteer anything."

Listening to him made Alexandra extremely uncomfortable. Her father was couching his words behind language that implied *this is what I'd do*, but the result was the same. He was suggesting how she should deliberately distort the facts. That she should lie. Did he seriously think she would commit perjury or do anything that could be interpreted as obstructing justice?

"Dad, I'll be under oath. I have to tell the truth as I remember it."

His entire body tensed. "I'm not telling you what to say," he retorted. "I'm just offering an opinion on what I feel is the right way to handle a situation like this."

"Look, Dad, I don't want to cause you any problems. I just wanted to bring you up to date. I was also hoping you'd be more forthcoming." She hesitated, then went on. "Even if you don't want to tell *me*, don't you think it would behoove you to tell the A.G.'s office what happened twenty years ago, *before* it comes out in a court of law?"

He stood abruptly, looming over her, his voice taut with anger. "No, I do not, Alexandra. The smart thing to do is to not make this any worse than it has to be." He peered at his watch. "I've got to go. I've got a speaking engagement in fifteen minutes."

Sitting there watching his retreating back, Alexandra was filled with conflicting emotions. She remembered that day in his office when he wouldn't tell her anything about the case or his reasons for rejecting it. He'd insisted there was no truth to any of Erica's statements and that the woman was crazy. He'd volunteered nothing. He hadn't even told her of Bob Frazier's existence until his back was against the wall. And she was positive that he hadn't been truthful about his reasons for visiting Erica. If there was evidence to exculpate himself, wouldn't he have told her by now?

It was painful to think that her father would lie to her, and even worse, ask her to lie for him. She'd tried to help him but he'd refused to level with her. There really didn't seem to be anything more she could do.

Alexandra was convinced that the source of money for the bribe had to be the one hundred thousand dollars that George and Erica Collins had borrowed and that had not been accounted for in any of their records.

If they had paid that money as a bribe to a D.A., as Erica had claimed, who had that D.A. been? As much as she wanted to believe that her father hadn't taken part in the scheme, she didn't hold out much hope. There were really only three possibilities: Bob Frazier; her father; or the two of them together.

Somewhere there would have to be evidence suggesting that money was being received by either Thomas Kendell or Bob Frazier.

Irene Frazier seemed to lead a very simple life. If her husband had taken the bribe, what had he done with the money? Thomas had mentioned that the Fraziers' son, Ian, had been born retarded. According to Mrs. Frazier, her son was twenty-six and lived not far from her. Maybe he was in some kind of a home or an institution. How many places could there be within a certain specified area?

Alexandra began by calling the Department of Social Services and explaining that she was a deputy D.A. on leave, doing research on a case. No one asked her any questions beyond that. And saying that she was a deputy D.A. opened a lot of doors.

Several hours later, Alexandra had the information she needed. As she drove in through the gates of the Sunnyslope Home, she saw a two-story building of Spanish style at the end of a long driveway. The lawns had seen better days. Thick vines covered the walls of the building and there were bars on all of the windows.

She'd called ahead and made an appointment, so she didn't have to wait long before she was shown into the administrator's office.

"I'm checking into an old case involving Bob Frazier," she explained. "Can you tell me what it costs to keep Ian Frazier here?"

"Three thousand dollars a month," said the administrator.

"Does Mrs. Frazier write you a check for that sum?"

"No. The funds are paid by a trust."

He supplied her with the name and address of the trust and she wrote the information down before going on. "When did Ian first come here?"

As Alexandra circled the date he gave her on her legal pad, her pulse started racing. By her calculations it looked like the boy had entered the home approximately three weeks after Thomas had rejected the Collins/McGrath case. Of course, that could merely be a coincidence, but she doubted it.

Driving away, she was pretty sure whose money had paid for Ian Frazier's care for the last twenty years. What was left to determine was her father's part in the deed.

Attorney General Clifford Wolsey sat in his office in Sacramento speaking with Karen Hunter in Los Angeles as she filled him in on her meeting with Patrick Ross and Alexandra Locke.

"What do you think?" asked the Attorney General.

"As I've told you before," Karen said, "I feel that our case against George Collins may not be strong enough without Alexandra Locke's testimony."

He didn't like the way that sounded. "Even with the testimony of Jeffrey McGrath's daughter?"

"Sally McGrath Potter could be a problem on the stand," she explained. "However, I believe Alexandra Locke would make an excellent witness. I'm also convinced that she has other evidence that would help us convict Collins."

"Don't forget that it's Thomas Kendell I really want," said Wolsey.

"I understand," she replied. "But at the moment we don't have enough on Kendell to do anything. I'm hoping that once George Collins realizes the magnitude of the evidence against him, we can use that as leverage to make a deal with him. If we make it attractive enough, I think Collins will gladly tell us about his wife's part in the scheme as well as the details of any bribe they paid. And then you can go after Thomas Kendell."

"Good." The Attorney General cleared his throat. "What are the chances of Patrick Ross prevailing on their argument that Ms. Locke's notes are not the work product of the D.A.'s office?"

"I think it's a fifty-fifty proposition. But if the judge sides with her and it's upheld, the courts could rule that all of our evidence is contaminated." She paused. "And if George Collins walks out of the courtroom a free man, you'll never get your chance at Kendell."

Wolsey frowned. When Ned Taylor had first told him about Alexandra Locke's arrest, he hadn't imagined that he could do anything more with the information other than use it to embarrass Kendell. And there was no doubt it had helped his friend Frank Sanchez do well in the primary. On the other hand, he had high hopes that the Collins/McGrath case, if handled properly, could provide the necessary ammunition to bring Thomas Kendell down.

"I definitely don't want Collins to walk," the Attorney General said to Karen. "So do whatever you have to."

31

"I SPOKE TO MY secretary, Geena, at the district attorney's office," Alexandra told Patrick, barely able to contain her anger over what she'd found out.

"Go on," he urged, leaning forward over his desk, his gaze focused on her.

"She told me that all of my personal papers, books and other things were already packed up in boxes and in her car when Elizabeth Nathan insisted that she hand them over to her." Alexandra's eyes darkened with fury. "I can't believe the nerve of that woman!"

"That does take audacity," he agreed, "but it sounds like it supports our argument against the admissibility of your notes. What else did Geena say?"

"Elizabeth claimed that I said the notes on my cases were mixed in with my personal papers and that it was okay for her to look at them. She also

promised to personally deliver the boxes to me."
Alexandra gestured with her hands. "Geena was
shocked to learn that Elizabeth had never even discussed the matter with me, and that my things had
arrived by UPS."

There was a thoughtful expression on his handsome face. "So Elizabeth lied to gain access to your
papers?"

"Absolutely! It must also have been Elizabeth
who copied my notes before sending them on to
me," Alexandra said. "Although, I still don't understand how she even knew of their existence."

He tapped his pen on the desk. "Maybe your father told her and he was the one who suggested
that she copy them?"

"That's a possibility," she admitted, frowning.
"But I can't see why my father would involve her."
She mulled over the implications of her father and
Elizabeth working together for some unknown reason. "Geena also told me something else. Apparently, one day while I was in court, Elizabeth
showed up looking for two cases Geena had never
heard of. Geena followed her into my office and
had to stop her from going through my files." She
rolled her eyes for emphasis. "Geena offered to ask
me about the cases when I returned, but Elizabeth
said no, and that she'd speak to me herself. Of
course, she never did."

"Did she specifically ask for either the Collins or
the McGrath case by name?" he queried.

"Unfortunately, Geena didn't remember, but she
thought they both sounded familiar."

Playing with his brass paperweight, Patrick was pensive. "The fact that she obtained possession of your personal papers by lying to your secretary will definitely help us with the A.G.'s office," he finally said. "I think we're in a much stronger position now to make a deal with them."

The next afternoon, Alexandra and Patrick were back at Karen Hunter's office. It was a repeat performance of the day before. Alexandra sat there, her nerves taut, as the Senior Assistant A.G. and Patrick each went through their moves.

"Counsel, your client has no choice but to cooperate with us," Ms. Hunter insisted. "Her continued refusal to do so is impeding a murder investigation."

"With all due respect," Patrick countered, clearing his throat, "my client is ready and willing to cooperate. All we ask is that she be given certain assurances before she shares any information she might have. We feel this is only fair under the circumstances."

Ms. Hunter drummed her fingers on the top of her desk as if debating with herself.

"Oh, by the way," Patrick said in a droll voice, "I almost forgot to mention it. My client's secretary says that Ms. Locke's notes were packed up with her personal papers and already in the secretary's car for delivery to her, when Elizabeth Nathan lied to her and removed them. My client never gave her consent."

The Senior Assistant A.G.'s face showed clearly

that she was discomfited by this information, even though she did a remarkable job of trying to hide it. "Do you have that in writing?" she asked, watching Patrick carefully with what Alexandra thought was a newfound respect.

He smiled at her politely. "I've got her signed declaration in my briefcase." He reached down and got the document for her.

Alexandra could feel every nerve ending in her body on alert as she waited to see what was going to happen next.

"Very well," Karen Hunter finally said, looking unhappy with this turn of events. "I'm not authorized to enter into any type of formal agreement; it will only be an unofficial promise." She leaned forward and began clicking off her points. "Your client must cooperate fully; she must be truthful in relating everything she learned from Erica Collins; and, she must share all evidence uncovered by her investigation. In addition," she added in a firm voice, "she must make herself available to testify against George Collins in any and all proceedings."

The woman stopped to take a deep breath. "In return, we'll fully investigate the possibility that someone planted the drugs to stop Ms. Locke from pursuing the Collins/McGrath case." Her gaze was steady as she waited for his reply.

Patrick shook his head. "I don't like the idea that there's no formal agreement."

Karen Hunter's mouth formed a stubborn line. "That's the best I can do, Counsel."

*   *   *

Alexandra and Patrick had been given an hour to make their decision, and they had walked to a small park.

She had brought some trail mix with her in a plastic bag. "Munching on this kind of food helps me think," she explained, holding the bag out to him.

"Whatever gets some nourishment into you is okay with me," he replied, taking a handful of raisins and nuts. "You've barely been eating lately."

The fact that he had noticed gave her pause. He sounded worried about her. "I know. Between all this, and with my mother so sick, I've been too nervous to eat."

They found a low wall and sat down. "So, what do you think?" she asked.

"I don't like it," he said immediately. "If we take their deal we're basically at their mercy. If they feel you've given them everything they want, they *may* keep their promise. Then again, they may not."

"I know you're playing devil's advocate," she nodded. "And I suppose from a defense lawyer's standpoint, it's best never to trust prosecutors too much." Her eyes momentarily challenged him. "But I've been on the other side all my life. I understand where Karen Hunter is coming from. She doesn't want me on the stand explaining that in exchange for my testimony, the drug charges against me are going to be dropped. It would destroy my credibility."

"That may be true. But while you're an extremely ethical prosecutor, Alexandra, not everyone is like you," he pointed out. "As a defense lawyer, I've seen my share of deals go bad after my client gave a prosecutor what they wanted. And you've seen plenty of corrupt law enforcement officials. Are you willing to put your life in Karen Hunter's hands?"

"I'm not sure," she admitted.

"If we call her bluff," Patrick argued, "I think they'll lose the admissibility of those notes as evidence at a higher court level."

"Maybe so. I only know that it could take years to fight them all the way to the Supreme Court. And in the meantime, I've got to go ahead with the trial on the drug charges or my career is over." Her hands curled into fists at her sides. "And if I'm convicted, my life might as well be over."

"And if you make the deal?"

"At least I have a chance to be cleared," she replied. Her mind was a crazy mixture of hope and fear. "If I live up to my side of the bargain, I want to believe that they will, too. The A.G.'s office has a lot of resources at their disposal. They can find out who planted those drugs a lot easier than I can." She stopped to take a deep breath. "Besides, the more we fight them on technicalities, the more it looks like I'm guilty."

"And what about your father?" he said, his eyes searching her face. "If you testify, you'll be asked about him."

"That bothers me more than anything," she

confessed, feeling her neck growing tense. She rubbed it with one hand while she went on. "Yet I've given my dad so many chances to level with me, and he still hasn't. I don't want to hurt him, but how much longer can I keep trying to protect him?"

He appraised her. "Do you want my opinion?"

"Yes." She nodded.

"I think you have to do what's best for yourself," he said quietly. "But that doesn't mean that this deal is the way you should go. I want to be sure that you fully understand the pros and cons of an agreement like this."

"Thanks to you, Patrick, I've looked at every issue backward and forward. I go to bed at night thinking about it, and I wake up in the morning thinking about it."

Patrick shifted his position on the wall. "If you don't feel ready to make this decision yet, I'll get you some more time."

"I'm sure we could squeeze another day or two out of Karen Hunter, but the bottom line is—I can't live this way anymore." Unable to hide her anguish, she swallowed with difficulty and then struggled to find her voice. "If I make a deal with them, I'll be taking back some control of my own life. Whether it turns out to be the correct decision or not," she said, shaking her head, "I've got to take the chance." Her eyes pleaded with him. "Can you understand that?"

"Yes and no," he answered honestly. "As a defense lawyer, I've learned the game of patience. It sounds to me like your emotions are getting in the way of your head."

"You could be right," she said, staring directly into his eyes. "I've made a lot of snap decisions in my life, and I've lived to regret some of them."

"And I've probably done the opposite," he acknowledged, his gaze meeting hers. "But that doesn't mean I don't have my regrets, too."

She took a deep breath. "What's important now is for me to do what I feel is right," she said softly, "no matter what the consequences are."

George was picking up the morning newspaper lying by his open front gate, when he saw a car pull up and two men wearing suits got out.

"Doctor George Collins?" asked one of the men.

"Yes?" he responded.

The other man flashed a badge. "We've got a warrant for your arrest."

George's mouth went dry and his stomach contracted with fear. "What for?" he managed to get out.

"Murder," the second cop said, coming up to him. "Please put your hands behind you."

George did as he was told and the cop snapped the handcuffs in place. The other cop then pulled out a card and started to read him his Miranda rights.

When the cop was through, he jerked on the handcuffs. "We're taking you in."

"May I at least tell my wife what's happened?"

"Sure." They both accompanied him up the driveway and to the front door.

"Lorna," he called out. "Come downstairs, darling. I need to speak to you."

His wife, wearing a cream-colored satin robe, appeared at the head of the landing. "What's wrong?" When she saw the men standing with her husband, she seemed to freeze as her eyes glittered with fear.

George twisted around so that she could see the handcuffs. "Call our lawyer."

"What are they arresting you for?" she gasped, rushing down the stairs.

"Murder," one of the cops said as she came to stand beside George.

Lorna paled. "George, what are we going to do?" She seemed to be on the verge of panic.

He gave her a warning look to be quiet. "Call our lawyer, Walter Underhill," he repeated, as calmly as possible. "He'll handle everything." He leaned over and gave her a quick kiss on her forehead. "Don't worry, Lorna. I promise you—it will be okay."

"Where are you taking him?" she asked the cops, her voice cracking slightly.

"Parker Center," one of the cops said.

George tried to bolster his wife's spirits by flashing a confident smile. He knew that the longer they stayed here, the more chance there was that Lorna would blurt out something he wouldn't want the cops to hear. "Let's go," he told them, turning toward the door.

After pulling herself together and dressing carefully, Lorna showed up at the studio where Michael was directing a picture and demanded to see her son.

"Sorry," his assistant said, shaking his head. "They're shooting. He'll kill me if I disturb him. As soon as they break, I'll let him know you're here. Can I get you something while you wait?"

"Yes," she said, her eyes blazing angrily. "You can get me my son—and *now!*" She gave him a look to convey that she refused to take no for an answer.

"But I've already explained . . ."

She was not in the mood to be subtle. "How would you like to lose your job?"

The assistant seemed to be weighing her threat.

Lorna prodded him some more. "I promise you, my son *will* listen to me."

A short time later, Michael came rushing into his office. His face was flushed as if he'd been running. "Mom, what's wrong? What's happened?"

As soon as they were behind closed doors she told him. "George has been arrested."

Michael appeared to sway on his feet and had to quickly sit down. "When?"

"This morning. It's been on the news. I thought you would have heard."

"No," he said. "I've been on the set. I haven't heard anything." He wiped his brow. "Let me get things squared away here, and I'll go with you." He stopped for a moment. "Have you contacted a lawyer?"

"Of course. Ever since that damn prosecutor, Alexandra Locke, entered our lives, George has been communicating regularly with Walter Underhill. He knows exactly what's been going on."

Michael looked worried. "Did Underhill say he could get George out on bail?"

Fear shot through her. "He wasn't sure."

"Dear God," Michael muttered, rubbing the dark stubble on his chin. Finally, he glanced up at his mother. "How are you managing?"

"Not very well." She gave a small shudder. "We may have failed to keep Sally from going to the district attorney's office," she said grimly. "But we absolutely can't allow her to testify against George."

"Tell me what you want me to do. I'll go to the cops and tell them anything you want me to say."

"I'm not sure what to do," she admitted, tears filling her eyes. "I'm frightened." She put her hand to her throat. "What if they arrest me, too?"

He came over and put his arms around her. "I understand that you're frightened. But don't worry about being arrested. What could they possibly have against you?"

Lorna contemplated telling him, then changed her mind. "Perhaps I'm being overly dramatic," she said, realizing she had to calm herself down or all would be lost. Then, taking a deep breath, she felt her resolve returning. "Let's go to Walter Underhill's office. He should have some ideas. The man gets a fortune for every second he spends with us. We might as well get our money's worth."

*   *   *

As Alexandra sat by her mother's bed at the City of Hope, she saw how weak Roberta was becoming.

"I don't want any more chemo," Roberta said, gazing at her daughter. Her eyes no longer looked hazel, but like pools of black ink. She was on a lot of morphine for the pain.

"Do you want me to get the doctor?" Alexandra asked, her heart breaking.

Roberta reached for her daughter's hand and nodded. "It's time for me to go home. And I want you to arrange for nurses and . . . hospice care, too."

Alexandra choked back her tears. "Whatever you want."

"Important . . . die at home with your father and you both there with me."

"Okay," Alexandra said, barely trusting herself to speak. She didn't want to cry and make this harder for her mother.

"Your father's . . . going to object . . ." Roberta's words trailed off as she gazed imploringly at Alexandra. "I can't make him . . . understand. He feels as if I'm abandoning him."

"I'll talk to him," Alexandra promised.

"Sleep now," Roberta said, closing her eyes.

Now that her mother couldn't see her, Alexandra allowed the tears to roll down her face.

When Thomas arrived several hours later, she explained to him what had been decided. At first Thomas wouldn't go along. Instead, he'd rushed into Roberta's room and tried to make her change her mind, telling her over and over again how much he loved her. Standing at the doorway, Alexandra watched as her mother kept shaking her head.

Finally, Thomas decided to speak to the doctor, and Alexandra went with him.

"I've got to convince her to give it one more try," Thomas kept saying to the doctor.

"Mrs. Kendell is lucid," the doctor reminded him. "In these types of cases we like to follow the patient's wishes." He paused, his eyes conveying sympathy. "In my opinion, another round of experimental therapy will not help her," he added in a firm voice. "It will only make her last days or weeks more difficult."

"She's suffering too much already, Dad," Alexandra said quietly, her eyes begging her father to accept the inevitable. "I know this is hard for you. It is for me, too." Her voice cracked. "But doesn't Mom deserve the dignity of deciding her own fate?"

Thomas seemed to shrink before her eyes as he slumped down heavily in the chair. He looked beaten. He just kept shaking his head as if he could shake away the truth that his wife was dying.

32

ON THE FIRST DAY of George Collins's preliminary hearing, Alexandra paced back and forth in
the corridor waiting to be called to the witness
stand. The hallway was crammed with reporters
and television crews jostling each other for a better
position from which to view the participants.

"Thanks for being here," she said to Patrick,
who was standing next to her.

Looking handsome in a navy-blue pinstriped
suit and a light blue shirt, he'd made himself a
human shield to block the photographers from getting at her. "No problem," he said, smiling.

"I can't believe how fast things are moving," she
whispered.

"It surprised me too," Patrick whispered back.
"It's not what most defendants opt for."

George Collins had asked for his preliminary
hearing to be set for ten court days after his arraignment. There were many reasons to delay a

hearing, thought Alexandra. Usually, the more time the lawyers had, the better the defense they could put on. But if one was rich like George, and willing to spend a lot of money, the defense could get ready very fast while the prosecution might not be able to mobilize that quickly. This sometimes gave the defense an advantage and the prosecution couldn't do anything about it. Under the due process clause of the Constitution, the right to a speedy trial belonged to the defendant.

"It's a smart move on George's part," she said. "He's hoping my arrest makes me a less credible witness. And while that information won't be allowed into evidence, anyone who's picked up a paper or turned on their TV will know, including the judge. George wants me testifying under a cloud of suspicion."

"There are a lot of people who believe in you," Patrick told her, an earnest look on his face.

Before she could respond there was a commotion at the other end of the hallway. It was George and Lorna Collins, flanked by George's legal team. George was dressed in a somber suit and tie, while Lorna was decked out in a smartly tailored black suit and high heels.

"I almost went into hock posting twenty thousand dollars bail," Alexandra said ruefully, "and George posted three million like that." She snapped her fingers to make her point.

"That's our justice system," Patrick stated. "The rich post bail and remain free pending their preliminary hearing and trial. The poor wait in jail."

"At least we got my preliminary hearing postponed until after the outcome of George's case."

"Yeah," Patrick replied, looking less than overjoyed.

She knew that he wasn't satisfied with the deal they'd made with the attorney general's office, but she felt it had been the right decision. She just prayed that the A.G.'s office kept their word and investigated her allegations of being framed. While it meant that she was still in limbo and unable to work, at the moment she preferred to spend as much time as possible with her mother.

Thinking about her mother, she sighed. A little more than two weeks ago Roberta had returned home, where she was being cared for by round-the-clock nurses.

Although Thomas and Alexandra had to tell Roberta something about what was going on, the information they disclosed had been minimal, and Roberta was really too sick to absorb most of it. Alexandra shuddered at the realization that it wouldn't be much longer before Roberta closed her eyes forever.

"There's Harry Isen," said Patrick, gesturing toward a small, wiry man with dark hair and a neatly clipped mustache. Karen Hunter had appointed him as the prosecutor for George's hearing. The man was carrying two huge briefcases. Next to him, someone else pulled a cart loaded down with cardboard file boxes.

"Have you had many dealings with him?" Alexandra asked.

"No. But Tricia told me he's had a lot of experience. He's also someone who won't get flustered by the relatively high profile of the defendant and all the media attention being paid to the case."

That was an important factor, she thought. Sometimes lawyers and judges got so carried away with their instant fame that they spent too much time in front of the cameras and not enough time doing their homework. The courtroom was only a part of the working day. Afterward, there was usually hours more of work: looking up citations, preparing witnesses for the next day, doing the paperwork to issue subpoenas or file motions, not to mention returning dozens of calls.

The bailiff had opened the courtroom doors and was allowing certain people inside. Due to the intense media interest and the limited seating capacity, reporters had to have an assigned seat. That's why so many of them were taking turns sharing a pass.

George Collins and his entourage went through the door, but his wife stayed behind. Since Lorna was being called as a witness, she wasn't allowed into the courtroom prior to her testimony.

One of the members of the defense team escorted Lorna to a bench. When her green eyes met Alexandra's, she gave her such a look of contempt that Alexandra felt chilled from its impact.

"I'm glad you got Isen to call me to the stand first," she said quickly to Patrick, hoping that if neither side contemplated recalling her, she could remain in the courtroom afterward. "I'll go nuts sitting here not knowing what's going on."

Patrick glanced at his watch. "I want to check with Isen to make sure we're still on schedule. Will you be okay for a minute?"

"Of course," she replied, wishing she meant it.

After he left, her attention was drawn to another pair getting off the elevator. It was Michael McGrath accompanied by his grandfather, Lester. She sighed with relief when neither of them looked her way.

Soon Patrick was back. "One slight change. They're calling Lester McGrath to the stand first. You second. Isen said they wanted to put a human face on the victim, and who better to tell the court how wonderful Jeffrey McGrath was than his father?"

"Damn," she said. She really couldn't fault Isen. It was something she would have done as a prosecutor. But that didn't make it any easier for her to accept. Now she'd have to wait even longer out here in the hallway.

"Looks like Michael McGrath's being allowed in," she said gesturing toward the doors. "I guess they're not planning to call him as a witness." She paused before asking, "Are you going inside to hear Lester's testimony?"

"No. I'm sure he'll paint Jeffrey McGrath as a paragon of virtue and the best son a man ever had. Standard stuff. I'll stay with you until you're called."

Alexandra flashed him a grateful smile. They

made small talk with another lawyer Patrick had worked with on a recent case. Before long, the time had passed. Suddenly the bailiff appeared in front of her. "Ms. Locke, they're ready for you now."

Glancing up at him, she nodded. Then she drew in a long breath and prepared herself for what was coming.

As she walked to the witness stand, Alexandra felt extremely uncomfortable. In spite of Patrick's kind words to the contrary, she was convinced that, because of her arrest, everyone in the courtroom, including Judge Terrance Washington, had prejudged her credibility and found it lacking.

The clerk swore her in and she sat down. Her mouth was dry and she forced herself to swallow.

After Isen had asked some preliminary questions, the prosecutor finally arrived at the heart of the matter. "Now, Ms. Locke, did there come a time when you were in Erica Collins's hospital room that she mentioned Jeffrey McGrath's death to you?"

"Yes."

"Would you please tell this court what she said?"

"Erica stated that twenty years ago her ex-husband George Collins had killed his best friend, Jeffrey McGrath, and that she had helped him get away with it."

There was a slight murmuring in the courtroom. Isen took a step forward. "Did Mrs. Collins say how she had helped her husband, George, get away with this crime?"

"Objection, hearsay," said Walter Underhill, George Collins's defense attorney. He was objecting regardless of the fact that before this hearing got started, certain disputed issues had already been hammered out. One such issue was the admissibility of Erica's statements as made to Alexandra. The judge had already ruled that because Erica had implicated herself in a crime by making a declaration against penal interest, certain portions of her statement would be allowed into evidence as an exception to the hearsay rule. Underhill was merely preserving the record for later.

"Overruled," stated the judge. Nodding at Alexandra, he said, "You may answer the question."

"What Erica Collins told me was that they had paid a young deputy D.A. one hundred thousand dollars in cash to keep George Collins out of prison."

"And did Erica Collins mention who at the D.A.'s office it was that they allegedly paid this money to?"

"Not exactly."

"What do you mean?"

Alexandra's stomach tightened. She wished she didn't have to respond. "She merely mentioned the deputy D.A. who had been in charge of the case."

"And what was the name she gave you?"

She had no choice but to answer. "Thomas Kendell."

"Thomas Kendell is your father, isn't he?"

"Yes," she replied, her voice low.

"Did Erica Collins indicate what her marital status was with Doctor Collins when she spoke to you at the City of Hope?"

"Yes. She referred to him as her ex-husband and said they were divorced."

Isen put his hands behind his back as he asked his next question. "Did Erica Collins ever explain why she hadn't gone to the authorities about this crime?"

"Yes."

"Would you please tell us what she said?"

"Erica stated that she was afraid."

"Did Erica say what it was she was afraid of?"

"At first it sounded like she might have been afraid of her husband—"

"Objection," shouted Underhill, jumping to his feet. "I move to strike the entire answer as nonresponsive."

"Sustained," said the judge.

"What words did Erica Collins use when she said she was afraid?"

"She said she didn't know what she was getting into back then and didn't want to go to prison."

When the prosecutor went back to his table to pick up a yellow legal tablet, Alexandra glanced out at the courtroom. She noted that Michael McGrath was seated behind George, his gaze focused directly on her. He was frowning. Their eyes locked for a moment. She quickly looked away and concentrated instead on the prosecutor, who had returned to his prior position.

Responding to Isen's next several questions, Alexandra explained that Erica had said she should have told the authorities about the crime twenty years ago. That she was dying of cancer. That her husband had murdered a man in cold blood and that she didn't want to die with it on her conscience.

"And did Erica extract a promise from you to look into the matter?"

"Yes."

In response to more questions, Alexandra told the court how she came to be in possession of a key to Erica Collins's storage locker and what she had found when going through Erica's things. When Alexandra got to the love letter, she was asked by the prosecutor to identify it. The letter was then marked as an exhibit and entered into evidence. Finally, Alexandra was asked to read a portion of it.

There were titters in the courtroom at the graphic language in the letter. Alexandra glanced over at Michael McGrath to see his reaction. His face was beet red and he was scowling.

She went on to tell the court about her visit to George Collins's office and the things he had told her. The defense lawyer objected many times, and there were numerous sidebar conferences with the judge while the admissibility of these statements was argued.

She then related to the court the details concerning the financial records she'd found in Erica's locker and what they'd indicated. When she identified the copy of the insurance check, she caught the look of surprise on Michael's face.

After what seemed like eternity, Isen finally turned toward the judge. "No further questions for this witness, Your Honor."

Alexandra was glad that this was only a preliminary hearing. That meant both sides would be careful not to expose their entire case. The prosecution merely wanted to present enough information to hold George over for trial and the defense merely wanted to show enough of their strategy to keep the reporting by the media even-handed. It was a fact of life in today's electronic age that a person's guilt or innocence was heavily weighed in the media long before the trial ever took place.

Underhill, the defense lawyer, stood up. He was in his early fifties and had large jowls and small eyes. He also had a reputation for being a skillful examiner, and an expert at going for the jugular. As he approached her, Alexandra felt a sense of unease. This man's job was to do everything he could to discredit her, and she steeled herself for his assault.

"You've testified that Erica Collins acknowledged to you that she was dying?"

"Yes."

"Didn't she seem to be bitter about that?"

"Objection," Isen stated. "Calls for speculation on the part of the witness."

Not waiting for the judge to issue his ruling, Underhill said, "I'll rephrase. In your opinion, Ms.

Locke, didn't Erica Collins seem to be bitter about the fact that she was dying?"

Alexandra thought back to that evening in Erica Collins's room. "Yes," she replied.

"Didn't Erica Collins threaten to go to the media if you didn't help her?"

"Yes."

"And didn't she also threaten to turn over her information to someone else?"

"Yes."

"Who was that?"

"Frank Sanchez."

"Isn't he the man who is opposing your father for L.A. County District Attorney?"

"Yes."

"Did it ever dawn on you that Erica Collins could be seeking revenge against her ex-husband?"

"Yes."

Underhill asked the judge for a moment to confer with his client. After a short, whispered conversation with George, Underhill straightened up and came toward her again.

"Ms. Locke, you've told this court that Erica mentioned your father was the deputy D.A. who was in charge of the case. Is that correct?"

"Yes," she admitted.

He gave her a warm smile that she knew was intended to disarm her. "Did you have any thoughts at that moment as to whether or not Erica could be lying?"

"Objection," Isen said, jumping up. "That calls for speculation on the part of the witness."

Judge Washington looked over his glasses and pronounced his ruling. "Sustained."

Underhill wasn't going to be deterred. "Isn't it true, Ms. Locke, that you and your father have not been on the best of terms for the last fourteen years?"

"Objection," said Isen again. "Relevance."

"Your Honor," Underhill said, his voice pitched to sound like a reasonable man, "I'm merely trying to find out if this witness had an ulterior motive for wanting to see her father implicated in a crime." He motioned with his hands. "It goes directly to her credibility."

The judge seemed to be considering Underhill's argument. "Very well," he finally said. "I'll allow it."

"May we have the question read back?" asked Underhill.

The court reporter found her place and reread the question. "Isn't it true, Ms. Locke, that you and your father have not been on the best of terms for the last fourteen years?"

Knowing that she had no choice but to be truthful, Alexandra felt cornered. "Yes," she said in a barely audible voice.

There was a buzz in the courtroom as people commented to one another. Sitting there stiffly, Alexandra kept her gaze focused on Underhill, who was smiling widely as if he'd just won a large victory. Finally, the judge asked for quiet.

"Isn't it also a fact that your father didn't want you to apply for a job with his office?"

She hesitated briefly before responding. "Yes."

"But you went ahead with your application anyway, didn't you?"

Alexandra knew he was trying to imply that she'd joined the office to spite her father. Hoping she could get away without a yes or no answer, she gave it a try. "He acquiesced when he understood how important it was to me."

"Your Honor, would you please instruct the witness that a simple yes or no is sufficient to my questions?"

The judge reprimanded her.

"Yes," she finally answered.

"Ms. Locke, did you tell anyone else what you learned from Mrs. Collins?"

"Yes."

"And who would that be?"

"The prosecution. My lawyer. My father."

"How much time passed between Erica's statements to you and your giving this information to the prosecution?"

She knew where he was heading and was powerless to stop it.

"Approximately two months."

Underhill smiled at her. "And how much time passed between Erica's statements to you and your telling your lawyer?"

Isen objected. "That's privileged."

A sidebar conference was held and the judge decided she didn't have to answer. But Alexandra knew that everyone in the courtroom had heard that she had her own lawyer and must have figured out why.

Coming closer, Underhill asked another question she was dreading. "And how long was it after Erica Collins told you her story that you mentioned her accusations to your father?"

Having no choice, she said, "A few days."

The defense lawyer looked askance at her answer. "So then you're telling this court that you told your father about Erica's accusations a few days after you heard them, but you waited almost two months to tell the Attorney General's office?"

"Yes," she admitted, "but there were—"

"Your Honor, please instruct the witness again on answering yes or no."

Isen stood up and objected. "Asked and answered."

Underhill was undeterred. "Then I ask the court to strike the last part of the witness's answer after the word 'yes.' "

The judge did as Underhill asked.

"Now, Ms. Locke," said Underhill, getting ready to draw blood. "Isn't it likely that the reason you waited so long to tell the Attorney General's office was because you didn't believe Erica's story?"

"Objection," called Isen. "Lack of foundation."

"Overruled."

Underhill waited for Alexandra to answer.

"I had my doubts," she conceded.

With a flourish, the defense lawyer again waved

his hands. "I have no further questions," he said in a dismissive tone of voice, as if to say that Alexandra wasn't worth any more of his time. Underhill then went back to his seat, patted his client on the back and sat down.

Judge Washington eyed the prosecution. The deputy attorney general stood up and came forward.

"Ms. Locke, can you please tell this court your reasons for waiting so long before turning this evidence over to the attorney general's office?"

"Yes. I was looking for corroborating evidence."

"And once you found that evidence, did you turn over everything you had in your possession?"

"Yes."

"And Ms. Locke," said Isen in a strong voice. "When you told this court that Erica Collins implicated Thomas Kendell as the D.A. who was in charge of the case, were you speaking the truth?"

Her stomach clenched as she said, "Yes."

"No further questions," Isen said with a satisfied smile of his own.

A sigh of relief escaped Alexandra's lips as she realized she could leave the stand. Answering the questions about her father had been difficult and she was glad it was over—at least for now. Although Underhill had made some points, neither side had used all of their ammunition. When the time came for the actual trial, she'd find herself pounded mercilessly by the defense solely for the benefit of the jury.

Next, she watched anxiously while the judge determined whether either side expected to call her to the stand again during this hearing. Finally, the judge informed her that she would be allowed to remain in the courtroom. As she stood, Alexandra felt all eyes were on her once more as she headed for the empty seat next to Patrick.

A short time later, Alexandra listened to a man testify that he'd been the McGraths' insurance agent before Jeffrey's death.

In answer to the prosecutor's question, the agent explained that Jeffrey had purchased an insurance policy from him for one million dollars approximately a year before his death.

Isen held out a document that had already been introduced into evidence. "I ask you to take a look at People's Exhibit 10. Do you recognize it?"

"Yes," the agent said. "It's the insurance check the company issued on the policy after Jeffrey died."

"And who was the beneficiary under this policy?"

"Lorna McGrath, Jeffrey McGrath's wife—I mean widow."

"Do you know of your own personal knowledge if this check was ever delivered to Lorna McGrath?"

"Yes," the agent replied, nodding his head.

Alexandra glanced over at Michael to see how he was taking this testimony. Michael had shifted forward in his seat and his hand was gripping the chair in front of him.

Isen rubbed his hands together. "Can you please explain how you knew of this delivery?"

"Of course," said the agent. "Lorna McGrath received that check because I personally gave it to her."

Michael McGrath's face was ashen. Alexandra thought back to the conversation she'd had with him and his mother in the restaurant at the New Otani Hotel. Lorna had said that her dead husband hadn't had any life insurance. Now, seeing how upset Michael appeared, she guessed that Lorna must have kept the truth from him and his sister. Why, she wondered, would a mother want her children to believe that their father had not provided for them?

Frank Sanchez had been trying to keep abreast of all the developments in the Collins case. He was especially eager to learn if Thomas Kendell had been accused in open court of having participated in a cover-up.

Planning on observing the proceedings as a spectator, Frank saw the crowd gathered in the hallway outside the courtroom and realized he wouldn't get inside unless he used some sort of ruse. He was still deciding what to do when the doors opened and several people came out. It looked to him like a recess had been called.

"Frank."

He saw it was Elizabeth. How long had she been inside? he wondered as she joined him. Elizabeth had just started to tell him something when Alexandra Locke came over to where they were standing.

She appeared shaken. In spite of the fact that he was personally gaining a lot of headway in the polls from her misfortunes, Frank felt sorry for her.

Looking Frank squarely in the eye, Alexandra said, "Did you know that Elizabeth lied to my secretary so that she'd turn over to her several boxes of my *personal* papers and other belongings— things that were already packed up for me and in my secretary's car?"

Frank's eyes narrowed as he glared at Elizabeth. "You told me you found those notes in Alexandra's office. That they were in files belonging to the D.A.'s office."

"What difference does it make now?" Elizabeth said, shrugging her shoulders. "Alexandra has obviously waived any objections she might have had by testifying here today."

He was still appalled.

"After promising Geena to personally deliver the boxes to me," Alexandra continued on, "Elizabeth copied what she wanted and then sent my things to me by UPS." She paused before turning to address Elizabeth. "How did you even know about the Collins/McGrath case?"

"Sally McGrath Potter came to see me," Elizabeth replied smugly.

Looking from Elizabeth to Alexandra, Frank was trying to figure out what was going on.

"Was it your decision to copy my papers?" Alexandra asked Elizabeth. "Or did my father or Frank put you up to doing it?"

"I never asked her to copy anything," Frank insisted, shaken by the suggestion.

"And I'd never follow instructions like that from Thomas," Elizabeth snapped.

After Alexandra walked away, Frank focused his attention on Elizabeth, ready to give her a piece of his mind.

She spoke first. "What's important is that Alexandra took the stand and implicated Thomas in taking a bribe." Elizabeth's eyes gleamed with excitement. "Finally, he's going to get his."

"Maybe, maybe not," Frank said. "Don't you think if they had any real evidence against Thomas, besides the words of a dead woman, they would have arrested him by now?"

She glanced around quickly, as if making sure that no one was close enough to overhear. "The A.G.'s office is confident that after this hearing, George Collins will be so concerned about the weight of the evidence against him that he'll change his mind and make a deal. For a lighter sentence he'll divulge Thomas Kendell's part in everything, including the bribe."

Frank was surprised. "Just where are you getting your inside information?"

"Oh," she said shrugging. "I've got my sources."

"Who?"

"Really, Frank, I'd tell you if I could, but I promised not to say."

"I see," he said, not at all pleased by her arrogant attitude.

"Anyway, don't look so glum. Thomas is going down for the count," she assured him with a knowing smile. "And his daughter is going with him."

33

———— ~ ————

ALEXANDRA WATCHED as Vince Donovan, the retired sheriff's deputy she'd spoken to on the telephone, took the stand. After qualifying the witness, Donovan began testifying as to what he'd observed when he'd arrived on the scene and found that Jeffrey McGrath had been shot. Since Alexandra already knew the answers to the questions he was being asked, she gazed around the room, trying to judge the reaction to his testimony.

After Donovan was through, other sheriff's deputies, including Joe Barton, were called to the stand. Then there were those from the crime lab, who testified to collecting and preserving crime scene evidence.

Finally, Isen called the medical examiner as the next witness. An older, heavyset man in a conservative, ill-fitting gray suit, he peered out at the courtroom from behind rectangular black plastic-framed glasses, so old they had come into fashion again.

Before he got to the matter at hand, Isen led the man through a lengthy set of routine questions to establish his qualifications. "Were you the medical examiner who physically examined the decedent twenty years ago?"

"Yes," the medical examiner acknowledged with a nod of his head. "I also personally supervised all of the necessary tissue and organ studies."

"And what did you first see when you observed the decedent?"

"A large shotgun wound to the chest."

Isen came to stand in front of him. "Did you notice anything unusual about the position of the decedent's wound?"

"Yes, I did."

"Would you please tell this court what that was?"

"I found that the shotgun pellets entered the decedent's body from the front to the back of the torso."

"Did this cause you to question the explanation the defendant, George Collins, gave for how this shooting occurred?" asked Isen.

There was a hush as everyone seemed to be waiting expectantly for his answer. "Yes," the witness replied, taking off his glasses and wiping them with a handkerchief that he had removed from his pocket.

"Can you explain why you questioned his explanation?"

"It was my observation that if Jeffrey McGrath had tripped and fallen as the defendant said, the buckshot wouldn't have gone through his chest at a ninety-degree angle."

"And what did you base this observation on?"

"The fact that when a person trips and falls, the body is at an angle to the ground as opposed to being in a vertical position as when the body is standing up."

"Now, using these same angles in your explanation, sir, can you tell us at which angle the pellets in this case entered the decedent's body?"

"At more of a horizontal angle."

"And from these observations," Isen said, his voice rising to let everyone know that the next question would be even more important than the last, "did you form an opinion as to what had in fact happened?"

"Yes, I did."

Isen smiled at the witness. "Would you please tell this court what that opinion is?"

The medical examiner cleared his throat before speaking. "The decedent's wounds were consistent with those that would occur if the decedent had been standing up at the time he was shot and someone had fired at him from close range with the gun pointed directly at his chest."

As people started whispering in the courtroom, Judge Washington pounded his gavel and declared a recess.

For over an hour, Alexandra had been sitting there in the courtroom watching the defense lawyer, Walter Underhill, grill the medical exam-

iner, who was still on the stand. She didn't personally care for the man's style. Too much of a show-
man. Lots of defense lawyers liked to think that
they were performing on a stage, but she thought
it was overkill. Especially at a preliminary hearing
with only a judge and no jury present. Finally, the
man seemed to be winding down.

"In your many years of experience, have you
ever seen shotgun pellets hit a bone and be deflected?" asked Underhill, gazing around the room
expectantly as he waited for the answer.

"Yes."

"Then isn't it possible, sir, that shotgun pellets
that are deflected could end up traveling at a
ninety-degree angle?"

"I've never seen that happen," the medical examiner insisted.

Underhill frowned as if the medical examiner
had not told the truth. "But can you say with any
degree of certainty that it's impossible?"

"No," the medical examiner admitted, shaking
his head. "I can't say it's impossible, but as I
said—"

"Your Honor, please instruct the witness to just
answer the question."

The judge looked over at the medical examiner
and gave the desired instruction.

Pacing back and forth, the defense lawyer now
turned to ask his next question. "Can you state unequivocally, Doctor, that there's absolutely no way
a random shot can end up looking like a shot that
was deliberate?"

"As I said before, it is extremely unlikely for that to happen."

"Your Honor," Underhill pleaded, rolling his eyes for the benefit of the court, "would you please strike the last answer as nonresponsive and order the witness to give us a simple yes or no?"

The judge told the medical examiner to so answer. Underhill nodded and turned back to the witness.

Forced to comply, the medical examiner shifted uncomfortably in his seat. "No," he admitted, with an unhappy expression on his face.

Looking pleased with himself again, the defense lawyer waved his hands in a dramatic gesture. "I've no further questions," he said before taking his seat.

Underhill had just used a time-tested legal maneuver employed in courts across the land. It was called the "stop while you are ahead" move. Alexandra herself had used it many times before.

The next witness was the criminalist. Isen stood and after qualifying the man as an expert, he began to question him about the weapon.

"Can you tell this court what type of gun fired the fatal shot into the decedent's body?"

"Yes. It was a twelve-gauge, double-barreled shotgun."

"Is this a common type of gun?" asked Isen.

"Not as common as a one-barreled gun. But both are frequently used in hunting season."

Isen smiled. "In your experience, when hunters are going out to shoot small game such as rabbits and squirrels, what type of ammunition do they use?"

"For small game they'll usually use a fine shot."

"And what was the type of ammunition found in the decedent's body?"

"Buckshot."

Isen took another step forward. "And in your experience, what kind of game is that type of ammunition more commonly used for?"

"Big game, such as deer."

The prosecutor stopped to check his notes. "When a twelve-gauge shotgun is fired at a person from close range, what type of a hole does it make?"

The criminalist lifted one eyebrow. "A very large hole," he said dryly.

"Can you usually tell from what distance a shotgun has been fired after the fact?"

"Usually yes," replied the witness. "Double-barreled guns frequently have one barrel smooth-bored and the other chokebored. To determine accurately the distance from which the gun was fired we find it necessary to make test shots with the particular weapon used."

"And why is that?"

"Because when the shotgun has been held in direct contact or very close to the skin, we see burning, singeing and charring of tissue much the same as in contact wounds due to revolvers and pistols."

Giving a few seconds for the information to sink in, Isen then said, "And could you perform these test shots in this case?"

"No," the witness said, shaking his head.

"And why was that?"

"Because the shotgun that fired the fatal shot had been smashed against a tree afterward and couldn't be fired."

There was a smattering of talking in the courtroom as Isen prepared to ask his next question. "In view of your years of experience, do you have an opinion as to why someone would want to smash a shotgun against a tree?"

"Objection," said Underhill. "Calls for speculation."

"Your Honor," Isen said, "I'm merely asking for an opinion from this witness."

"Overruled. Please answer the question."

The court reporter read back the question. "In view of your years of experience, do you have an opinion as to why someone would want to smash a shotgun against a tree?"

"Yes," replied the witness.

Alexandra wondered why the judge had overruled the objection. In her opinion, the admissibility of this evidence would be reversed at some later date.

"Can you please tell us what your opinion is?" asked Isen.

Looking directly at George Collins as he spoke, the criminalist said, "It would seem to me that the person who smashed the weapon against the tree was trying to keep the shotgun from being test fired after the incident."

"Thank you. No further questions." Looking pleased with the responses he had elicited, Isen sat down.

Underhill rose and came toward the expert. "Are you saying, sir, that you've never seen ordinary hunters go after small game with buckshot?"

"No. I'm merely saying that it's overkill."

"But it's done nevertheless, isn't that correct?"

"Yes."

"Isn't it true that if a shotgun is fired from beyond ten feet that the pattern of shot will become more scattered in proportion to the distance?"

"Yes."

"And was that apparent in this case?"

"No," the witness admitted.

"So then you agree that this shotgun was fired from a very close range?"

"Yes."

"And isn't it true," asked Underhill, waving his arm, "that whether a gun was fired by someone tripping with their own gun or by someone standing directly in front of them, forgetting the angle of the shot, the pattern will be very similar? In other words, it will look like the shotgun was fired from very close range?"

"If you delete the angle from the equation, the answer is yes."

"We've had previous expert testimony that the angle of a bullet or more particularly, buckshot, can be altered if that shot is deflected," Underhill said. "In your opinion, isn't that possible?"

"I suppose so, although—"

"Your Honor," Underhill protested, frowning, "could you please direct the witness to answer the question with a yes or a no?"

The judge glanced at the witness and nodded. "Please so answer."

"Yes."

"I've no further questions at this time."

Alexandra knew that at the actual trial both sides would bring in more experts to present their theory of how this shooting had taken place. And she assumed that George Collins's attorney had already hired the best experts that money could buy. So far however, by just questioning the state's experts, Underhill was doing a fair job of raising reasonable doubt.

That night, George was having dinner with Lorna in their large kitchen. Because she wasn't allowed to be in the courtroom until after she testified, he was trying to bring her up to date on everything that had happened earlier in the day.

"I can't stand having to wait in the hallway," she lamented, draining her glass of red wine and asking George to pour her another. "How do you feel it's going?"

"I think Underhill made some good points," he said, filling her glass to the brim. "He got Alexandra to admit that she didn't get along that well with her father, which didn't help her credibility as a witness. Hopefully the judge knows about her arrest on the drug charges. We've got the top lawyers in this city, Lorna. I'm sure we're going to beat this."

George stopped to take a gulp of his drink. "We also made some good headway in disputing the prosecution's theory regarding the manner and mode of Jeffrey's death."

In spite of his positive words, Lorna still looked uneasy. "Has anyone spoken to Sally?"

"No," George admitted with a frustrated sigh. "Michael said he called her, but Arnold answered and told him that Sally refused to come to the phone."

"I'm worried," Lorna admitted. "I'm afraid that she's going to be the prosecution's star witness."

"She hasn't testified yet," George reminded her in a firm voice while he stroked her shoulder. "And I am willing to bet that she won't do it."

"I hope you're right." She took several more long sips of her wine.

The doorbell rang and George went to see who it was. He was surprised to find Michael standing there. He looked very upset. "Come on in," George said, stepping aside.

"Where's my mother?" Michael asked, his eyes darting around.

"In the kitchen," George replied, noticing that his stepson was more tightly wound than usual. "We were just having some supper. Would you like to join us?"

"No thanks." Without another word, Michael quickly moved past George and headed for the kitchen. George hurried after him, reaching the room in time to hear Michael hurling a question at his mother.

"Why did you tell me that my father didn't have any life insurance?"

Lorna sighed. "It's a long story."

"I've got plenty of time," Michael shot back. Pulling out a chair, he turned it around and straddled it so that he was facing her. "I think I deserve some answers."

Taking a few steps forward, George tried to intervene. "Whatever is bothering you, son, I'm sure we can talk this out." He put his hand on Michael's shoulder in a comforting gesture.

Michael looked pained. "I don't want to be disrespectful to you, George," he replied, his lips pressed together in a grim line. "But this is really between my mother and me."

Realizing that he couldn't reason with Michael in his present state, George lifted his hand and briefly considered leaving the room. But when he saw how upset Lorna had become, he decided to stay.

"I'm waiting," Michael stated, his green eyes glowering at his mother.

Lorna took several more gulps of her wine before she spoke. "You've got to understand, Michael. I was in a state of shock after your father's death. Your grandparents had never liked me. I was afraid if they knew about the insurance money, they'd get their fancy lawyers to put it all into a trust for you and your sister, with themselves as trustees."

Michael shook his head several times as if he didn't understand. "What was wrong with that?"

"It would have meant they'd totally control us, and I just couldn't live like that." Lorna reached out for her son's hand, but he jerked back from her.

"If it was our inheritance, why did you turn it over to George?"

"I was the beneficiary of the policy—it was my money to use as I saw best."

"That doesn't answer my question."

Lorna stiffened. George could tell that his wife's patience was quickly disappearing in the face of Michael's accusations.

"I'm waiting," Michael stated, remaining intractable.

"Very well. I turned it over to George because I trusted him. We were in love. I believed that if George was generous to you and Sally, the two of you would more readily accept him as a stepfather."

Michael looked at her with an incredulous expression on his face. "You wanted George to buy our love?"

"No," she replied curtly. "I just wanted you children to see him as a man who would take care of us." She paused and reached out again. This time he didn't shake her off. "I never meant to hurt you, Michael," she said, her voice softening. "Everything I've ever done has been because I love you."

"I know that," he mumbled, his face still glum. "But it was a shock to find out about the insurance for the first time in the courtroom. Why didn't you at least warn me?"

"I can see now that I should have," she acknowledged, peering over his head at George.

George felt it was time for him to step in again. Once more he put his hand on Michael's shoulder. "You know, son, your mother was just trying to get away from Lester and Frances. I realize they're your grandparents, and I don't want to speak ill of them, but they were never nice to your mother. Certainly you were old enough to notice that?"

"Yes," Michael admitted. He stopped for a moment as if thinking. Then, fixing his penetrating gaze on Lorna, he said, "Why did you lie when Alexandra Locke asked you if you were seeing George *before* my father died?"

Her face flushed. "I couldn't very well give that information to the prosecution," she explained. "It would have been . . . misunderstood."

George saw that his stepson was trembling. "You don't look at all well, Michael," he said gently. "Are you sick?"

"I just haven't been sleeping," Michael conceded. He let out a long, audible breath and his shoulders slumped. "This whole hearing has me on edge. You're being accused of murder. Mom is sitting there every day looking scared out of her mind. Sally won't talk to any of us. How do you expect me to feel? It's awful." His voice rose. "I want the whole damn thing to be over."

"Now Michael," George said, "you and your mother are both worrying over nothing. I've got the best legal team money can buy. They're going to get me off—I promise. If you two really want to help me," he added, giving each of them a purposeful glance, "then pull yourselves together."

The next day at the morning recess, Patrick left Alexandra's side to use the telephone. She was standing alone in the corridor when an angry-looking Michael McGrath came down the hall toward her. Her heart started hammering in her chest. Would he acknowledge her presence, or keep on walking?

He stopped. "Are you satisfied now that you've successfully ruined everyone's lives, including your own?" His angry tone was laced with bitterness.

"I did what I thought was right," she said softly.

Michael shoved his hands into the pockets of his loose-fitting jacket. "Because of you, no one in my family is talking. My mother and my sister are estranged. George is being accused of a crime he didn't commit. And you've even done a good job of destroying your father's career. Doesn't family mean anything to you?"

"Of course it does," she said, upset by his scathing remarks. "But too many facts about your father's death didn't add up. At least it's all out in the open now. I believe George is getting a fair hearing, and if the judge finds that there's not enough evidence, he won't be made to stand trial."

His eyes darkened. "Do you really believe that crap?"

"Yes," she replied, her gaze challenging him to contradict her.

34

PATRICK WAS HEADED back to where he'd left Alexandra in the corridor. About ten feet away, he suddenly stopped. Michael McGrath was standing next to her, and although Patrick couldn't hear what either of them was saying, it looked as if they might be arguing.

Why did it bother him so much to see the two of them together? Sure, McGrath was handsome in a dark, moody sort of way that Patrick supposed some women could find attractive. What he had a hard time admitting, even to himself, was how much it disturbed him to picture Alexandra and Michael McGrath in bed together.

Did that mean he was jealous? And how was that possible unless he still cared for her? Even though she was constantly on his mind, Patrick still searched for other explanations. He rationalized that it could be Alexandra's case that he found so interesting. There were many unusual aspects, including the dilemma regarding her father. He'd been obsessed with other cases before—it was one of the hazards of being a trial lawyer. Yet this situation was somehow different.

His reverie was broken when the bailiff announced that the recess was over. Quickly crossing the distance that separated Alexandra and Michael from himself, Patrick joined the two of them.

"Is everything all right?" Patrick queried, glancing from one strained face to the other.

Michael was the first to speak. "I was just asking your client if she was pleased with all the misery she's caused." Without saying another word, he turned and walked away.

Alexandra paled, but other than that, Patrick was unable to gauge how Michael's words had affected her. It was this that bothered him most of all.

That evening after Alexandra spent several hours with her mother, whose condition was worsening, she went home to her little apartment over the garage. It seemed that she was rarely here anymore except to sleep.

Getting ready for bed, she turned on the TV. The noise helped to keep her from thinking too much. Flicking through the channels, she recognized two prominent local attorneys on a news-magazine show, discussing George Collins's preliminary hearing. When one of them mentioned her name, that got her attention.

The man went on to say that he felt Alexandra's testimony at the hearing had not been believable.

The other attorney countered that Alexandra had nothing to gain by fabricating a story like the one she'd told on the witness stand.

When they were asked to discuss the evidence that had been presented so far, both seemed to agree that George Collins had done some inexplicable things at the scene of the shooting.

After thanking the two lawyers for being on the show, the newswoman smiled at her viewing audience. "We'll be right back after this station break, with the Attorney General of California, Clifford Wolsey."

The announcement made Alexandra angry. It seemed as if everyone was using both George Collins's arrest and her arrest to their own political advantage. Clifford Wolsey took every opportunity to impugn her father and to praise deputy D.A. Frank Sanchez. In her opinion, it was wrong for the Attorney General to comment on an ongoing case, especially one that was being prosecuted by his own office. And even more so when his office was also handling the drug case against her.

Seeing Clifford Wolsey's face grinning out at the viewers, Alexandra was sickened by the man's blatant jockeying for power. Having no other viable way to protest, she turned off the set.

Feeling extremely uneasy, Patrick took a deep breath and then rang Nancy's doorbell.

"Patrick!" Nancy exclaimed, her eyes brightening with pleasure as she opened the door to her condominium. "It's after eleven. I wasn't expecting you." She smiled at him. "But it's a nice surprise."

"I'm sorry it's so late," he began. "But I've been driving around, and I lost track of the time."

"That's okay."

"I guess there's no right way to do this," Patrick said, running his hand through his hair as he stood there uncomfortably.

As if she were anticipating what he'd come to say, she tried to forestall him. "Come on in and sit down; we'll have a drink," she said, smiling sweetly.

He shook his head. "I don't want anything, thanks."

"Well, come in anyway. I'm sure we can talk out whatever it is that's bothering you."

Patrick walked into her living room but chose to remain standing. Stuffing his hands into the pockets of his leather jacket, he searched for the right words. "I've been thinking about us, Nancy. And I need to explain how I'm feeling." He paused before going on. "You've been asking for a commitment from me. And you're definitely right—it's more than time. The problem I've just realized, is that I can't make the commitment because I'm not . . . in love with you."

The smile dropped from her face as the color drained from it. Watching her reaction, he felt terrible that he had to hurt her, but he didn't feel he had any other choice. It would be worse to keep on pretending that everything was fine.

After a few seconds, she seemed to find her voice. "So, I was right—you're still in love with Alexandra?" Her words were spoken harshly. "How long have the two of you been carrying on behind my back?"

He shook his head again. "It's not like that, I swear." His steady gaze met hers. "I *am* in love with her," he admitted in a low voice, "but she doesn't know. That's because I've only just figured it out for myself."

Hands on her hips, Nancy guffawed. "You expect me to *believe* that?"

"It's the truth," he said solemnly. "It seems that I've been afraid to face my real feelings. Instead, I've come up with all sorts of excuses to myself— which has been getting harder and harder to do."

The corners of her mouth turned downward. "If she hadn't come back to L.A., we'd be getting married and everything would be fine."

"Please don't blame Alexandra," he said. "Something about the relationship between you and me wasn't right. I think we both knew it, Nancy, we just couldn't admit it to ourselves." He reached out for her hand. "I'd like for us to remain friends—partners, too, if that's possible?"

"I'm not sure," she told him, refusing to take his hand.

"That's fair," he replied. "Take as much time as you need to decide."

"I think you'd better go." Her voice, stripped of her usual confident bravado, was filled with hurt.

His eyes searched her face for a moment, trying

to see if she was going to be okay. Then, with a quick nod of his head, he left.

Walking back to his car, Patrick felt terrible about having to hurt Nancy. But she was strong, and even though her ego was damaged, he was confident that she'd get over it. Nancy had many wonderful qualities and he was willing to bet that she'd find someone who really loved her for the good person she was.

As for himself, it was as if a heavy weight had been lifted from his shoulders. He took a deep breath. No matter what happened with Alexandra, he knew that he'd done the right thing, for both Nancy and for himself.

Alexandra had just drifted off to sleep when the phone rang.

"Your mother's asking for you," Thomas said in a barely audible voice.

"I'll be there in twenty minutes," she promised, her heart hammering in her chest. She was angry at herself for leaving her mother's side. Earlier in the evening, Alexandra had seen how weak Roberta was getting. She'd wanted to sleep on the couch at her parents' house so as to be close to Roberta in case she needed her. It was as if she'd sensed something, but her mother had insisted that her daughter go home.

When Alexandra got to her parents' house, the hospice nurse let her in. She could see immediately that her mother's color had worsened. Her eyes were closed and her breathing was shallow.

Thomas sat by the bed, holding Roberta's hand. He looked haggard, his eyes red-rimmed, with big dark circles underneath them.

"Has she said anything?" Alexandra asked, a feeling of dread welling up inside her.

"Not since she asked for you," he replied, shaking his head.

She sat down on the edge of the bed and brushed a few wisps of Roberta's remaining hair away from her face. "Mom, it's me, Alexandra," she said softly. "I'm here."

There was a brief fluttering of eyelids as Roberta opened her eyes and smiled weakly at her daughter. She reached for her hand. Turning to Thomas, Roberta whispered, "Give . . . me a few minutes with Alexandra alone."

Thomas seemed reluctant to leave the room, but when Roberta repeated her request, he stood up and moved slowly toward the door. "Call me if anything changes," he said to Alexandra.

"I will," she promised.

Roberta's eyes had closed again. Alexandra continued to stroke her mother's brow as she waited for her to speak. In the meantime, an icy band of fear twisted around Alexandra's heart. Silently, she prayed that her mother wouldn't suffer too much.

After what seemed like an eternity, Roberta started to speak. "I've been debating . . . having this . . . conversation with you." Her voice was so low that Alexandra had to lean over to hear her.

"But I want you . . . to know the . . . truth

about the past. That affair wasn't all your father's
. . . fault. He needed things . . . that I couldn't . . .
didn't want to . . . give him." She paused, her
tongue wetting her dry lips. "At first I was upset
like you were. But then . . . I came to understand.
He lied to . . . protect me because . . . he loved
me." Her grip on her daughter's hand grew
stronger. "If not, your father . . . would have left
me."

As Alexandra listened to Roberta's words, she
tried to keep her fragile control from slipping.

"I know he hasn't been very supportive . . . during your recent troubles," Roberta said, her voice
hoarse. "Try and forgive him. He's not strong . . .
like you are."

It was hard for Alexandra to comprehend that.
In her mind, Thomas had always been incredibly
strong, imposing his will on everyone else.

"Please, Alexandra, I love you both . . . so
much. When I'm gone, each of you . . . will be all
the family the other one has. Promise me, you'll try
and work . . . things out?"

Alexandra was shaken by her mother's request.
She saw tears filling Roberta's eyes. As if from far
away, Alexandra heard herself speaking, "I'll do
whatever you want, Mom. I love you."

"I love you . . . too." Roberta sighed. Weakly,
she added, "I think you should . . . call your father."

Leaping up, Alexandra ran to the door, throwing it open. "Come quick!" she cried.

He rushed back into the room. "I love you,

Roberta!" he cried, his voice anguished. "Please don't leave me."

Her mother looked at her husband with loving eyes, then over at her daughter. "I love you both . . ." she said quietly, then closed her eyes.

Alexandra could see that Roberta was still breathing, but as she picked up her mother's hand and squeezed it tightly, Roberta seemed unresponsive to her touch. Not sure what it meant, she hurried out of the room to get the nurse.

After checking Roberta, the nurse told them that most likely Roberta had slipped into a coma. There was nothing to do now but to wait.

Thomas pulled Roberta's frail body gently up off the pillow and toward himself, murmuring to her and crying. Alexandra had never seen her father like this. He'd always appeared as if he were in complete control of himself and his every emotion. It was both frightening and heartbreaking at the same time.

Her own sorrow was deep and the pain in her heart unbearable. Alexandra laid her head against her father as he held Roberta, and she wept for them all.

Several hours later, Roberta's breathing became even more shallow. Neither Alexandra nor Thomas had left her side for more than a few minutes. Eventually, it became clear to Alexandra that this time her mother was not going to wake up.

Dawn was just breaking when Alexandra watched her mother take her last breaths. It was very peaceful. One minute she was there—the next she was gone.

"It's over," she said quietly to her father.

"No!" Thomas cried. Again he pulled Roberta's body close to his own.

After a short time, Alexandra remembered her mother's words. Forcing herself to be strong, she pushed aside her own grief as she patted her father's shoulder and tried to comfort him.

"I said I wanted the camera shooting from *that* angle!" Michael yelled, making a V-shape with his hands.

Because the preliminary hearing was taking up most of his days, Michael had set up a shoot on his new movie for the weekend. It was more expensive to work on Saturdays and Sundays, but under the circumstances it couldn't be helped. He had a schedule to maintain.

His cameraperson came over and tried to talk to him. "Hey, Michael, I know you're going through a rough time in court and all that, but you're making everyone on the set nervous. Why don't you take a break?"

"Because I don't want to," Michael snapped. "We're behind enough already." He rubbed his throbbing temples. "I just need some aspirin." He hollered at his assistant to get him some orange juice and the aspirin bottle.

Michael knew his cameraperson was right. He was a total wreck from yesterday. Despite Lorna's explanations, he still couldn't understand why his mother had lied to him about the life insurance and her affair with George.

Mulling these things over the night before, Michael had managed to consume a fifth of vodka, and today he was paying for it.

"Here," his assistant said, rushing over.

Shaking out the pills, Michael swallowed them with some juice and turned back to the set. "Okay, let's try that shot one more time."

A few seconds later, he was standing up and shouting again. "No! No, dammit! That's not what I want. Aren't any of you paying attention?"

Ignoring the confused looks he was getting, he stormed off the set and went back to his trailer. It was impossible to concentrate on the movie when he was faced with the prospect of his sister taking the stand Monday morning. He had to find a way to stop her.

Michael knew that the defense would crucify Sally. She really believed she was doing the right thing, but his sister's mental problems made her an easy target. Why couldn't she understand that she was simply risking too much?

35

GRIEF STRICKEN, Alexandra stood on the green hillside of the cemetery and watched her mother's coffin being lowered into the ground. She already missed her so much. She was glad that she'd spent the last nine months on the West Coast because of the extra time it had given her with Roberta. The fact that her own life had been turned upside down during the same period didn't change that.

She sneaked a sideways glance at her father. The man she had always seen as so capable, so unemotional, so distant, had been inconsolable since Thursday night. Alexandra hadn't realized the depth of the love he'd felt for her mother. It made it easier for her to understand Roberta's last words. All this time, Alexandra had seen her mother as the weak one and her father as the strong one—but it seemed as if she'd been wrong.

There was a huge turnout. Police cars were every-where. In spite of the scandal swirling around her father at the moment, the crowd was a reminder that he was still a prominent law enforcement figure. City, county and state elected officials as well as law enforcement personnel had shown up to pay their respects. An unwelcome contingent of media had also shown up and was hovering nearby. Thankfully, due to the solemnity of the occasion, most of them were standing at a respectful distance.

When the men began filling in the grave with soil, Alexandra started to tremble. Patrick reached out and steadied her with his arm. It meant everything to her that he was standing by her side during this difficult time. Tears slid down her cheeks as she silently whispered good-bye to her mother.

By six o'clock Monday morning, Sally had thrown up three times. Now she was in the bathroom again.

"Sally, open the door," Arnold called.

Couldn't he even let her be sick in private? she wondered as she washed her mouth out and then unlocked the latch.

There was a worried frown on his tired face. "You have to eat something, or you'll never make it through this morning."

"I'll be all right," she insisted, brushing her hair and applying more blush to her pale cheeks.

"It's not too late to change your mind," he said, following her as she went into her closet.

She pulled a dress off a hanger and slipped it over her head. "They're expecting me. I can't just not show up."

"With your medical history and background, all it would take is a doctor's letter and you'd be excused. I'm sure of it," Arnold pointed out.

For a brief moment, Sally wavered. She could get undressed and go back to bed. Slip under the warm sheets and forget the terror of having to tell her story in front of all those people.

"I don't think you should do this," he said again.

Sally knew that if she chose not to go, Arnold would handle everything. He'd feed her and take care of her just like he always did. It was tempting. Then she thought about her sessions with Doctor Abbott. For the first time in her life Sally felt that she was making some progress. She was actually starting to feel good about herself. Besides, Doctor Abbott was going to be at court with Sally. She couldn't disappoint her.

"Your mother and George will never forgive you. They will cut us off," Arnold warned as if sensing that she was vacillating.

Glancing at her face in the full-length mirror that hung on the back of the door, Sally knew that was a real possibility. But she also knew she had no choice. It was time to grow up; it was time to tell the truth.

Downtown in the Criminal Courts Building, Lorna had been waiting for over an hour when she finally saw her daughter get off the elevator and head down the hall for the courtroom. Sally was being escorted by Arnold and a middle-aged woman. Pushing her way through the crowd, Lorna tried to get close enough to be heard. "Sally! Sally! We need to speak," she called out in a firm tone.

Sally continued to look straight ahead as if she hadn't heard her mother.

Arnold glanced over and his eyes locked with Lorna's. Breaking away from the others, he came over.

Lorna glowered at him. "You were supposed to make sure this didn't happen. You promised to stop her."

"Honestly, Lorna, I've tried everything to get Sally to change her mind. It's no use." He wiped the sweat from his face before leaning closer to whisper into her ear. "That woman with us is Doctor Abbott, Sally's new shrink. I don't know how she's done it, but Sally only listens to her. It's like I don't even exist anymore."

Ignoring Arnold now, Lorna spoke over his head. "Don't do this, Sally!"

Still her daughter did not turn around. When the courtroom doors closed behind Sally, Lorna was left standing there shaking her head in disbelief. Where had her daughter suddenly found the courage to do this?

Sally's scheduled appearance had brought out an even bigger horde of reporters, television crews and onlookers, as everyone strained for a glimpse of the witness who was rumored to know something that would send her stepfather away for life.

Seated in the fourth row, Alexandra watched with trepidation as the tall, slender young woman made her way to the stand. Alexandra was still numb from the trauma of her mother's death. It had been difficult to pull herself together enough even to be here today. But she knew it was what her mother would have wanted.

After Sally was sworn in, the prosecutor, Harry Isen, asked Sally if she remembered where she was on Christmas Eve the year of her father's death. In a voice so faint the judge had to ask her to repeat herself, Sally replied, "Yes, I do." From there, although there were several nervous moments, she proceeded to tell her story.

"I remember that night because I'd been in bed for several hours. Mommy . . . I mean Mother, was downstairs with George wrapping presents for Michael and me to open in the morning." She paused to take a deep breath. "I wanted to see what I was getting so I snuck down the stairs trying not to make any noise. As I got to the bottom I could hear Mother and George doing something on the floor. I tiptoed behind the couch and peeked out. Their backs were to me."

The prosecutor urged her on. "Would you please tell the court what it was you saw."

"Yes. My mother and George were piling large stacks of money into a briefcase."

There was a burst of whispering in the courtroom and Judge Washington admonished everyone to be quiet.

"What else could you see?" asked Isen.

"They were marking down the piles of money on a pad of paper before they put them in the briefcase."

Isen took a step forward toward the witness. "How did you know that's what they were doing?"

"I heard them counting out loud."

"Objection. Move to strike as nonresponsive," said Walter Underhill, the defense attorney.

"Sustained," the judge replied.

The deputy attorney general rephrased his question. "After seeing them putting the money in the briefcase, what did you then hear?"

"I heard them both counting the money out loud. Mother told George the last stack made it one hundred thousand dollars. And then George said that was good. As he closed the briefcase, Mother started to cry. George put his arms around her and told her not to worry. She said she couldn't help it. She was scared. What if something went wrong and the cops didn't go along with the deal? And he said, 'No one's going to jail for killing Jeffrey, I promise you. This money is for the deputy D.A. He will take care of everything.'"

By the time she finished her recitation, Underhill had gotten to his feet and begun shouting, "Objection! Objection! Hearsay!"

"Sustained," said the judge.

Underhill nodded. "Move to strike."

"Stricken."

Isen turned back to his witness and calmly went on. "What happened next?"

"Mother asked, 'What if things go wrong and

they find out about the bribe? We could both end up in jail.' And then George told her again not to worry."

"And after that?"

"Mother got up and walked George to the door. I wanted to get out of the room without her seeing me, so I ran up the stairs and jumped into bed. When she came into my room a little bit later, I pretended to be asleep."

Glancing over at the defense table while Sally was testifying, Alexandra saw that George was furiously writing down notes on the yellow legal pad in front of him and passing them to his lawyer.

Isen went on. "Until just recently, did you ever tell anyone what you had seen that night?"

"No."

"Not even your brother, Michael?"

"No."

Isen looked around the room before asking his next question, as if wanting to make sure that everyone was listening. "Why didn't you tell anyone?"

"I was afraid. It sounded like my mother did something bad. Something she could go to jail for. And I didn't want that to happen."

"Did you have any idea at that time why your mother and George had to bribe someone?"

The defense lawyer objected. "Calls for speculation, Your Honor."

The judge sustained the objection.

"Let me ask you this question," Isen said, appearing unperturbed by the judge's ruling. "Why did you think your mother had done something wrong?"

"I overheard one of the kids at school say that my daddy hadn't really tripped and shot himself, but that George had killed him. And I'd heard George say no one was going to jail for killing Daddy. So I guessed that he was paying someone to stay out of jail."

"Objection, Your Honor. Calls for speculation."

"Sustained." The judge also struck the offending words from the record.

"Did you ever tell your mother what you had seen or heard?"

"No."

Isen lifted one eyebrow. "Why not?"

"Because I was afraid she would be angry."

"Can you tell this court why, after all these years, you came forth now to tell your story?"

"I didn't feel it was right that George had gotten away with killing my father. I felt that I had to tell the truth no matter what."

"Are you still worried about hurting your mother, Sally?"

"Yes," she nodded. "But I've also got to do what's right."

"Objection," said Underhill. "I move to strike the last part of her answer as not responsive."

Judge Washington agreed and ordered the court reporter to so strike the record.

Smiling, the prosecutor stated, "No further questions."

"We'll take a fifteen-minute recess," the judge

said. He turned to Sally and told her she'd be expected back on the stand right after the break.

There was a look of relief mixed with trepidation on Sally's face as she left the stand.

So, Alexandra thought, after all the innuendo and speculation, finally a witness who could state unequivocally that both George and Lorna had actively participated in preparing the cash for a bribe. But had it been for her father? Or Bob Frazier? Or could it have been for both of them?

In the courtroom corridor, Alexandra saw reporters using their cell phones to call in their stories. She and Patrick found themselves standing off to the side.

"Pretty powerful stuff," he said.

"Yes," she conceded. "I'm afraid the defense has no choice now but to tear Sally apart. They can't let her testimony stand. It's too damaging."

"You're right," Patrick agreed. There was a worried frown on his face as he regarded her. "How are *you* doing?"

A large sigh escaped her lips and she realized what a tight rein she had been keeping on her emotions. "Okay, I guess. Although I still can't believe she's gone." Tears welled up in her eyes and he nodded sympathetically.

When someone came over to speak to Patrick, Alexandra turned to wipe away a stray tear and noticed Michael McGrath across the hallway talking to his mother. He looked as if he hadn't slept in days. Despite the fact that he had spoken to

Alexandra so harshly, she sympathized with his situation, knowing that he was probably worrying about the upcoming cross-examination of his sister. Alexandra didn't blame him for being concerned. It was bound to be brutal.

For one long, terrible moment, she sensed the chill of Lorna's gaze on her. No doubt Michael's mother blamed Alexandra for everything that was happening.

"Judge is coming in," said the bailiff, letting everyone know that it was time to return to the courtroom.

When she turned around, Alexandra felt someone else's gaze boring into her. It was Lester McGrath. Obviously, he also held Alexandra responsible for ruining their lives.

There was a lot of tension in the room as Sally once again took the stand. She looked even more frightened when Walter Underhill grabbed some papers and approached her.

"What kind of light was on in the living room that night you say you saw your mother and George on the floor?"

"I think there was a lamp on."

"You're not sure?"

"I mean . . . I don't remember."

"You don't remember?" he echoed sarcastically.

She nodded and the judge told Sally that the court reporter could not record nonverbal messages.

"I don't remember," she said again.

"You said it was Christmas. Was there a tree?"

"Yes."

"And where was this tree?"

"In front of the window."

"Was this in the same room where your mother was?"

"Yes."

"Where were your mother and George in relation to the tree?"

"They were on the floor right next to it."

"Were there any ornaments on the tree?"

"I think so."

"You mean again you're not sure?"

Sally appeared confused. "There were lots of things hanging on the tree."

"Can you describe some of them for us, please?"

"Uh, I think there were some red and blue balls. Some silver ones too." She frowned. "And some candy canes."

"Is that all?"

"Yes," she nodded.

"What else do you remember about the tree?"

"That's it."

"Oh," he said, turning around to look at the spectators. "You mean there were no lights on the tree?"

"Oh yes. I forgot. There were lights."

"You 'forgot.' " He rolled his eyes. "And what color were these lights?"

"I'm not sure. I think they were white."

"But you're not sure?"

"Right."

"What else can you tell us about the tree?"

"That's all."

"What about the color?"

"It was a green fir tree."

"And what kind of a base did it have?"

Sally seemed confused again. "I don't understand."

"Was the tree standing inside a big bucket?"

"No."

"Did it have wood pieces tacked at the bottom to give it balance?"

"I don't remember."

"Was there any kind of a covering on the floor under the tree?"

"I'm not sure."

"How about presents? Were there any presents under the tree?"

"Oh yes. I forgot. There were a lot of boxes."

"How many?"

"I'm not sure."

"More than five?"

"Yes."

"More than ten?"

"I don't know."

"What color paper and ribbon were on the boxes you saw?"

She shrugged and the judge again admonished her. "I guess there were all kinds of colors."

"You guess? You mean you don't remember?"

"Not really."

"Yet you seem to remember every detail of a conversation you say you clearly overheard, although the people who were speaking had their backs to you?"

Sally tilted her chin. "I could still hear them."

Alexandra watched as the defense lawyer went on, forcing Sally to falter in her description of every bit of minutia in the living room that night. Alexandra acknowledged to herself that Sally's memory seemed poor, and that Underhill was doing a good job of showing the disparity between her clear memories of the conversation between her mother and George and her recollection of the other details.

"Now Sally, you say this conversation you heard was a few weeks after your father died, is that right?"

"Yes."

"That was over twenty years ago. How can you be so sure?"

"My father died right after Thanksgiving. I remember, because we always put up our tree right after Thanksgiving. And the night I heard their conversation was Christmas Eve. So it had to be a few weeks."

The defense lawyer went back to his table and consulted a note George had handed him. Then he faced her again. "With whom have you discussed the testimony you planned to give here today?"

Sally pointed over at the prosecutor. "Mr. Isen."

"Anyone else?"

"Uh, a deputy D.A. by the name of Elizabeth Nathan."

Alexandra wasn't surprised to hear this bit of news. From her earlier conversation with Elizabeth

Nathan, she'd realized that Sally must have tried contacting her at the D.A.'s office and that she was turned over to Elizabeth instead.

"Did either of these two people tell you to provide testimony on specific details and to twist your story as you've done here today?"

Harold Isen jumped up. "Objection! Argumentative."

"Sustained," said Judge Washington, giving the defense lawyer a cautionary look.

"Let me rephrase," suggested Underhill. "Now Sally, have you ever told this story about your mother and George when you failed to mention the incident happened on Christmas Eve?"

"No."

He took a step closer. "Are you absolutely sure about that?"

Isen said, "Objection. Asked and answered."

"Overruled." The judge ordered Sally to answer.

"Uh, I think so."

"Isn't it a fact, Sally, that when you recently told this story to your brother, Michael, you said it had happened several nights *before* Christmas?"

Sally glanced over at her brother with a stricken expression on her face. "Uh, maybe. I don't remember."

Underhill was doing a good job of showing that Sally's memory of the events could have been improved upon or enhanced by someone else, thought Alexandra. And she couldn't help wondering what role Elizabeth Nathan might have played in that regard.

The defense lawyer plowed ahead, making Sally describe everything about that night, from the weather to the colors of her nightgown. Over and over, she seemed hesitant before answering. There were moments when Alexandra thought Sally would burst into tears.

"By the way, Sally, did you ever play Monopoly as a child?"

"Yes."

"So you know what Monopoly money looks like?"

"Yes."

Underhill paused. "Are you sure that the money you saw that night wasn't Monopoly money?"

"It looked real."

"Please answer the question," he said in a gruff voice. "Are you positive it wasn't Monopoly money?"

"Objection. Not relevant," Harry Isen said, standing up. "This witness has already testified that she recognized the money for what it was. This is an attempt to confuse the issue."

"Overruled." The judge spoke to Sally. "The witness will please answer the question."

Sally straightened her shoulders. "I'm positive it was real."

Good for her, thought Alexandra.

"Now Mrs. Potter, let's talk about my client, Doctor Collins." Underhill walked behind George and put his hands on the man's shoulders. "How *do* you feel about your stepfather?"

She shrugged and the judge reminded her again

that she had to verbalize her answers. "I don't think about him much," she finally said.

"Isn't it true that you have never liked him?"

"I suppose."

"Your Honor," said Underhill, "would you instruct the witness to answer my question with a yes or a no?"

After the judge spoke to her again, Sally replied, "Yes."

"That's 'yes' that you've never liked him, right?"

"Yes."

"Is that because he married your mother?"

"I didn't like him before that, too."

"Why is that?"

"He had funny eyes. He was always looking at me when he came over. It made me nervous."

It didn't seem as if the defense lawyer had been expecting that response and he quickly went on. "I imagine you were very upset when your father died, is that true?"

"Yes."

"You loved your father very much, didn't you?"

"Yes."

Underhill waved his arm. "So when another man started paying attention to your mother, you didn't like it, right?"

"Yes."

"Did you feel your mother was doing something wrong when she started seeing George?"

"Yes."

"Did you feel your father had loved your mother?"

"Yes."

"Did you feel your mother loved him back?"

"Yes."

"Did you have a hard time understanding how she could want to be with another man?"

"Yes."

Underhill's voice had become like that of a kind uncle. "So it wasn't just George you didn't like. You would have felt the same way about any other man that tried to date your mother?"

"I don't know. My mother never saw anyone else but George."

Zing, thought Alexandra, knowing Underhill hadn't expected that response, either.

The defense lawyer got tough again. "Did you think that your brother felt the same way toward George as you did?"

"Objection. Calls for speculation."

"I'm merely asking for her opinion," the lawyer explained.

"Sustained," the judge said.

"Let me rephrase the question," said Underhill with a phony smile. "Did your brother ever tell you how he felt about George?"

"Michael said he liked George."

"How did that make you feel?"

"Bad. I didn't want him to be so nice to George."

"Did you tell your mother that you didn't want her seeing George?"

"Yes."

"What did she say?"

"That she was lonely and had a right to be happy."

"And what did you respond to that?"

"That my father had made her happy and that she didn't need another man."

Underhill paused for effect. "So when your mother told you she was going to marry George, you weren't thrilled about that prospect, is that right?"

"Yes."

"Did you do anything to protest their marriage?"

Sally's face looked confused. "I'm not sure I understand."

The defense lawyer folded his arms across his chest and raised his voice slightly. "Did you say anything or do anything to show your mother how much you were against the two of them getting married?"

"I cried a lot. My mother and I had a lot of fights. But she wouldn't listen."

Underhill continued to push her. "Did you do something desperate to stop the wedding two days before it was to take place?"

Sally glanced over at a woman in the audience, and Alexandra saw her give Sally an encouraging smile. "Yes."

"Would you tell the court what that was?"

"I swallowed a bottle of sleeping pills."

"You took an entire bottle of sleeping pills?" Underhill allowed a hint of disbelief to creep into his voice.

"Yes."

"Where did you find these pills?"

"In my mother's bathroom." Sally's voice broke and she put a tissue to her eyes.

"How did you know what they were?"

"I saw my mother take them. She said she couldn't sleep and needed pills."

"Were they clearly marked as sleeping pills on the label?"

"No. They had a long name. But the instructions on the bottle said, 'As needed for sleep.' I remember I checked because I wanted to make sure they would work."

"Then what did you do after you took the pills?"

"I lay down on the floor to die."

36

―――――― ～ ――――――

WHEN COURT RESUMED after a brief recess, Walter Underhill began where he had left off, hammering away at Sally, trying to show that she had been irrational in her attempts to prevent her mother from marrying George.

Alexandra felt bad for the young woman, yet she knew Underhill was doing exactly what needed to be done.

"Before the recess, you told us that you had taken a bottle of pills and then laid down to die?"

"Yes," she said softly.

"What happened next?"

"I don't remember."

"What is the next thing you *do* remember?"

"Waking up in the hospital."

"Was this incident you just told us about the only time you tried to commit suicide?"

Sally glanced down at her hands. "No," she said softly.

Underhill looked at her sternly. "How many other times have you tried to kill yourself?"

"Objection. Relevance."

The judge looked at Underhill. "Counsel, why is this relevant?"

"Your Honor, it goes to her mental state at the time and her ability to recollect things that happened at that time."

"Overruled," said the judge.

Alexandra felt that the judge made the wrong call.

"We're waiting for your answer," Underhill stated.

"Five," Sally admitted.

There was a murmur throughout the courtroom and the judge asked for order.

Alexandra cringed as the defense lawyer made Sally describe each attempt in minute detail. Sally was becoming more and more distressed and kept biting at her nails and looking over at the same woman. Before long, she was also crying. The judge asked her if she wanted another recess, but she said no.

Glancing across the room at Michael, Alexandra tried to gauge how he was taking this. His face was grim.

On and on the defense lawyer went, making Sally describe each time she'd had a nervous breakdown and had to be hospitalized. She kept wiping at her eyes as she responded.

"Either before, during or after one of these so-called nervous breakdowns," said Underhill, "has anyone ever prescribed pills for you?"

Sally gazed at the prosecutor before answering. "Yes."

"What kinds of pills?"

Sally listed a number of barbiturates, antidepressants and antianxiety pills, although she had a hard time remembering when each had been prescribed or for what particular symptom.

"Are you on any medication at the present time?"

"I'm taking an antidepressant."

"Is that all?" Underhill's voice had an edge to it.

"I take birth control pills, too," she said, blushing slightly.

"Let's go back to the time of your father's death. Do you remember how you learned about it?"

"Yes. A sheriff came to the house and told my mother. I was right behind her at the front door."

"What did your mother do?"

"She started to cry."

"Where was your brother, Michael?"

"Upstairs."

After crossing his arms across his chest, Underhill said, "Did this sheriff explain how your father died?"

"Yes."

"Do you remember what he said?"

"That there had been an accident and that my father had shot himself by mistake."

"Did you have any reason not to believe what he said?"

"No."

"Was there a time when you changed your mind about how your father had died?"

"Yes."

The defense attorney took a step closer. "Do you

remember when it was that you changed your mind and began to think that George had killed your father?"

"I'm not sure."

"Isn't it true," he demanded, "that the first time this thought ever entered your mind was when you overheard another child talking about that possibility at school?"

"Probably," she said.

"So it never entered your mind before that?"

"I'm not sure."

His voice became soft again. "You loved your father very much, didn't you?"

"Yes."

"And you felt guilty because you were still alive and he was dead, didn't you?"

"Yes," Sally said.

"Isn't it true, Sally, that you would have objected to any man your mother started to see?"

Alexandra recalled that that question had been asked and answered before. She also wondered why Isen wasn't objecting more.

"I don't know. I just didn't like George."

"And your way of protesting your mother's marriage was to try and kill yourself?"

"I don't know." Sally was becoming increasingly agitated.

"After that you wanted to get rid of George, didn't you?"

"Yes. I mean, I wanted him not to live with us anymore."

"So you just kept throwing tantrums and crying, hoping your mother would divorce him?"

"I guess so." She shifted uncomfortably in her seat.

After obtaining this concession from her, Underhill attempted to hammer her again on her many hospitalizations.

"Objection. Asked and answered," said Isen.

"Sustained."

"Your nervous breakdowns, Sally, were your way of making your mother get rid of George, weren't they?"

"I don't know," she said, weeping.

The judge finally called for another recess. Sobbing, Sally was led out of the courtroom by her husband and the woman to whom she had looked for encouragement.

As soon as the recess was called, Michael rushed out of the courtroom and over to his mother in the hallway, where he proceeded to fill her in on what had just transpired. "We've got to stop this before Sally falls completely apart!"

"I know it must be hard to watch," Lorna said in a soothing tone of voice, "but she'll get through it—I promise."

"She won't," he insisted. "That goddamn defense lawyer is out to destroy her!"

Lorna quickly glanced around as if to make sure no one was listening to them. "It won't be much longer. Just be patient."

Either she wasn't hearing him or she didn't want to hear him, thought Michael. "Listen to me,

Mom," he said, gritting his teeth. "That fucking lawyer has gone too far. Now get him to stop before I . . . kill him!"

Her eyes widened in alarm. "Keep your voice down and pull yourself together, Michael," she hissed under her breath. "I know you're upset. And I am too. But Sally's testimony was very damaging to George. The lawyer has to do what he can to lessen its impact. Surely you can understand that?"

"No. It's got to stop. Underhill will do what you say," he said, gesturing with his hands. "Go over there and tell him that's enough. He's made his point."

"I can't do that. Not yet. Right now the most important thing is to get George out of this mess."

He leveled her with a withering gaze. "Even if it means destroying your daughter?"

"Of course not," Lorna said, shaking her head. "But she's stronger than you think."

Michael started pacing back and forth before he turned to face her. "If you won't stop it—then I will."

She gave a large sigh. "If you're that upset, I'll talk to them and see if they can't tone it down. Okay?"

"Promise me," he demanded, his eyes darkening.

"I promise."

"Now," he ordered.

Twenty minutes later it was as if Michael and his mother had never even spoken. If anything, Walter Underhill seemed to be going at Sally with renewed vigor. Michael was furious. Why couldn't any of them understand that this kind of questioning was destroying Sally?

Michael's sister was soon crying again as Underhill pounded away at her. He was doing his best to show that she was irrational and that her feelings of dislike toward George were also irrational.

"Isn't it true that you really hated George?" Underhill asked.

"Yes," she screamed. "I hated him! So what?"

Underhill had a smug, self-satisfied look on his face. "Did you hate him enough to try and frame him for your father's death?"

"No," she snapped. "But I had every right to hate him. He killed my father," she said loudly.

"Move to strike the witness's answer as nonresponsive," said Underhill, his face flushed.

"Sustained."

Suddenly Sally stood up, her eyes looking wild as she pointed her finger at George. "I hated George because he molested me. He raped me!"

George turned white. Pandemonium broke out in the courtroom. Sally began crying again. Faced with chaos in his courtroom, the judge called another recess.

Michael couldn't stand what was happening to his sister. This time when he found his mother in the hallway, he practically dragged her into an alcove away from the others. "You lied to me! You promised you'd talk to the lawyers."

"I couldn't," she replied, shaking her head. "I

explained to you that the defense lawyer has to do his job."

"No," Michael cried. "He's killing Sally! I can't let this go on and watch my sister be destroyed."

"It's almost over," she said, trying to shush him.

He put up his hand to stop her. "It's enough. Things have gotten out of control. Sally just accused George of raping her." His voice was harsh, and he saw the fear come into her eyes. But he didn't care.

"I'm tired of all the lies." His face was grim. "I'm going to find Isen and tell him what really happened."

As he turned to rush off, Lorna grabbed her son's arm. "Don't be a fool, Michael," she warned, her voice filled with panic. "You'll ruin everything."

"There's no other way," he said, shaking her off.

Alexandra was just returning from the ladies' room when she heard a commotion from the other side of the corridor. Turning around, she saw Michael McGrath and his mother arguing. He was practically screaming at Lorna. Then he shook his mother's hand off and rushed across the hall to where Harry Isen, the prosecutor, was standing.

"I have to talk to you," he said loud enough for everyone to hear. "My sister's on the verge of a nervous breakdown. I can't tolerate the lies. It's time to tell the truth. It wasn't George who raped my sister, it was my father."

Michael's voice rose to a pitch that carried all the way down the corridor. "And it wasn't George who shot him. It was me!"

*   *   *

Alexandra couldn't believe what she'd just heard. From the very beginning she'd sensed that the McGrath family and the Collins family were hiding a lot of secrets. This must have been what they were so afraid of having the world find out.

"My God," she said to Patrick as she joined him. "I just heard Michael McGrath and his mother arguing before he rushed over to Isen. He accused his real father of raping Sally, then he said that he was the one who had shot his father. Do you think it's possible that Michael killed Jeffrey?"

"It would make all the pieces fit," Patrick ventured, looking equally surprised.

She suddenly realized that if Michael had been the murderer, then he was the one with the most to lose by her investigation into his father's death. And carrying that logic further meant that he also had to be the person who had planted the drugs.

It was bedlam in the hallway as reporters rushed to call in the latest developments on their cell phones. Out of the corner of her eye, she saw that Michael was being led off to an attorney's conference room. Sally, too, was ushered into the same room. Her wails could be heard all the way down the hall.

"You know," Patrick said, rubbing his jaw as if he'd been thinking things over, "either Jeffrey McGrath was a real monster, or his son Michael is going to desperate lengths to save his stepfather."

37

~

As ALEXANDRA PACED her small apartment that night, her mind was in turmoil. It was windy outside. The branches from a tree next to the garage were scraping against her bedroom window, reminding Alexandra of the night they had found the drugs in her apartment.

Earlier in the day, the judge had announced that pursuant to an agreement, George Collins's preliminary hearing was being postponed for two weeks so that the A.G.'s office could investigate the statements made by Michael McGrath regarding the death of his father.

For her part, Alexandra didn't know if she could wait days, let alone weeks or even months, to find out what part her father had played in the whole messy affair. She needed to know now. Making a decision, she searched for a home phone number for Michael. Then, hands shaking, she dialed.

After several rings, he answered. "It's Alexandra Locke," she said. "I was—"

"Haven't you done enough?" Without waiting for her to answer, he hung up.

As Alexandra replaced the receiver she considered what she should do. After a moment, she picked up her purse, grabbed a jacket and ran down the steps to her car.

She knew the name of the street where Michael lived, and from his description of his house it wasn't hard for her to find. The house sat far back from the road behind massive trees and shrubbery. From the street, it appeared dark and silent.

The Spanish architecture was the type that had been popular in the heyday of Hollywood in the early thirties. Michael had told her once that a famous silent film star had lived there. Although he'd described the floor plan as being on three levels, from the front she saw only two, and figured that the house must have been built into the hill at the back.

Alexandra gathered her jacket around her to ward off the chill in the air and made her way up the steep, tree-shrouded driveway. The moon, a bright silver, appeared in a break of trees. Glancing up at the sky, she wondered if her mother was watching her—protecting her.

When she finally reached the structure, she was stymied. One set of stairs went up to a second level; another stairway seemed to wrap around the side of the house. There were no lights on anywhere.

Climbing the stairway to the second level, she

peered inside but saw nothing. Heart pounding, she knocked on the door and waited. Still nothing. She tried again. The only sound was the wind in the trees and the rustling of the bushes.

She retraced her steps and took the stairway that went around the side of the house. Halfway up, she felt something brush against her legs and she let out a small scream. Then with a sigh of relief she saw that it was only a cat. It stood a few feet away and silently watched her, its eyes glowing yellow in the night.

The trees grew close to the house and a number of branches hung over the stairway. She continued on until she reached some sort of a patio. Seeing no bell there either, she knocked on the door. Again, silence. Total blackness. The second time she knocked, it was louder, and she also called out his name: "Michael?"

She guessed he was there but didn't want to see her. She was about to leave when she heard a loud creaking sound. Where was it coming from? she wondered. As she crossed the patio littered with fallen leaves and broken branches, she found herself at the back of the house.

Now the creaking noise became even louder. She saw something moving between the trees. Her heart thudded in her chest. Terrified, she peered into the darkness until she made out the outline of a hammock swinging back and forth in the wind. Momentary relief flooded her before the fear returned.

"Michael?" she called out again.

Only silence. Then finally he spoke. "Turn to your left and you'll see another stairway down."

Her pulse was racing as she followed his directions. In the darkness his profile seemed gaunt. Dressed in the slacks and shirt he'd worn to court, he was reclining on the hammock with his left leg swinging down over the side. He held a glass in one hand, and as she approached she could hear the clinking of ice.

He didn't seem at all surprised to see her. "You never listen, do you?"

"I guess not," she replied, hearing the tremor in her own voice.

"Well, too late now." He sat up. "Come with me."

At the doorway to the house, Alexandra stopped. She'd come here wanting the truth, but suddenly she was reluctant. The house was big and dark, and Michael was behaving so strangely.

He must have sensed her hesitation. He turned to look at her. "If you want answers, I suggest we go inside."

Taking a deep breath, she calmed her nerves and walked through the doorway.

"I'm drinking vodka. Care to join me?"

"No, thank you."

She followed him down a long hallway, passing several rooms before going under a high archway. Suddenly she was standing in the middle of a room that was at least two stories high. Moonlight was streaming in from the upper windows, and in the glow she saw shelves built into both sides of the

room, reaching all the way to the ceiling. They
were filled with books.

"What a beautiful room," she said, hoping she
didn't sound as nervous as she felt. "Can we turn
on some lights?"

"No," he responded, sharply. "Have a seat, I'll
be right back."

Being left alone made her even more jumpy.
Where was he going? What was he doing? Had he
gone to get a gun? Don't be silly, she told herself.
He's a famous director. He's not going to hurt you.
But if he had murdered his father, another small
voice said, anything was possible. She barely knew
him. He could be distraught and planning to kill
himself. What if he decided to take her with him?
Why had she come here without thinking this
through? She was getting frantic.

The cat came into the room and curled up on the
floor, watching her. As Alexandra's eyes became accustomed to the lack of light, more of the room
came into focus. She noticed there were large paintings on the wall behind her, filled with dark, unrec-
ognizable shapes. This house definitely reflected
the moodiness of the man she'd met several months
ago. Now, with all that had happened, it seemed
like years had passed.

By the time Michael returned, her nerves were
stretched taut.

"Sit down," he ordered.

Gingerly, she took a seat on the couch, not taking her eyes off his shadowy face.

Michael sat down across from her on a window

seat. He had brought a bottle of vodka with him. "I suppose your first question is, did I really kill my father?" There was a slight slur to his words and she realized he already must have had a lot to drink.

She swallowed hard and said, "Did you?"

"Yes," he replied matter-of-factly.

"Because he molested your sister?"

"It was rape. And more than once. And then there were the other things he did." Even in the moonlight she could see the scowl on his angular face. "My father was a very abusive man."

"But Sally claimed that it was George who raped her."

"Victims of incest often can't handle the truth. It's too terrible for them to accept that their own father could be hurting them. So they repress it." His voice was tinged with bitterness. "Sometimes, as in my sister's case, they even transfer those memories and deeds onto someone else."

Alexandra shook her head at the toll this ordeal had to have taken on Jeffrey McGrath's family. "Why didn't you just tell the truth twenty years ago?"

He leaned back against the arched window and put one foot up. "That's not easy to answer."

There was a lengthy silence. Was he debating whether or not to tell her what had happened? she wondered. The room was so quiet she could almost hear the sound of her heart beating.

Finally he spoke. "I'd gone to where George and my father were hunting. There had been a terrible incident the night before, and I had to speak up. So I confronted my father about Sally, and about beating my mother, too. I threatened him. Of course, it was the braggadocio of a fifteen-year-old." The words were spoken slowly, as if he were reliving that day as he told her. "It was obvious that he was angry that I had dared to accuse him, especially in front of George, who was stunned at my accusations. He became enraged and went for his gun, but I picked up George's gun and shot him first."

Alexandra sat forward. "Then it was self-defense?"

"Who knows," his face clouded with uneasiness. "My father might only have meant to scare me. Or he might not have shot to kill. George was afraid the cops might not see it our way. He told me to leave and promised he'd make it look like an accident."

Michael stopped to take a gulp of his drink before going on. "I went straight home and told my mother. When George came we all talked. They were worried that even if I admitted to killing my father in self-defense, my life would be ruined. And Mom didn't want anyone to know about the incest or the abuse."

Alexandra's eyes had now become accustomed to the dark and she saw his features twisted in pain.

"George had already told the cops that it was an accident. Mom asked what if they didn't believe him. That's when George offered to take the blame, if necessary, and she jumped at the offer. I guess they didn't think things out too clearly." He exhaled loudly. "By the time they did—it was too late. We were all caught in the lies we had told."

"Did your grandparents know the truth?"

"They knew that my father was abusive but they blamed my mother for it. As to how my father died, while they definitely suspected that something wasn't right, they had no idea I was responsible."

She took a deep breath. "Then you must have also known about the bribe?"

"Not for many years," he said. "It wasn't until George slipped one day and said something that I learned how we'd escaped the legal consequences."

Alexandra's voice was shaking as she asked, "Was it my father who was bribed?"

Michael gave her a long, appraising look. "I honestly don't know. Only George does, and he's not saying. It's all he has to bargain with. He's asking for immunity from prosecution and if he doesn't get it, he'll invoke the Fifth Amendment against self-incrimination."

Relief that he hadn't named her father was followed by disappointment because she still didn't know the truth.

Michael had turned sideways and was staring out the window. "I hope my mother and George won't be punished too harshly. They were trying to protect me." He gave another heavy sigh. "I've hated all the lies and what they've done to everyone. I'm glad I finally told the truth, even if it means I have to go to prison."

Alexandra doubted that either George or Lorna would see prison time for not telling the truth about how Jeffrey had died. Too many years had passed. As for Michael, a lot would depend on how the evidence squared with his description of the events and his reasons for his actions. It was entirely possible that he, too, could escape prosecution for shooting his father.

The bribery situation, however, was another matter. Like murder, there was no statute of limitations on bribery. And she guessed that if someone from law enforcement had been involved in a cover-up, it would not be treated lightly. That's why George was going to use his knowledge to get immunity for himself and probably for Lorna as well.

Holding his glass to his mouth, Michael drained it. "Sure you won't join me?"

"No." She wished he wasn't drinking so much. It wasn't going to help. Again, there was silence. "That night when you followed me home," she finally said, "had I really left my car lights on?"

His laugh was caustic. "If I'd been planning on spending the night, I would have pulled my car in behind yours in the driveway. By leaving it on the street I got a rather expensive ticket."

Alexandra had forgotten about the parking limits in her neighborhood. Her eyes were grave now. "Did you plant the drugs in my apartment?" she asked, a catch in her throat.

"No," he replied.

Did she believe him? She wasn't sure. "It had to be someone in your family."

"God, I hope not," he said, his voice raw with emotion. He turned to face her and then added in a softer tone, "I heard about your mother. I'm sorry."

His words of sympathy caught her off guard. "Thank you. It's hard to believe she's gone," she admitted when she finally trusted herself to speak.

Michael set his glass down and picked up the vodka bottle. She didn't want to watch him drink himself into oblivion. It was time for her to leave. She reached for her purse and stood up. "So then you have absolutely no idea who was involved in planting those drugs?"

"No," he said, shaking his head. "I'm sorry. I know this case has ruined your life. I never meant to drag you into my family's problems. In the beginning, all I wanted was to stop your investigation." He let out a long, audible breath. "Of course, I didn't count on being so attracted to you. I only wish . . ." he hesitated briefly before going on, "I only wish we could have met under different circumstances."

Alexandra saw the way his shoulders slumped. He sounded overwhelmed by the events in his life. "That would have been nice," she responded. She went over to him and held her hand out. "Thank you for being so honest with me."

He nodded silently and turned away. As she went out the door, she knew that the pain she'd seen on Michael's face would be with her for a very long time.

38

A LONG TIME AGO, Roberta had told Alexandra where all their important papers were kept in the house in case anything ever happened to Thomas and to her.

While her father was at work, Alexandra let herself into the house. The quiet surrounded her. It was difficult being here now that her mother was gone. Every room she entered brought back painful memories. She tried to push back the gloom and think of happier times.

In the closet in her parents' bedroom she reached behind the clothes and ran her fingers along the wall. When she found the hidden panel, she pushed it with both hands and the panel opened, exposing a small space, large enough to hold two fireproof filing cabinets.

Sitting down on the floor, Alexandra discovered that the small key Roberta had given her opened

them both. Taking a deep breath, she began first
with the bottom drawer.

Walking over the green lawn toward her
mother's grave, Alexandra saw that Thomas had
already arrived. "Thanks for meeting me," she
said.

"I was coming here anyway."

She put the pink roses on the fresh dirt that des-
ignated the spot where Roberta had been buried.
They had ordered a grave marker, but it wasn't
ready yet. Alexandra communed silently with her
mother for a few minutes.

When she sat down on the bench next to her father, she noticed how much older he looked. His
face was haggard and his eyes were puffy. "How
are you doing?"

"Okay," he replied with a slight shrug. "And
you?"

"About the same." She inhaled deeply and tried
to fortify herself for what was going to be a difficult conversation. "I wanted to see you," she explained, keeping her voice on an even keel,
"because I have it on good authority that George
Collins is making a deal. Sometime in the next few
days he's going to tell them everything he knows."
She gave him time to absorb her news. "I thought
you might like to tell me first."

He eyed her warily. "What do you want to
know?"

"Let me tell you what I've found out and then
you can fill in the blanks." She mentioned the insti-

tution Bob Frazier's son was in and what else she'd just discovered. "The trust fund that pays for Ian Frazier's care was established three weeks after you rejected the Collins/McGrath case. It was set up with an initial deposit of one hundred thousand dollars cash. The other one hundred thousand dollars came from Bob Frazier's insurance after he died."

When her father didn't seem that surprised by her revelations, Alexandra was forced to ask the next question.

"You knew about it, didn't you?"

Thomas sat there staring off into the distance. The seconds passed slowly before he began to talk. "Like I told you before, Bob asked me to reject the case for him because of a conflict. When I found out about the expensive institution where he had just put his son, I accused him of making a deal. Bob admitted to me that George had caved in and told him the truth about what had happened."

He shook his head as if remembering. "Bob felt sorry for the boy who'd tried to protect his nine-year-old sister. Poor Bob was also at the end of his rope concerning his own son. So he and George decided to help each other." Thomas rubbed the knuckles of his left hand in the palm of the right one. "He begged me not to say anything."

She assumed he still wasn't finished and waited quietly.

"I was only trying to help a friend—" His voice broke off in midsentence. "Who was hurt by it, anyway?" he asked, sounding almost angry. "Is it better now that everyone knows Sally was raped by her father and that Michael killed him?"

"A bribe is wrong," she said softly, "no matter how noble the purpose."

His face clouded over, but he didn't respond.

"Why didn't you come forward after you confronted Bob and learned the truth?"

"I was trying to decide what to do when Bob blew his brains out."

"And what stopped you after that?"

He looked pained.

"I want to know."

"Fine." He gave a sigh of exasperation. "I was afraid that if word about the bribe got out, it would look like I'd been involved because I signed the rejection letter."

She wasn't buying that. "You could have proven you didn't receive any of the funds."

Thomas squared his shoulders. "There's no law that says I had to tell anyone what I knew."

"What about your ethical obligation?" she countered. Without waiting for him to reply, she went on, "You knew that Bob had used his position to do something that benefited him and that it was wrong. You also had to assume that he'd either destroyed or suppressed evidence. As an officer of the court, shouldn't you have gone to your boss at the time and told him the truth?"

"Come on now, Alexandra," he said, "these ethical versus legal situations aren't always that cut and dried."

"Yes, they are. As a prosecutor, you have an

obligation to be above reproach." Suddenly, Alexandra abandoned all pretense at civility and allowed her anger to surface. "I'm tired of the excuses—the subterfuge!" She reached into her briefcase and handed him the missing Collins/McGrath file she'd found hidden in her parents' things. "You lied to me about this and you're still lying—especially to yourself."

Thomas put his head down and sat immobile for a time. "Don't you understand?" he said finally, his voice low. "If I had told anyone about what Bob had done, for the rest of my life there would have been those people who assumed that I had taken some of the money. I had plans. I wanted to be D.A. and I didn't want anything to ruin my chances." He paused. "And I figured that no one was getting hurt."

Alexandra felt ill. "So it was a political decision?"

"I guess that's one way of looking at it."

"Why did you lie to me about taking the file?"

"It was Dale's idea to get it. We were afraid of what might happen if Frank Sanchez got hold of it. I . . . just couldn't seem to tell you."

She wasn't satisfied yet. There were more unanswered questions. "Why did you really go to see Erica?"

"I wanted to find out why she'd accused me of taking the bribe. I needed to know if she was deliberately lying, merely surmising I'd been involved, or if Bob Frazier had indicated that I was involved. Unfortunately, Erica was so sick at that point that she didn't even realize I was there. I learned nothing."

"What do you think George Collins is going to say?"

"I don't know," he said, his brow creased with worry. "I never talked to him. But if Erica thought I was in on it, then maybe he did too." He looked discouraged. "It doesn't matter anymore. There will always be people now who will believe I was involved."

Standing up, Alexandra pushed her hands into the pockets of her jacket. It would be her father's word against George's word. Did she believe him? Yes. Still, waiting twenty years to tell the truth wouldn't be viewed favorably, but she didn't have to say that—he already knew. She inhaled deeply. There was one more issue to cover. "Did you have anything to do with the drugs found in my apartment?"

A horrified expression appeared on his face. "I wouldn't ever hurt you that way. My God, Alexandra, you're my daughter. I love you."

It had been a long time since she'd heard those words. In time maybe she'd learn to appreciate them more. For now she was still too upset with him.

"I realize now that the drugs must have been planted because of the Collins/McGrath case." Thomas's eyes were focused on her. "I'm sorry. I should have believed you from the beginning."

Some of her anger dissipated. "As I'm sure you already know, Frank Sanchez and the Attorney General are old friends. Patrick feels the drug case against me has been at least partially politically motivated. They really wanted you."

There was astonishment on his face. "You don't think Frank Sanchez planted those drugs, do you?"

"I hope not. I saw both Frank and Elizabeth after Sally collapsed on the stand." She repeated their conversation. "Frank sounded angry at Elizabeth for turning over my personal papers to the Attorney General's office."

"Elizabeth Nathan?" He scratched his chin as if trying to remember something.

"Yes. Elizabeth said she went searching for my notes after Sally visited her. But I was told by my secretary, Geena, that Elizabeth was looking for the Collins/McGrath file even before I was arrested. Do you have any idea how Elizabeth found out about the case?"

He seemed perplexed. "Carol Eberhardt told me once that she'd caught Elizabeth Nathan listening at my door. I brushed it off as paranoia. But maybe Elizabeth heard us arguing about the case and that's how she found out."

Finally, it all made sense, thought Alexandra.

"Could Elizabeth have been behind the drugs?" Thomas asked.

"Again, I'm not sure. Although it sounds like both the A.G. and Elizabeth could have been responsible for all the leaks to the press."

"That's unconscionable," he said, shaking his head.

She gave a bitter laugh. "They'd probably say it was only politics."

Thomas reddened in embarrassment as he caught her meaning. "I shouldn't have blamed you. In fact, I know you tried to protect me. I appreciate what you did."

"That's okay," she said, glad finally to have him acknowledge her efforts. They sat quietly for a few moments, each lost in their own thoughts.

Clearing his throat, Thomas broke their silence. "Could you tell me, Alexandra, what your mother said to you there at the end?"

Alexandra felt a stab of pain. She didn't want to betray her mother's confidence. But Roberta had never told her not to tell him. "Mom said things hadn't been entirely your fault and that she forgave you because she'd realized you truly loved her. She also wanted us to work our problems out because we only had each other."

His eyes watered. "Anything else?"

She hesitated.

Thomas gestured with his hand. "Please. It's important to me."

She took another deep breath. "Mom also asked me to forgive you for not supporting me during my troubles. She said you weren't that—strong."

Thomas seemed to crumple, as if the air had been let out of him, and he buried his face in his hands. After a few minutes he stood up and walked a short distance away.

Alexandra realized how well her mother had known her husband. She'd recognized that Thomas had felt powerless when faced with her cancer and how difficult that was for a man who was used to controlling everything. She'd also known that Thomas was weak. Alexandra wondered if Roberta had been aware of the bribe too—or had she merely suspected her husband's willingness to cross over the line for his career?

She watched as he fumbled with a handkerchief and heard him blow his nose. When he came back, he seemed more composed, although his eyes were red.

"Thank you for telling me," he said simply.

Alexandra nodded.

A slew of emotions crossed his face and she sensed that he was struggling with some kind of a decision. "I'm going to resign," he finally said.

It struck her that this man who had done so much in the pursuit of power had just as suddenly found it was all meaningless. The only person who had always stood behind him was gone. Even worse, Roberta had seen him for who he was. "I think that's a good idea," she murmured softly.

"I'm sorry, Alexandra. I should have come to your defense the minute you were arrested. But I'll do whatever is left in my power to help you."

Sensing that her father was asking for a chance at redemption, she took a small step forward. "Actually, there is something you can do."

"Name it."

"When I spoke to Michael McGrath yesterday, he said something that jogged my memory. The parking on my street is by permit only. I've gone over my schedule and come up with a window when the drugs could have been planted. Can you get a list for me of all the parking tickets that were issued during that time period on my street and several blocks in each direction?"

"No problem." He cleared his throat again. "Listen," he said hesitantly, "maybe we can work on doing what your mother asked of us?" There was a tremor in his voice. "I know that I want to—I hope you do, too."

Alexandra sighed. "I can't pretend to understand what you've done, Dad, because I don't." She stopped and gazed up at the sky, trying to sort out the rest of her feelings. There were clouds and it appeared as if it might rain. "You're my father," she said when her mind had cleared. "I want to honor my promise to Mom. It's just going to take some time. Okay?"

He looked her in the eye. "That's more than fair," he replied.

39

~

IT TOOK ALEXANDRA, working with one of Patrick's investigators, some time to go down the list Thomas had provided of cars, license numbers, names and addresses. Through painstaking questioning they had eliminated everyone who seemed to have a legitimate reason for being on or about her street during the crucial forty-eight-hour period.

Alexandra was becoming discouraged. The person who planted the drugs probably hadn't even gotten a ticket, so she'd wasted everybody's time for nothing. Finally, the list was narrowed down to three possibilities. No one from the Collins family, the McGrath family nor the D.A.'s office was on that list.

Unable to stand the uncertainty one second longer, she had convinced Patrick to accompany her in checking out the last three people. When two more were eliminated as suspects, Alexandra looked at Patrick. "I guess I was wrong," she muttered dejectedly.

"We have one more place to try," he reminded her.

A little while later they drove up to an apartment complex in North Hollywood. It was an old building, but looked well-maintained.

He checked the mailboxes. "Billy Nash lives in number 16." A young man wearing jeans and a sweatshirt answered the door. Alexandra thought he couldn't be more than late teens or early twenties.

"Billy Nash?"

"Yeah?" the young man replied, gazing from one of them to the other.

Patrick explained that he was a lawyer and had some questions. "We understand that you got a parking ticket on Norman Way two months ago?" He showed him a copy of the citation.

"I'm sure I paid it," Billy replied, looking at the piece of paper.

"That's not why we're here. We have some questions to ask you about that night."

Alexandra saw the young man swallow as he shifted his weight from one foot to the other. "Like what?"

"What were you doing there?"

Billy shrugged and managed a slight smile. "Visiting someone."

Patrick squared his shoulders. "Who?"

The young man's Adam's apple bounced nervously. "I . . . I uh, I think her name was Lois."

"Lois what?"

"I don't remember."

"What's her address?"

"I'm not sure."

"Do you have it written down someplace?"

"No. I don't think so." A slight film of perspiration had appeared on his brow.

"What does this Lois look like?"

"She's uh . . . blond, I guess."

"Long hair or short hair?"

"I . . . don't remember."

"Tall?"

"Kinda."

"Describe what her apartment looked like inside."

"Let's see . . . I . . . uh, there was a couch."

"What color?"

"Uh, maybe red."

"Did she have a television?"

"Yeah."

"What kind?"

"I dunno."

"Did she live alone?"

"I uh . . . I'm . . . not sure."

"Will she vouch for you and where you were that night if we go see her now?"

"I . . ." He suddenly reddened and couldn't go on.

"You see this woman," Patrick pointed to Alexandra.

"Yeah."

"She's convinced you broke into her apartment that night."

Now the kid looked really scared. "I didn't break into anybody's apartment."

"If she identifies you in a lineup it will be your word against hers."

Patrick was bluffing, but Billy didn't realize that as he shifted his weight again. "I don't know what you're talking about. I gotta go." He slammed the door in their faces.

As Alexandra walked away with Patrick, he said, "The kid knows something. I'm sure of it."

They got into Patrick's car and waited. Five minutes later, Billy ran out of his apartment and hopped into a black Honda Civic. Trying to stay behind him without being obvious, they followed him onto the 101 Ventura Freeway. After several miles he switched onto the 405 San Diego Freeway going north.

"Do you seriously think he's going to lead us to the culprit?" Alexandra asked.

"He seemed pretty scared," Patrick replied. "Sometimes when people get like that they do stupid things. Besides, I doubt he's a professional."

Soon, Billy Nash exited the freeway. After they had been driving for several minutes more, Alexandra suddenly sat forward. "I've been here before. This is the street that passes Cal State Northridge. Arnold and Sally Potter live just beyond the university."

She reached for the cell phone and called Thomas. When he came on the line, she asked him to have someone from the police department meet them at the Potter residence. "Maybe we're going to get lucky," she said, excitedly.

In front of the Potter house, Billy brought his car to an abrupt stop, got out and ran up the steps. Sally came to the door, and a few seconds later, the professor stepped out onto the porch and joined her.

Patrick's car window was open and Alexandra could hear arguing.

"Come on," said Patrick, as they started for the house.

When the professor saw them approaching, he turned to Billy. "Get inside," he urged, trying to shove Billy toward the door. But Patrick stepped onto the porch and blocked their way.

During this ruckus, Sally had just been standing there listening. Alexandra took a chance and spoke directly to her. "Listen to me, Sally, I think Billy's the one who planted the drugs in my apartment to keep me from investigating your father's death."

Sally gazed from one face to the other. "Did you do that?" she asked Billy, simply and forcefully.

"I . . ." the kid was really sweating now, and he looked like he was going to be sick.

A patrol car had pulled up and an officer joined them on the porch. Having been briefed, he turned to Alexandra, "If you identify him as the person who broke into your place, I'll take him in."

Alexandra wanted to say yes, but she couldn't. "I think you better read him his rights."

When the cop told Billy that he had the right to

remain silent, the boy started trembling. "I was just trying to do the professor here a favor."

"Don't say anything, Billy," shouted the professor. "I'll get you a lawyer."

Ignoring him, Alexandra spoke to Billy. "How much did the professor pay you to break into my apartment and plant the drugs?"

"He didn't pay me," Billy said, shaking his head. "I was flunking. I told him I'd do anything if he'd just give me a pass. He said I could help him by stopping someone who was selling drugs to children. Later, when I found out the truth, I felt bad. But when I complained, the professor told me to keep my mouth shut."

"I'm not listening to any more of this nonsense," the professor muttered, heading for his front door.

"Hold it right there," the cop ordered. "You're under arrest." He backed the professor up against the house, placed the handcuffs on him and read him his rights.

"I insist on calling my lawyer," Arnold Potter said loudly.

"You'll get your chance down at the station just like everyone else," said the cop.

"Who called the tip in to the drug hotline in the first place?" Patrick asked.

"The professor did that," Billy told them, as the cop put a pair of handcuffs on him.

After a backup unit came and the police pulled away with their suspects, Alexandra focused her attention on Sally. "Thanks for your help."

The young woman smiled sadly. "All this stuff happened only because you tried to find out the truth about my daddy's death."

"I'm sorry it turned out to be such a difficult experience for you," Alexandra said.

Sally shook her head. "Actually, it's been okay. There were always so many lies in our family. Now we're all starting to talk. And I've been making some real progress with my therapist." She stopped briefly before going on. "Arnold shouldn't have tried to hurt you. But I think I understand why he did it. He was afraid of losing me. He figured if he could just stop your investigation, things could stay the same between us."

"Are you terribly upset about it?"

"No," Sally admitted. Her blue eyes were guileless as she gazed at Alexandra. "I've been a little girl for too many years. It's time I was finally on my own."

40

ON HER WAY TO pick up Patrick, Alexandra had stopped at the gourmet market and bought a delicious picnic lunch. Patrick had put it in a big cooler, and after they got to the beach, they had dragged it across the sand, close to the water.

The sun, wind and salt water, along with the food, had finally taken their toll on Jenny and she now slept curled up on a beach towel, protected from the sun by a green-and-blue striped umbrella.

Alexandra was sitting with Patrick only a few feet away, his arms wrapped tightly around her. For the last several minutes they had been talking about Thomas.

"I keep thinking how much easier things could have been if my father had just explained the situation to me from the beginning."

"That's true. But my guess is he couldn't admit to you that he was less than perfect. His image and your respect were too important to him. And once he lied to you, he couldn't acknowledge it because that too would have been a sign of weakness."

"My mother tried to tell me that. Only she wouldn't come right out and say it."

He nodded.

"But you know my mother, she loved him no matter what."

"Isn't that what love is all about?" he asked. "Accepting a person's faults as well as their good points?"

"Yeah. I guess you're right," Alexandra replied, watching the waves rush toward the shore and then roll back out to sea.

Pulling herself back to the present, she glanced over at the mounds of sand that represented a large sand castle and the moat surrounding it. "What do you think of our elaborate design?"

He chuckled. "You're both my champs."

"Jenny's a real sweetheart," she said, smiling. "I can see that you're doing a wonderful job of raising her."

"It's easy. She's such a good kid. That's not to say that she doesn't drive me crazy sometimes. But I really do love being a dad."

"Jenny knows that," Alexandra said softly. Trailing her hand through the sand, she turned toward him. "It's beautiful here. But why did you insist we come all the way to Long Beach when there are beaches a lot closer to where we live?"

"Because," Patrick said, grinning, "it was here

on this beach that I realized I loved you." He ran his fingers lightly over her lips. "I don't think I ever stopped."

His touch sent small shivers up her spine. "I was young and foolish," she said, shaking her head. "When I think of all the years we've wasted, I want to kick myself."

"Don't do that. Now that we're both a little older and wiser maybe we can finally get it right."

She laughed. Looking from his handsome face to his precious sleeping child, she felt lucky to have been given a second chance.

Also available from

MIMI LATT

POWERS OF ATTORNEY

USA Today bestseller

PURSUIT OF JUSTICE

Pocket Books
A VIACOM COMPANY

Visit
❖ **Pocket Books** ❖
online at

....

www.SimonSays.com

....

Keep up on the latest new
releases from your favorite
authors, as well as author
appearances, news, chats,
special offers and more.

SIMON & SCHUSTER
A VIACOM COMPANY
www.SimonSays.com

Pocket
Books

2381-01